a CON SPIR ACY *of* TALL MEN

Noah Hawley

Harmony Books / NEW YORK

Published by Harmony Books, a division of Crown Publishers, Inc.,
201 East 50th Street, New York, New York, 10022
Random House, Inc. New York, Toronto, London, Sydney, Auckland
www.randomhouse.com

HARMONY and colophon are trademarks of Crown Publishers, Inc.

Printed in the United States of America

DESIGN BY LYNNE AMFT

Library of Congress Cataloging in Publication Data
Hawley, Noah.
A conspiracy of tall men / by Noah Hawley.
p. cm.
I. Title.
PS3558.A8234C66 1999
813'.54—dc21 97-39842
CIP

ISBN 0-609-60280-2

10 9 8 7 6 5 4 3 2 1

First Edition

for

BETH

a mystery of an altogether different color

Acknowledgments

I would like to thank the following people without whom anarchy and chaos would quickly overwhelm life as I know it: my mother, my father, my brother. Thanks to the Weintraubs and to JDS for his faith and perseverance. A special thanks must also be given to all the authors who have inspired me. If novels are truly a dialogue between writers, then I humbly submit this book to the timeless debate.

BOOK *one*

City of Machines

Linus is afraid of money. Not the smaller bills, the Washingtons and Lincolns, the Jacksons and Grants, but the larger sums, the cashier's checks with multiple zeros, the stock portfolios and escrow accounts, afraid too of what they buy, the new cars with their leather stink, the first-class seats on airplanes, the cellular phones and fax modems. He is afraid of office towers, where currency is acquired, afraid of suburban mansions and large screen TVs. He is alarmed by purebred dogs. Expensive suits make his teeth chatter, shoes that shine, organic fruits and vegetables purchased at gleaming, politically correct supermarkets, monogrammed handkerchiefs, pipes and cigars, flat platinum credit cards, symphony tickets, bread machines and espresso makers, ski weekends and barbecues with salmon and free-range chicken, bed-and-breakfasts, four-wheel-drive vehicles owned by anyone not living on the side of a mountain, laser disc players, multiple CD changers, summer houses and winter houses, spontaneous weekend getaways, the games of tennis and golf, penny loafers, angora sweaters, dry martinis and ten-year-old scotch, bay windows that don't look out over parking lots or weed-cluttered yards, but over real bays, Jacuzzi bathtubs, all of Western Europe (especially France and Switzerland), electronic organizers with global position satellite locators, season tickets to anything, waterproof watches, corporate vice-presidents, crystal, gold. He is suspicious of comfort, not to mention luxury. He fears the implications of wealth, though he has never really had any. "I'm too cynical to be rich," he says. He equates financial success with a certain soullessness.

This has been his philosophy since the early days of his youth. It is a byproduct of his own juvenile poverty politicized, and yet somehow he has found a certain comfort now in his middle age, sipping home-brewed coffee in the living room of his own home, looking out a bay window at a small section of San Francisco Bay. He is well aware of the contradictions, the small discrepancies between politics and life, between phobia and happiness. Does he wake up afraid, lying under sheets that are one hundred percent cotton or occasionally real linen? Can he be terrified of the sound of his own wife steaming milk under the gleaming silver nozzle of their espresso machine? No. As with all people he has altered his perceptions to retain both his dogma and his lifestyle, but there are problems. His life is not all contented moments of calm reflection. There is a noxious cloud that follows him, a sense of foreboding. The truth is, he is a man pursued by sinister forces, plagued by suspicious happenings, troubled by disquieting phenomena.

Things are happening to Linus. He has grown one and a half inches since October. A fact verified by his last physical. For a thirty-five-year-old man this is startling, and it makes him question the viability of his wardrobe. He can often be seen tugging down his pants legs, a look of alarm on his face. If this keeps up, he thinks, I will soon have nothing at all to wear. Not that he is a man preoccupied by fashion. On the contrary. It is the inexplicable nature of the occurrence that bothers him, the absurdity. The truth is, Linus is afraid that his life will soon be overrun by the minor mysteries of his body and mind, that he will no longer be able to work because of such distractions.

At the same time, there is twenty-one dollars and sixty-three cents less than there should be in his checking account. This is similarly something that can't be accounted for. Even by men with doctorates. Even by bank presidents. When he comes home at night particulars are not where he left them, books lying on tables open to different pages than they were that morning, coffee cups stacked on wholly new shelves. His wife has gone to visit her mother, so she cannot be blamed. She is in Chicago, fighting wind chills and the insistent demands of the elderly. Linus is understandably at a loss. It would seem that scientific reasoning no longer applies in his life, that the laws of nature and physics have been suspended as he moves onward into middle age.

He has been married six years this December, the time simply rushing past him as he waits on street corners and supermarket checkout lines. It is his plan to bring Claudia flowers on their anniversary, to go for a drive to a seaside bed-and-breakfast. This is something he plots in secret, smiling and nodding when she suggests her own itinerary. It is only fair, he thinks, that I have secrets. There is so much kept from me, tiny plots and greater schemes. Everyone has his or her own agenda. This much is clear. He wonders if he will ever know why his body has chosen to grow, why his hair has decided to thin. Not in one spot, but all over; a general wearing away, an erosion of brown, like water driving at a jut of rock. He has resigned himself to ignorance.

There is no alternative, he feels, but to blame all these things on some greater conspiracy, which he does. Linus, you see, believes there is a clandestine cabal running the world. A machination comprised of bankers and businessmen, military leaders and intelligence agencies. He believes in UFOs, in the secret agenda of the Freemasons, the monopolies of industry. At least this is what he tells his students, who scribble down all of his paranoid imaginings as if they were science or math, as if the very act of teaching them made them irrefutably true. Linus is a professor of conspiracy theory at Modesto College in San Rafael, California. He teaches, among other things, a graduate-level class on JFK, gives seminars on magic bullet theories and the hidden etymological meaning of the words "Dealey Plaza," shows slides meant to prove the faking of the 1967 Apollo moon landing, explains how the symbols on the dollar bill reveal the presence of a secret government leading the world toward unified socialism and biblical Armageddon.

On this particular day he is making his way from the main history building of the college to his office, which is sequestered underneath the cafeteria in a building known as "the Landfill" because of the creeping smells that emanate from its windows and doors around mealtime. As he walks he is holding his head back, pressing one hand to his face, clutching a wad of wet Kleenex. This is his third nosebleed this week. The joke is that he has been given an implant by extraterrestrials. His students have tried to convince him to comb his body for unexplained scars and triangular marks. It is only by the strongest power of will that he has not done so so far.

Above him the sky is cloudy, a gray glove, fingers drumming restlessly. Walking with his head elevated like a man applying eyedrops, he stumbles his way down the stairs into the narrow hallway that leads to his office, a small square of yellowed wall photos and overburdened bookshelves.

He manages to dig out his keys, to wrestle the rusty lock and shove the door open. He drops his briefcase, throws himself into his scarred wooden desk chair, which bends back alarmingly on well-stretched springs. He has not bothered to turn on the light. His eyes are tearing. He tastes blood, salty, filled with heavy metals and his own spiraling DNA. The clock on his desk says 11:45, insistently, in red digital numbers, as if the only thing an occupant of the room must be aware of is the time. Linus, it should be noted, is not a big fan of time. There is too much of it, he thinks, and to no good end. However, it would behoove Linus to pay some attention to his clock, for by this point his wife is already dead.

He has lunch with Edward and Roy at a vegetarian bistro just off Route 101 in Mill Valley, parking his car in the lot and crossing the ruptured asphalt to the front door, noting that Roy's '84 Monte Carlo is already parked outside. Inside the greetings are brief and businesslike. Edward and Roy live a few miles away. They're neighbors who conspire each month in Roy's basement to publish two separate government watchdog newsletters. As paranoid intellectuals go they're a lot like Lucy and Ethel, mulishly determined to pursue every harebrained scheme. Edward is twenty-four, but already retired. He's saved a startling sum of money working as a software engineer for several Silicon Valley start-up companies at the top of the decade. He lives off this now, investing and allotting. He's still just a narrow youth, from some angles almost two-dimensional, with a slight crest of curly brown hair and a dress code comprised mainly of black jeans and combat boots.

Roy is more substantive physically. He has a masculine build, wears his dirty blond hair trimmed at the ear, harbors a crooked mouth and a square jaw. His hands are weathered. He gestures in expansive swings. Unlike Linus, who has the rest of the afternoon free except for a student conference at three o'clock, Roy has to be back to work in exactly an hour. A new, tyrannical boss at Radio Shack, he explains, "As if I were a scientist at a Lockheed missile facility instead of an overage computer geek selling second-rate electronic equipment to a steady trickle of the condescending middle class."

Here among the tabouli salads and unprocessed soy drinks the three conspiracy theorists meet each week to discuss developments in the interconnected network of plots driving the world toward a new order. The words that emerge from their mouths are rooted in the language of suspicion, the discussions of secret technologies, of alien abductions, of governmental machinations traceable to the highest levels. They are representative of the uneasy outcasts, some with academic credentials, who fill the nooks and crannies of the American experience. They seek the truth the way soothsayers read entrails. In order to understand them you must first understand that there is no such thing as History with a capital *H*. Everything is a matter of perception and interpretation. Facts can be manipulated, photographs altered. As Linus has explained to his students: People do not come to believe things after seeing them. They see things only when they already believe them. Be alert. Watch the skies.

"There's an online conference on corn circles and cattle mutilation tonight, Professor," says Edward, who has taken out a small tube of antibacterial spray and begun wiping off his silverware. They sit in a booth by the window, vinyl seats the color of beef blood. "Sixty percent rise in mutilated cattle since February. This guy who's running the conference has an impressive collection of downloadable photos. Can you read .gif files on that lumbering Goliath of yours?"

Edward is referring to Linus's file-cabinet-size computer, which runs at the speed of an overweight, asthmatic civil servant.

"Print them out for me, will you?" says Linus. The nosebleed has stopped, but he is wandering around Northern California with a small clump of toilet paper jammed up one nostril. They order salads and shrimp cocktails. Edward and Roy won't eat beef because of the growth hormones the government injects into cows. It's a sore spot with Roy, who was a meat eater for twenty-nine years until Edward wore him down with slides and spreadsheets. Now he suffers through fish, chicken, and vegetables with a subterranean resentment that borders on the spoiled. Edward mentions that antibiotics used in livestock feed are creating strains of drug-resistant food-poisoning bacteria: "So now when you get salmonella poisoning from that Egg McMuffin, you'll need to start thinking in terms of eulogies." They offer to show him documentation that the hormone injections are part of a plot to control the human mind by introducing particular pharmaceuticals through diet.

"Write me up a paragraph, will you? Include sources."

Edward and Roy, despite Roy's innocuous job at Radio Shack and Edward's mostly shut-in status, are cutting-edge anarchists, publishers of anarchic newsletters, organizers of the new virtual revolution. Linus, in contrast, feels sheltered in the fat nest of academia. Sometimes he doubts his phone is even bugged. He picks it up and listens for the comforting clicks and whirs of government surveillance. This is how people in his profession confirm their importance, by identifying the size of the file with their name on it in a gray-green file cabinet in Washington, D.C. Linus hasn't published an article or done an interview in almost six months. He has been distracted by his own life. His friends have become his lifeline to the daily rumbles of secret groups, plots and subplots. Through a mixture of cleverness and cash they have set up one of the premier databases in the country for tracking clandestine government projects.

"Think of it this way," says Roy. "Knowledge is power, therefore ignorance is slavery. Correspondingly, terrorism becomes the fear of the unknown. Innocent activities take on sinister characteristics. We stop trusting our mail. What could be a teddy bear could also be a bomb. We learn to fear crowds, for crowds are the target of desperate individuals. Terrorism strips us of our identities. Crowds strip us of our humanity. We are the smudgeable ink rushed into newsprint. We are yesterday's papers, yellowing in trash heaps and collecting dust in the living rooms of yuppies."

He takes a sip of his Orangina, which is the closest thing to a Coke he can get in this restaurant.

"The answer, if your intent is to make people feel empowered—though without actually empowering them—is to overload them with knowledge, with information. In this way they feel as if they are inside a loop of knowing. You show them the type of information they need to feel secure, whether or not it's true, and in this way you have a population that is content. They believe that they possess answers to the questions they ask, and that they have access to the information they need. Now you are free to do whatever it is you like. Our job is to decipher the truth from the flood of data, to extrapolate meaning from an assault of news and facts meant to overwhelm us and keep us from ever finding out just what is going on. Witness the Internet. What is the information age if not a ploy to make us feel informed when every year we know less and less about the things that really matter?"

Linus chews the ice cubes from his glass.

"How's the missus?" Edward wants to know. He smiles nervously. There are spaces between his teeth that should never have survived adolescence.

"She's in Chicago visiting her mother."

Edward blows his nose into his napkin. He has a sip of water to try to judge if it hurts his throat to swallow. "Talk about ice and snow," he says. He's on the verge of a cold or the flu. His joints hurt, his nose is running. Edward has taken the bold step of retiring at twenty-four in part because of his health. Roy calls him a hypochondriac, but then Roy doesn't appreciate the full danger of the bacteriological world.

Linus folds and refolds his napkin, distracted by his own hands moving.

"Claudia also has some business. A client of her agency. Some meeting or other. A presentation maybe." He shakes his head. Claudia is in advertising. She is the head of a creative team at a midsize agency. He carries pictures of her in his wallet. He feels she endows his money with a certain holiness. Linus himself is, at best, unremarkable looking, not unattractive, just bland and not given to the best grooming habits, while Claudia, aside from being compelling visually, is someone who says the cleverest things in all the appropriate places.

Recently she has been showing irritation that he has not yet blossomed into some greater academic, become the chairman of some committee or the national authority on a subject other than the ridiculous paranoid sophistry he is renowned for. He is beginning to think she wants a husband who is more cosmopolitan. A Rockefeller, a Kennedy, a bright, handsome young urban professional who drives a German-engineered sports car and knows how to choose wine. To this end he has purchased a book on vineyards. He is planning to learn a foreign language as soon as the semester is over. Study French, perhaps, or Russian. He vows to buy a tuxedo and take her to the opera. To throw out all of the corduroy pants and the jackets with off-colored elbow patches. But he wonders: How can you teach the underside of American history in a twelve-hundred-dollar suit? Though Claudia's friends will take him more seriously once he begins to dress like an Italian stockbroker, his own friends will take him less. He could lose credibility in his field.

There are corners and then there are corners and this is a sticky one, but Claudia has become very obstinate recently. She wants to be happier than she is. Work problems, she tells him, though it is he who suffers the brunt of them, whatever they are. He plans to bring her flowers on their anniversary. To take her somewhere nice. Though it seems to him they have been growing apart, he is sure this is just his suspicious mind. That underneath his fear everything is fine. She still looks at him sometimes over dinner, in restaurants, still gives him the same brilliant smile. It's just a rough period, he thinks, just a little matrimonial turbulence.

"She's fine, really," says Linus, dwelling. Roy and Edward exchange a look. The shrimp cocktails arrive.

"Ah," says Roy. "Fresh frozen."

Linus met Edward and Roy at the opening of the Conspiracy Museum in Dallas. Rectangular rooms filled with apprehensive men looking over narrow shoulders, drinking bottled water purchased independently to deter any governmental tampering with their bodily fluids. At the reception, the two led an impromptu seminar on how to avoid government security forces when visiting the Area 51 UFO testing area in Nevada.

"You need a four-wheel-drive vehicle," they said. "Some good infrared camera equipment, plenty of beer."

After the reception, which Claudia had found a way to avoid, Linus ended up in the museum parking lot with Edward and Roy drinking champagne from stolen bottles, slipping his shoes off to air the holes in his socks. There was a small series of confessions then between them, as if the three were participants in some prison support group or twelve-step program. First Edward, arms like pool cues, volunteered that he belonged to an unofficial organization of men known as *skinny nervous guys:* poorly shaven, Adam's apple a little too prominent, awkward around women, uncomfortable with direct confrontation. Then Roy confessed that his wife left him for a Pontiac salesman from Boise a week before their third anniversary and the next day the bulldozer he was driving slipped into a ditch and broke his leg. He was trapped inside for ten hours staring at the carcasses of trees and the sinister circuitry of his crippled machine. When his leg healed he took the insurance settlement and moved to the Bay Area, bought a house in San Rafael, and did nothing but take computer classes for a year.

"There's something about being pinned under a giant motor next to the carcasses of five-hundred-year-old trees that strips you of the ability to keep on killing," he said. He felt the need to study machines in detail. He said, "It's important to try to understand the things you fear most."

The house he bought in San Rafael was small and run-down, a crippled runt in a neighborhood of villas. Two weeks later Edward moved into the Victorian next door. All it took was one beer for them to discover they shared a morbid fascination with the misty plots of ruling bodies and the secret doings of science. Soon afterward, financed mostly by Edward's software portfolio, they invested in computer equipment and desktop publishing software, which they used to monitor government agencies from Roy's basement and publish a bimonthly newsletter called *Saucer Watch* and a weekly titled *American Conspiracy.* In the newsletter Edward and Roy ran abductees' stories, sightings, and conspiratorial speculations, driven mostly by the brainstorming of friends and frequent trips to desert military sites that are usually surrounded by barbed wire and patrolled by dogs.

Linus swallowed what remained in the black Freixenet bottle. The world was full of stars and spinning pinwheels. He considered the possibility that he might be having an out-of-body experience.

"More booze," said Roy, staggering to his feet and throwing the last empty champagne bottle into a Dumpster, where it broke with a rich, heavy crash. "We should stop our girlish whining and go find more booze."

Edward moved his head somewhat ambiguously. Linus managed to get to his feet with the assistance of a brick wall and the sleek cold corner of the Dumpster, which he leaned on for support despite its rich, aroma of restaurant leftovers and wet cardboard.

"I miss my wife," Linus slurred. This was his confession. He was a man who could no longer sleep alone without landscaping the pillows beside him to simulate a human form.

The three of them wandered off onto the streets of Dallas, brushing clumsily at the seats of their pants and listing badly, first to one side, then the other. Buildings passed by in darkness, cars with their bright anonymous lights. Edward told them how Marilyn Monroe's home had been bugged by J. Edgar Hoover and somewhere there was a tape of what really happened the night she died. Roy offered that one couldn't get too close to the Kennedy brothers and live to tell about it. Linus lurched on toward the promise of fermented liquids. In this way they found themselves standing on the corner of Houston and Elm, swaying slightly and waiting for the light to change. None of them had to speak. They all knew they had arrived. It was an evening in October and late, 2:00, maybe 3:00 A.M. There was little traffic, the occasional headlight, a low wind pricking past their faces. The overpass beside them was a dark tunnel. Linus pulled his coat a little tighter, tried to think of something to say. They stood in the shadow of the world's most famous book depository. Above them the light turned green.

"Bang," said Edward.

"Pow, pow," said Roy.

Just as eloquently, Linus turned around and threw up into the road.

The next thing Linus will remember in the days to come is rising from his desk when his office door opens. He will already have been sitting with the student from his "JFK and the Long Arm of the Mafia" class for maybe fifteen minutes, having returned to campus directly after lunch. He will remember putting up his hand in midsentence to stop her from talking. Two men in brown suits have entered after a slight knock. They wear no expressions. Their faces are young, but no younger than his. One of them has a small notebook out, a pen. They ask him if he is Linus Owen. This seems like a reasonable question and so he agrees that yes, he is, and who might they be? They do not answer but ask to speak to him privately. He excuses his student, who, imagining she is witnessing some secret meeting between her conspiracy professor and intelligence operatives, will scurry back to her dorm to spread the word of his clandestine tryst. The men identify themselves as Sikes and Peterson. They are with the FBI. Linus offers them a chair, though there aren't enough for all three of them. There is a feeling in his stomach, dread.

"Mr. Owen," says Agent Sikes. "We have some bad news."

Claudia, thinks Linus for no reason. Instinct, maybe. Telepathy? Somehow he knows.

"I'm sorry. There was a plane crash this morning. A flight from New York to Brazil."

Linus is confused. He is experiencing a hundred emotions.

"But my wife is in Chicago," he says, a feeling of relief spreading through him.

"Your wife is Claudia Owen, maiden name Morris? Parents, Raymond and Astrid Morris?"

"Well, yes, but...but I don't see how. I spoke to her Tuesday. In Chicago."

"I know this is difficult, Mr. Owen," says Agent Peterson. "But your wife was on a plane flying from New York City to Rio de Janeiro that crashed yesterday at five P.M. Eastern Standard Time.

There is plenty of evidence to suggest that it was her. Identification was found on the body."

Linus sinks down into his seat when Peterson says the word *body.* He begins to recite the names of California wines in his mind, Mondavi, Stags' Leap, Kendall Jackson. There are cabernets and chardonnays and dark red burgundies. He will learn French *and* Russian, Spanish, even Portuguese. He will become as sophisticated as Jacqueline Onassis.

"Do you know why your wife would be on a flight to Brazil when she was supposed to be in Chicago, Mr. Owen?" they ask him. Sikes is poised to write. Linus shakes his head. He picks up the phone and dials his mother-in-law's number. A woman's voice answers and for a moment he is certain that it is Claudia, and he sits up straighter.

"Claudia, Claudia, it's Linus."

But the woman is weeping and she says, "Linus, Linus, how could this happen? How could they have taken my Claudia, my baby?"

And Linus has the feeling of tumbling miles above the ground, the feeling that this time his parachute isn't going to open and he will end up a very small and sorry stain on the thin blade of reality.

He sits there with the phone, without thought, unable to decode, unable to believe.

"It's impossible," he keeps repeating. "Astrid," he says into the phone, "Astrid, what happened? Calm down." He repeats what she said in his mind: *How could they have taken my baby?* Who? Who took her? He says this. She cries harder.

"Astrid, who took Claudia?"

"Sir," says Agent Sikes, "your wife's ticket was paid for by a man named Holden, Jeffrey Holden. The two were seated together on the plane. This is from the passenger log. The ticketing clerk remembers them, a man and a woman, the woman tall with long brown hair, quite pretty. He says the two were together, holding hands. Sir, I realize this is difficult. Mr. Holden appears to have been a client of your wife's company. Maybe this was a business trip. Did your wife mention anything about a business trip?"

"Astrid," says Linus, holding the phone so tightly that there will be grooves in his hand when he finally lets it go, "what happened to

Claudia? I thought she was visiting you. How did she end up in New York?"

The agents wait, step back, allow him to finish the call. On the other end of the line his mother-in-law tries to compose herself.

"She got a call Tuesday evening. She said it was business and that she had to go home, back to California. She said she would call me when she was back. She didn't say anything about New York. Why did she go to New York? I don't understand. Linus, what's going on here? How could she be dead flying from New York to Brazil? What's in Brazil? Linus? Linus?"

Linus feels an emptiness, a total lack of being.

"I don't know anything, Astrid. I don't know. Let me talk to the police and see if I can learn any of the details. I'll call you later." He hangs up the phone with defeat. Right now the details seem a hollow reward, a terrible trade of love for knowledge. He looks up at the agents. He feels weak and totally exhausted, all of the verve and energy he has mustered to prepare for her return fallen away like a seat belt that failed in a car crash.

"Okay," he says. "Okay, what happened?"

■

The facts are these. Claudia left Chicago on Wednesday morning. She flew to New York. The airline says she arrived in New York at 12:53 P.M. She boarded flight 613 for Brazil at just after 2:00 P.M. Eastern Standard Time, and she was not alone. As the FBI has explained, her ticket had been purchased that morning by a man named Jeffrey Holden. The two boarded together and sat side by side in seats 18 F and G. Holden worked for a company called Hastings Pharmaceutical, for which Claudia had been involved in preparing a television and print advertising campaign. The flight departed at 2:31 from New York's JFK. It flew south on a path that took it over Washington, D.C., past Virginia, and down over Florida, where it crashed just outside of Orlando, allegedly from a sudden decompression in the fuselage.

"We think there may have been a bomb on the plane," says Agent Sikes. "Can you think of anyone who may have wanted to kill your wife?"

And Linus begins to laugh. He says,

"Agent Sikes, I am a professor of conspiracy theories. I could come up with more names in the next ten minutes than you could write down. But my wife wasn't that kind of woman and...and... No. No one." He is overcome for a moment by the enormity of it, by the realization that with Claudia's death he too has ceased to exist. "Who could have wanted to kill her? What was she doing there? I just don't understand." He tries to shake it off. He looks like a man disagreeing with the world. "I just don't understand."

The three of them stand there awkwardly. Because they are in a basement office the ceiling is quite low, and Linus can see that Sikes, who is tall, feels the need to crouch slightly, to stoop.

"Sir, I'm going to have to ask you to come to Florida and identify the body."

Linus thinks of the smooth planes of her back, the long cylinders of her legs. "Is she...?"

Agent Sikes clears his throat.

"Sir, I won't lie to you, a body that's been in a crash like that is not pretty. If it's any comfort, she must have died instantly."

Linus continues to shake his head like a dog worrying a bone.

"Agent Sikes, when death is involved, an instant can be the longest second of your life."

"I understand, sir. I do. But perhaps your wife had some identifying marks. Perhaps on her back or her legs."

Linus tries to swallow but can't.

"What are you saying?"

He looks at them. He can see the pores on Agent Sikes's face, the beginnings of afternoon stubble. The office is as small as a matchbox, the three of them huddled together. Linus feels he may pass out, weak and so far removed from his body. Agent Peterson clears his throat.

"In this case a facial identification won't be possible." He says it cleanly, quickly, as if trying to cut down the time this will take, the time they will have to spend cramped together in this little room breathing the sour air of Linus's grief. "It just won't."

Linus nods. The words have almost no meaning.

"I see," he says. He thinks of his wife waiting for a plane at JFK airport, thinks of JFK waiting for *Air Force One* on the morning of November 22, 1963, thinks of death waiting for the winged to drop, for gravity to call all bodies down to earth. *They took her,* he thinks. They took my Claudia. But who are they? And why must I now brush the thinning hair from my eyes and climb into a brown four-door sedan to begin the painful process of identifying the dead?

■

By the time Linus packs some clothes together and makes it to the airport, the FBI knows more. While he is in the air hurtling toward Orlando, they are learning certain details about the torn metal and scattered bodies. They are finding that at some point before the crash a large hole appeared in the bottom of the plane. The metal from this area is buckled and blackened. By the time his flight arrives in Orlando, they are positive that a bomb was responsible for the decompression and the crash. They have collected samples of the fuselage and the shattered luggage, fragments of bone, and mutilated seat cushions. As Linus climbs woodenly from the airplane, dangling carry-on luggage from two unfeeling hands, government agencies are finishing the gruesome task of removing the bodies from the trees and bushes, from the long torn spread of ground.

On his own flight Linus has thought of nothing but the feeling of the plane suddenly diving toward the earth, of the terror and the overwhelming certainty of his demise. He thinks of Claudia descending into darkness, of the wind sucking, the ground looming, of the screams and prayers and silent implosions that make up dying. He wants to share this experience with her, as he has shared all others in the ten years they have known each other. Listless in his complimentary first-class seat, he welcomes his own end, for he does not feel he deserves to live if Claudia is dead, her mortal worth being so much more than his. She was a vibrant and powerful force while he is just a little man preoccupied with plots and conspiracies that are, in the end, irrelevant, next to death, next to the end result of dying.

He is met as he disembarks by two agents from the FAA. They walk him over to a car and from the airport drive over Floridian highways toward the hotel, where he will stay, free of charge, compliments of the airline, whose officials speak with concerned faces and use words like *saddened* and *loss*. Halfway there, watching the anorexic palms swaying beside the road like world-weary cheerleaders, Linus tells the agents to take him to see Claudia. He tells them he is not in the mood for hotels and the isolation of strange corridors. I just want to get this over with, he says. I'm sorry, but I need to know. More than anything, I just need to know.

Leaving the highway, they are mostly silent. Linus answers whatever questions they have on the subject of Claudia's trip. He finds himself in a loop of *I don't know* and *It makes no sense.* The investigation is continuing, is all the agents will tell him when he tries to wrestle the details from their tight-lipped faces.

"Is anyone taking credit for the bombing?" he wants to know.

"What makes you think it was a bomb, Mr. Owen?"

They leave their backs to him and over the headrests he stares at their close-cropped necks.

"This is what the FBI said. A bomb."

"We're looking into all possibilities."

They are just voices and skulls. Occasionally there is a profile. Linus rubs his face with one hand, feels a stubble rising, wants to distract himself from the coming morgue, the identification, the body. What will be left? he wonders. How much of my wife will remain? Or is it just a question of moles and scars, a process of elimination?

"I'd like to see a roster of passengers," he says.

One of the agents, the one sitting in the passenger seat, turns around and looks at him.

"Now that's an unusual request, sir. Why would you ask for that?"

Linus puts his hands in his lap, forces air through the gap in his front teeth.

"When Pan Am flight 103 went down over Lockerbie there were five CIA agents aboard. They were carrying a suitcase with five hundred thousand dollars inside, as well as an intricate drawing of a Beirut building and a greeting card with an encoded message that seemed to indicate some secret plot would come to fruition on March 11, 1989. A second crew of CIA agents arrived at the crash site posing as Pan Am employees, probably to collect and destroy evidence. No definite answer exists as to who planted the bomb, but there is some speculation that the plane was blown up by an element of the CIA that didn't want either the negotiation for the release of the hostages in Lebanon or their rescue to come to pass. What I'm asking is relatively simple given these facts. If no one has claimed responsibility, and no apparent reason is present to explain the explosion, then it is safe to assume that there is some clandestine agenda at work. So, again, I'd like to see a passenger roster, please."

The agents exchange a look, but Linus's attention has wandered away to the landscape whirring by outside. He speaks, as much for the distraction of his own voice as for the communicatory value of it.

"Actually it is clear that German intelligence, the Mossad, and CIA-1 had heard word of a bomb attack in the making. A German drug agent who knew of the warnings spotted a suspicious suitcase as it was loaded onto the plane. He called CIA-1 to let them know that a bomb may have been on board. When CIA-1 checked with Washington Control, the message back was, 'Don't worry about it. Don't stop it. Let it go.' "

Linus is temporarily blinded by sun flashes from the windshields of approaching cars.

"Mr. Owen," the driver says carefully, "you can be sure that whatever the cause of this crash and whoever is responsible, we'll find them. There will be no, uh, cover-up. For the moment, however, let's keep wild speculation about the CIA to a minimum, shall we? It's very early in the investigation, and in order to keep the rumors from taking over we're being pretty careful where conjectures of responsibility are concerned. That's all. We have no ulterior motives. Rest assured, the minute there is documented information we'll tell you."

"I'll also need my wife's luggage, her carry-on. Is that possible?" Linus looks up and over at the agents, whose backs are toward him once more. He feels there may be something in Claudia's things that will explain why yesterday she was on the other side of the country emigrating to Brazil.

"Whatever luggage can be recovered from the site will be returned to the next of kin," says the one in the passenger seat. "It may take a while to sort it out, though."

They ride the rest of the way without dialogue, the sun pouring down over the car, crowding the air inside with moisture. The agents explain that investigators and rescue workers have taken over the gymnasium of a junior high school near the crash site. It has been turned into a makeshift morgue. If there had been any survivors, it is there they would have gone for medical attention, but there were none and so the medical supplies have been returned to the hospital, the boxes of bandages and vials of morphine, the anticoagulating agents and liters of whole blood. Linus imagines the bodies of children in team uniforms strewn across waxed wood floors. He thinks of the children he will now never have. There has to be something, he thinks. Something left to hold on to for me. He can think of nothing. They leave the highway and wind their way through rows of robin's-egg-blue houses and trailers. The shoulder of the road is overgrown with weeds. Occasionally the husk of a battered automobile can be seen lurking in the underbrush like a starving beast of prey collapsed from the impotency of old age.

On the plane Linus read the published version of events in the *New York Times* and the *Washington Post.* Quotes from airline officials and federal watchdogs. Editorials about the increase of domestic terrorism. There was speculation about Muslim extremists, increased security at all airports, pictures of the wreckage. Linus scanned all this quickly, avoiding the pictures out of guilt and shame and something akin to self-preservation. No one on his plane spoke of the crash, though most could think of nothing else. This was the denial they needed to survive the ride. Passengers tight-lipped and white-knuckled. The drink cart made extra trips up and down the aisles. Linus breathed the stale air, the recycled oxygen of people with more to live for than he.

The airline had offered to send a counselor with him, for comfort or warmth or understanding, but Linus refused. Patronizing little men with compassionate eyes and television rhetoric could drive him into a rage greater than anyone could know, and if there was one thing Linus needed, it was to suppress his emotions, to compose himself and go on with the wrenching task of finding out whether his wife was really dead and who killed her.

Ahead he sees a conflagration of emergency vehicles and unmarked government cars. The rectangular jut of a concrete gymnasium looms above the short palms. Linus's mouth is dry. His throat tightens. Instinctively he checks to make sure that both of the rear doors are unlocked. He feels a savage need to escape, to run off into the Florida marshes and sink into the stink of the Everglades, a hermit living in one set of unwashed clothes, cooking shellfish snatched from the muddy depths of soggy bogs, speaking to no one, pondering only the unwelcome prospect of heavy rain.

"I'm sorry we have to put you through this, Mr. Owen," says the agent in the passenger seat again, as if sensing that the air has become charged with fear and sorrow. "Your wife did have identification on her, but since we can't figure out why she was on the plane at all we have to be certain. You know her employer was just as surprised to learn that she was traveling with Mr. Holden."

Linus thinks nothing, except that he is not about to trust any government agency to tell him why his life has suddenly turned to so much shit. As they round a corner and the facade of the Willmont Junior High School comes upon them, Linus sinks his fingernails into the meat of his palms, squeezes. Perhaps he is trying to cut his own lifelines before he has to face the prospect of his dead wife. After this, it is clear, nothing will ever be the same. I will be a man who has looked upon the husk of the woman he loves. The car stops in front of the gym. The three men climb out woodenly. Linus is in a daze. The closure of the car doors reverberates in his head. They stand for a moment in the hot Florida sun. Linus feels the sweat on his back, the undersides of his arms. He is wearing a blue suit, a shirt and tie. He wanted nothing more than to look like a Rockefeller or a Kennedy for his wife and show his respect. The pants hang a quarter inch above his shoes. Even now he is growing. Even now. Agent Neilson, the passenger, leans over to him as if he is about to offer consolation or some words of advice.

"Gum?" he says, holding out a battered pack of Trident.

Linus begins to walk toward the cinder-block exterior of the gymnasium. It is as if he is walking through a tunnel wide enough only for him to pass. The tunnel leads straight to the front doors of the gym. An official of the airline comes out to greet him, agents of the FBI and the Justice Department. He ignores them. Soon there is a crowd of suits and dresses around him. Their voices sound like static or the humming whir of insects. The doors are opened before him and then he is inside a lobby filled with trophy cases and clots of grieving relatives. This is the sound of disaster, the sobs and curses of those left behind. There are whole families and shuddering couples, stunned individuals, male and female, dazed, wandering, corralled by representatives of the media. Who would do this? they ask. How could this happen? As if until this moment everything in life happened for a reason, as if before now there were no surprises, no fear, no expectation of catastrophe. The whole event is being broadcast to networks and foreign television stations, the hard robotic noses of cameramen stalking the crowds followed by the cold glint of anchormen and -women, polishing their teeth on the distress of others.

His own entrance is captured by representatives of CBS and NBC but will wind up on the cutting-room floor of the evening news. As he crosses the lobby, a cameraman for CNN swings out from nowhere, leveling his optic eye like a weapon of truth, pinning Linus for all time against the battered wall of broadcast journalism, a man's face frozen in sick repose. He falls back before Linus's unyielding footsteps. Inside the lobby the ceilings are high, the floor carpeted with an orange short-hair wall to wall. On both sides are concrete staircases winding up to the second floor. Straight ahead is a set of doors that leads into the gymnasium itself, with its basketball nets and painted-on courts, wall-mounted braces for volleyball nets and cold metal scoreboards. There will be the rise of metal bleachers, tall mesh-covered windows. There will be the smell of preteen sweat and the echoing remains of the squeaking sneakers of sprinters and the skirting red flash of dodge balls.

Linus is still surrounded. He moves through the crowd like a presidential candidate protected on all sides from some surprise attack. He says nothing, just walks straight to the gray metal swinging doors and pushes them open.

Edward lets the phone ring twenty-one times before hanging up. He wiggles one of his incisors between two fingers, feels pain creep into his eye socket. He considers the disturbing reality that he may have to make a dentist appointment, walks over to the glass doors, and stares out into the Radio Shack parking lot. He has stopped by to visit Roy at the crap factory. Since yesterday's lunch he has reevaluated his burgeoning cold and decided that it is probably viral meningitis, though his *Physician's Desk Reference* indicates he should be experiencing a serious elevation in body temperature as a result.

"Any answer?" says Roy, coming out from the back office.

"Nothing. Not at the school or at home. Touch my face. Do I feel hot to you?"

"Stop it. It's not like him not to call when he says he will. This is a man who calls, if you know what I mean." Roy clucks his tongue against the roof of his mouth. He's wearing a wrinkled white oxford shirt with blue slacks and a tie as wide as a bolo. His hair is tousled and unwashed. He looks around the store with undisguised contempt. Radio Shack is Roy's way of hiding from the future. It is a job he took last summer to acquire enough money to eat, a three-day-a-week display of postdivorce tentativeness that allows him to get out of the house and away from the photo albums that sit under a great weight of laundry in the back of his closet. It's a job he can sleepwalk through, which is what he wants at this stage of his life, pushing thirty-four, a lonely former logger from Washington State who had a revelation about technology one night while lying on the top of a double-wide trailer after a visit from a UFO.

"Now don't get paranoid," cautions Edward, watching a couple emerge from their car and walk past Radio Shack to the Liquor Barn.

"Hah. As if." Roy picks up the phone, dials for himself. Twenty rings. No answer. Edward crosses back behind the counter and opens up this month's issue of *Fair Play* magazine, starts reading an article on JFK's forged autopsy records. The hardest thing about being retired at twenty-four is all the extra time, but Edward's fear of germs limits his choices. He tries to minimize his exposure to other people. About twice a week he'll come down when Roy's boss is not in the store and keep Roy company, but he can't see himself going back to work in an office, and traveling is definitely out of the question, all those hours spent breathing recycled air on squalid airplanes traveling to countries where prehistoric viruses sneak from clotted rain forests and cleave the unwary traveler with fevers and bloody bowels. So when he's bored he'll drive down to Radio Shack and sit on his ass reading declassified documents and worry about his health.

"Ed." Roy taps his shoulder. "Ed, look at this."

Edward looks up. Roy is pointing to the fifteen television screens that litter the store, a barrage of unphased colors all carrying the same picture: Linus, white faced, overexposed, crossing through the lobby of what looks like an gymnasium.

"Volume," hisses Edward. Roy runs around the store looking for a remote. At the bottom of the screen the little red letters CNN appear. The picture changes to the scattered metal of yesterday's plane crash.

"Holy shit," says Roy, still stalking around in circles looking for a remote. "Holy shit, holy shit, holy shit."

"Where's the fucking remote, Roy?" Edward lunges toward one of the Realistic monitors and slaps at the control panel, adjusting first the color, then the picture, then finally the volume.

"...Officials are now confirming the presence of an explosive on board the Brazil-bound jetliner, though no one is yet claiming responsibility. Earlier this afternoon the president issued a grim warning to whatever person or group is responsible for an act of terrorism that claimed the lives of over one hundred and seventy-six people."

The president can be seen moving his mouth, his teeth white, perfectly spaced. Edward remains standing inches from the screen, his hands dangling at his sides, while Roy has stopped running in circles and stepped behind the counter, where he is dialing Linus's home number, watching as the TV screens change to a jittery helicopter shot of the wreckage.

"Son of a bitch," he's saying. "Son of a bitch."

He listens to the empty rings, the sound of the answering

machine, Claudia's voice. He's trying to figure out the connection, why Linus would be included in footage relevant to yesterday's plane crash.

"What are they saying?" he asks. Edward shushes him.

"Maybe they brought him in as an expert."

Edward looks at him as if he's Cro-Magnon. Sometimes, when they grow sick of each other, Edward and Roy will stand on diagonally opposed porches and shoot Nerf missiles at each other from launchers the size of Hoover carpet steamers.

"He didn't say anything about anyone going to Brazil."

"Will you shut up and let me listen? Why don't you call the airline, see if they're releasing a passenger list yet, call CNN, see if they can tell you why he's on there."

Roy taps his foot nervously on the ground. If he were home he could turn on his computer, make some connections.

"I think I should close early," he says. "I think we should get out of here and head home so we can do some serious investigating."

Edward, eyes still on the bank of televisions, nods. He doesn't say anything about how Roy will most likely be fired for leaving the store in the middle of the day, says nothing about what Donna the shift manager will say when she comes back from lunch to find the Closed sign hanging on the door. In his opinion, Roy is wasting his life in this palace of mediocrity. He has pushed him for months to stop hiding out in a run-down shopping mall and get his life going again. So when Roy suggests he close up, Edward says absolutely. Let's get a move on, he declares. He knows that retail is an early grave.

Together they slap off all the televisions and power strips, let the store go dark. Roy flips the sign, locks the door, and then they're sprinting across the mall parking lot. Neither one of them has any sense that the presence of Professor Owen on television is a positive moment for the future of Owen-kind. Edward's leaves streaks of black on the asphalt. It is a ten-minute drive to their headquarters. When they get there they will find one cryptic message on Roy's answering machine. It will be just minutes old and they will listen to it three times, raising the volume level each time until Linus is almost shouting across the short distance of Roy's living room.

"Claudia's dead," he says. "And I need you to help me find out why."

Linus received his undergraduate degree from Yale, took his master's and Ph.D. in history and political science from UC Berkeley. He once wrote a paper titled "Government Hit Men from Mars—Or, What Really Happened to Jimmy Hoffa." As a child he was no different from the others. He played stoop ball and stick ball in the Park Slope neighborhood of Brooklyn. He smoked dope when it was appropriate, chased girls when it was possible, learned to skateboard and to play electric guitar badly. His father belonged at one time or other to the Garment Workers Union, the Health and Hospital Workers Union, the Plumbers and Electricians Unions. He drove trucks for the Teamsters. His mother didn't work, but stayed home to tend to the lives and minds of her children. This was the late 1960s, the early 1970s. Now it is the 1990s. Someday they too will seem like a strange, dead era inhabited by ghosts and memories and strange displays of fashion.

Linus wasn't alone in all this. He had a younger sister and an older brother, Alice and Ford. Alice got into some trouble a few years back with the white horse they call scag, hit bottom, got into rehab, relapsed, pulled her act together, and now she's thinking one day at a time. She's still skinnier than is healthy, still looks strung out, but she's recovering, feeling better every day, and there's a new boyfriend who's straight this time and he takes her out to decent places, to see movies or bands, and they don't even smoke pot but maybe have the occasional glass of wine. Alice is waitressing in New York, living in Park Slope two blocks away from her mother. Linus's father is dead now, has been since 1991, when the booze and the red meat and the cigarettes put the final stranglehold on his heart. World Federation Wrestling is how Linus likes to think of it. His father was in the cage, undergoing the cruel merciless death match with Angina the Terrible, Fibrillate the Masked Avenger, Emphysema the Breathless. He tries to see his father in the light of national television, as a man swollen with muscles and masculine power facing down the unvanquishable enemy. When he does this he pictures his father's opponent as a conglomerate of shadowy businessmen. These are the tobacco tycoons, the presidents of Jim Beam and Johnny Walker Red, the CEOs of the insurance companies who wouldn't insure his father after the second heart attack, after the pneumonia. The match is rigged. R. J. Reynolds III has a wrench in his glove, a sock full of quarters. They crack his father's skull when his back is turned.

Linus's brother, Ford, is an investment banker at Harrison Freidlow. He lives in New York City, forty-two stories above the ground, looking out over the park, drinking cappuccinos prepared for him by his French au pair, never coming down except to ride in limousines and yellow cabs smelling of frankincense and distant beaches to restaurants and health clubs and the wood-paneled interior of his fifty-seventh-floor office. From the altitude of towering skyscrapers he has gotten used to the idea of looking down on people and so this is what he does now with everyone. He suffers the conceits that money brings, that sense of smugness, of immortality. He has a beautiful blond wife and a darker more mysterious mistress whom he visits with some regularity on his lunch hour. His hair is brown and full, unlike Linus's receding follicles. He owns more than two hundred ties and over thirty pairs of shoes. He has enough underwear to last until the turn of the century, and far below the ground, two stories beneath the lobby of his penthouse apartment, he has an Infiniti J30 and a Jaguar housed in the extravagant recesses of a luxury garage.

Linus speaks to him infrequently, the occasional phone call, a quick visit around Christmas and Easter. Claudia inquires about Ford regularly, if only because Linus's family is still the one mystery he possesses, but Linus does not have the strength for prolonged interaction. This is because Linus and Ford are magnetically opposed, men of repellent polarities, and Linus cannot stomach the smugness, or the elitism, cannot swallow the perfect teeth and Vassar affectations of Ford's wife, Madison. It is the stability Claudia admires, he thinks, the social gaiety, not the opulence. She likes the idea of parties with visiting dignitaries and dinners with the Buckleys. She is growing tired of the homemade meals shared with UFO abductees and estranged government employees. He thinks she likes the idea of having an eighteen-year-old Parisian fashion model looking after her two brilliant children, children Linus and Claudia are planning on having shortly. He wants them and so does she, but she has asked him to find a better-paying job so that she can quit hers and stay home to raise the kids, whom they agreed to name Carter and Reagan in a moment of mordant humor. Linus says yes, that he is looking, but he isn't really. There is guilt at not doing so, but it is overwhelmed by fear, the fear of selling out, of taking risks, of becoming Ford. Also, he sees himself as a government watchdog. Who will teach the nation's children the truth if he moves on? Who will send every new generation out with a complex understanding of how international conglomerates are controlling the world market, the world governments? This dichotomy of need makes Linus even more reluctant to speak with his brother, who exhibits all of the surface symptoms of being a good, providing father, while simultaneously mounting businesswomen and hookers on trips he takes to foreign and domestic cities under the pretense of raising investment capital and wooing clients.

Ford speaks with Alice with even less frequency than he speaks with Linus. Though she lives just twenty minutes away by cab, they do not see each other except at family gatherings and sometimes by chance on street corners. If anyone at Harrison Freidlow knew that Ford's sister was a recovering heroin addict he would not live it down. It's bad enough his father was a blue-collar union man, bad enough that his mother is still sewing patches onto dresses and socks, when he sends her enough money to buy whatever she wants. The business of money has made Ford very rich, but no one in his family seems to appreciate him for it. He considers himself cursed with a lineage of imbeciles and communists. It's amazing, he thinks, that I ever made it out of that recessive gene pool with any brains or looks at all. Whenever he calls Linus, usually on Sunday mornings when the rates are cheapest, he says, "How's my crazy brother? Still teaching the dogma of the paranoids and the kooks?"

Claudia tries to tell him that there is nothing more important than family. Linus looks at her skeptically and hands over the phone so that she and Ford or she and Madison may catch up, trade anecdotes, play siblings. It is the same with Linus's mother, who grinds away at him like a drill, always asking, "When am I going to see some grandchildren from you? When are you going to stop being crazy like your father and come back to Brooklyn, stop teaching those rich hippies and get a real job like your brother? Can't you see your wife is getting old? She needs a baby. I can tell. I'm a mother. I know these things."

The only one Linus will talk to is Alice. He calls her from his office every Friday afternoon.

How are you today? he asks. With heroin, as with alcohol, they tell you every day is important. Linus is not big on recovery dogma, but he is willing to use the language if it helps his sister.

I have my cat in my lap, she says, some tea. Brian is out getting the paper. He feels the need to read the paper ever day. He's got to work at seven.

Brian drives a truck for the *Village Voice*. He delivers papers once a week in the cold empty corridors of the early morning. The rest of the week he loads boats at the shipyard.

How's your job?

They get the food when it's hot, and if they're lucky a coffee refill. The tips are for shit, really. Worse and worse every day. Do you know who the worst tippers are? Businessmen. Businessmen tip like schmucks. I bet that brother of ours leaves twelve cents on a ten-dollar meal. I mean you'd think these guys were scrimping and saving to buy their kids some chemotherapy.

Do you need anything, money?

Alice laughs, a husky tired laugh that is not the sound that younger sisters are supposed to make, without innocence or joy.

What does your wife think, you offering your junkie sister a percentage of your kid's college fund?

I could send fifty, maybe a hundred? That's not going to make a dent. Besides, hers is the real salary. Mine hardly gets noticed. One zero too few, I think. Also, Claudia has a heart the size of Texas. You know, a real giver, which is why I love her, I guess. Anyway, she always tells me that there's nothing more important than family.

But Alice never takes his money, and so far she's been clean for nine months. It's this Brian, Linus thinks, and the fact that deep down his sister is a good person, scared of disappearing into the void of need and despair.

He means it when he says that Claudia's heart is big. She has none of the cynicism he thrives on. She is always the first one to call when she discovers a discarded wallet, to pledge fifty dollars to public television. Despite the fact that she works in advertising, she is not manipulative or calculating. If she has a fault, it is that she wants what everyone else wants, a nice home, some security, children. She wants their lives to progress, for their careers to move forward. She pushes him, not because she wants him to be someone else, but because she wants them both to continue to grow, to continue to thrive, so that neither one of them will lose interest, will move past the other. Linus knows this, but he also knows that he has found his niche, found his calling and his trade. He tries to tell her that he can still grow in his present position, but more and more when he looks for her beside him, he sees her far ahead, pulling away on a freeway of promotion and lifestyle changes. Slow down, he thinks. Come back. But she does not turn and instead it is up to him to catch up.

They met when he was in graduate school, a setup through a friend. She was already working in advertising, already writing copy for companies eager to market merchandise to ever-widening populations. The first time they met, Linus knew he would never see her again. She was too pretty and too well put together. He was twenty-six, she twenty-five, and he was one year away from his doctorate in alternative American history, while she lived in the Pacific Heights area of San Francisco and drove an Audi. She had friends named Jasper and Evan, while his peers went by code names, Hoffa and Haldeman, Hinckley and the Gipper.

They went to the Museum of Modern Art for their first date, wandering among the Mondrians and the de Koonings. She talked about lines and space and he noted how no one was willing to step right up to the paintings, to smell them, feel the weight of the paint on the canvas. "I like the process," he told her. "I like to see how the fat chunks of red and brown coagulate on the surface, to step up close and see the...well, face it...the ugliness of each brush of color." He told her jokes about his crazy Brooklyn family. His hair was short then, but full, and he looked even vaguely respectable in khakis and a nice pair of oxblood wingtips. It was his sense of humor that won through to her, he thought, his quick wit, and that day he felt alive and electric like she was pumping amps and volts through the weight of her eyes.

"I would have to say that art has finally been reduced to just another form of advertising," she said to him as they stood in a clot of bodies staring at the Diebenkorns. "In New York they have these murals scattered through the parking lots of SoHo. No image, just a signature. It says, *Rene: The best artist.* Here's a guy whose sole artistic statement is his own superiority to other artists."

Behind them a man on a cellular phone said, *It's more of a burning sensation.*

"I think art has turned into an excuse to wear provocative clothing. I picture the modern artist like the mad scientist testing a potion of incompatible elements on himself, the plaids and stripes, the blacks and browns. That and the importance of being seen in the right restaurants."

Claudia wore a black dress of suggestive length. Her shoes were expensive. She had a walk like a cocky man. She told him that she was fascinated by the human urge to sell.

"Did you know Hitler was the first public figure to use loudspeakers? His rise to power was a perfect example of the art of promotion. He designed all the Nazi uniforms, the banners. He had a vision for the future of modernism."

"Hitler's brain still lives in a jar in Langley, Virginia. Scientists ask it questions, mostly having to do with who he likes in the fourth race at Belmont."

Claudia smiled.

"That's funny what you said, mad scientists testing potions on themselves."

So although he'd thought it would be otherwise, he saw her again later that same week, and again the following. All the words that he spoke seemed to be the right ones, all the places they went and the things they did. She introduced him to her friends, who, as promised, were mainstream and unthreatening, and he showed her his, who were disheveled and hyperverbal. It became clear that they came from different environments, and he used to joke that they were rats from different behavioral-analysis labs congregating illegally in the damp newspaper of some abandoned cage.

They slipped into marriage easily, painlessly, just the solid impact of their families failing to find common ground at the rehearsal dinner and the reception.

With help from a small inheritance on Claudia's side, they bought a home in Tiburon the second year they were married. Linus fought for a less pretentious area, but in the end he was won over by the view of the Bay and the city skyline they could see from their deck. It's not a big house, just one story, two bedrooms, a large living room, full kitchen. The mortgage takes up a big part of their monthly income, but they have managed to put away a small sum in a fund they call their infant account. The unspoken agreement is that when the balance reaches thirty thousand they will take the appropriate actions to begin its use. By Linus's calculations this means about six more months until the concept of birth control becomes one of other people's concern.

And now they have been married almost six years. Linus is amazed at his ability to be responsible. He makes sure the garbage is out when it's supposed to be, makes sure the bills are paid on time, even writes each check number and the amount in the space allotted in his checkbook. As conspiracy gurus go, he is unique in that he lives well and has adopted the vestiges of the American dream, with a wife and plans for children. Despite politics, he tells people, we all must have lives that are worth living. There is no excuse for bitterness and loneliness other than our own self-subversive natures. Still, he is considered an oddity by his peers, and more often than not Claudia will stay home from the conferences and symposiums to allow him to appear more personally radical than he is.

The truth is, he has begun to get excited by the notion of his own child, has been planning how he will meet each milestone in the pregnancy, each event of Reagan's or Carter's life, the birthdays, the first tooth, the first bicycle. He has begun to make a list of the books and toys he loved as a child, begun to collect them secretly, storing them in his office so as not to tip his hand as to how much he wants this child. Not that he is keeping secrets from Claudia. It is just that they have agreed to wait until a certain dollar figure is reached, and he knows that if he confesses that he can't wait, then they won't, and he feels that structure and planning are essential to good parenting, and he doesn't want to start off on the wrong foot with impulsive actions and spontaneous decision making.

Still, he has squirreled away copies of all Tove Jansson's Moomin stories, has collected *Paddle to the Sea* and *The Phantom Tollbooth.* He is ready to teach his son or daughter how to play catch, how to ride a bike, how to read, ready to teach him or her the well-hidden secrets of twentieth-century living, the trysts and cabals of governments, the conspiracies of science and technology, the atrocities of puppet bureaucracies and corporate takeovers, and the poorly disguised knowledge that when it comes to sentient life in this universe, we are not alone.

In the gymnasium there is mostly silence. Curtains have been erected in geometric patterns, closing off the bodies from one another, creating the illusion of rooms, of dignity. A thin corridor cuts its way between the hang of white sheets. Padding through it, Linus has the sensation of being in heaven. The air smells burned in a way that Linus can only assume signifies death. He takes the mentholated gel the coroner offers him and wipes it under each nostril. At the strong medicinal smell his head jerks up involuntarily. The gym is lit with a diffused glazing that refracts off the curtains, erasing shadows and any perception of depth.

The coroner looks grim. He has met Linus at the door, accompanied by two agents from the National Transportation Safety Board. All three look tired, overcome by the fumes of mass extinction.

"Mr. Owen, I'm Agent Crawford and this is Agent Parker."

Linus nods. He has met so many agents, they are quickly becoming a composite sketch of authority. The coroner swallows, offers his hand.

"Bill Bowen."

Linus hands him a shake as limp as any traveling salesman's. He has chewed his lips down to raw skin and the metallic flavor of his own blood. The gym is cold, over–air conditioned to prevent premature spoilage, and Linus feels the breeze on his exposed ankles.

"Can I see her?" he tries to say, clears his throat, tries again.

"Of course," says Bowen. He takes Linus's arm. "I want you to know that your wife died very quickly, if it's any consolation. Not that it would be, but still. Some people take comfort in that."

"Yes," says Linus, fumbling with the choreography of language. "Some people do."

The four walk slowly down an aisle of white fabric. To the sides are openings in which the long plastic-shrouded forms of the dead look like fallen trees, piles of garbage, casualties of war.

"Do you feel like you might faint, Mr. Owen? Any light-headedness, dizziness, nausea?"

Linus runs his hand through his hair. His scalp is greasy. His hand comes away coated with sweat.

"I'm—I think I'll be okay."

Bowen continues to guide him by the arm, snaking through the rows. The two agents are quiet, clearly uncomfortable. If this were TV they would pull each other aside, light cigarettes, say, This is the part of the job I hate.

"You should know that your wife's body is intact. She died from the impact, but there was some fire damage after death. I will need you to consider the peculiarities of her form. An identification based on her body, not her face."

"What about dental records? I thought you could do this from teeth, from imprints."

"It takes time, sir. Yes, it does. And the not knowing. Well, I think you would agree that if we can settle this now..."

Linus wipes his sweaty palms on the sides of his pants. There is a part of him that would be willing to live in doubt for a very long time. A part that wants to pack up a mental U-Haul and cross the rocky borders into the northwestern state of denial.

"My wife has a mole under her right breast. There is also a scar from sitting on a broken bottle on the back of her left thigh."

Bowen nods. That will make it easier, he thinks. He squeezes Linus's arm and stops him short, turns to face him. He is an older man, bald on top, going gray on the sides, wearing a flaccid gray suit. There are bags under his eyes. He has been county coroner for fifteen years and today he has seen more bodies than in all that time.

"If you feel like you might pass out, Mr. Owen," he says, "I want you to tell me. The sight of death can produce many different reactions. You may want to run or weep, or you may become unreasonably angry. I have been coroner for fifteen years. There is no wrong reaction, and you should let yourself feel whatever you will feel. This is a gruesome, gruesome thing, but it must be done. Try and make the identification quickly. The memories you have of your wife should be those of her alive, of better times. This should not be how you remember her. If you cannot make the identification quickly, or if you're not sure, we won't press you. It can damage one to look too long. Are you hearing me?"

Linus nods. The blood is roaring in his ears. Behind Bowen he can see a toe, part of a foot. His mouth has gone dry. Bowen stares into his face to try to judge if Linus is in any state to proceed.

"Okay," he says. "Frank, Ted, I'm going to ask you to wait out here. Mr. Owen and I will step inside and take a look, then you can take him out and get him a drink, find him a quiet place to sit. When he's feeling better you can talk to him about what's happened here. I can't make you give him a chance to catch his breath, but that's my advice."

"We're not monsters, Doc," says Agent Crawford. "Mr. Owen can talk to us when he's ready."

Bowen nods.

"Let's go then, Mr. Owen."

The body is laid out on a long folding table, like the kind used in Holiday Inn conference rooms. Inside the curtained walls there is barely enough room to stand. Linus stops at the feet.

"We have kept her face covered. It will not help you in recognizing her and it's better that you don't see." He rubs his cheeks with his thumb and forefinger.

Linus looks down slowly, then up again, faster this time. He puts his hand under his chin, squeezes his own throat, feels the blood pounding in his head. Above the curtains he can see the tattered white net of the backstop, the black scuffed metal of the hoop. He can see the sun, bright squares choked back by the wire mesh that coats the windows. It is absorbed by the cold glare of the fluorescents. He is trying to strangle the lump in his throat but succeeds only in forcing it higher until his eyes water and he puts his teeth neatly through the skin of his lower lip. A thin line of blood runs over his mouth and works its way down his chin.

"Okay," he says. "Okay. It's her."

And on his way out through the rippling maze of soft white curtains he breaks down, hunches over, at first still shuffling forward under the firm lift of Bowen's arms, and then, quickly, mercifully, he loses consciousness and slides to the floor.

■

"Mr. Owen, this interview is really more of a formality than anything else. So if you don't feel up to it..."

There is the sound of helicopters nearby, black metal vultures scanning the Everglades for the last castoffs of debris. A piece of wing, of tail, a shoe, the torn sweater off somebody's baby. Linus looks at the glass of water they have given him, but it's empty, just a damp cup with the clear smudge of his fingerprints visible on the stem. He has regained consciousness, has been allowed to go to the bathroom and splash water on his face. That he is in shock is not in doubt; it is the extent to which he is unable to function that has yet to be demonstrated. Linus is in a sixth-grade classroom, tucked behind the teacher's desk. Behind him the blackboard still carries pictograms of chalk, the details of homework assignments, quotes from Crane's *The Red Badge of Courage*. The agents, four in all from various agencies, stand around him, clearly uncomfortable with Linus's inability to control his grief. There is always the possibility that his emotions might rub off on them. Disaster survivors are as contagious as the poor. He sits up and shakes his head.

"No, I can continue."

Agents Parker and Crawford of the NTSB are there, though if you were to examine Crawford's records closely enough you would find that he is really employed by the NSA. The other two agents claim to be from the FBI. One is blond, skinny, and dressed in the type of suit Linus had envisioned buying to impress his wife. The other wears a mustache and something cheap and blue. They have told him their names are Forbes and Buckley (no first names), but Linus thinks they could be anybody, CIA, DEA, the list is endless. The truth is, Forbes works for the CIA, though even Buckley is not aware of it. He spends his days doing things he cannot tell his wife about.

Buckley, by comparison, is relatively tame. His secrets are more modest and mundane. He is afraid that he might be a homosexual, because sometimes he fantasizes about making love to men. To counter this he will only have sex with the lights on, so that he can be sure that he is making love to a woman, can condition himself to associate orgasm with the bodies of a biblically sanctioned gender. When he was twelve his brother sodomized him in the basement of a summer home. Now Buckley cannot eat oysters or scallops. Bouillabaisse makes him gag. But still, there are the memories, and a jumble of conflicting emotions.

There is also a representative of the airlines hovering in the back of the classroom, who speaks only when some issue of liability is raised, and then only to say, "The airline is happy to attend to any needs or wants you may have," or, "This is a terrible tragedy and we just want you to know we're there for you one hundred percent." His name is Morgenstern, Louis Morgenstern, and Linus dislikes him as intensely as is possible for someone he's just met, not for any particular cruelty or personal infraction on Morgenstern's part, but because he is a kiss-ass in a cheap suit, whose job it is to keep people from suing his airline. This makes his words of comfort and support as disingenuous as Hallmark cards.

"Can you think of any reason your wife might have been on that plane?" Agent Forbes asks him.

"I wish I could. Some kind of clue. I just can't think of anything. She went to her mother's. She was supposed to stay at her mother's." Linus has been racking his brains. He has combed through his mind until there is nothing left but question marks, rows and channels and canals of question marks.

"Had she been to New York recently? Before this trip."

"Six months ago. She had clients. Presentations to make. I don't keep up with her work so much."

Agent Forbes loosens his tie. He feels like he's been wearing it since Tuesday. Later in the afternoon a padded envelope will arrive carrying the sum total of Linus's works, his two books, five articles, seven letters to the editors of various newspapers and magazines. Back at his hotel room, Forbes will ingest one quarter of an unmarked purple pill. He will take a shower, open Linus's dossier, and begin to dictate notes into a handheld microcassette recorder.

"The people in Mr. Holden's office tell us that your wife was there in July on business."

Linus tries to do the mental mathematics, thinks, The summer, she did go in summer.

"That would have been the trip. Yes."

"Have you ever met Mr. Holden? Heard your wife speak of him?"

Linus shakes his head.

"I've thought about it. I mean, who is this man? Someone said... I mean, holding hands came up, but...I've never heard his name. I'm sure of that."

The agents nod. Agent Parker from the National Transportation Safety Board clears his throat.

"There is the possibility that this was a personal trip," he says.

Linus is not interested in considering that possibility.

"Fuck you too," he says, but only because he's from Brooklyn, and not very polite when aspersions are cast on his family. The truth is, he is unwilling to think about the possibility of Claudia dying for the romance of another man.

His outburst breeds an uncomfortable silence. These are men who under different circumstances might be pushing his head down into the frigid pouch of a toilet bowl, a fact of which everyone in that room is aware. Behind closed doors Linus is referred to by investigators as "the anarchist." However, grief allows him a certain leeway, despite his unpopular political views.

"Mr. Owen," says Forbes, raising his pointer finger as if to admonish a child.

"Right," says Linus in a clipped voice. "Sorry. But listen, I have some questions here too, some requests."

"Whatever we can do to help you, sir," says Parker.

Linus pulls himself up in his seat. He doesn't like being surrounded like this, doesn't like them all looking down on him. He gets to his feet, puts his back to the blackboard, then as they make room for him he crosses to the window, looks out at the rows of emergency vehicles, the sea of unmarked law-enforcement vehicles.

"Do we have any idea who planted this bomb?"

Forbes leans his rear on the edge of the desk, crosses his arms.

"No. Right now no one's claiming responsibility."

"Well, that hardly makes a difference. What sort of warnings have you had in the past few days? What kind of threats? I mean this country has more intelligence agencies than congressional pension plans. There are records, surveillance files, information passing through phone lines, modem lines. It's not plausible that you have no idea, not even a clue."

"Be that as it may, Linus," says Forbes, taking out a cigarette and lighting it. "My answer stands."

Linus nods. It's not that he expected anything else. But it is the nature of human beings to hope.

"Fine, so you're going to lie to me."

"Mr. Owen..."

"No, that's okay. Why should today be any different? So my next question," he says, before they can interrupt him, "my next question is, who else was on that plane?"

Forbes looks at the two men from the NTSB. They shake their heads and make faces, as if to say, What the hell kind of question is that?

"I'm not sure I understand your question, sir," says Forbes.

"I'd like to see a roster of the passengers on that plane. Most likely the bomb was directed at someone, or a group of someones in particular. Despite whatever assertions are made about random acts of terrorism, it is my experience that there is no such thing."

"And what experience have you had with random acts of terrorism, Mr. Owen?" asks Agent Buckley, pulling his hands from his pockets. He has withdrawn a notepad and a pen. He is poised as if ready to write.

"Very funny," says Linus, rubbing at one bloodshot eye. They just seem to be tearing on their own now, his body going about the business of mourning despite his wishes or attempts for control. "Look, I'm sure you're familiar with my work. Despite my outdated wardrobe, I am at least partially famous with law enforcement and government intelligence agencies. Perhaps you've even read the article I wrote on the psychology of crowds and crowd control. Fear can be a very effective tool. But I'm sure you know this. Sometimes we even bomb ourselves if it will move the country in the direction the Pentagon wants it to go. Take the Gulf of Tonkin. I've already discussed Pan Am flight 103 with some of your colleagues, but I'd be happy to go into it again if you're interested."

"Mr. Owen," says Agent Forbes, who doesn't like to be lectured to, especially by radicals. He puts out his cigarette in the bottom of a metal trash can, steps forward. "We're not interested in a confrontation with you right now. We realize you're upset. We would like to get through this as painlessly as possible." Privately he is thinking of all the other things he could be doing.

Linus nods.

Forbes and Linus, as much as they would deny it, have something in common. They both have brothers they can't stand. Forbes's brother (Forbes's real name is Richard Wermer, born on 14 June 1962, SSN 312-56-7841, and his real hair color is closer to brown) is an auto mechanic in Allentown, Pennsylvania, who drinks too much and has been arrested twice: once for driving under the influence, the second for knocking out two of his wife's teeth.

Forbes's own wife calls him Richard. She too thinks he works for the FBI. This insistence on secrecy has infected other parts of his life, until he cannot be sure some days which truth she believes, what stories he's told her. For example, there is a scar that runs the length of Forbes's right leg. When Julie asks him how he got it, he tells her it happened in a skiing accident on a trip he told her he took with his friends to Aspen, but in fact he was bitten by a rabid dog in San Salvador, a skeletal mutt that jumped out from a maze of trash cans and tore him up. He had to shoot the damn thing to get it to let go, screaming and cursing, its jaws like a vise grip cutting off his leg. The local doctor, smelling of moonshine and American cigarettes, rubbed ethanol alcohol into the eruption of his groin and sank twenty-one rusty needles into his stomach. Sometimes Forbes fantasizes about putting a plastic bag over his wife's head when he fucks her. He is excited by the notion of asphyxiation. Perhaps this is because he cannot breathe a word of the truth to anyone.

"So you can provide me with a copy of the passenger roster."

"We will release the passenger list to the media within a few hours. The airline has been very cooperative in helping us figure out exactly who was on that plane."

In the background Mr. Morgenstern perks up at the compliment. He is considering how he can work this reference into his next press conference.

Linus shakes his head.

"No. I want to see the unabridged list. The original one, before you've taken off all of the questionable names."

"Mr. Owen, don't you think you're being slightly paranoid?"

Linus sees red, pictures his wife's body, her face covered by plastic. She was missing two toes on her right foot. Two toes. He has to come to terms with the fact that part of her will have to be left in Florida, like a nagging concern that jabs at you from the bottom of your consciousness. He makes his hands into fists, says:

"I won't even justify that with a response. All I'm saying, without getting into a lengthy discussion about the history of American covert operations and cover-ups, is that I have questions that must be addressed. And we can do this one of two ways. Either I can make myself the biggest pest you ever had, and as you know I have no qualms about being called a kook, or you can give me what I need and I'll shut up."

Linus chews his lip, though this just reopens the skin and the bleeding starts again. He has tasted his own blood a lot in the past few days. Perhaps this is some indication that he should consider more carefully the implications of his own mortality.

"First of all, Mr. Owen," says Agent Buckley, putting his pad away and buttoning his jacket, "I doubt very much you would shut up, even were we to give you what you want. People like you are only interested in furthering their own causes at the expense of the American people. Second of all, the passenger roster will be released within two hours and I'm sure a representative of the airline would be happy to provide you with one personally, as soon as it is available. So there's no need to argue over something we are all in agreement you will receive."

Mr. Morgenstern, hearing the word *airline,* leaps forward to assure Linus that he will personally deliver a copy to him, as the agents, through the medium of eye contact, begin to move together in the direction of the door.

"Mr. Owen," says Forbes, buttoning his jacket, "again, our condolences. If you need anything more, please don't hesitate to contact us, but I would caution you that we are very busy trying to get to the bottom of this matter, and the less distractions, the quicker justice can be done here. Someone will contact you regarding the issue of your wife's remains."

Linus is on the verge of chasing them from the room with a litany of epithets about his rights, when Forbes uses the word *remains.* It is like a brick wall that jumps up and hits him in the chest. He stands there not knowing what to do with his hands. The agents file from the room as Linus stares after them.

"Sir, I'm gonna make sure you get a copy of that roster first thing. First thing," says Morgenstern, stepping up to offer him his arm for support should it be required. Linus shrugs him off. At that moment one of the FBI agents in the main office placing a long-distance phone call on a sticky rotary phone accidentally reclines against a mechanized panel, and the oppressive drone of the school bell bellows forth its instructive cry, signaling to the classrooms of bomb-squad technicians, the blue-brown clots of federal agents clustered near water fountains and battered lockers, the topiary of lifeless bodies filling the gymnasium that the end of this period has come at last.

When Linus gets back to his hotel he is ambushed by representatives from the airline. Since identifying Claudia, he has avoided interviews with the press, slipped out of the comforting crush of therapists, and declined invitations to join a survivors' group. I have survived nothing, he tells them. I am a walking dead man. This type of comment, surrounding the specter of mass extinction, spooks even the most leechlike, and in this way Linus has managed to cut through the crowds. He is driven back to the Marriott by Agent Perry, just out of the academy, still puffed up by the ideals of truth and justice like a caricature of Eliot Ness.

"Are you familiar with J. Edgar Hoover?" Linus asks him.

"Sir?"

"Liked to wear women's dresses. Kept files on the sex lives of the politically famous. He had Polaroids of Lyndon Johnson sodomizing a farm animal."

Perry looks over at Linus and considers making him ride the rest of the way in the trunk. He was born in Miami a bastard with no father, and has struggled out from under the great weight of prejudice to prove his merit in the hierarchical jungle of the FBI. When he was nine years old he killed a rat with an M-80, then threw up afterward. It has been the straight and narrow path ever since.

"Word is you're a communist, sir," Perry says.

"Is anyone still a communist? Is that what it says in my file, a communist?"

"I haven't seen your file, sir."

"Neither have I, but I hope it says something better than communist. We're talking about millions of dollars of taxpayer money spent on domestic intelligence, all so some guy in a bad tie with no neck can write the word *communist* on a man's file without any substantial elaboration."

"I wouldn't know, sir. Last time I checked I had a neck."

"Very good, Perry. Very good. You get the FBI wit-of-the-day award."

Perry is thinking that if he took the spare tire out of the trunk there would definitely be room for one passenger inside. He is also wondering if he's been given the chauffeur's job because he's black. All I need is a fucking cap, he thinks. He is as eager to do real law-enforcement work as a thirteen-year-old boy spying out his first breast. At night he reviews federal statutes, lying naked on the floor of his one-bedroom apartment.

"I'm sorry for your loss, sir," he says, intent on rising above. He has to practice his patience. It is the FBI thing to do.

"Sorry for my loss? How humane of you, Perry. My wife is dead, you realize. She's not a bet or a set of keys that has been misplaced, not a credit card to report stolen. She's just a husk now." Linus rubs one eye with his fingers. "And I am well on my way to becoming a bitter old man."

Perry clenches his jaw, checks his side- and rearview mirrors. Mr. Owen has just experienced a real tragedy, he thinks. I can take the slings and arrows. It's only five or six more miles. Linus, beside him, is watching the asphalt slide by under their wheels. It is hypnotizing him into a sort of trance.

"Have you ever *lost* someone, Perry, a wife?"

Perry thinks of Francine, how she smelled stale at the end, how shocking it was to discover that mold can actually grow in the hidden folds of fat people.

"My mother died last year, Mr. Owen."

"My father died five and a half years ago."

Perry adjusts the side-view mirror, switches lanes.

"It's not a competition, sir. She was my mother, after all."

Linus nods, leans over, and presses his face against the cool glass of his window.

"You're absolutely right, Perry. I'm being a total ass."

They drive for a while, watching the cars flash by; thoughts soon forgotten.

"Had you been married a long time, sir?"

Linus rolls his face to the other side, feels the glass pressing his flesh.

"Almost six years."

"It's obvious you loved her very much."

Linus says nothing. He is thinking of the mornings he spent lying in bed watching her dress. Every day, first the socks, then underwear, then the bra. What to wear? The riffling of drawers, the sideways shuffle of clothes on the hanger. Every day her wet hair, the damp towels that held her smell well into afternoon, the litterings of mascara cases and lipstick tubes on the counter. The way she looked in jeans or skirts, that sudden flash of ankle.

"Do you realize that the world is run by people so wealthy they will never know what it's like to go hungry, to worry about their children going hungry?"

Perry pulls in behind a red Ford pickup truck. He's driving fifty-five miles an hour exactly.

"Hadn't thought about it much, sir."

"When I was a boy and my father would go on strike, we'd eat onions sometimes for dinner. Sometimes just beans, just day-old bread."

Perry changes lanes again. He is a man who's never happy being where he is.

"I used to survive on Doritos and sweet potatoes, sir. My mother was on welfare most of the time. She was disabled." Francine had been classified as disabled because of her weight, because just standing up was a chore. Three hundred pounds in the end. A little less than twice his weight and he was no weakling, her body a mighty structure collapsed in on itself. Her breathing an animal rasping, clawing its way out from under the burden of her breasts. A hundred and thirty-one dollars a week, and there'd been five kids to feed.

"Right. My wife came from privilege, so she didn't understand. But you would. When you've suffered the drain of malnutrition you become a certain kind of person. I mean, it's never good for a child to go hungry, but I think it helps them to understand."

"Understand?"

"That the world is not a nurturing space, that they shouldn't take for granted what they have. In this way children do not grow up with the misunderstanding that life is fair."

"I guess I'd have to..."

"Because it's not fair, and we forget sometimes. We get caught up in our lives, and things become static and we feel safe. And love is what makes it okay that life is not fair. I know it sounds schmaltzy, but it's true. Love makes it okay, but life has this final injustice to hand you just when you feel you have come to accept the world you've been given, and so planes crash, elevators fall fifty-two stories, fires burn out of control. There is the phone call in the middle of the night. When we would go hungry in Brooklyn and my parents would conspire in the kitchen to come up with some way to feed us, there would come this real feeling of family. That was when we were closest, when we were just trying to stay alive." He trails off, lets the sound of the road fill the void.

"Later on, though, when I was ten or eleven, my sister and I discovered that my brother was hiding food. That he'd been beating up kids in school for their lunch money and using that money to buy candy bars and hot dogs and boxes of sugar cereal, and he wasn't sharing. He wasn't making up a lie to tell my parents so that we could eat. He was just hoarding and feasting. There were wrappers and half-filled bags of M&M's in his footlocker. Obviously this wasn't right. Something had to be done. Unfortunately, Ford didn't agree. There was a bloody nose in it for me, a twisted arm for Alice. The threat of further violence. That was the price of our silence, his brutality. He was much bigger than us. He's still bigger. And, I mean, you want to talk, but the fear of pain keeps you quiet, makes the hunger slip to a pale retreat. When I got older I swore that no bully would ever make me hold my tongue again, not my brother and not the FBI and not the threats and ridicule of the people with the most to hide. I tell you this because you've gone hungry too. You know what it is to feel that emptiness. There is no shit in the phrase, A hungry man is an angry man. No shit. Sometimes there's strength for nothing else."

Linus picks his face up off the glass, wipes his forehead on his palm.

"You know, Agent Perry, my wife was what made it okay that the world is a brutal place. In the end that is what love is. And now..."

There is just the road and the thick sour smell of the sun.

When they reach the hotel Linus climbs out into the Florida heat. His suit is soaked through in the back. Agent Perry watches him struggle to arrange his crumpled clothes around him. It is obvious that Linus is one step away from breakdown. Feeling the sweat soak in under his own arms, Perry leans over and rolls down the passenger side window.

"Mr. Owen."

Linus runs his hand through his thinning hair like a man trying to restore his dignity after a long bout of public ridicule. He leans over and places his palms on the hot metal of the door.

"Agent Perry?"

"When my mother died I was just finishing up at the academy. They called me back from Virginia. She'd had a heart attack. My mother was, well, she was a big woman, sir, heavy. Her heart was just this small little engine trying to run this monster truck. They had her at the funeral home and we didn't really have much family other than my little brothers and sisters who were still just kids really, and Mama didn't get out much, because of her weight, so it was just me and my aunt Lottie. We had to hire pallbearers, a lot of them." Agent Perry is sweating more in the heat of the open window, the collar of his shirt going yellow. Linus feels like his legs are wavering, his body becoming heavier, but he wants to listen, wants to hear some words that might actually have meaning.

"After they buried her I walked out of the cemetery, walked away from that place and crossed streets and avenues, going nowhere, you understand, just walking. And somewhere along the way it got dark and then I'm walking past the highway, all the way downtown, and I'm not thinking, just walking, and I go up the on ramp and cars are passing me honking, guys are yelling at me, but I'm still going, and I make my way up onto 95, and it's like this river, this fast-moving river of lights and I'm still going, not on the shoulder but in a lane, my own lane, with cars swerving around me and the sound of shrieking tires. It's like wading through a hurricane, and all I'm thinking about is Mama and how she used to put enough thread in my ratty old socks to make two new pairs and then as I'm thinking I just make a left, I turn left and head out toward the median. The speed limit is fifty-five. It's maybe eight o'clock at night, not rush hour, but still, heavy traffic, and I am walking across the highway, I think because I was looking for a sign that God wanted me alive."

Linus feels as if he's going to pass out again, either from the heat or the import of everything that has happened to him. He is a man standing under a pillar of sunlight meant to knock him to his knees, but he won't go down.

"I sort of woke up when I hit the median," says Agent Perry, sweat now dripping from his chin to darken the fabric of the passenger seat. "I guess I said, What the fuck am I doing here, you know? But you know what else? Even though I made it through that without a scratch, I didn't think it was a sign. I just thought I was a crazy fool, a crazy fool who got lucky, because I still didn't want to believe that somehow I was supposed to live after she died. But look, sir, I don't mean to make you stand out there in all this heat. My point is, Look, here I am today. It still hurts, sure it does, but you get over it. It stops hurting so much."

Linus clears his throat. He's trying to remember how to talk, something about his tongue, his mouth opening, closing.

"I don't want to get over it," he mumbles.

And Perry nods and reaches for the lever to roll up the window. He puts his hand on it and stops and looks Linus in the face, who is pale and splotchy and looks near death himself.

"You don't have a choice, sir," he says. "One day it just happens."

■

Inside, Linus finds that the convention atmosphere of the junior high school has carried over to the lobby of the Marriott. Through the revolving door he comes, hitting, upon entry, a solid wall of air conditioning that slaps his face, grabs his body, sucks him inside. He wades through the reporters, makes his way to the elevator, closes his eyes as it rises through the atmosphere of hothouse vegetation that someone in Marriott management thought would make the hotel more inviting. He leans his head against the elevator doors. Recently it is as if his head has become too heavy for his body to support without help. He is not alone, but he doesn't care. A tourist and his wife, two children. Are you okay, buddy? You all right there? His nose starts to bleed.

He feels the blood run down his lip, tastes it on the edges of his tongue. His hand comes up reflexively to catch it before it can ruin his suit. He puts his head back, opens his eyes. Above him the numbers are climbing, 13, 14, 15, 16. He feels a little dizzy, but that can be blamed on a lack of food and water. It's always good to eat three meals a day, he thinks, especially if you're going to have a heavy itinerary of corpse identification and confronting authority figures.

"Hey, buddy, you don't look so good." A hand on his arm. The man's wife is digging in her purse for a handkerchief or a Kleenex. The two kids are sniggering under their father's arm. They have been whispering the word *fart* to each other for the last half hour. There is an electronic sound. The doors open on 17. Linus steps off, his head back, holding the woman's Kleenex to his nose. In front of his room he finds two representatives from the airline checking their watches. At first there is relief in their eyes when they see him, but it quickly turns to alarm when they notice blood dribbling over his fingers.

"My God, Mr. Owen, are you all right?"

They take his arms and get his door open, lead him inside. Linus goes into the bathroom and locks the door. Outside, the airline reps hear the click of the bolt sliding home. They exchange looks.

"Mr. Owen, maybe we should call a doctor." The man has hair that sits on the collar of his white oxford. He nods to the woman, who is wearing a brown skirt suit and has a mole under her right eye. The woman goes to the phone to call down to the front desk. Linus throws the blood-soaked Kleenex in the trash. The glasses on the toilet tank have paper jackets.

"It's just a nosebleed," he calls to them. He doesn't want to be monitored by a physician. He closes his eyes and tries to make the airline people disappear with his mind. Outside, the woman accidentally drops the receiver, the clatter of plastic. "I get them all the time," he says, when it's clear they're not going to go away.

Airline representative Jack Evers motions to his partner to put down the phone. He used to sell real estate in Tallahassee, so he is under the mistaken impression that he knows how to read people. He has a wife, Linda, who does part-time modeling work to promote local tourism, and a son, Marshall, away at college. A weird adopted boy he doesn't like too much. In Jack's office at the airline is a postcard with his wife in a thong bikini, her ass cheeks shiny and brown, standing on the fluorescent edges of the word *Florida*.

"Sorry to bother you, sir, but we were hoping we could do something to make this experience less...well, painful."

The woman has crossed to the bathroom door. She puts her ear to the wood. They don't need this guy flipping out on them. It's hard enough to handle all of these grieving families, to take the edge off the malice they feel toward the airline, without having some rogue husband blow the whole thing up in their faces.

"Sir, my name is Sally Fields. Like the actress. This other voice belongs to my co-worker Jack Evers. We're from the airline. I realize you've spoken to a lot of people today. We don't want to take up too much of your time, but we're concerned with the condition of all of the families of our passengers. We just want to make sure you have everything you need, that your questions are being answered—basically, that you're not lost in all the hullabaloo." She looks at Evers, shakes her head. He shrugs, mouths the word *mental.*

Sally is a single mother, a divorcee. There was a time when she had everything she wanted, a fabulous husband, kids, a beautiful home, but now she lives in a three-bedroom apartment in a questionable part of town and her husband lives in Key West with a twenty-year-old girl with breast implants. She would agree with Linus's assessment on the fairness of life.

In the bathroom Linus wets two pieces of Kleenex with cold water, jams them up his nostrils. His eyes have started to water. He is wondering how he's going to get these people out of here so he can call Edward and Roy. He considers the possibility that his room and phone are bugged. It's a chance he'll have to take. When the bleeding is under control he washes his hands, dries them, checks his jacket pocket for his keys, loosens his tie. His sweat-soaked clothes are drying, but the air conditioning makes him feel chilled, like he's being frozen. He looks at himself in the mirror, hair like the lawn of an abandoned house, eyes red rimmed, shirt wrinkled and speckled with blood. He is a man with nostrils enlarged by wet wads of paper. He clears his throat and opens the door. Jack and Sally are caught standing too close to the door and they step back, embarrassed.

"Are you okay, sir? Can I get you anything?" Sally maneuvers herself past the bed to one of the brown chairs that decorate the room. Jack goes into the bathroom and slips three glasses from their jackets. He fills them with water and brings them out, sets them on the table. Linus takes off his tie. Sally pulls out a chair for him. She looks at Jack, who nods, and goes into her routine.

"Mr. Owen, as a representative of the airline, I just want to say how sorry we are for your loss."

Linus smiles.

"Uh, we think...we think it's good for all of the family members who've suffered a tragedy like this to feel like they have someone they can talk to, someone to help them get through this terrible period of mourning. Some people have friends or other family members. Some people like to seek help from professional sources. I just want to let you know—"

"Sally, right?" interrupts Linus.

"Yes, right." Sally sits up in her chair. She is prepared to be as receptive to Linus's needs as is humanly possible.

"Listen carefully, Sally. I'm going to make you a deal. I don't want therapy. I don't need help from a professional, and I'm getting real tired of the airline protecting their ass and pretending it's sympathy."

"Mr. Owen." This from Jack Evers, who stands stiffly, not drinking his water.

"Pipe down there, airline boy." He keeps his eyes on Sally. "So listen. All I want is a list of the passengers who were on that plane. It doesn't really matter why. You can think I'm crazy if you want to. I'm not going to argue, but here's the tricky part. I want a copy of the original list, not the one that your bosses are editing now for public consumption. I want to know who was on that airplane. Every single person. And if you get that to me, *if,* then I will be more than happy to sign a waiver absolving the airline of all responsibility in the crash. I will give up my right to sue. Sounds simple, right? And it is. The list and I go away and you can stop coming around here kissing my ass. The alternative, so I'm clear, is that I personally lead the other victims' families in a bloodletting of your airline, the likes of which you've never seen. I will sue you into the next century without fail. Am I making myself clear?"

Sally's face is screwed up. She is in shock that this man is sitting here addressing her like she's guilty of some kind of criminal offense. She would like to keep patronizing Linus on the grounds that he is grief-stricken. He is, however, making it extremely difficult. But there is something else too. She's not dumb. She does see benefits to his offer, even if he is crazy, a way to get this over with quickly. A waiver could potentially save the airline a lot of money, could be a public relations coup to show to the other families, to the public. She looks at Jack. He looks ready to haul Linus to his feet and rebloody his nose. She warns him off with her eyes. He is as intelligent as a sack of hammers but has proven himself willing to step out of her way when he can't figure a situation out, which happens whenever people stray from the script he's memorized.

"Perhaps if you took a calmer tone we could discuss this like adults," she says.

Linus plucks the Kleenex from his nose and drops them on the table. They sit there like small dead rodents. Sally flinches from them. She looks at Linus, whose eyes are hard. She stands up, brushes her skirt flat.

"I'll have the list here in an hour. You will sign the waiver then, and, Mr. Owen, I seriously recommend you get some professional help. Your behavior is absolutely bizarre."

Linus picks up his glass, drinks. Blood from his nose drips down, one, two, three, and dissolves in the tilted reflections of the water. He stands up, licks the crimson from his lip.

"One hour then."

After Sally and Jack are gone, Linus climbs into the shower in his clothes and lets the hot water pummel him into unconsciousness.

■

"There are four names on the original list that aren't in the paper," says Edward.

It is 9:00 P.M. Linus is sitting on the edge of his bed. Edward and Roy have him on speakerphone. They have spent the day calling in every favor and marker owed them by the counterintelligence community. Around 6:15 Linus faxed them the list that was dropped off by Mr. Morgenstern of the airline. Morgenstern looked as though he had been warned that Linus might be violent, so he kept a distinct distance except when he was handing over the documents. Linus read them over and signed the waiver Larry P. Owen, which was not his real name.

"Any of these names strike a bell?" asks Linus. His nosebleed has stopped. He has eaten a small dinner, left the dishes piled on the tray on top of the television.

On the other side of the country, Edward and Roy shake their heads. There is a discarded pizza box squatting on top of their printer.

"Aliases probably," says Roy. "We're working on a lead we have through..." He stops himself, pauses, considers the possibility that the phone might be tapped. "Well, there could be video."

Video, thinks Linus. He pictures small surveillance cameras lurking in the shadows of airport walkways.

"How long until you know?" He fingers his lower lip, which is sore where he bit through it earlier.

"Soon, we hope." Edward has asked his video connection to

direct-modem the footage to him the moment he receives it. He will stay up all night watching his computer wait.

"Listen, Professor," says Roy, and by the tone of his voice Linus can tell what's coming.

"Don't tell me how sorry you are," he interrupts. "I mean, just don't."

There is an awkward silence. It costs the airline ninety-two cents, of which the hotel will take fifteen.

Roy clears his throat.

"We're looking into a rogue wing of the CIA that could be involved."

"Well, until we can figure out exactly who was on that plane, I think we're just spinning our wheels." Linus stands at the window, watching the cars pass by on the highway below. On the horizon silver clouds are sneaking through the atmosphere, moving to smother the moon.

"I'm going to New York in the morning. It's important to keep moving. Who is Jeffrey Holden? This is what I must find out. Call me as soon as you know anything." He hangs up without giving Edward or Roy a chance to say anything. It will be two hours before Linus is able to sink into a restless sleep.

What is the nature of a conspiracy? *Webster's* defines it in three ways: (1) the act of conspiring; (2) a group planning to commit an unlawful or evil act; (3) the persons involved in such a plan. Secrecy is the unspoken element of these definitions. Why it is not included is hard to say, perhaps this is no small conspiracy in itself, but whatever the reason, Linus would say that secrecy lies at the heart of all successful conspiracies. Clandestine figures plotting nefarious activities in smoke-darkened basements and hotel rooms. As a society we are intrigued just by the concept. Our imaginations are easily sparked by the subtle plots of devious men. It is a symptom of fear, fear of a loss of individuality. If a group can combine, can plot, their goal can only be the erasure of the individual. From routine conspiracies to commit murder to government conspiracies to conceal truths, the underlying principle is control. Control of the individual by the group. Politicians use this fear when they speak of the conspiracies of Jewish bankers, cabals of international businessmen. Even the unremarkable conferrings of Planned Parenthood take on a sinister quality when portrayed in the proper light. These are the nuances Linus explores in his classes, not simply the rhetoric of specific plots, but also the need ingrained in people to believe in them and the usefulness of this need to larger groups that would seek to manipulate them. The wheel inside the wheel, he says. The chicken and the egg.

Remember, he tells his students. There are conspiracy theorists on both extremes of the political spectrum. The far left sees CIA agents in every corner and so does the gun-toting militiaman who believes in family values and the NRA. The reasons are different, but the fear is the same. In investigating any conspiracy theory you need to examine closely the element of fear, your own especially. But here are two tips: Follow the money, and follow who benefits. In any battle in which the outcome is suspicious we always blame the winners, for they are the obvious perpetrators of any devious plot, but sometimes the responsible parties are more mysterious. A successful conspiracy points in any number of directions. So with JFK, a model on which other conspiracies are based. So many suspects, manufactured evidence pointing fingers in every direction. Uncovering a conspiracy can be a question of layers. There are the obvious scapegoats. It is always safe to blame the CIA, but it is naive to assume that this means anything anymore.

The first step in getting to the heart of a conspiracy is to find the key player or players. They will usually hide themselves behind enormous numbers. This is because they are cowards. They see their power as rooted in the silent control of others, but really it is that they are afraid to associate themselves with their actions. They are not the brave freedom fighters who make public their distastes but instead the back stabbers, Brutus in his lair.

What is the nature of a conspiracy? It is the darker side of human beings. It is a philosophical animal, the pursuit of which is a never-ending series of questions. It is the paranoia of the pharmaceutically disturbed, the insecurity of crowds, the resentment of the dispossessed. The nature of a conspiracy is to move furtively, to cover its tracks, to strike without evidence of ever having acted at all. It is a perfectly normal day that leaves a man lying dead in a pool of blood in the middle of a park. It is a locked room inside of which a terrible crime has been committed with no apparent point of entry. It is the ever-increasing use of the word *why.* A conspiracy is the reason we are here, in this room and on this earth. The trick is to ignore the smoke and the mirrors. The trick is to always ask questions. If the clue seems too obvious or the evidence too conclusive, you must ask yourself, Is this what I am to believe or what they want me to believe? In tracking the conspiracy it is essential that we disassociate ourselves from our desires and beliefs, for these can be played on. We can all be led in the directions we want to go. The key is in putting aside our personal prejudices and judging the evidence by its weight alone. Only by being dispassionate can we succeed.

■

The plane ride to New York is short compared to the flight from San Francisco, and Linus spends his time going over the notes he has made from his conversations with Edward and Roy. He had asked them to find out all they could on Jeffrey Holden and Hastings Pharmaceutical. The result was delivered to him in the airport by a static-haired nineteen-year-old who had seen too many cold war spy movies and who slipped a sealed envelope to Linus under the low wall of a bathroom stall. An encoded file transfer between Roy and his colleagues in Miami. The nineteen-year-old had driven for three hours, eyes glued to his rearview mirror, taking back roads and city streets. He wore dark glasses indoors.

Linus himself makes no real effort to conceal his departure for New York. He pays for the flight with his credit card in his own name. His need for secrecy is low at this point and he doesn't want to alarm the FBI or others by disappearing. It will be hard enough to keep their eyes off him without raising alarms in their minds by running.

On the plane Linus tries not to think too much about the last time he was in New York. He and Claudia had come for Alice's rehab graduation. Alice said they were silly, but for once Linus had insisted on attending a family function and they sat on rusty metal folding chairs in the fluorescent basement of a halfway house and clapped and shouted as Alice was handed a small piece of paper signifying her release to the ranks of the sober and the undependent. Afterward Linus and Claudia took Alice to lunch at Odeon and Claudia grilled them both on Linus's childhood. Alice just laughed and told her that Linus had never had a childhood, just a series of years spent at a reduced size.

"He was so serious, always. Just a scruffy boy with a furrowed brow, always concentrating, like everything was threading a needle."

Linus and Claudia stayed at the Marriott in Times Square. Linus declined Ford's offer of housing and Ford returned the favor by skipping Alice's graduation.

"It's not so much a family," said Claudia, "as a series of tactical maneuvers."

That night Claudia came down with a case of food poisoning after a bad Indian meal on East Sixth Street. There followed two slippery days crouched over an anonymous porcelain toilet, Claudia purging and Linus holding her hair. In the midst of this, Linus visited an acquaintance of his downtown, Fisher Cody, who had written a book on the assassination of Abraham Lincoln that Linus had used the preceding semester. Correspondence had bred phone calls, phone calls lunch invitations, and finally Linus sat in a crowded West Village falafel shop wiping hot sauce from his lips. Fisher Cody wore old jeans and a denim work shirt. He was heavyset, full bearded.

"Imagine a murder at a conspiracy-theory convention," he said by way of greeting.

"Like a kitchen fire at the firemen's ball."

Linus kept the lunch short. He didn't want to leave Claudia alone in the hotel room for too long. He hadn't wanted to come at all, but she had insisted.

"I have hair ties," she'd said. "And if you want to know the truth, you're driving me a little nuts pacing around the hotel room."

Fisher taught modern assassination theory in the NYU history department. He had coined the phrase *ratings martyr* to describe the role of television in the modern political arena. At lunch he grilled Linus on the Berkeley environment and the left coast culture.

"I feel it's important to relocate every three years," he said. "This way you avoid becoming too much of a fixed target. I never forward my mail. Let the bill collectors come after me. They can hitch a ride with the secret death squads."

Upon request, Linus produced a picture of Claudia. A picture he had taken on a trip to Big Sur; cliff side, the sun dropping into the ocean. There was a look in her eye, a moment of contentment that was visible in the chemical stain of developer and high-gloss paper. It was the first year of their marriage, when the air was still weightless below their feet.

"She's very pretty," said Fisher.

"She's a miracle," said Linus, and the vehemence of his words surprised him. This casual scene of two men, acquaintances gathered for lunch in an informal setting, and he was suddenly laid emotionally bare by an outburst of what he could only reflect on later as fear. He and Claudia had spent much of the past week fighting. He was cajoling, attempting to placate her, but this made things worse, for what she required was a good fight and did not want to be catered to. She became disagreeable on a semantics level, arguing his asides, contradicting her own requests. It appeared that she was trying to articulate some deeper dissatisfaction and yet did not have the proper forum to do so, so she confronted him on the minutiae of missed left turns and moldy shower curtains.

Now, at Kennedy airport, Linus calls Fisher Cody and sets up a meeting for later that evening.

"Call 415-555-1057 from a secured line," he tells Fisher. "Ask for Oswald. You will be prompted on what to do from there. Bring the information you receive to our meeting. I'll call you later with the location."

He makes his way into Midtown, a taxi skimming across pitted highways, careening through minor traffic skirmishes, the feel of a car with a crippled transmission driven by an unintelligible man with a name made up exclusively of consonants. On the BQE he sees the mechanical humps of Manhattan rising up over the horizon. The weary brownstones of Queens, their laundry lines weighted down with the underwear of the heavily accented, storefronts and soot-soaked brick and concrete apartment buildings. The black snow of last week's blizzard is piled in filthy mounds along the sides of the road. Linus does not have a winter jacket, wears a ratty corduroy sports coat, his hands jammed between his knees for warmth. He wears a skinny tie, his hair askew and depressed at odd angles, a result of falling asleep on the plane. He looks at the skyscrapers of New York, the sky a defeated gray, and can think of nothing constructive. The search for answers is a reflex, driven not by a need to know but by a need for action. Keep moving, keep busy, keep looking. They cross the Fifty-ninth Street Bridge, pass the Roosevelt Island tram, head across clotted avenues. The Christmas season has passed and now there is just the tired wait until spring. The remaining months of unwanted freeze cause the city to contract. People feel squeezed by the ice-heavy outdoors. The weather threatens to crush them, its bitter, dirty embrace.

Linus listens to the unintelligible words of his driver, the half-muttered curses and Americanisms that litter his speech.

"Lincoln Town Car," he says. "Piss pocket."

Linus considers the trip he has planned to Hastings Pharmaceutical. He is not certain how to proceed. It seems obvious that he must speak to someone in authority, Holden's supervisor, but he has no real expectation of getting meaningful answers. That would presume the existence of meaning in the universe, and Linus is unconvinced and unwilling to concede such a basic point.

"Standard dual air bags," says the driver. "Antilock brakes."

Linus tips him ten dollars, emerges from the well-heated interior to the February frost of East Fifty-third Street. He stands with his suitcase beside a street-bound steam pipe, stares down Lexington

Avenue. People wash around him. From above he seems like a tiny island threatened by a rushing river. His eyes are red. For a moment he doesn't know which way to go, cannot remember why he has come, and then he starts across Fifty-third toward Madison Avenue. He hoists up his suitcase. His hands have already gone numb. His face stings with the pull of the wind. And for the hundredth time in two days his eyes begin to tear, though this time it is from the cold.

We live in a world of surveillance. There are cameras in our ATMs, cameras in the supermarket checkout lines, cameras in drive-through windows and office-building lobbies. Satellites circle the upper atmosphere carrying telephoto lenses sensitive enough to read the numbers on a postage stamp. For most people these petty invasions are overlooked or rationalized as a necessary aspect of a dangerous and technocratic environment. For people like Edward and Roy, however, a more sinister character can be assigned. They feel watched, actively studied. The shutter-covered eyes of anonymous observers are there not to oversee societies in general but to spy on them, on Edward and Roy and others like them; a tool of a suspicious government utilized to monitor the actions and intentions of its citizenry. Edward, for instance, believes that televisions have been equipped since 1991 with two-way communications capabilities that transmit the likeness of each increasingly porcine couch vegetable to the calculating eyes of pale men in dark glasses. He recognizes that automobiles are designed with a secret computer chip that can be controlled via satellite (your VIN is linked to your name in a global database). He has even argued with Roy over the existence of a computer system called B.E.A.S.T., which he says is located in Brussels, Belgium, and records all ATM and debit-card transactions within fifty-seven seconds of their occurrence.

It's clear my phones are tapped, he thinks, that somewhere in the house there are bugs planted by government agents. He and Roy have invested in expensive bug-identifying equipment as well as a device that emits a sonic frequency meant to disable listening devices, but even still, there could be men sitting in a cable truck in the Safeway parking lot with a long-distance unidirectional microphone listening to him think at any moment.

Surveillance is something one can learn to live with, much like hunger or long-term imprisonment. Edward and Roy have adapted their routines to maintain their privacy. Tape recordings of conversations have been made. Playbacks are routine. Two years ago Roy built a special room inside his house. It is a five-by-seven booth in one corner of the living room that has been completely soundproofed. Roy thinks of it as the cone of silence, much like the one the Chief and Maxwell Smart used to lower when they wanted to plot free from the eavesdropping of K.A.O.S.

Because they are both surveillance conscious, Edward and Roy have developed an encryption software package that enables them to send and receive information via modem by randomly switching codes every fifteen to twenty seconds. Each change is signified in the data by a number. To decode the data the number is then referred to by a second piece of software once the download is complete. They have distributed the software to a select few peers in various locations. The decoding software is updated every two weeks. There are advantages to modern electronics.

"Consider the new technology," says Edward, rolling around their basement office in his desk chair. "Grim-faced seventeen-year-olds discovering new means of communications in computer labs and rec rooms across the country. Forget us. You and I are too old to even compete where the new thinking is concerned. Computers are a language best understood by ungelled minds. We reach an age where we can only think about things in one way. As soon as this happens we drop out of the game as far as technological innovation or even comprehension is concerned."

Roy drinks Sprite out of a glass that is questionably clean.

"There are books and magazines. They make instructional videos. I'm not voluntarily stepping aside so some prepubescent homework jockey can claim the throne of technological relevancy."

"Instructional videos? We're talking about a different dimension of thinking, an inventiveness that springs from the suspension of disbelief. I hear that NASA is raising a community of orphans in a secret lab in Virginia. They assault them at playtime with questions about new launch procedures. They force them into directed play. Pretend you're on a spaceship. Describe the technology, the computers and modernized weaponry. They have two research scientists with doctorates and Ph.D.s taking copious notes. They utilize the pure imagination of the young to develop tomorrow's technology. How can you compete with a child who has not yet developed the tools for rational thinking, who can instead imagine devices of infinite possibility? We joke about our parents not being able to program the VCR, but this is far more serious. We're talking about a secret language of ones and zeros. It's a kind of babbling baby talk interpretable only by the very young. New technology is like a Narnia adults can't see."

Roy disagrees. He rolls back in his chair, chucks his empty soda can into the trash. There is a yellowing array of newspaper clippings and photos that scatter the walls like buckshot. The whole room could use a painting, at the very least a cleaning, and the shelves that house *Saucer Watch*'s collection of political and conspiratorial books are unorganized and overflowing, a library suffering from a bleeding back wound that refuses to clot.

"You have a degree in C programming, in Java and Unix. You can't tell me that you're a computer illiterate. And me—I built these computers from the case up."

"You plugged ready-made pieces into motherboards and power packs. I can type code onto a screen. These kids can envision parallel universes. They drive fire trucks on Mercury. For them a wooden spoon can be a hypno-death ray. How does it work? the scientists want to know. Tell us about the ray. A child babbles off something about a spinning laser. He mentions the importance of color in producing the hypnotic effect. In government laboratories they get to work translating his notes into gaskets and tubes."

To decipher the responsibility for the bombing, Edward and Roy split assignments. Edward will investigate Hastings Pharmaceutical and Jeffrey Holden. Roy will disassemble the passenger list, try to match faces to names, decipher aliases. He will also monitor the theories and chatter on the Internet. He starts by taking the passenger roster and running it against a database of government employees, which he has appropriated from public records.

Next he runs the roster against a different database, this one made up of a list of "known" government agents. The list includes defense contractors, military advisers, CIA agents, and other outed members of the intelligence community. This database comes from Virginia. It is updated regularly and distributed in secret once a month through a post office box in St. Louis. No one knows who authors it, but the names have always proven accurate and Edward and Roy have come to rely on it as a legitimate source of information. While the names are checking, Roy drives to the San Rafael bus terminal, where he uses a pay phone to contact an agent he knows at the National Transportation Safety Board. The discussion is brief. Three hours later Roy will receive a Quicktime video via modem of the JFK boarding call for flight 613 to Brazil. The footage will be grainy and hard to decipher. He will enhance it using an outboard video processor, adjust the brightness and the contrast. He will then create stills of as many recognizable faces as possible. These stills he will modem to a third party, in Oregon, who will modem them to New Orleans to a woman with diverticulitis, who will finally send them to their intended recipient in Washington, D.C. The stills will then be checked against four file drawers' worth of government ID pictures copied and smuggled from the offices of Willmont Frank, the official photographers of the United States government, by a disgruntled summer intern in 1994. While this is taking place, Roy will check his hits on a third database he calls the "alias database," which is a reference source compiled by the editors of *Fair Play* and *Lone Gunman* that includes phony names used by suspected government agents in conjunction with nonsanctioned government activities, from the hobos arrested in Dallas in 1963 to the mysterious motel guests never identified who took the rooms adjacent to Danny Cabrillo the night he *committed suicide.* It pleases Roy to know that if the world has become a place of surveillance, then he is watching them as much as they are watching him.

At the same time he can't help but wonder where his ex-wife is and if she's safe. He has become something of a hater of women since the divorce, deeply suspicious of the cruelty that motivates the female mind. Despite this he feels certain lingering emotions. He was, after all, still in love with Lorrie when she left him. In the last six months he has spoken to her only once, a phone call placed on a melancholy evening near Christmas. The conversation was brief. They were having some kind of Christmas party. He could hear music in the background, talking. The new husband was curt when he answered the phone. It is possible that Lorrie had painted her marriage to Roy in such a negative light that Duane believed there was some kind of emotional abuse involved, when really Roy and Lorrie had just woken up one morning to find that he was no longer a high school halfback and she was no longer the most popular girl in town. Instead they struggled for cash in a troubled economy. He worked as a salesman for a theater supply company in Portland and she sold shoes at a department store. The future became a questionably ominous door sealed at the end of a long hallway.

I can't talk long, she'd said.

I just wanted to say Merry Christmas.

That's nice, Roy. Merry Christmas to you.

There'd been an uncomfortable silence in which Roy understood the monumental error in judgment that had inspired him to pick up the phone. Their marriage was like a hostage situation played out to its tragic end in a past life. They were strangers now and this conversation was about as personal as a wrong number.

Well, I hope you're happy, he'd said.

I am, Roy, she'd said. I'm also pregnant.

At thirty-four, Roy Biggs has become bitter and suspicious where affairs of the heart are concerned.

As he checks the databases for name recognition, Edward reviews the material he has gathered regarding Hastings Pharmaceutical. By unspoken agreement neither of them brings up the specter that hangs over their inquiries, the reality of Claudia's death, though they are both preoccupied with it; Edward because he was secretly in love with her and Roy because of his own fears that his antigovernment activities will one day get him killed. In his mind, her death was an organized attempt by a secret governmental society to get Linus to be quiet. It was a warning by the masters of industry to stop asking questions and go along. The next step, he thinks, is for some military death squad to drive out of the desert and disappear Linus into the barren void of *Don't ask*.

Contrary to Roy's preoccupation with the political implications of Claudia's death, Edward can't stop thinking about the pass he made at her last Christmas, about how he'd had too much to drink and she was wearing this tight brown ribbed sweater and her eyes were so bottomless and green and he'd had another scotch just to make sure he was as close to clinical brain death as possible and had cornered her in the kitchen with a handful of what he claimed was mistletoe, but what was really a clump of fern he'd pulled off one of their plants in the living room, and he'd waved it over his head and lurched toward her until she'd kneed him smartly in the groin and left him pitching and shivering on the kitchen floor with a handful of grass in his hair. Thank God she'd never mentioned it. Linus, he was sure, had no idea of what an ass he'd made of himself, and for that he could only love Claudia more. In fact, he fantasizes that she had protected him for some deeper romantic reason. There was always next Christmas, he'd thought, except now there would never be Christmas again, just cold and snow and the unfulfilling geometry of store-bought presents.

Through a friend who once worked for Visa, Edward is able to review Holden's credit history. From the credit history he is able to retrieve Holden's social security number, date of birth, and driver's license number. Within two hours he has assembled a pamphlet of facts about Holden that reaches as far back as his elementary-school records. Just a cold stack of paper summarizing the meaningless details of modern existence. They paint no real picture except for the clinical sequence of events that marched from birth to death.

"Married ten years. Two kids."

Roy eats half a doughnut that has been sitting on top of his monitor since yesterday.

"Service record?"

"Nothing military. Looks like a Connecticut childhood, prep schools. MBA from Princeton."

"We got a picture?"

"They're sending us one from Hastings. Think we're a trade journal wanting to do a memorial."

Roy looks at his screen, frowns.

"Here's something weird," he says. "I ran a routine check on every passenger, credit history, verify current address."

"Right."

"Well, I have one passenger here who doesn't exist. Teddy Waren."

Edward rolls over in his chair, verifies it with his own eyes.

"To get on an international flight you have to have a passport, a ticket, and a picture ID. This is the law."

"So we assume he had all three."

"Teddy Waren. He have a middle name?"

Roy looks at a printout on his desk.

"Just a middle initial. O."

"I had an uncle who joined an ashram. Changed his last name to O. He wrote us a letter saying he was surprised initially by the roundness of it."

"Maybe this is your uncle O."

Edward opens his drawer, takes out a bottle of maximum-strength disinfectant. He swabs down his keyboard, cleans the phone, the doorknobs. Roy looks around the room for more misplaced food.

"My uncle O is seventy-one years old. His brain is similar in weight and function to a bag of mushrooms."

Edward rubs his eyes with the heels of his hands. He has been staring at a computer monitor for six hours. He looks at his watch.

"Almost time to meet J-Card."

Roy wipes his fingers on the seat of his pants. Edward goes back to his computer. Occasionally he will breathe from a pocket inhaler. A sharp suck for air, a second. It is almost six years since the operation. He will no longer even speak to doctors, has attempted to manufacture his own healthiness through the applied use of homeopathics and self-designed medical devices. He is five foot nine, weighs only 125 pounds. In 1989 his left lung collapsed five times in four months. The problem was deteriorating tissue. Doctors in surgical masks assaulted him with anesthetics. His chest was cracked, a portion of the lung removed, the remaining lung sewn into a smaller pocket. In the recovery room he contracted a staphylococcus infection. There followed a two-week barrage of antibiotics. His parents were confronted with the words *touch and go.*

The only mistake Roy made in calling Edward a hypochondriac was in underestimating Edward's motivational drive and attention to detail. Edward is actually a superhypochondriac. He is convinced that he will be the first man in the United States to fall victim to Marburg or Lassa hemorrhagic fever. He believes he will soon succumb to a deadly strain of meningitis, an outbreak of Ebola, a particularly virulent episode of tuberculosis. Every time he takes a shit he checks for blood or irregular consistency. Every time he sneezes he takes his temperature. He has been known to wear a particle mask and rubber gloves in public. He has memorized the shapes and sizes of viruses, in case he is ever in the position of having to identify one through a microscope.

"The words *multi-drug-resistant bacteria* inspire panic," he says. "I sweat, my pulse rate skyrockets. That's how close I feel we are to the next plague, like the words themselves could start it."

"I was reading the other day that the next wave of terrorism will be biological, hooded men in labs creating genetically mutated viruses."

"Don't get me started. Do you know how easy it would be to take a flu virus and insert the gene coding for Machupo virus, better known as Bolivian hemorrhagic fever? Given access to virus samples and a high school chemistry set, a twelve-year-old illiterate could mastermind the end of life on this earth in about an hour."

In the car driving to the meeting, Edward leans his head back on the rest. His window is down. Every once in a while he flicks his eyes to the side-view mirror to check for pursuit.

"A man's wife goes out of town on business," he says.

Roy checks his rearview mirror, changes lanes, clicks his tongue against his teeth. He makes himself imagine.

"Let's say she stays with her mother."

"Chicago, home of the blues."

"The White Sox, the Bulls."

"Branch offices of the CIA, NRO, NSA."

"Same as any major city."

"So she stays with her mother."

"A few days, some shopping, maybe a drive into the heartland to see a bedridden aunt."

"And then on the last night."

"There is a phone call."

"Check the number. Who called."

"The call was made from a telephone located at 1625 Third Avenue."

"Hastings Pharmaceutical."

Edward hangs his hand into the wind.

"Hastings Pharmaceutical."

"We have this? This is confirmed?"

"Tapped the AT&T mainframe at two thirty-seven."

"So Tuesday, the woman has finished her business in Chicago."

"The Windy City."

"She is thinking about coming home."

"Maybe. Maybe she is thinking of not coming home."

Roy purses his lips, switches lane. The sun begins its weightless descent into the foothills of Marin.

"The phone call comes."

"It's ten o'clock in the evening."

"The woman talks on the phone. How long?"

"Fifteen minutes."

"Perhaps the mother is downstairs."

"A piece of pie, staring at an empty chair."

"The woman comes back into the kitchen."

"She has taken the call on an upstairs extension."

"The element of secrecy."

"Sorry, Mom, she says."

"That was the office."

"Right, that was the office. They need me back tomorrow."

"A meeting."

"They need me back tomorrow for a meeting."

"The mother looks sad. She'd been hoping for another day, two."

"She offers to drive the woman to the airport."

"A cab. The daughter volunteers to take a cab. She looks distracted."

"Is anything the matter, dear? This from the mother."

Edward stares into the lengthening shadows. He is afraid he will cry. His sister committed suicide eleven years ago. She had hair the color of pumpkin pie.

"Everything's fine, Mom. Everything's just fine."

"She pokes at her pie but doesn't eat."

"In the morning she packs her things."

"The cab comes at nine forty-one."

"She gives her mother a huge hug."

"An abnormally large hug. The mother is certain there is some problem."

"Are things all right with you and Linus, dear? she wants to know."

"The woman smiles, but the smile is tragic really, a small animal dying bravely by the side of the road."

"Do you ever think about Dad? she says. Her father died of a heart attack in 1974. He was a pharmacist."

"The irony does not escape us."

"The mother sighs. The question is a decoy meant to preoccupy her with her own thoughts."

"Linus isn't dead, dear, she says. Sometimes in marriage things are rocky. Stick it out. He's a very decent man."

"The woman doesn't answer. She stares out into the street through a living-room window. Then she too sighs and turns and gives her mother another smile. She opens her mouth."

"She wants to say more."

"The taxi arrives, honks its horn."

"The daughter gets up, gets her bags. The mother hovers around her, making sure she has everything."

"This is her only child. Her husband died before she could give birth to more."

"At the door the daughter, laden with luggage, smiles again."

"It was great seeing you, Mom."

"Oh well."

"The mother says, Oh well."

"You still want me for Thanksgiving? she asks."

"The daughter nods. Of course."

"Then she's inside the cab."

"The mother goes back into the house, the daughter to the airport, where she does not board a plane to go home to her husband."

"Whom she has not called."

"Whom she has not called. Instead she takes a plane to New York."

"She has made the reservations the night before."

"After the call from Hastings Pharmaceutical."

"She sits on the aisle."

"In the back, third row from the end. The weather is clear."

"Perhaps she reads a book."

"Maybe she's too nervous to read."

"What makes her so nervous?"

Roy drives across the Golden Gate Bridge, pays the toll, makes the first available U-turn, drives back toward Marin. Below them the bay waters are orange in the setting sun. He pulls off at the vista turnout. The parking lot is full of tourists, busloads of them. They stand in starched white shorts and take pictures of clouds. Roy parks the car between a Hyundai and a red Chevy minivan. They roll up the windows by hand, checking the mirrors for signs of surveillance vehicles. At the edge near the telescopes they find J-Card. He is wearing a sweatshirt and black bike shorts. He has a red handkerchief tied over his head.

"Get out of town," he says.

"We drive all this way."

J-Card grimaces.

"People are going missing."

Edward and Roy exchange a look.

"Flight 613," says Roy.

"Professor Owen's wife was killed."

J-Card winces.

"Listen. There are federal agencies you've never even heard of looking for answers on this one."

Edward raises an eyebrow.

"I've heard of quite a few."

"People are being disappeared." J-Card flicks his eyes around the parking lot. He has placed his back to the side of a hill. He looks as if he is expecting assassins to come by boat.

" 'People' is vague."

"Your people. My people. Conspiracy people."

" 'Missing' meaning...?"

"Dumb. You guys are so dumb. I slept in a Dumpster last night. The word is that the feds are looking domestic on this and they're looking at people like you and me."

"Why?"

J-Card squats down. He has a desperate need to make himself a smaller target.

"There must have been some pretty heavy guys on that plane, that's all I'm gonna say. I've heard Men in Black. I've heard Com-12, NRO. People are getting visits from Delta Group. Landladies go up to collect the rent and find a strange smell, sign of a scuffle. Big black cars have been seen trolling suburban streets."

"We watch the government. We don't plant bombs on airplanes."

J-Card shrugs his bony shoulders. Crouched down, he looks like an athletically minded caveman shielding a small fire.

"Last night I'm on the phone with Reilly. He tells me he's heard some crazy shit coming out of Washington. Like what crazy shit? I say. Hold on, he tells me. I thought I heard something. The phone goes down. I hear noises, then silence. A phone booth I'm in and I feel like a paper target at a shooting gallery. A different voice comes on the phone, cold. *Who is this?* I went to sleep in a Dumpster behind Pizza Hut. Me, a rat, and four hundred half-eaten slices of pizza. You can't be too careful."

"A new angle," says Roy as they follow the highway back toward the house.

"Dark forces."

"I guess we can expect a visit from our local congressman."

"Boogeyman. A visit from our local boogeyman."

They ride the distance from the highway to Roy's house in silence. The world has gone dark, just the pale shafts of light their headlamps throw, the grinning squares of windowpanes from the houses by the road. Edward keeps his window rolled down, though by now he is cold in his T-shirt and shorts.

"Instead of going to San Francisco she goes to New York," he says.

Roy checks his rearview mirror. There is an itch in the middle of his back, like that of a prisoner running for the freedom of a prison wall.

"Actually she goes to Florida."

Edward chews a hangnail. His face glows in the sudden headlights of a passing car. He thinks about how much bacteria has attached itself to his person since he woke up that morning.

"I always hated Florida. It's like a really sunny happy commercial for death. Come join us, the smokers, the Cubans, and the elderly."

Outside the house are two unmarked black sedans. Roy does not slow down, makes a right at the corner, heads back to the highway.

"Where to?"

"I guess we should spend the night at Rooster's."

"What if Rooster's been routed? We need a safer place." Roy eyes the mirrors.

"How much cash do you have?"

Roy checks his pocket, keeping his eyes on the road.

"Sixty-one dollars."

"I've got thirty-five."

"A motel."

"Should have an underground parking lot. We don't want them spotting our car from the street."

They ride the bridge again, the freckled lights of the city. People commit suicide facing town, jumping out of the anonymous dark. Roy watches the sun. They drive Lombard Street to the Golden Gate Motel, park on the top floor of a rectangular structure, their car set at an angle on the far side, away from the street. They check in separately, first Roy, calling himself Marty Ray, then twenty minutes later Edward, using the name Forest James. They have rooms next door to each other. It's nine o'clock at night. They sit chewing ice cubes in the dark, watching out Roy's window as the traffic on Lombard Street roars by, lending fumes of exhaust to the air.

"The woman flies to New York."

"She's thinking about her husband."

"How can she not? She's wondering, Am I doing the right thing?"

"But what is she doing? Is it criminal or just unfaithful?"

"Picture a man in sunglasses contacting her in a Chinese restaurant three months prior."

"Your country needs you."

"Maybe she's been recruited to investigate allegations against a certain pharmaceutical company."

"A mole, you're saying."

"I'm trying to paint a pretty picture using the light I have."

"The wife of a conspiracy professor working for the government, though? Better she service whole football teams using every available orifice."

Roy scrunches his face.

"An affair then. With Holden."

"And Brazil?"

Roy crunches another ice cube between his teeth, which by now are numb and feel foreign in his mouth.

"A fresh start?"

"A fresh start."

They sleep in the same room, Roy on the bed, Edward on the floor smelling the fireproofing on the carpet, kept awake by the rusty squeak of bedsprings. How could I have made a pass at my best friend's wife? he wonders. He watches the shadows pan across the ceiling. In the bathroom the faucet, like a short man with a deviated septum, gives off a steady drip. Edward closes his eyes and wonders what will be left for them at their homes in San Rafael. He imagines everything has been confiscated. He is mouthing the word *confiscated* when he hears the front door opening. He humps his way under the bed like a Marine crawling through mud, stares at the crack of light that has entered the room. There is a click as the chain is cut and then the sounds of the street come in with four pairs of shoes. The door closes. Edward holds his breath.

Roy wakes up disoriented, looks at the clock, starts to sit up. There is a man in a chair at the foot of the bed.

"Fuck!"

He is aware of movement from the corners of his eyes and then a hood is placed over his head. He is rolled, hands taped. Edward continues to hold his breath. He listens as they remove Roy from the bed, feels rather than hears the sudden creak of bedsprings released. The door is opened again. Two pairs of shoes leave. Edward listens to the steady thump of his own heartbeat. I should never have tried to kiss her, he thinks. Bad karma. Then the bed is lifted away and he rolls in time to see two sets of hands descending.

They are driven in the trunk of a gray Chrysler to a warehouse in Emeryville, hustled from the car, tied to chairs. Their hoods remain on, almost suffocating them. The room sounds big. Different smells, sawdust, oil, a strong aroma of fish. Edward speaks through muffled sackcloth.

"Roy?"

"You know what I was just thinking?"

"What?" The hood is a thick, heavy fabric. Edward can't even make out sources of light.

"How J-Card didn't look like he spent the night in a Dumpster."

The hoods are removed. Two men in suits are sitting on a sofa in front of them. The sofa has obviously been brought in from outside. It is a three cushion full length, set with its back to a stack of crates. The fabric pattern is floral. The men wear Halloween masks, famous presidents. One is Richard Nixon, the other George Bush.

"Republicans," says Roy. He turns his head and looks at Edward, whose hair looks like it's been run over and flattened by a truck. It is clear that there are other people standing behind them, but neither Edward nor Roy can turn his head far enough to see them.

"Fifteen dollars says Nixon works for the National Reconnaissance Office," says Edward. His face is sweaty and red after having spent so much time covered, lying facedown in the trunk of a car.

The two men turn and look at each other. Roy clears his throat. He is having a hard time feeling his fingers. Nixon leans forward, brushes sawdust from his shoes.

"You may call me Mr. Yee. This is Mr. Clean."

"Mr. Clean?" Edward gives Roy a sidelong glance.

"We are going to ask you some questions. You are going to give us some answers."

"Mr. Clean?"

"You publish a tabloid called *Saucer Watch.*"

"That's not a question."

"You are Edward Bender and Roy Biggs. You live at 1301 and 1303 Chestnut Road in San Rafael, California. You see, I know things."

Edward glances at Roy again, but Roy is busy getting his breathing under control. Nixon's hair is a plastic shield.

"Mr. Clean and I work for a certain government agency."

"Department of Housing and Urban Development," guesses Roy.

"The Postal Service?" says Edward.

Mr. Yee reclines. Mr. Clean leans forward.

"Number seven will now administer a small electric shock," he says. His voice is that of a high school science teacher, flat and weary of the petty antics of adolescents.

Both Edward and Roy flinch as small electrodes are attached to the bases of their necks. The wattage is low, but they see flashes of light and feel as if their hair has caught fire. Mr. Clean sits back. His real name is Stanley Brewer. His father was a Little League coach who died in a bus accident along with all seventeen members of his junior high school team. Stanley is truly relaxed only when wearing one of his masks. Sometimes at night when he cannot sleep, he slips one on, reclines on his bed, listens to the sounds of his breathing captured in the enclosed space. The smell of rubber soothes him.

"We are men employed by the federal government," he says. "The rest is irrelevant."

"As a taxpayer then," grunts Roy, clears his throat, which has gone dry, "I'd just like to remind you that you work for me."

"Ah," says Mr. Yee. "I can see that this is going to turn into a conversation about money. Mr. Clean and I are not interested in conversations about money."

"Mr. Clean?" says Edward. His hair is now standing straight up.

Mr. Yee sits back, crosses his legs. He resembles a Nixon as yet uncaught and unpursued. Underneath the mask is Special Agent

Daniel Boyle of the National Reconnaissance Office. He is a slightly puffy man who bears an uncanny resemblance to John Denver.

"I will save you the trauma of a long questioning and simply ask you, What are the answers?"

"How about one question to get us rolling. I'm not even sure what we're talking about here."

Mr. Clean makes a hand gesture and this time the shock is sharper, the crack of a bat against the backs of their skulls.

"It used to be," pants Edward, "that a couple of federal agents would come by the house. They'd have notepads. Nobody considered the idea that men with masks might come and kidnap you. That idea is so Central American dictatorship."

"And yet here we are." Mr. Yee stands up, takes off his jacket, lays it carefully over the back of the couch. Mr. Clean remains perfectly still.

Roy exhales. He is sweating freely, his armpits, forehead, groin. He is considering going back to school to get a degree. He is contemplating working toward a life as a productive and unquestioning citizen. Mr. Yee approaches, walks between them, disappears. They can hear him pacing behind them, the slight tap and shuffle of his heels. Mr. Yee has chosen the name Mr. Yee because he believes it gives his persona a sinister Asian quality. A man who looks like John Denver must sometimes go to great lengths to impress others that he is a terrible and sadistic person.

"A bomb on a plane," he says suddenly, his head beside Edward's ear. "An explosion. One hundred and twenty-seven passengers." He enunciates each syllable as if speaking to the deaf.

"Flight 613," says Edward. "A plane flying from New York to Brazil. Somebody put a bomb on board. We don't know who. We were hoping you would provide some clues. Our friend's wife died."

Mr. Clean rolls up one starched white sleeve. He has been divorced twice. The second time for putting a pillow over his wife's head while she slept.

"Professor Owen. He is a suspect."

Roy snorts.

"The collective intuition of the federal government."

"We are looking for Danton."

"Danton?" Edward looks at Roy from the corners of his eyes.

"It is a group. We believe Professor Owen is a member. We suspect you as well may be members."

"Danton," says Edward. "I'm drawing a substantial and uncomfortable blank."

"Roy?" Mr. Yee places one cool hand on Roy's shoulder. His voice betrays friendship, though it is the insincere tone of the bully. At the office the other agents call him Mr. Freeze. He is a man who is never invited to parties or out for drinks.

"I've honestly never heard of it."

Mr. Yee takes his finger, runs it across Roy's neck, which is now wet with sweat. Roy sees colored lights out of the corner of one eye. He wonders if this is what J-Card meant by "people are missing."

Mr. Clean stands up, brushes at the legs of his pants.

"Tell us about Teddy Waren," he says.

Edward turns to look at Roy.

"I thought he was one of yours. Teddy Waren, secret agent. This was my sincere belief."

"We'll take polygraph tests," volunteers Roy.

Mr. Yee picks up Edward's hood from the floor. He holds it up in front of his face.

"It's hard to know where these things have been," he says. "Look at the fabric, how old. Imagine how many people have worn this, their breath wetting the fabric where your lips are." He takes the hood, pulls it down over Edward's head. Edward bucks and jerks.

"When they're not in use," says Mr. Yee, "we keep the masks in cages with the monkeys."

Roy pulls at his restraints, pauses, counts to ten, tries to get control of his breathing. Mr. Clean crosses from the couch. He picks up Roy's mask.

"Next time think up better answers."

They are dumped outside Roy's house, untied but not unmasked. By the time they get the hoods off they are alone, lying in the cold dewy grass of the front yard.

"I think I pissed my pants," says Edward, climbing slowly to his feet. His lips are dry and cracked, face a disgruntled red. Roy lists cautiously toward the front door.

Inside Roy's house everything appears undisturbed. Even their coffee cups remain unmolested, resting on stacks of paper. Files persist in their drawers, computer programs open as they were left. Roy and Edward exchange a series of looks. A scan for bugs reveals the presence of fourteen newly placed listening devices. Roy moves to his computer to check the results of his database searches. There are ten names, flashing white against gray.

"Here's something worth thinking about," says Roy. Edward goes to look for something alcoholic, returns a few moments later with a half-empty bottle of Absolut. He pours vodka into two Daffy Duck glasses, hands one to Roy.

"To a long life."

Roy drinks, winces.

"I've got three CIA agents including Aquarius and the Fifth Column and three more employees of Hastings Pharmaceutical."

Edward drinks down to Daffy's waist.

"What else?"

"I have two employees of Dow, one Hooker Chemical chemist, and a known executive of MK-ULTRA." Roy walks over to the windows and pulls down the shades.

"Chemical weapons perhaps. Do we think there were test tubes on board, strange orange isotopes?"

"We are, as of yet, unclear."

Edward places his hand to his head. It continues to shake despite his best efforts to relax.

"I predict a clot of defense contractors sitting in first class."

Roy closes his eyes. He can see the Halloween masks of Mr. Yee and Mr. Clean.

"Maybe we should quit while we're ahead," he says.

Edward sits in his chair, exhales.

"And in your opinion we're ahead. At this moment. As we speak."

"Men in masks just attached electrodes to our necks. This is no joke."

Edward watches Roy's face shimmer in the glow of his monitor. He will be twenty-five in two months.

"So just walk away, you're saying."

Roy scratches his forehead.

"We could live a lot longer."

"And Linus is just left floating in the wind?"

They sit silently for a moment, thinking. Roy wonders how he ended up in this place, when five years ago he was a trusting man with a funny wife in a starter home in Portland. Edward thinks of Claudia, of his own weaknesses and fear. They both evaluate with suspicion each creak and shift of Roy's rickety house.

"We're talking about Linus," says Edward. Roy says nothing. He sits for another minute wishing his options were better, then he prints the list, looks at his watch. He is certain they cannot stay here. He does not have great hopes for their leaving without a tail, however.

"If only the machines could think," he says, staring at his monitor.

Edward wipes the mouth of his inhaler with disinfectant, places the bottle back inside the drawer, carefully wiping the drawer handle before touching it with his hand. He has started saving money to buy a plastic bubble in Arizona in a complex of men and women who one day fell allergic to modern living after a new chemically treated carpet was installed in their offices. They now live in airtight domes breathing pure oxygen and wearing only clothes made from natural fibers. For Edward this sounds like what heaven must be. He picks up the stack of paper they have assembled and throws it onto his desk.

"Thank God they can't," he says.

When a man's wife dies he forgets many things. He forgets when to eat and when to sleep. He forgets how long each day is. It slips his mind to keep himself clean. His brain becomes a sieve through which his thoughts leak into empty air. Linus, hauling his tired suitcase into the lobby of 1625 Third Avenue, his aging blue suit crushed and wrinkled by travel, his face unshaven, hair displaced, appears a survivor of alien abduction wandering off the runway of a flying saucer, disoriented and uncertain of his existence. Though technically he is dressed for the occasion—that is, for the visit to the corporate headquarters of a major pharmaceutical conglomerate—his appearance is just wrong enough to incite people to stare a few seconds longer than is polite. A security guard in the atrium considers stopping him, but Linus walks purposefully toward the elevator banks, and people who appear to know where they are going are rarely interrupted. The memory of Howard Hughes lingers. In New York it is not uncommon to find that the crazy shopping-cart pedestrian who accosts you is a millionaire.

Entering the elevator, Linus presses 49. The doors close. Next to him a secretary in a gray pinstripe pants suit takes out a hairbrush and begins brushing her hair, shifting and adjusting her outfit to amend her reflection in the wavy chrome of the doors. Just as the woman faces her image, so must Linus. As the elevator rises he is accosted by his own appearance. He sees a man, his tie askew, pants wrinkled, shirt buttons undone. His hair is a tumbleweed brutalized by a twister. Who can this be? Linus puts a hand up to his head. The man in the reflection does the same and Linus rediscovers himself like a baby learning its own dimensions from the scoop of a spoon. Alarmed, he puts his suitcase down quickly and attempts to straighten himself out. The buttons are fastened, the pants pressed hurriedly flat with the palms of his hands. He attacks his hair with fingers moistened by saliva, but it resists the shape and form of fashion, springs back into the strangled configuration of a dying fern.

"May I borrow your brush?" he asks the secretary, who fastens him with a frightened stare, more so because he has chosen to speak to her at all than by the specifics of his request. She is in the process of stuffing the brush back into her purse among the chewing gum wrappers and business cards of single men. Reluctantly she pulls it free and hands it over. Linus attacks his receding locks with gusto, reddens his scalp, plows his tired coif into submission. The pain of the bristles feels good to him. Death has made him a masochist. He realizes that he requires the sharp cut of discomfort to wake him up, otherwise he will simply sleepwalk through the remaining hours and days of his life.

The doors open on 49 and Linus hands over the brush, then steps clear into the main lobby. A gleaming brass and oak sign behind the reception area announces that he has arrived in the empire of Hastings Pharmaceutical. There is no Abandon Hope All Ye Who Enter Here sign, though even if there were it would not apply to Linus, who gave up whatever hopes he had the moment the two FBI agents walked into his office. Instead there is a sleek lobby, a de Kooning on the wall, a smart carpet, wood paneling, elegant molding. The receptionist is brunette and slim. The air she exudes is that of a fashion model waiting for a photographer to change a roll of film. She quickly assesses Linus's attire, his carriage and gait. It is clear that he is not a VIP or bank president. She smiles in a perfunctory fashion.

"Can I help you?" she asks, and her voice is deep and throaty. Her presence is meant to imply that Hastings Pharmaceutical is a company concerned with beauty, with purity, with goodness. To Linus she is a wheel of cheese.

"Jeffrey Holden," he says. The receptionist's face rearranges itself into a posture of grief.

"I'm sorry, sir, but Mr. Holden was, well, was killed two days ago in a plane crash."

"Yes, I know."

She looks surprised, as if the photographer has suddenly requested she place a bag over her head.

"I'm afraid I don't understand."

"I'd like to speak to Mr. Holden's superior."

The receptionist, whose nameplate suggests she should be addressed as Nancy, looks down at a personnel sheet she keeps on her desk. Her hair is set in a French twist made fashionable by *Dr. Quinn: Medicine Woman.*

"That would be Mr. Loyal. May I tell him who's calling?"

"Linus Owen."

She smiles. The taking of names and making of appointments has brought her back to familiar territory.

"And may I just tell him what it's regarding?"

"Tell him I'd like him to explain to me why my wife is dead."

At this point her expression implies that the famous fashion photographer has pulled out a sexual appliance and requested she utilize it.

"Excuse me?"

"I'd like him to tell me why my wife is dead. I can't be any clearer than that."

She darts her eyes first left, then right.

"Just a moment, please."

She picks up the phone, and Linus crosses to the waiting area and puts his suitcase on top of the coffee table. He lowers himself into a chair, stares at the de Kooning that hangs on the wall. Grief has disposed quite neatly of any need for tact he once felt. It is as if by having nothing to live for he is free to say everything he desires. A man in an olive-green suit emerges from a closed door. He is frowning, but in a way that is meant to be empathetic.

"Mr. Owen?"

Linus lifts himself up, takes the hand that is offered him.

"I'm Jerry Loyal. My sympathies. Your loss is just terrible."

Linus takes his hand back, hides it in his pocket, looks around. Jerry Loyal is too suntanned to be trusted.

"I'm sorry. Have I lost something?"

"Pardon?"

"Forget it. It's just the phrase everyone keeps using."

Loyal makes a face, like that of a man contemplating an undercooked meal.

"Of course. I understand completely." He looks down at Linus's suitcase, examines his wrinkled suit.

"Well, please come back to my office and tell me what I can do for you. Things are so shaken up around here since Jeffrey was killed. None of us quite know what to do with ourselves."

He leads Linus back through a door with no knob. They are buzzed in by the receptionist, who throws Linus one last look of radiant sympathy, as if to the paparazzi at the funeral of a famous movie star. Linus plods past unaware.

Behind the door is a long mahogany hallway with offices lining both sides. Men in suits cross in and out with faces that imply that there is nothing more important than the task of running a major pharmaceutical corporation. Linus hauls his suitcase along. He looks like a man who has turned himself in for mail fraud after years of living under an assumed name in a small town in tornado country. The hallway opens into an arena of cubicles, the random geometry of the low statused whose snapshots of children, dogs, and lovers are indelicately tacked to particleboard walls.

Linus wades through the startling aroma of photocopies.

Jerry Loyal's office sits atop hardwood floors. He has an impressive collection of flowering plants. His desk is metal and glass. From his window Linus can see all the way to Queens. He offers Linus a seat, slips behind his desk. His own chair is like a rubber hammock, all crisscrossed straps. There is a teak humidor on his desk filled, no doubt, with expensive Cuban cigars.

"Now, please tell me what I can do for you. I notice you still have your luggage. Do you have someplace to stay? I could have my secretary book you a room if you haven't had a chance."

"I haven't gotten that far yet."

Jerry Loyal picks up the phone and tells his secretary to reserve a room at the Waldorf.

"On us, of course," he says to Linus, but Linus has no interest in discussing lodging.

"I flew up to New York to ask you a question."

"You could have phoned. Not that I'm not happy to meet you. I'm just saying. The price of a plane ticket."

"Oh, don't worry, when an airline kills your family you get to fly wherever you want for free."

Jerry Loyal continues to smile, though not without some effort.

"I didn't know that."

"Not that I'd suggest going that route simply to get free miles."

"Mr. Owen."

"One question, though, and then I'm going back to San Francisco. For what, I don't know, but I will leave." Linus feels incapable of being undramatic. Everything he says feels like the proclamations of tragic Greek heroes.

"Ask two. Ask three. I'm at your disposal." To bolster his statement, Loyal buzzes his secretary again and tells her to hold his calls. He leans back in his chair. His face contorts to express the appropriate mixture of decorum and concern. Linus can see him standing on the terrace of a penthouse apartment on Central Park West. There is a brunette in the background, twisted up in ivory sheets. It is the receptionist. In the office Linus checks Loyal's hand for a wedding ring. When he finds one he envisions Loyal and Nancy conspiring in an Italian restaurant. Loyal promises for the hundredth time that he will leave his wife for her. Nancy smokes angrily and cuts her pasta with a knife.

"Mr. Loyal."

"Jerry."

Linus sighs. He is sweating, though for no reason he can name. Jerry Loyal sits opposite him like a prep-school bully who has decided, for less than trustworthy reasons, to be magnanimous.

"My wife was in Chicago three days ago. On Wednesday she flew to New York and met Jeffrey Holden. She had no plans to do this. Neither her mother nor I had any indication that she was going to do this. The question that remains is, Why did she do this? Not to mention why she then, four hours after landing in New York, boarded a 747 heading to Brazil using a ticket paid for by Jeffrey Holden."

Loyal nods, exhales as if to say, This is what I was afraid of. His every movement appears to be calculated for a hidden camera.

"Mr. Owen, may I call you Linus?"

Linus shrugs. The question of names is a formality in which he is no longer interested. Loyal in any case doesn't wait for a response. He says, "Well, Linus, the truth is, I can't tell you what your wife was doing in New York. I have been over Jeffrey's appointment book, grilled his secretary." Linus has an image of Jerry Loyal in leather chaps beating a fifty-year-old woman with a riding crop. "And I can't find any indication that Jeffrey had any plan to meet your wife. What's more, Jeffrey was in the office on the morning of the nineteenth, but he left at noon to begin what was scheduled to be a two-week vacation. However, and here's where it really gets odd, Jeffrey told me last week that he was going to take his vacation in Europe. He showed me his itinerary. There were to be five days in London, four days in Paris, three days in Cannes. Nowhere in any of our conversations did he say anything about going to Brazil. As you can see, the whole thing remains quite a mystery."

Loyal picks up a pencil off his desk and begins to twirl it absently between his fingers. Linus rubs the palm of his right hand on his thigh until the skin is numb. He doesn't speak, but waits for Loyal to continue. He is thinking about how he almost fell at his own wedding. How far would it have been, a matter of inches? He tries to imagine the plummet from thirty-seven thousand feet.

"The authorities, of course, have gone into all this with me. I have shown them Jeffrey's books, introduced them to the staff." Loyal shrugs, as if to convey: What else can I say?

"Tell me about Hastings's relationship with my wife, her company. Have you ever met my wife?"

"I have. She was here in July to work on a marketing and advertising campaign with our department. She was a beautiful woman." He shakes his head to make clear that he considers the loss of the aesthetically pleasing to be of greater significance than the death of the obese and hirsute.

"As far as you're concerned, Mr. Loyal, my wife was a brick in a burlap sack."

Loyal flushes.

"I'm sorry. I meant no offense. I was simply saying."

"Well, don't. If I need the sexual camaraderie of greasy men in slick suits I will call my brother and have him buy me lunch. Claudia was here on business. So let's stick to business."

Loyal places the pencil back on his desk. He speaks quietly, managing to sound disappointed, as if addressing a small child.

"Listen, Linus. I appreciate your dilemma, really I do, but there's no need to be curt."

"As long as we understand each other."

"That, I believe, is my line."

The two stare at each other. Loyal has raised one eyebrow to intimate a certain emotional detachment. Linus pictures himself leaning across the desk and stabbing the pencil into his throat. The action seems almost rational. He sits back in his chair and chews his lip. He finds himself thinking about Claudia in this office. He envisions her surrounded by men in gray suits, flushed by the attention, her delayed laugh. They are drinking coffee from porcelain cups and loitering in the language of sales, profit margins, product appeal. Claudia is cursing like a longshoreman. The thought of her so near fills him with a sudden weightlessness. Once again he feels numb, placeless, as if he is simply a cloud, a formation of water molecules formed in the sudden temperature change of atmosphere.

"Could I have some water?" he asks.

Loyal reaches immediately for the intercom again. He is silently grateful to be given the opportunity to show that there is a sympathetic man under his tough exterior. In a few minutes a secretary comes through the door with a tray containing a crystal pitcher and two glasses. Loyal pours water for Linus, hands it to him. Linus sits forward, accepts the glass, drinks. He is studying Loyal's office, though there are no clues to be found in the minimalist decorations and perfect corners, except that Jerry Loyal is a man who enjoys controlling his surroundings. After the secretary is gone and Loyal has retaken his seat, Linus puts the glass back on the tray, straightens his tie. He knows that Loyal considers him something of a pathetic rube. The thought neither angers nor preoccupies him.

"I would like you to speculate as to why my wife came to New York. Say anything that comes into your head."

Loyal weighs this request, purses his lips, takes a sip from his glass.

"I really can't say," he announces finally.

"Were Mr. Holden and my wife involved in any business negotiations?"

"Well, the summer campaign was ongoing."

"And what was the campaign?"

"Hastings has developed a new antidepressant. Your wife's firm was helping us get through the FDA approval process. She was preparing a marketing campaign for the ultimate sale of the product, print and television campaigns. We have recruited a famous doctor to write a book."

"And did you get FDA approval?"

Loyal betrays a slight smile.

"Just last month, thank God. These FDA hearings can be a nightmare."

Linus still cannot wrap himself around the concept of Jeffrey Holden, a man who died next to his wife thinking thoughts that will never be known.

"Tell me about him."

Loyal shrugs.

"Recently divorced, a tennis player. Had a great golf swing. He was around forty-three, didn't drink, two kids." He shrugs again. From his description, Holden is the archetypal executive.

"Do you have a picture? I just can't see him in my mind. It's very important that I be able to see him in my mind."

Loyal frowns. He can think of no reason not to show Linus a picture, but still it is against his better judgment to do so. He begins to decline.

"Mr. Loyal, my wife is dead. You're a married man. Imagine it. One day she is your wife on a family trip, the next she is dead in a field in Florida. There's no reason. There's no warning. And yet there's a man who may have the answers as to why your wife was in that place at that time. Can't you see how important it would be to understand that man, to know him?"

Loyal sighs, brushes back his hair, climbs to his feet. He motions for Linus to follow him. Silently they walk across the hall to Holden's office. The door is closed, lights off. Loyal flips them on as he enters. The office is still cluttered with the evidence of labor, files open on the desk, Post-its stuck to the base of a computer monitor.

Loyal crosses quickly to the wall behind Holden's desk and removes a framed photograph from the wall. He hands it to Linus, who has moved parallel to Holden's big oak desk. Linus's hands are sweating. He wipes them on the pockets of his coat, takes the picture. He sits down behind the desk and switches on the halogen desk lamp. Loyal stands uncertainly over him.

"That's Jeffrey and his ex-wife. As I said, the divorce just went through. He hadn't gotten around to taking the pictures down."

Holden was tall. That is the first clear distinction between him and the stereotype Loyal had described. His eyebrows were full and almost joined in the middle of his brow. He was handsome in a way that comes from a peculiar arrangement of facial features. His eyes were narrow, but his mouth was full and he was smiling. He had all his hair. It was fashionably parted on one side. His suit was expensive. He looked like a man who knew how to choose wine.

"Did he speak any languages?" Linus asks so softly that he has to repeat himself before Loyal can answer.

"German, Spanish, and French," says Loyal, and it is obvious that he thinks it a very strange question. Linus nods absently.

The wife is thin and pretty and blond. Her cheekbones are sharp. She wears a low-cut black evening gown. She has the frown lines of an attorney. Linus imagines that she is a woman who has developed a small addiction to Valium.

"His wife worked long hours."

"They both did."

"What did she do?"

"She worked for the Justice Department."

Linus nods. As far as he is concerned there's no such thing as a coincidence. That Holden's wife has a connection to the government only deepens his suspicions. Loyal takes the picture from the desk and places it back on the wall. It is his way of instructing Linus that their time is almost at an end.

"What do you do, Mr. Owen?"

Linus leans back in his chair, slouches down, places his forehead in the palm of his hand. He has not slept or eaten in forty-one hours.

"I'm a professor."

"Really?" Loyal crosses to the door. His eyes say, Okay, let's go. "What do you teach?"

"Mr. Loyal."

"Jerry."

"Jerry. I have to apologize, but I really need another glass of water. It's just all too much for me. I think I might pass out."

"Oh dear, well." It is clear that Loyal does not want to leave Linus alone in Holden's office, but he also does not want to appear overly suspicious. He stands for a moment, undecided, turns, turns back, clears his throat as if to speak. Then he nods and opens the office door.

"I'll be right back."

As soon as he's gone Linus begins opening drawers. He is looking for some evidence of Claudia. Outside he can imagine Loyal running back to his office. He pictures hidden cameras, listening devices, heat and motion sensors. Security guards will burst in at any moment. In the top left drawer Linus finds an envelope addressed to Holden's home. He slips it into his pocket without examining the address, then closes the drawer. Loyal returns with the pitcher and Linus's glass.

"I hate to seem insensitive, Linus, but I have a very important meeting in about ten minutes, so if I could escort you out to the lobby. Please feel free to rest there as long as you like. Nancy can call you a cab to take you to the hotel. Remember, anything you want while you're there is on us, as condolence for your"—it is clear that he intended to say *loss*—"well, for the terrible thing that has happened."

He pours Linus a glass of water but offers it to him in such a way that Linus must stand to get it. Linus imagines Jerry Loyal raising children who will jump from the roofs of buildings in their early twenties.

"The antidepressant," says Linus.

"A breakthrough. A miracle of science."

"That's what they said about thalidomide. Are you guys still making that?"

Loyal smiles but in a way that looks like a frown held up at gunpoint. He refills Linus's water glass, then, holding it, walks from the room. He is the Mussolini of the carrot and the stick. Once in the hallway he puts his hand on Linus's shoulder and guides him back through the cubicles toward the reception area.

"Thanks for coming by, Linus. It was a pleasure to meet you. If there's anything I can do for you please don't hesitate to call."

He opens the main door and Linus could swear that Loyal gives him a little push over the threshold. His suitcase is standing by the reception desk. Nancy is looking at him with sad but somewhat suggestive eyes. Linus turns to say one last thing to Loyal, but the door is already closing, Loyal's back visible down the hall. Linus is left standing there, a man in a rumpled suit holding a half-full glass of water. He looks at Nancy, who gazes at him encouragingly, as if he is a baby on his first day wearing big-boy pants. Linus puts the glass on the counter, where it leaves a water ring. He straightens his tie, picks up his suitcase.

"He's never going to marry you," he says to Nancy as he waits for the elevator to arrive.

"I know," she says.

Linus rides down alone.

In a strange city it is easy to forget who we are. There is so much unfamiliar motion, noises and traffic, faces composed in unfamiliar patterns. In New York, like Calcutta, there is a teeming quality to the streets that robs us of our separateness, forces us too close to one another. We succumb to the crowd, become part of it. In walking back across Fifty-third Street at rush hour Linus slips into the flood of commuter bodies. He is herded toward the subways at Lexington Avenue, driven toward the bus stops. It is the stampede toward television, the mad rush of people freed from the confines of their professions to make it home in time to watch this show or that, to order food that will be delivered by pubescent Asian boys on rusty bicycles. It is the rush toward bars and restaurants, the careen toward alcohol, toward dealers and brokers and bartenders. In the hundreds of bodies Linus is lost, his personal circumstances erased by the need of the crowd to flee. He feels the emotion emanating from them, though their faces blur, their bodies pass by too quickly to catch. That it is Friday adds a certain reckless quality to their flight.

Some will end the evening asleep with spouses, some alone. There are those who will not sleep at all, running toward morning as if in dawn there is some greater salvation. A few of the frantic pedestrians who pass Linus on the street will find themselves bruised and battered by morning, the result of muggings, hate crimes, the force of a boyfriend's or husband's loping kick. And there are those who will be dead. They walk just like the others, on the balls of their feet, unaware that the fate they rush toward is their own untimely end. It is New York after all, and all too easy to succumb to the indifference of random gunfire, the hunger of flames that spring up as a result of faulty wiring in low-income housing, the seductive urge to fly from the steeples of tall buildings. In this sea of madness Linus spins, unsure of what to do, where to go. The crowd moves him but it is simply physics. He is just an object in motion, swept along by the urgency of bodies.

On Lexington he stumbles and is shoved into a doorway. He

stands for a minute catching his breath. He is in the foyer of a bar, neon lights announcing the presence of numerous brands of beer. Linus watches the crowd surge past the doorway. He is exhausted, almost without the strength to lift even one tired foot. He goes inside and orders a drink, sits alone in a booth, while around him men with loosened ties and women with sweat stains on the armpits of silk blouses jockey for romance on the racetrack of happy hour. Linus rubs at his eyes. His suitcase sits on the floor next to him like a small child in some Depression-era documentary, looking up at its father pitifully, as if to say, Where are we going, Papa? Why do we have to keep moving so much? Linus has no answers for the boy. He drinks his beer. It is the first thing other than water he's put down his throat since Tuesday. He suffers no appetite, just an unhealthy need to keep going. After about ten minutes he takes the folded envelope from his pocket. It contains a phone bill that documents several long-distance calls to a San Francisco number that Linus recognizes as his own. The sight of his number there on the paper causes his mind to leave his body. It floats up toward the ceiling, detached as if by a sudden explosion.

That is me, he thinks, looking down at himself, a stunted dirty man in a cheap suit with no prospects except for the unenviable task of living on alone, though he is beginning to suspect that he has been alone for some time now, that Claudia had absented herself in more ways than one from their marriage. The thought makes him thirst for another beer, but his body is so far. He tries to will his hands to move, but they just hold the phone bill in front of his eyes so that he has no choice but to look. They turn the bill on their own accord until the address is clearly visible, and from this his body receives another shock, a physical jolt of dismay, for the address on the envelope is the same as his brother Ford's. Jeffrey Holden, it would appear, lives two floors beneath Ford and Madison and Ashley and Dana, beneath their dog, Muffin, and their cat, Mittens. They are neighbors.

He imagines his brother riding the elevator with Holden, two men in expensive suits greeting each other in a small enclosed space. It is at this moment that Linus begins to see the conspiracy. It is not a conspiracy of government groups, though surely they are involved in some way, but a conspiracy of friends and family. It is the clandestine plottings of the people he loves behind his back, the secret agenda of deceit carried on the shoulders of people he thought he could trust. It is clear to Linus now, sitting friendless with just his suitcase in an anonymous bar in a city of 8 million people, that he has been duped, that his whole life has been a lie. He struggles his way back down inside his arms and legs and orders another beer.

An hour later he stumbles out onto the street, now occupied with less frantic motion. He is drunk, an easy feat on an empty stomach, and he zigzags toward the gutter. He manages, through some miracle of God and science, to get a cab, fumbles open the door, tumbles inside. He rides in swirling silence uptown to Fifty-ninth Street, then across to Central Park West. The cab skirts the park, climbs along its tree-lined edge. In the backseat Linus falls asleep to the motion of wheels on pavement. When they arrive at West Eighty-seventh Street, the cabdriver, under the mistaken belief that Linus is dead, notifies the doorman to call an ambulance, but continued shaking of his shoulder is eventually enough to rouse Linus from the black pit of unconsciousness and he stumbles from the cab, clutching his suitcase like a life preserver. The doorman eyes him suspiciously. Linus has visited Ford here only once before and so there is no recognition, and, given his current state, no connection to that distant and saner day. Linus's mouth tastes like the inside of a movie theater. He stands swaying in the marble lobby, listening to the tinkle of the fountain, the swaying of ferns. He announces that he's come to see his brother. The doorman, as tactfully as possible, wonders aloud if perhaps his brother has a name. The words *Ford* and *Owen* come to Linus, but he speaks them as if they are a request for assistance to a policeman in a foreign country. The doorman—his tag indicates his name to be Rick—looks at a list of names on the desk in front of him.

"Mr. Owen said to send his guests up without calling," he says, almost to himself. Linus blinks, exhales. He is oblivious to the fact that the doorman is torn between following the tenant's instructions and obeying his own doorman instincts.

Linus nods and looks toward the elevator, where a small Italian man with a mustache sits on a collapsible stool watching them. Linus points at him and winks for reasons that remain unclear. The doorman appraises Linus with his eyes.

"Okay," he says reluctantly. "Go ahead up. It's apartment 4901."

Linus says thank you. His suitcase, which he has held this whole time, has cut off the circulation to his fingers. He switches hands clumsily and marches over to the elevator, where the small man has risen and folded his stool. Linus is advised to watch his step, which of course he can't.

"Big party," the elevator man says, once Linus is aboard and he has swung the gate closed. He puts his hand on the lever and the elevator begins to rise.

Linus nods, places his hand on the wall to keep the room from spinning. The words *big party* are meaningless, a collection of vowels and consonants. It is as if the elevator man has said to him *tig arty* or *fib smarty.* The numbers pass, 14, 21, 36. As they pass the 47th floor, Linus thinks of the phone bill and Jeffrey Holden. He wonders if his wife, on her visits to New York, ever disembarked from the elevator at that floor, walked across the fluffy pile carpeting to another man's apartment, knocked, and slipped inside. It does not occur to him that she may have had a key.

At 49 he stumbles over the lip the elevator has left between its floor and that of the hall. His suitcase flies from his hand and clatters across the hardwood floor of the foyer. Linus manages to keep his feet but when he moves to put his weight on his left ankle he feels a sudden strange pain and then finds himself sitting like a marionette that has been dropped in desperate haste. The Italian curses in his native tongue, steps out of the elevator, helps Linus to his feet. From the apartment down the hall Linus hears the piano-tinted voices of many people. He mistakes them for voices in his head, swats at himself. The Italian steps back, watching him warily. He believes Linus to be a crazy man. The evidence is in the eyes. Linus manages to find his feet. Muttering, he thanks the elevator man, collects his suitcase, limps off down the hall.

At 4901 he presses the doorbell, slicks his hair back with one gritty hand, as if this one gesture will make him presentable. When Ford answers Linus has it in mind to punch him in the nose. To strike him for all the years of bullying and condescension. The voices are louder now, rising in steady tones, like the prolonged sigh of some enormous animal. Linus puts down the suitcase, balls his fists. He favors his left ankle, places his weight on his right, draws back his hand. The door opens suddenly, a man's face appearing. Linus hauls back and lets fly.

He expects a certain jarring pain to travel the length of his arm, but instead he finds himself once again sitting on the floor. A room full of people ceases talking and turns to look in his direction. The piano music stops. He is as oblivious to their bodies as he was to their voices. Son of a bitch, he says, then again louder. Son of a fucking bitch. In the middle of the crowd, Ford, dressed in a charcoal Armani tuxedo, seeks out his wife's eyes. All he can think of is the senator by the piano and the president of Disney by the stairs. Madison grimaces and pantomimes a face as if to say, Do *something*. Ford grits his teeth, takes a deep breath, and heads for the front door, beside which Linus is sitting at the feet of a very astonished investment banker. At the same time, Madison signals the pianist to play something, anything, and he starts into a Beethoven sonata.

"Linus," says Ford, swooping in low and putting his hands under his brother's armpits. "What are you doing here, buddy? I thought you were raising revolutions in the West."

He lifts Linus to his feet and steers him in one smooth movement down a hall and into a bedroom, snatching up the suitcase as he goes. Linus's breath smells of beer and nothing else. His suit is creased beyond belief, shirttails untucked, face dirty with stubble and the spreadable ink of Jeffrey Holden's telephone bill. Ford has no idea what's going on, but he is certain that because of Linus his party is absolutely ruined.

"Linus," he says, then again in a drill-sergeant snap, when it appears that Linus is lost in some distant reverie.

"Ford," says Linus, focusing his bloodshot eyes, "beware the Men in Black."

And then gracelessly, and for the second time in two days, he passes out, tumbling over his own luggage to the floor below.

He wakes thirty-six hours later under scrutiny from the wide eyes of two small girls. His body, unlike the weightlessness of Friday night, now feels unmanageably dense. He is in a room with white curtains. There is a small framed Julian Schnabel painting hanging above a triangular dresser. When the two girls see that he is awake, they look at each other. These are my nieces, thinks Linus. He has no memory of anything after his visit to Hastings.

"Daddy says you've been asleep for days," says Ashley. Linus props himself up on his elbows. He feels in many ways as if he has been in a coma for seven years. He expects presidents to have changed. He will walk out the front door and find hovercrafts and colonies on Mars.

"Morning," he mumbles. His mouth appears to still be sleeping.

"Daddy says he's never seen such a mess," Ashley announces. She is seven, her sister five. Dana sits at the bottom of the bed, chewing her lower lip.

"Cock," she says. Ashley looks over at her, but speculatively, as if she is a scientist watching fruit flies breed. "Poop," adds Dana.

"Is Ford around?" asks Linus, pulling himself up farther. He is wearing an old T-shirt and someone else's boxers. He reaches up, touches his hair tentatively, as if to make sure it's still there. Ashley makes a face, then leaves the room. Dana begins bouncing on the bed on her hands and knees.

"Motherfucker," she says, though without front teeth this comes out *muthafucka*.

Linus finds a pair of jeans hanging over the back of a divan. He slides them on and walks barefoot out into the living room. Dana follows behind, sucking her thumb. In the kitchen he discovers Madison drinking a cup of coffee. She is wearing black slacks and a sweater. When Ford graduated from Harvard Business School he set out to find the perfect wife. His criteria were simple. She was to be the embodiment of East Hampton in the summertime. In Madison he found the perfect match. Her hair has the thick blond sheen of dune grass. Her manners are Harvardian, her teeth bright white, cheekbones high and bred of privilege. She is the kind of woman who looks stunning in either a Vera Wang black silk evening gown or shorts and an eggshell-colored cable-knit sweater. Linus in hand-me-down jeans and someone else's T-shirt stands for a moment and studies her, reminded quite suddenly of his own beautiful wife, whom he will never see again except in sudden mirages on the faces of other women. With delicate precision she picks up her coffee cup, puts it to her lips.

"Cock," says Dana in her five-year-old voice, which makes the word sound like the joyful exclamation of Barney.

Madison turns around, jumps when she sees Linus standing there, the coffee spilling over the newspaper she has been reading. Dana giggles and runs from the room.

"Jesus, Linus," she says. He steps forward to apologize, but she has already moved to get a dishcloth to clean up.

"You've been out like a light for almost two days," she tells him after they've both sat down with new coffee. Linus stares out the bay window at the park. The kitchen is stylized modern, metal and expensive Spanish tile. The stove is a circular island in the middle of the room.

"I don't remember anything. The airport, a taxi, and then..." He puts his hands up to signal emptiness.

Madison, her lips thin and fragile and pale, wipes her mouth with the corner of a cloth napkin.

"You were as drunk as I've ever seen."

"Drunk," says Linus, mystified, as if she has accused him of speaking in tongues.

"You took a swing at Paul Stanley. Missed totally, but then there you were spread out on the floor like a sack of rice."

Linus sighs, toys with the handle of his coffee cup. He looks down at his feet, the rolled cuffs of his pants.

"Claudia's dead," he says quietly. Above the park a flock of pigeons banks and dives. The city looks silent from this height, a perfect balance of architecture and motion.

Madison stares at him. She has a haircut appointment set for eleven.

"You're joking."

Linus puts his cup down, half full.

"I need to use your phone."

Madison can think of nothing to say.

"Ford will be home soon. He said. Just a breakfast meeting." She thinks about the death of her mother. The smell of Fresca. She has never touched Linus, not even a handshake or an awkward hug. She is not a physical person. Other than to have the children she and Ford have had the sex life of monks. Linus stands up nervously, walks toward the living room. Madison feels she should do something, offer some kind of physical consolation. In the end she simply watches him go.

Claudia was born in Albuquerque, New Mexico. Like many other children birthed in a place their parents were just passing through, either on business or pleasure or during a short domestic stay in the course of a career change, she emerged in a world as foreign to her parents as the world of people and color TV was to her. Her father, Raymond, the owner of a small chain of drugstores, had come to Albuquerque for a sales convention of pharmaceutical manufacturers. Astrid was eight months pregnant. She went into labor in the lobby of the Albuquerque Holiday Inn, a sudden rush of water spreading circular stains across fire-retardant carpet. Face constricting, she clutched her husband's arm for support. Two days later the baby Claudia was transported by car across staggering miles of painted canyons, rock formations, the slick black macadam an arrow pointing toward a distant airport. She was a magic baby, a struggling new life slick and crisp against the jutted horizon. A sense of infinite possibility surrounded her. The faces of her parents crowded her small shape.

In Chicago she learned to wiggle and walk, to speak in short, incomprehensible grunts. Hair stuck out in wisps and streaks across the broad expanse of her still-hardening skull. She grew in sudden bursts, sometimes swelling inches lengthwise in a matter of minutes. Everything was new, small eyes circling, darting in hungry arcs. Wearing a beard of tiny spit bubbles, she slid from infancy.

When Claudia was seven she was struck by a car while crossing against the light. Her body was thrown twenty-seven feet. A Davy and Goliath knapsack saved her from permanent injury, though she lay in a coma for seven days. During this time she had a number of out-of-body experiences. Before they were married she told Linus stories in which she hovered in the air of a hospital lobby. A man was arguing with a vending machine. The nurses wore faded white orthopedic shoes. A doctor slept in a metal folding chair leaning against a water fountain. As she watched the slow progression of wheelchair patients down ramps of imperceptibly small grades, Claudia, a specter, a shade, elected not to die. *I remember suddenly wanting to come back,* she said. Until that point she had been undecided, lured in many ways by the warm cocoon of sleep. As she hovered, her parents stood by the front door of the hospital, smoking. They said nothing, but the tips of their fingers touched as they breathed ash into the chilly autumn air.

"I floated through walls and doorways," she told Linus one night while they were still dating as they lay in bed submerged like children who have made a fort from blankets and pillows. "My feet never touched the ground."

"But out-of-body. Did people have out-of-body experiences before 1975?"

"I met a Scientologist at a party once who told me that people who have had near-death experiences are more in tune with their own sexuality." She rolled over onto her side, dragged a finger up the bony jut of his spine.

"The only thing worse than the pickup lines of cult members is the cafeteria food in New York City public schools."

Claudia rubbed her teeth with her index finger, then inspected the results.

"Can't you be serious for a minute?"

Linus stared at the ceiling, wondered if he really couldn't.

"I'm serious about you," he said.

Claudia rolled onto her other side, rested her head on Linus's concave chest. They were both sweating. Linus had made a tent post with his knees and bowed the bedding around them. She played with the delicate hairs on his shoulders. They had been to see a Woody Allen movie at the Alexander Theater, then began making love in the hallway outside her bedroom, stumbled onto the bed. Somewhere in the middle Claudia had her first awakening to the idea that she and Linus would be together a long time.

"What is it about intercourse that makes you want to reveal your most embarrassing secrets?"

"The facial expressions. We figure, How much more unappealing could we get?"

In the fourth grade Claudia developed a strange affinity for the Southwest. She believed that the place of her birth held some special resonance for her, a romantic sunlit vista to which her parents had traveled for only four days. While he was courting her, Linus used to tell Claudia stories of the desert. He described Oppenheimer's long late-night drives through moonscapes of shale and sand, Native American tribes whose cultures were based on the credos of the aliens who had visited their ancestors, secret military bases.

"The desert has anonymity," he said. "It is a place you go to get lost."

Claudia turned nine. Her parents began to believe she would live. A collective sigh of relief was released. By high school she had returned to normal in many ways, though she was still given to moods of absence and removal. She could sometimes be found sitting in her room staring off at some invisible point. She was easily hypnotized by spinning objects. The microwave could drop her into a trance, water flushing from the toilet. At birthday parties she was the one who could be made to cluck like a chicken or dance wearing shoes that were too big. She grew lovely beyond belief, her hair long and straight, eyes cool and slightly unreadable as if she harbored unreasonably some universal secret. Breasts developed. She was pursued like a burning automobile chased down a desert highway by seven lonely fire trucks. In the face of the antics of high school boys she remained serious. Her sense of humor was practical and often turned off. There were times when she felt she must make a conscious decision to be social, as if it was a mode or speed her brain had to be adjusted to match.

"I never understood why people laughed at television, *The Honeymooners, Mary Tyler Moore, Dick Van Dyke*. It was just words and gestures. I couldn't add up the quips and one-liners into anything amusing."

"My father would laugh beer from his nose on a regular basis, great geysers of Black Label squirting in astonished spasms."

"Your family has a fine tradition for the spraying of liquids from the head."

Linus clawed his way out from the heavy humidity of the covers, tasted the clear air on his tongue. Claudia wriggled out, went into the bathroom. Linus could hear her peeing through the door.

"I've noticed that you almost never laugh. When I first met you I thought a beloved grandmother had just died."

A flush. Claudia came back brushing her hair.

"Sometimes it takes me over an hour to get a joke. I burst out laughing in elevators and scare old people. I'm now convinced that when I first met *you,* seventy percent of the residents of my building thought I had some kind of dissociative mood disorder."

Linus rolled over onto his stomach, dug around under the pillows for his shirt.

"In Brooklyn there was this guy Tommy Maza who told everyone the CIA had put an electrode in his head that made him say dirty words to schoolchildren. Nicholas Colletti's father beat the shit out of him with a cork-filled baseball bat."

Claudia sat down on the bed, tucked a leg under her hip.

"Now see, I don't think that's going to strike me as funny anytime during the next seventy-two hours, but you never know. I could be in a taxicab counting my change and suddenly spit."

Falling in love is like discovering that you are suddenly a much larger person than you realized. You drink a figurative potion, succumb to an elusive transformation. You become a monster with two heads and four arms and four legs and one heart. Where once you were separate beings, now you are joined literally, like Siamese twins, and as we know, though it is possible to separate twins like these, it's rare for more than one of them to survive the operation. Therefore, once the joining is complete, a great risk arises from any impulse toward renewed singularity. Your cells begin to conspire together. You take on a joint smell, surrendering your individual odors to the overwhelming sense of togetherness. When faced with an empty house Linus would invariably make his way to the bedroom, lie on top of the crumpled comforter, breathe in the air of pillows touched by married hair, blankets pulled by married hands. To be alone again, even for an hour, no matter how much of a relief, is still a kind of loss. He would wander through the empty house, positive that he was forgetting something, but it was only Claudia, her absence. How crazy this could make Linus, for when the time came that Claudia worked late into each night for months at a time, he began to grow a threatening insecurity that sprang from this sense of forgetfulness. Her absence became a nagging doubt, a distraction.

For a year now it seems as if he has been unable to concentrate, preoccupied by small sounds, by the awareness of his own body, his own actions. When a man who has been coupled for so long becomes solitary again, it is as if he has forgotten how to live naturally, how to talk and think and act. Every motion must be checked for accuracy. The unconsciousness of his motions are now glaringly apparent. Much like the obsessive-compulsive who must count to twenty-five four times before walking through a doorway, Linus found himself monitoring the lifting of a fork, the tying of a shoelace, the brushing of his hair. Is this how I do it? he would wonder. This doesn't feel right at all.

Claudia for her part must have felt the loneliness too. The distance brought on by her absence was distance that was not easily crossed even when she was near again. They spent so much time apart that each began to fill in the emptiness in other ways. They found they had less in common with each passing month, for Linus's response to Claudia's overworking was to throw himself into his own work, to increase the number of radicals and suspicious philosophers he met for dinner, to plumb the depths of American greed and depravity. He radicalized while Claudia slid more toward the middle, relaxed into a comfortable language of marketing talk and fancy lunches, sparked inside by the creative atmosphere of the agency, the challenges, the deadlines. She formed fast and close friendships, felt an excitement from her coworkers, a team spirit that disappeared when she climbed into her car to go home. And Linus became resentful, and Claudia became defensive, and the whole thing started to seem like a bad TV movie, and so Claudia would stop for a drink after work with the guys and Linus would stay out late with Edward and Roy and their marriage became in this way a self-fulfilling prophecy. Who knows where it would have gone from there? When Claudia took that trip to Chicago, Linus felt that it was a cooling-off period, a time for each to reflect on their lives and rediscover their need for each other. He would like to think that there was a way back and that they were at the point of turning. That together they could step away and regroup, restart the trip into forever. Now he wonders what was really going on. A man named Holden would seem to be the final clue to a cruel hoax in which Linus wakes up to the fact that maybe his marriage was a con game in the end, filled with polite chitchat and sullen mood swings.

But oh, when things were new, when they were young and in love; the honeymoon and those first years starting out. They would spend entire evenings in restaurants without realizing, would drive or walk home with a great sense of fulfillment, as if everything in the world was where it should be. It bred confidence in both of them. They became more aggressive in their careers, because they knew they had the support of the other, had overcome the hardest hurdle in life, which is the finding of a partner. Linus blasted out those first two books. The words just seemed to fly from his head. Claudia got a promotion after a brilliant campaign for a major supermarket chain. Linus traveled back East for a series of lectures. Claudia moved into a corner office. They both felt weightless. Linus for the first time in his life felt lucky.

Ford takes Linus to lunch at Café des Artistes on Central Park West. He talks about the end of the world.

"The final cataclysm will begin when Russia allies with the Arab nations against Israel," he says. He orders for both of them, an endive salad, grilled ahi, tiramisu.

"You may not have much of an appetite, Linus, but if you don't eat you will simply continue to pass out." Linus takes the cloth napkin to his lap. It has been handcrafted into the form of a swan. He wonders how much longer the numbness will last. Everything appears to be occurring in the third person. There I am, he thinks, having lunch with Ford. He's wearing a suit though it's Sunday. I'm sitting in khakis that are too short for me. My tie is yellow. I look like a mental patient on a work furlough. At Ford's insistence he has showered and shaved. He must stop being what Ford has categorized as "self-indulgent."

"You must deal with this as if it is a problem of logic," Ford says, buttering a wedge of bread. "Think in terms of years."

Linus studies the cutlery.

"I'm still stuck in Thursday. I'm sitting in my office. I'm telling Sylvia Beckleman that she has failed to consider the fact that there was no blood at the site where they found Vince Foster's body. There is a very assertive knock. Three strong raps. That's the moment I can't get past. I feel that if I had simply kept moving, if they had never found me, then Claudia would have lived. Without the pronouncement of death she would have just lived. Conceptually, I mean." He presses bread crumbs idly into the skin of his thumb.

Ford signals a waiter that he'd like to see the wine list.

"After the Russians ally with the Arabs, the ten-nation European common market will sign a pact with Israel. In this case the common market is clearly the ten-horned monster in Revelation 13. The pact will be that described in the Book of Daniel."

"Is this meant to soothe me? Talk of the apocalypse? Let me finish for you. After the peace a seven-year tribulation begins. The leader of this new international empire is the Antichrist. My wife died, Ford. Don't tell me you've become a born-again Christian."

Ford orders an Italian burgundy. The salads arrive.

"What are the funeral arrangements? Do you need help with anything? Whatever you want." Ford cuts the bitter lettuce with his fork, chews. "I feel terrible."

"For my loss?" Linus mutters angrily.

Ford wipes his mouth with his napkin.

"She's dead, Linus, not lost."

Linus makes an angry gesture with his hands, as if to say, *Finally* another sane human. "Thank you," he says, then again more quietly, "Thank you." He puts down his fork, pushes his plate away. Ford, chewing, points the tines of his fork at Linus.

"Eat it."

"Or what, a full nelson?"

"Linus, you are a man spinning out of control. I realize this. Were I in your shoes I too might cease to function, but as your brother I refuse to sit and watch you fall apart."

"You may have no choice."

"About whether you fall apart, that is correct. As to whether I watch, that is a separate matter."

Linus picks up his fork, herds the lettuce around his plate. The tuna arrives.

"Mother and Alice will be at the house when we get back," Ford says, once it is certain that Linus is indeed chewing and swallowing and not orchestrating some elaborate funneling of food from the side of his mouth to his napkin. "I thought before we put you through the whole family ordeal that you might like a quiet meal where we could try to talk reasonably about what has happened and what you will do now."

"This to you is something that can be discussed reasonably," says Linus.

"Yes, actually. It is."

Linus stares at his plate for a long time. Ford chews idly, watching him. He does not move to take another bite or a drink of wine. He sits with his fork transfixed in midair. He watches Linus with the eyes of a man who earns his living making money in large quantities. Behind them a man on a cellular phone says, *I'm not going to start recruiting anyone until after the infomercial comes out.* Finally Linus nods.

"I just don't see how I can go back. How could I live in the house? How could I go back to teaching? It would be a lie."

"There are other things. Take some time off. Travel. Find something worth living for. There will be insurance money. You must think in terms of rescuing yourself, of saving your own life. This is what she would have wanted."

Linus finishes his water, places the glass back on the table next to his plate.

"We are all victims of anonymous forces," he says.

"Yes, but, Linus, your confusion is in seeing those forces as governmental. The power we're all dealing with is God."

"A conspiracy of the divine? Is this what you're saying? God sitting in a golden office with the angel Gabriel going over the schematics of New York City airport security?"

"If you like. I prefer to think of it as God having a higher plan for all of us. The problem with you and your kind is that you insist on assigning dark and sinister overtones to every minor mystery. The mysteries of the universe are for Him to know, not us."

Linus nods, puts his fork down, covers his brother's hand with his own.

"You know what, Ford. I think you're right."

Ford has a look of actual shock on his face. "You do?"

"Yes, I feel a sudden overwhelming urge to sacrifice a goat or a flock of ducks or something."

A sour frown.

"My response is to eat and pretend you didn't say that."

They both return to their food, Ford with a vigor that implies an untroubled colon.

"Fear is a sign of faithlessness," he says between bites. "Your paranoid culture is based in the atheism of cynicism and hopelessness. God asks each one of us to simply spread His name. Worship and know peace. We are rewarded with everlasting life."

"Not to mention the Jaguar, penthouse, and the summer home on Long Island."

"Material possessions. The true believer cares not."

"You know, Ford, the rich shouldn't be allowed religion. It belittles the faith of the poor."

Ford chews his lip a moment, furrows his brow.

"I have no response to that."

Under the table Linus steps out of his shoes, crouches down in his seat, disappearing beneath the tablecloth. He produces the shoes as if they are moneys owed to a loan shark, depositing them on the table between them.

"Walk a mile," he says. "Then see what kind of God you can believe in."

Ford brushes the shoes to the floor, snarls.

"Don't be a baby, Linus. Retain some small shred of dignity."

"Are you a respected leader of your community, Ford? It's quite possible that you could be the Antichrist of which we speak."

"You are having a complete mental breakdown, aren't you?"

"Beware the new religions. They signal the end."

Ford's face is flushed. He rocks in his seat as if suddenly he cannot get comfortable.

"Don't make light of my beliefs. Once the pact with Israel is signed, the Antichrist with the aid of the Committee on Foreign Relations and the Trilateral Commission will persuade all Western nations to unite under a one-world government, a single monetary system. We see it already in Europe. We will each be assigned a unique ID number. The need for credit cards and cash will disappear. A new system of credit transfer will be instituted involving the placing of a small biochip into the right hands or foreheads of all humans. We will be electronically branded for life. It is already happening. Nineteen hundred years ago John warned us about just such a global system of enslavement. Revelation, chapter 13, verses 16 through 18, states 'and he causeth all, both small and great, rich and poor, free and bound, to receive a mark in their right hand, or in their foreheads. And that no man shall buy or sell, save he that had the mark, or the name of the beast, or the number of his name.'"

"Six six six."

"Six six six."

"Aren't those the first three digits of Bill Gates's phone number? Seriously, Ford, you're far more of a freak than I am. You live your whole life based on the belief in a conspiracy of mythic proportions."

"I have the rational beliefs of my faith. I refuse to be compared to the pimple-faced radicals you associate with who believe that extraterrestrials are kidnapping them for sperm samples. What do these aliens want to do, breed a new superrace of the lazy and the chemically imbalanced?"

"If you start in with the Pledge of Allegiance I am pouring a glass of water on your head."

Ford stares at him for a few seconds. There is a greater contempt historic in his pose than can be ascribed to sibling rivalry. The question is how these two men can be related, truly of the blood, given their exotic separations of body type and character. Ford controls a portfolio worth just under $700 million. It is his curse to be anchored by the chains of familial obligations to a godless cynic and a drug addict. He bears this burden as a penance for crimes as yet unexplained.

"Eat your fucking lunch," he says.

Over coffee Ford tells Linus about how the death of their father affected him. The tiramisu is like a small office tower surrounded by carefully plowed snowbanks of powdered sugar.

"He always had such a smell. Our house smelled like him, that blue-collar underarm odor."

"He worked for a living. Hauled sacks of flour, unloaded boxes of cans and bottles."

"To live in a house with smells. It's embarrassing. The body should be dry and excrete little if anything in the way of aroma. When he died his casket had that same musty stink. As if he had keeled over in the midst of some manual labor as opposed to after a month of bed rest. I was frankly incredulous."

"He rotted from the inside. The smell was defeat. Another notch on the bedpost of the tobacco lobbyists and the booze magnates. The blood-profit agenda of drug pushers."

"He drank because he drank. He smoked because he smoked. No one held a gun to his head."

"He drank because he was an alcoholic. He smoked because R. J. Reynolds injects enough nicotine into their cigarettes to ensure that your body will never function happily again without a constant supply of it."

Ford shakes his head, stirs his coffee.

"You always blame people's problems on the ambiguous menace of third parties. The only person Dad was a victim of was himself. He killed himself very slowly over a great number of years and he knew all along what the risks were. There were no surprises. There was no brainwashing. He drank, he smoked, he died."

Linus ignores his tiramisu as if it is a South African landowner attending the cotillion of an Aryan offspring. The coffee he drinks black. It makes his teeth ache. He feels suddenly a great desire to grab Ford by the lapels and yell into his eye.

"Do you know Jeffrey Holden?"

Ford wipes his mouth with his napkin as if polishing a magnificent handlebar mustache. It is a sign of the languorous patience of the very wealthy.

"There's a Jeff Holden on the co-op committee, down on forty-seven."

"Yes. He was on the plane."

"Jeff Holden?" Ford looks surprised. "Really." A sip of coffee. "Doesn't he work for Eli Lilly or something?"

"Hastings." Linus tries to make it sound casual. He wants Ford's shock to be enormous. "He and Claudia worked together on an ad campaign."

"Really? How strange. Jeff Holden. Not that I knew him all that well, but..."

"He bought her ticket."

Ford's face goes very still. It happens suddenly and to Linus it is an eerie reminder of moments from his youth when Ford would go cold like someone had just turned off the heat in him.

"So it was a business trip. She was going to Brazil on business."

"Business." Linus says it as if it is an idea that deserves pondering. He leaves a silence at their table that is reflective and slightly anemic.

"Did you ever see Claudia when she came to town?" he asks. "Did Madison ever say, 'I could swear I just saw Claudia Owen getting off the elevator,' and you said, 'Oh, Mad, don't be silly'? Did anything like that ever happen?"

Ford has narrowed his eyes and the corners of his mouth have turned down.

"Linus..."

"Did you ever see a woman from the back walking down your block and you thought for a split second that it had to be her and then she turned a corner and you forgot about it, because of course she was in San Francisco with me? Did Jeffrey Holden ever talk about his divorce? You see, Ford, what I have to do now, rationally or not, is find answers to all the questions, otherwise I will never be able to talk rationally to anyone about anything ever again."

Ford touches his hair unconsciously with his hand to make sure it is still in place.

"Linus. I don't know what to say, except don't let your suspicious nature tear you down. Don't always expect the worst from people, lest that be all you get."

"I refuse to speak to anyone who uses the word *lest* in a sentence. Quoting scripture is bad enough. Terrible, in fact. What's happened to us, Ford? Where are the snot-faced innocents of our childhood?"

"Seek guidance in God, Linus. The Lord answers all questions in time."

Linus stands up. He is suddenly and uncontrollably furious. His voice is a thin razor wire of concentrated rage.

"Ford, I am going to smack you in the mouth if you say anything like that again. I don't want you to introduce me to a personal friend of yours, Jesus Christ. I don't want to hear how God is the answer to every question. What I want to hear are actual answers to tangible questions about why my wife, Claudia Owen, is now strangely toeless and completely dead. Why she flew to New York, why she left me..." He trails off, thinking first that this is not what he meant to say and then that maybe it was. The implications of it are too infinite to be quantified. He sits absently, succumbing to gravity.

Ford places his napkin on the table to signal that he is done. Waiters move in to clear their plates.

"Jeff Holden never said a word to me about his divorce. We talked about Christmas bonuses for doormen and the restoration of the marble in the lobby. Sometimes we talked shop. I gave him the name of a good lawyer and a great accountant. We never had dinner. We never had lunch."

"You never saw Claudia?"

"Never saw her. If she was in the building I never knew. None of the doormen ever said, 'Excuse me, Mr. Owen, I saw your sister-in-law was here earlier.' There was none of that. I think you need to go home, Linus. I mean stay as long as you need to, but then go home and grieve and let her go. She was your wife. She loved you. God loves you. I love you."

Linus's response is to place his head in his hands and begin to cry.

On the walk back to the apartment, Ford tells Linus that he spoke to an FBI agent who called while Linus was in bed yesterday.

"Claudia's things are being shipped up here. I have arranged to have them messengered to the house later today. Perhaps there will be something in there that can answer your questions."

Linus walks, placing one foot deliberately in front of the other. He flushes from time to time with anger, with sadness, with fear. He is the exhauster of mood rings, swinging from precarious emotion to small collapse. His mind is hard at work trying to override the debilitating flood of feelings, to shut them down. He has to figure out a way to get into Holden's apartment.

The sight of his mother is too much for Linus, who breaks down once again when they reach Ford's apartment, allows himself to be smothered, pushes his body against hers as if trying to force his way back to an embryonic state. Alice holds his hand and smiles her sad smile. She urges him to be brave, uses the rhetoric of AA. Inside she feels a tremendous self-loathing. Not pretty, not strong, not smart, she thinks. It is her own peculiar mantra. What use am I to help Linus, a thirty-one-year-old woman with no ideas for her own future except to survive each day without the debasement of my own weaknesses. Madison returns from her Swedish massage. She has bought a black-forest cake wrapped in a gold and green box. Her hair gives off a supermodel sheen. Linus goes into the bathroom to wash his face.

Claudia's luggage arrives later that afternoon, delivered by an expressionless airline employee with an invoice to sign. In return he leaves Linus two small Coach bags and a wardrobe. Linus, who has resolved himself to be clinical, carries them into the guest room and places them on the bed. He circles the mattress warily, eyeing each piece from all angles. This is the same luggage she took when they flew to London last year, the same she has carried since 1991. Its familiarity is intimidating. Linus believes there is a real possibility that each piece will be filled with pictures of Claudia's dead body. He swallows, steps forward, unzips the smallest bag. Inside, with her carry-on items, is a Ziploc bag containing the contents of her pockets and purse, her wallet, hairbrush, date book. Linus takes her key ring from the bag, examines each key. She has marked each one with a colored rubber shield to make them easier to identify. Orange, red, and green he knows to be house and garage. Blue is the office. The key to the Saab is easy to identify. This leaves three unknown keys, a yellow, a purple, and a brown. His heart rate is fast.

"I'm going for a walk," he tells Madison, who is reading the

Italian *Vogue* on the living-room sofa. She opens her mouth to say something, but Linus has already closed the door. He takes the stairs down to the forty-seventh floor. He is imagining their fifth anniversary party. Edward and Roy had edited together videotape segments of their wedding reception with outtakes from a seminar on alien abduction. Lecture descriptions of body appropriations and tampering were interspersed with footage of Linus and Claudia cutting their cake. Discussion of metallic implants was spliced together with stills of Linus's odd-looking cousins from Paramus.

At apartment 4720 Linus stops and examines Claudia's keys again. He selects the anonymous brown one closest to her house keys. It does not fit the bottom lock, but when placed in the top it throws back the bolt with an audible click. Linus, who has hit emotional bottom, feels nothing but a slight shifting of grief from sorrow to rage. The next key unlocks the bottom and he steps inside Jeffrey Holden's Central Park West apartment and closes the door behind him.

The layout of the apartment is similar to Ford's. A large living room with bay windows, kitchen and dining room facing the park. There are two full baths and a half bath off the kitchen. Holden holds mainly modern tastes, hardwoods, metal, and glass. There are photographs of his children in every room, an eight-year-old boy and a four-year-old girl, the boy in some prep-school uniform, the girl with braids and several missing teeth. There are magazines spread on top of a large glass coffee table. Linus looks for evidence of the wife, considers the absence of her things as a sign that it was Holden who filed for divorce, for the lovelorn man ambushed by separation keeps evidence of his betrayer at hand under the mistaken belief that his abandonment is simply a momentary lapse of reason. He wonders if it was Claudia who spurred Holden into destroying his family. He is struck by the ridiculousness of his predicament. Could Claudia really have been having an affair with this man of whom Linus had never heard? He considers the possibility that the whole thing is an elaborate hoax engineered by government agencies to keep him from discovering the truth. It's possible that the keys could have been planted on the ring. He shakes his head. All there is is circumstantial evidence. Remember, he thinks, if the clue seems too obvious or the evidence unarguably conclusive, you must ask yourself, Is this what I am to believe or what they want me to believe?

He searches the bedroom first, rifles through the sock drawers and closets. Designer suits and shoes. Could Claudia really have been so preoccupied with wealth? Holden wore boxers. His bedside reading betrays an interest in science, a collection of current essays on physics, a biography of Louis Pasteur. There is an etching of a 1930s New York street scene hanging over the bed. There is no evidence of Claudia in the room. The gratitude Linus feels borders on the ridiculous. He gets down on his hands and knees, searches under the bed. He goes through the shoes in the closet. He doesn't know what he is looking for, evidence of the affair or clues toward solving the bombing. He just looks for anything that seems out of the ordinary.

In the kitchen he finds a notepad with a few phone numbers scribbled on it. He puts it in his pocket. When Linus opens the door to Holden's study he finds Agent Forbes inside waiting for him.

"Jesus Christ," he says at the sight of Forbes sitting behind Holden's desk.

"Finding anything?"

Linus places his hands on his knees, breathes through his mouth. When his heart rate is down he straightens.

"What am I supposed to be finding?"

Agent Forbes puts his hands on the desk and studies them. His cuticles are brown.

"Pictures of Elvis, a plasticine statue of the Virgin Mary, underwear with streak marks."

Linus stares at him as if weighing him, considering the possibilities of him, his existence here in this place and time. There is a strong possibility, Linus feel, that he may be an apparition.

"Agent Forbes," he says, "and may I say, if that is your real name."

Forbes takes out a piece of gum. He is trying to give up cigarettes.

"Have a seat."

Linus examines the options, chooses to remain standing. Forbes, who flew up from Florida that morning, negotiates the gum from its wrapper and places it in his mouth.

"Oh, by the way, FBI Director Wallace wants me to tell you to say hello to your brother for him." Not even your own family can be trusted, is the implication. Linus understands. He is not surprised.

"The things money buys," he says. Forbes takes off his jacket, hangs it on the back of his chair.

"How are you, Mr. Owen? Really, deep down inside."

"There is no deep down inside. Deep down inside has been closed for renovations."

"Overwhelmed then. I understand. At a loss. Loose ends."

Linus begins searching the room with his eyes. He crosses to the desk, looks behind a stack of magazines.

"What are you doing?"

"I'm looking for a sign that says, The doctor is in."

Forbes chews his gum, first on one side, then the other. In his pocket is a bottle of pills.

"So why am I here?" he asks Linus, who fondles the keys in his pocket.

"A guess would be you are here to hide or destroy evidence that may be in this apartment. A second guess would be you are here to follow me, interrogate me, arrest me."

"Have you done something recently that might warrant a reading of rights?"

"I refuse to recycle. I am a conscientious objector when it comes to cans and bottles."

Forbes considers how he would feel were he to learn that his own wife was having an affair. To have to break in to another man's apartment looking for indecent Polaroids and stained sheets. For a moment he can't even remember his wife's name.

"You know what bothers me?" he says. "I know, you're thinking terrorism, drive-by shootings, the lack of leads on a critical case, but here it is. I don't understand foods that aren't supposed to be refrigerated until after they're opened. Mayonnaise, for example. All I can think of is a nice salmonella sandwich. I mean mayonnaise is not something you can just leave out."

"It's vacuum sealed."

"That's what I hear, but the thought is disturbing nonetheless. Here's a jar of mayonnaise like a food-poisoning time bomb just waiting to go off. And it's not alone. I go to the supermarket. Whole aisles of unrefrigerated explosives."

"I'm from Brooklyn. We eat mustard."

Forbes nods as if accepting sage advice from a Chinese apothecary.

"Have you ever looked at bacteria close up, like under a microscope? There's a whole other world taking place at the molecular level. The implications are alarming."

Linus raises his hand and waits to be called on.

"Can I be excused? I have other things I could be doing."

"I want to ask you some questions."

Linus reads the titles of the books on Holden's shelves. There is a copy of the *Physician's Desk Reference,* a college yearbook. He has diplomas on the wall. There is an antique globe on a dark wood stand beside the desk. The area carpet is Persian. There is a notebook left open on the desk. He sits on a divan and looks out the window.

"I take it as a bad sign if you think you can solve this crime by asking me questions. The term *grasping at straws* comes to mind."

"Still I have many."

Linus scratches his head.

"You know what interests me," he says. "Since we're on the subject of interest."

Forbes shrugs to make it clear that he has no opinion on the subject. He has come to New York for two distinct reasons, neither one of them having anything to do with helping Linus grieve.

"Pharmaceuticals."

"Well, sure. A very interesting subject."

"Also why you're sitting in a dead man's apartment. That I find truly fascinating."

Forbes nods his head. He considers the words *Big Mac attack,* followed very closely by *wimpy, wimpy Cinch-Sak.*

"As I said, I have questions." The gum goes flat. He continues to chew it. In the five years he has pretended to work for the FBI he has never once had an office there. He says,

"The first question is..."

"Have you at least put together a list of suspects?" Linus breaks in with irritation. "A short list. Two names on the back of a used envelope."

"Mr. Owen."

"Be reasonable."

"What?"

"Be reasonable. You were going to say be reasonable. I could see it in your eyes."

Forbes rubs his neck with the palm of his hand as if to show great weariness.

"I just spent the last four hours on an airplane. The woman on my right drank seven vodka tonics in a row. On the other side a fat man snored. I don't trust people who can sleep on planes. I spend the whole time gripping the armrests and pretending I'm at home watching *Columbo.*"

"That's because they crash. Great holes are blown in the belly, an engine fails, then another. They seek earth like bullets shot in the air on some hard-to-pronounce Mexican holiday."

In the last three years Forbes has begun to develop a fear of enclosed spaces. Airplanes make him feel constricted, taxicabs and automobiles are better. Windows can be rolled down. Elevators are the worst. He is a man who will climb thirty-one flights of stairs rather than be sealed inside a single elevator.

"Mr. Owen, I am willing to tell you certain things in exchange for your cooperation."

"Like the thing about the mayonnaise, or are we talking actual information?"

Forbes leans forward, rests his elbows on the desk. He is younger than his position with the CIA would suggest.

"The explosive was a C-4–based device. All of the component parts were plastic. It was stored with the luggage. We have reason to believe that it was housed in a tan or gray Samsonite bag."

"And we suspect whom?"

"Three words. Militant Arab extremists."

"My ass."

Forbes opens his briefcase.

"Perhaps you would like me to show you pictures of Jeffrey Holden screwing your wife."

A sick frozen feeling attaches itself to Linus's spine.

"Fuck your mother," he says.

Forbes takes a manila envelope out of his briefcase, shuts it, places it back on the floor.

"My mother is not the issue here."

"Ask away then, Lieutenant Columbo. I think you'll find all my answers are similar in tone and content."

Forbes makes a face. He is interested in setting Linus up with a certain set of facts and following him to their source. He is also aware that he must keep Linus off balance emotionally so that he does not dig too deeply into the facts he is given. Forbes rips open the top of the envelope and pulls out four sheets of paper, which he hands to Linus, who, thinking they are pornographic photographs, will not take them. Forbes drops them on the desk, waits for Linus to look at them. Linus struggles with his eyes, which strain toward the desktop. He forces them instead around the room. There are pictures of Holden's children, another etching. The light switch is on a dimmer.

"I thought you said these were going to be pictures of Claudia," he says when he can no longer restrain his eyes and focuses on the pages.

"I said perhaps you would like me to show you pictures of Jeffrey Holden screwing your wife. I didn't say I had any. This is a passenger roster. Something I believe you asked for. If you notice, I have highlighted four names on the list. One is a special operative of the Central Intelligence Agency. Another is a Pentagon attaché. The third is a Defense Department contractor for McDonnell Douglas. The last is a four-star general. We believe the bombing was directed at these four men."

Linus neglects to mention that he has his own copy of the list, one that contains a few more names. He says, "I'm waiting for the groundbreaking tie-in to pharmaceuticals."

"Try holding your breath. The truth is, we believe this was an attack against a group working on a top-secret project involving stealth technology."

To Linus this is just a series of consonants and vowels put together to cloud the truth.

"Skunk works, you're saying. The Aurora Hypersonic Spy Plane. The TR-3A Black Manta."

"Something like that, yes. I can't go into too many details obviously."

"Obviously. In the interest of a secure nation." Linus puts the list back on the desk, sits back in his chair.

"As you say."

"And in your scenario why is my wife on a plane with Holden flying to Brazil?"

Forbes gets up to open a window. He has begun to sweat. The room is undergoing a certain constriction. He walks into the bathroom and opens his pill bottle, inside which all of the small blue pills have been cut in half. He places one of these halves on his tongue, drinking water from the sink with cupped hands. He washes his face, wipes his hands on a tea-green towel, fixes his tie.

"In my scenario, Mr. Owen," he says, returning to the room and standing by the window, "your wife is running away with another man. She is leaving you. Abandonment is the long and short of it."

Linus nods. This has begun to seem like his scenario too. It may also, however, be a convenient interpretation of an otherwise dangerous set of facts.

"Militant Arab extremists?" he says.

Forbes shrugs. In his family there is a long line of intelligence-agency employment. His grandfather on his mother's side was the owner of a number of banks in South America and by 1955 had cultivated certain relationships with the CIA. His father is an executive at Boeing. Forbes himself was recruited straight out of college.

"What do you know about a group called Danton?" he asks. He can feel the pill starting to work, the room beginning to return to its original size. Now he must be careful to stay out of any situations that call for aggression on his part.

Linus shakes his head.

"Yours or ours?" he says.

Forbes smiles. He has read both of Linus's books, the last one in his hotel room in Tallahassee.

"Mr. Owen, I have decided to take a sudden liking to you."

"I don't know how to feel about that."

"Danton, we believe, is a group of left-wing extremists. Their place of origin is unknown. Their place of operation is unknown. Their membership is unknown."

"But you believe they exist despite this overwhelming lack of details."

"You know how things work, Linus. We operate on the suspension of disbelief, both of us. We hear rumors we have been trained to believe. We are suspicious people. Our first impulse is to think the worst. Someone tells you the government has made a deal with extraterrestrials. The government denies this. Your first impulse is to suspect a cover-up. For me, if I hear that perhaps there is a super-secret group known as Danton who are pursuing a campaign of violence against certain guarded government operations, I think, Well, this must be true, until it is proved otherwise."

"You use the word *campaign*."

"A figure of speech. Campaign. I mean a bombing of an airplane carrying Defense Department personnel."

"No one has sent you a letter, though. No late-night phone calls. This is Danton. We are responsible. That level of belief."

"We have only the vaguest speculation to go under."

Forbes begins to feel a certain distance from the room. He digs his fingernails into the palms of his hands, grits his teeth. He thinks, In 1492 Columbus sailed the ocean blue.

"So you're saying some left-wing militia has struck a blow for ordinary citizens everywhere," says Linus.

"I'm saying some left-wing militia has just blown up a hundred and twenty-four people, four of whom happened to be government employees. No victory, I would think, for the moral animal in all of us."

Linus considers the use of the words *moral* and *animal* by this man in this context. He raises an eyebrow.

"Tell me the truth. You don't work for the FBI, do you?"

"You may think of me as captain of the Keystone Kops if it makes you feel any better. Would you like me to run around in an oversize helmet crashing into lampposts and cable cars?"

"Give me the bottom line."

"We want you to work with us to find Danton."

"'We' being…"

Forbes smiles.

"The Fifty-first squad of the Keystone National Intelligence Agency."

"NSA, NRO, CIA."

"AFL-CIO, member FDIC."

"I'm being deputized."

"Not exactly. We need a man of your persuasion working from the inside. People trust you. They tell you things. People don't trust us."

"People shouldn't trust you."

"Either way."

Linus rubs his temple with his left hand.

"What exactly is a man of my persuasion?" he wants to know.

"Don't forget to pass along my greetings to your brother," says Forbes, standing up and putting on his jacket.

"What are you, looking for a date?"

Forbes smiles. He puts his hand in his pocket, rubs his thumb over the pill bottle. He hands Linus a business card with only a phone number on it.

"Mysterious," says Linus, placing the card in his shirt pocket.

"Are we agreed then? I have been authorized to offer you whatever services you can think of that might help you get to the bottom of all this."

"The words *wash my car* come to mind."

Forbes opens his briefcase, pulls out a copy of Linus's last book, *Make Us Rich: Government on the Eve of a New Millennium.*

"Would you autograph this for me? I'm a big fan."

Linus laughs.

"I just bet you are." He takes a pen from Forbes, writes, "To Agent Forbes, thanks for the documents."

Forbes examines the inscription and seems satisfied.

"After this we must meet in random places as if by accident. Call this number from a pay phone, leave an address. I will meet you within the hour."

"Take two taxis. Make sure you're not followed. This message will self-destruct in ten seconds."

Forbes opens the study door. His shoes are black, shined to a blinding sheen.

"Agent Forbes," says Linus. "Just where did you hear of Danton anyway?"

Forbes puts down his briefcase, strips the foil from another piece of gum.

"*Chicago Tribune,* January third, 1995."

"That's all you'll say?"

"That," says Forbes, picking up his briefcase and walking to the front door, "is all I'll say."

New York in February. The snow blackens quickly. It clumps as if rotting, cleaved by the tread marks of buses and cars. Enormous black pools of water form. Salt corrodes the boots of pedestrians, the wheel wells of automobiles. Underneath mountains of consumptive white, the windshields of cars struggle forth, ice ridden, flyers for discount clothing stores and 900 sex lines frozen to windshield wipers. The streets become clotted with the ranks of the homeless, androgynous mounds of humanity encumbered by layers of discarded clothing; five shirts, two sweaters, a torn parka or overcoat too short in the sleeves. The wheels of their shopping carts jam with clumps of ice and salt. They lope the uneven streets like rag-festooned beggars from medieval times and the dirty blue water from the squirt bottles of the window washers freezes in midair, their rags stiff and brittle, gripped in fingers that have lost feeling.

Beginning in November there is a great migration of the dispossessed to the subways. They descend in pairs or packs, together and alone. People are looking for heat. They ride the 4 and 5, the A, the C. They take the shuttle from Grand Central Station to Times Square and back. Hours pass, miles spent moving in place. Policemen roust them as they sleep curled into positions of defensive repose. The shelters fill, overflow. At night the temperature plummets. On the abandoned streets of February the homeless shiver after dark. They are the Sir Edmund Hillarys, the Ernest Shackletons of the modern age. They survive through the collection of clothes and garbage-can fires. In desperation windows are often broken, misdemeanors committed. The justification is the safety of a warm cell. After midnight the temperature drops to zero and below. At the airports ice smothers the runways. The windchill slices the skin. Businessmen in parkas and long corduroy dusters fight for room on crowded subway cars, where, conversely, the temperature can be measured in increments of Kelvin. Women in nylon winter coats and goose down stuff themselves like twitching sausages into the hot pockets between compressed bodies. Under their clothes, their sweaters and suits, they sweat in great rivers as the cars hurtle stammeringly downtown. Outside once more, covering the icy pavement toward office buildings, they feel the chill of the wind as it sneaks through the buttons of their coats, the weaves of their sweaters, and seeks out the dampened T-shirts and bras that now cling to their skin. The sky collects itself in muscles of constricted gray, shrugs ominous cloudbanks across the horizon. The days of blue sky are achingly clear, the cold weighing the soots and pollutants to the ground, where they seep into the snowbanks and corrupt the virtuous white until it has all turned a leprous black.

In Ford's Gore-Tex parka Linus swims his way downtown. He slips into the tide of Sunday shoppers descending from their Upper West Side retreats to the sparkle and hum of Macy's and Saks Fifth Avenue. He rides the B train to Thirty-fourth Street, walks over to the F, the train of his youth. He walks two cars up, gets out at Twenty-third, and gets back on three cars to the rear. At Broadway and Houston he changes to the number 6 and then switches to the 4 at City Hall. The train descends beneath the river, lights flickering on and off. Across from him a man in jeans with slush-soaked cuffs places a container with a medical-waste seal on the floor beneath his feet. On a cellular phone a woman says, *You're breaking up. I'll call you from the restaurant.* He gets off at Borough Hall in Brooklyn, ascends to street level. Traffic growls through the intersection at Court Street and Joralemon. Linus makes his way through the scattered bursts of snow to a Chinese restaurant illuminated by neon tubes. Fisher Cody has gotten them a table in the back, away from the windows. Linus strips off the Gore-Tex. His hair where he has sweated is flaked with ice crystals.

"You forget how brutal," he says.

"We get three nice months in New York. You've got May and half of April. You've got October and half of November. Other than that you may as well pay your therapist in advance."

Fisher orders moo-shu pork and sesame noodles. Linus has tea.

"I'm looking for a group called Danton. The wildest speculation and rumor is appreciated."

"Since you called me at the coffee shop this morning I've made a few phone calls. I have my suspicions, but you should be aware they're completely without foundation. I called Reilly in Indiana. I called Dowd in Arizona. I called Tuttle in D.C. We have a complete absence of data. The trick then is to guess wildly. Check around, see who's gone to ground, dropped out, disappeared."

Linus picks some flecks from his spoon, stirs his tea. He leans to where he can see the window, the faces in the restaurant. He feels watched. Cody lifts his hands from the table so the busboy can deposit his food.

"Lately I've been reading some material on the new extremism. Militia movements, the bombing of abortion clinics, the burning of churches in the South. The country has turned a hundred and eighty degrees since 1965. The radicals of the nineties are now right wing. In many ways the issues are the same, but their champions are the gun-toting, Bible-thumping snake handlers, the rural Baptist senator's nephews. Suddenly the government is too intrusive, too big. We're having spontaneous outbursts; small conglomerations of people who one morning decide they no longer recognize the legitimacy of the United States government. The Congress is run by special interests. Senators have become rock stars. The president has lost his magic status. The god-king is mortal. The emperor has no clothes."

He shovels rice onto his plate, lays out a pancake, sprinkles mooshu. He is a man who wanders the streets with small particles of food protruding from his beard.

"For the government it's as if a houseguest has suddenly peed into a silver tureen at a party in honor of Billy Graham. How rude of your citizens to suddenly question your authority. The response is inconsistent, but the outcome primarily fatal. Eighty people sit inside a compound in Texas for fifty-one days listening to the monumental strains of Nancy Sinatra played at a hundred ninety decibels. The attorney general does flyovers in a stealth helicopter. Every night we watch footage from cameras placed at discreet distances. We see heat lines, burnt brown grass. If we sit close to our screens we can see the tiny heads of ATF officers scampering from their vans to nearby humvees. Decisions are made, tear gas introduced. The whole compound burns to the ground in just under thirty-one minutes. In Montana another fifteen men pick up some extra ammunition and circle their wagons."

Linus sneezes, rubs his nose, sneezes again.

"People are finally beginning to realize that democracy is not in their best interest," he says. "In truth I think the United States Senate envies the new China. A repressive totalitarian regime controlling free enterprise. This way only the rich can surface."

"This is the right wing I'm talking about. Not the topic you came here to discuss. I assumed from our conversation earlier that the right wing is not useful to us, so I did my best to put it out of my mind, except in pursuing an interesting line of inquiry, which is, if the right wing is seceding from the center, then what must logically happen to the left? You see, without the totalitarian right to repress the radical left, and in fact using the right as a new role model for activism, isn't the left now freer to act in defense of its positions and beliefs? It offers a certain camouflage to the new left radical. You can blend in with the militia movements and lone gunmen. This being the case, I started to think about who the real wacko lefties are, the underground-flying-saucer-bases-CIA-brain-implant-world-bank-rules-the-world-listening-devices-in-our-teeth nut jobs. That list was pretty long, if you include the often overlooked states of Alaska and Hawaii, so I tried to narrow it down by eliminating the academics, the La Rouchians, the illuminati freaks, the Luddites, and the Internet newsgroup junkies."

"All in one afternoon."

"I canceled my three o'clock."

Cody places a wrapped pancake the size of a Polish hotdog into his mouth. The television over the bar gives off a blue light consisting of the opening credits of a situation comedy.

"At one minute past five I made my choice," he says through his food. He places a finger to his mouth and herds some of the escaping food back inside.

Linus leans over and stares at the traffic outside the window. He considers a Ryder rental truck stopped in front of the Key Food. He tries to decide if Cody is wired, whether this whole exercise is some government trick. Cody swallows, wipes his hands on his napkin.

"Richard Preston."

Linus is surprised, but not because it is a bad choice. It is simply the ability of Cody to be so decisive, to narrow the field of infinite possibilities to one risky name.

"The CIA works for five days around the clock and comes up with nothing and you give me Richard Preston after three hours of deliberation and some phone calls."

Cody shrugs, assembles another pancake.

"Remember he used to have this really creepy radio show every Monday night?"

"Out of Truth or Consequences, New Mexico, who could forget.

He called me to be on it once in maybe 1988. I'd just started teaching. My first book on secret technology and the myths of national security had just come out."

Cody chews intently, keeping his head down close to the table. He looks up at Linus over the bridge of his nose. Linus runs his finger along the lip of his cup.

"He said a psychic told him to call me. He asked me to fly to New Mexico and give my statement to the airwaves. I asked if I couldn't just do a phone interview. He hung up on me."

"Richard Preston published a series of articles in the late eighties on mind control and underground bases, Dulce, New Mexico, Pine Gap, Australia."

"Richard Preston." Linus shakes his head.

"Richard Preston."

Cody finishes his food, pushes the plate away. He is looking forward to the orange slices. Tonight he will watch a Knicks game on TV, finish a biography of Lenny Bruce. He says,

"I drove across country once. I wanted to see the Great American West. It was me and Myrna Blemel. Our goal was to have sex in motels in at least thirty-one states. We started with the Lazy River in Ohio. Not a great face, old Myrna, but some kind of body. In Laredo, Texas, I put on the radio. It's a hundred and fifteen degrees. The car is roasting like a peanut. Myrna is riding shotgun completely topless. All the windows are down. It's a nineteen seventy-one Chevy Nova. The car is rattling like a dime in a vacuum cleaner. I twirl the knob on the radio, hurrying past the ballads about pickup trucks and buck-toothed women. A televangelist berates me for placing my holy member in unholy places, which as far as he's concerned is probably anywhere within fifteen feet of Myrna Blemel. On 92.1 I find talk radio. Keep in mind I've just gotten out of school. My thesis is done. In the fall I start teaching Alternative American History at NYU. 92.1. It's two guys talking about how Star Wars technology is a cover for a secret satellite system meant to track the movement of American radicals. One of the guys is purported to be a former defense contractor. His voice is disguised mechanically until it is this Darth Vader–like growl. The voice of doom. I'm driving a hundred and ten miles an hour. I am a twenty-seven-year-old alternative American history professor with hair down to my ass rocketing through the shotgun state with a topless Jew. There's something about the desert that brings out the boobies, if you know what I mean."

"Preston."

"I'll never forget that day, that voice. Even through the explosive convulsions of my transmission I could hear something in his words. He was the smooth-throated hypnotist of the conspiratorial left. If he sang he'd be Sinatra. I haven't thought about him in ten years and then you called this afternoon."

"A hunch though. What am I to go on? You could make a similarly convincing argument for McDonald or Jerome. There is a point called the ultimate pinnacle of suspicion, where it is just as likely to consider that your mother shot JFK than it is to say Lee Harvey Oswald."

"That's the business we're in. If you're not going to follow your hunches, then be smart enough to follow mine." He orders a mai-tai. It comes with a pink umbrella. Linus watches commercials on TV.

"Paranoia is caused by a chemical imbalance. Suspicion is a sign of rational thinking."

"That's the difference between marriage and bachelorhood. At least you have your wife to keep you sane."

In the bathroom Linus runs cold water over his wrists. He goes into the last stall and sits on the toilet with his pants up. He leans his head back against the linoleum. On the stall door someone has carved, *Tony sucks dicks,* to which Tony has apparently responded, *Jerry Bruckner is the Marilyn Monroe of the hummer.* Next to Jerry's name is a phone number. Linus puts his face in his hands but he can't cry. He goes back to the sink, runs water over his face, wets his hair. In the mirror he refuses to meet his own eyes. On his way out he goes back into the stall and writes down Jerry Bruckner's phone number.

"Do you have a phone number for Preston?" he wants to know when he returns to the table. Cody has finished his mai-tai, paid the check. He lives a few blocks away above a Syrian bakery on Atlantic Avenue. He collects comic books and baseball cards. He writes letters to women in prison. It is his definition of dating.

"Nobody's seen Preston since 1991. He dropped out of sight."

Linus stands up, puts on his coat. "Piece of cake," he says.

Cody reaches under the table into his backpack and pulls out a folder and a tattered yellow pad.

"I put together a brief bio for you. The facts are sparse, born in Custer, Montana, to a single mother, educated locally. An only child. He won a scholarship at age sixteen to attend Stanford University, where he double-majored in anthropology and political science. The rumors are, he is very tall. I see him as a man with an important beard."

"With bits of moo-shu in it, I suppose," says Linus. Cody takes a moment to comb his beard for food. He turns pages in his notebook. Linus sits down, leaving his coat on.

"After college," he says, "Preston got his master's degree and doctorate at the University of Salt Lake City. His dissertation was on 'The History and Practice of Applied Fear as a Means of Governing.' I haven't been able to track down a copy yet. He became a teacher's assistant, then a professor. From 1981 to 1989 he had his own radio call-in show. During that time he became profoundly intrigued by government secrets. The desert called out to him. He moved out of Salt Lake City. He gravitated toward missile silos and secret air force bases. He began to take long trips into the desert, spoke to his listeners about UFOs. He began to make a list of words, the secret names of government projects. He believed the names themselves had power."

Linus watches traffic pass by on Montague Street. Brooklyn has become for him a time machine to which he has recently lost the keys. That child who once scaled fences in Park Slope has been orphaned suddenly by grief's equivalent of the Berlin wall. Cody clears his throat, finishes his drink.

Cody digs around in his pocket for a minute and hands Linus a piece of paper, folded.

"This is the Danton letter from the *Chicago Tribune*. It's a response to an article on land appropriations for Area 51."

Linus unfolds the paper, which is orange under the neon light. Outside, a heavy snow collapses on Brooklyn. The Ryder truck pulls away. A deliveryman on a bicycle propels seven bags of groceries into the darkness.

> *The Area 51 military base is a top-secret government facility in which the Pentagon, in conjunction with alien beings, performs medical and psychological experiments on United States citizens. The recent appropriation of land is a transparent ploy to try to hamper the ability of ordinary citizens to uncover the ruthless plots of the ruling class, which have in recent months been stepped up to meet a nefarious timetable centered in some way around*

the coming of the new millennium. The government continues to deny that such a base even exists, though pictures of it have been published by major newspapers and former employees have stepped forward to speak of the horrible crimes being committed there. These crimes must stop or the American people will be forced to fight back.

The letter is signed simply, Danton.

"It's hard to believe they even published this."

"It could be planted by the CIA, a setup for situations such as these. Create a left-wing group, distribute literature. When the time comes arrests are made, perhaps a suspect dies in jail. Look at Oswald handing out pro-Cuban propaganda from an office right upstairs from Clay Shaw."

"Now you're saying Danton is a fiction, a scapegoat, a wild-goose chase."

Cody lifts himself out of his seat, brushes rice from his beard. He puts his coat on, his gloves. He looks for all intents and purposes like a grizzly bear.

"Don't you ever watch *The X-Files*? Trust no one, baby. The truth is out there."

"I'm not sure I have the strength for paranoia anymore," says Linus as they make their way out into the snow.

On Monday Linus, Ford, and Madison fly to Chicago for the funeral with Alice and their mother, Ruth. The flight is half empty, the weather ugly. The plane bucks and skips. Linus stares idly out the window, gripping his armrests. He reads a series of mimeographed articles by Preston that Cody managed to dig up and deliver to the doorman at five o'clock that morning. Enclosed in the envelope is a handwritten note from Cody. It begins:

> *Preston submitted articles to national magazines who sent them back each in turn without comment. He finally published a piece in* Mother Jones *on the television habits of the UFO culture. In 1984 he moved his radio show to a local station in Truth or Consequences, New Mexico. He began to explore themes of nuclear consciousness. His article "Themes and Morals in the Disinformation Surrounding Secret Government Medical Experiments" gained him national prominence with left-wing panic-mongers. The radio station bought a new tower and increased its broadcasting range to four hundred miles. He began to receive calls from people in Santa Fe and Phoenix, people phoning in their fears and suspicions. A later tape provides this quote:*
>
> *"We have become increasingly concerned with the idea that our government has a distinct and separate agenda from the simple act of governing. This is a new religion, a secret black magic taking place. People begin to understand that their government is planning things for them. What is the point of these experiments, of exposing civilians to disease, chemicals, radiation? They must be preparing us for something. What is the need for super spy planes, satellite technology, electromagnetic pulses? Mind control. This is what we're talking about. A time when the earth is run by a ruling class, perhaps in conjunction with*

aliens. This technology is not for use against foreign governments but against its own people."

In 1989 Preston dropped out of sight. His radio show stopped. He went underground, some say into the desert of his obsession. The last thing he said over the airwaves was the following:

"Your children are not safe. Your bodies are not safe. We must defend ourselves from the slow corruption of microwave technology. The word abduction *contains new meanings every day. Do not be fooled. To the one-world government you are nothing more than laboratory animals, a bargaining chip in the secret negotiation with aliens. We must protect ourselves. This is all I can say. They are coming for me. They are almost here. I will return. Beware men in suits bearing gifts of technology. It is the machines that control us."*

On the tape there is a crash right here and a yell. You can distinctly hear a different voice saying, Shut it down. This is followed by static. A Gene Autry song comes on. I have no leads as to where Preston might be. He once told Livitz that he liked to drive highway 25 from Los Alamos to Las Cruces. Other than this he is a shadow on the wind. For more information look up my friend Luther K. in Victory, New Mexico. I'll let him know you might be coming.

As to the other matter you asked me to look into, I can tell you that Hastings Pharmaceutical does most of its product development and testing at a facility in San Bernardino, California, just off route 215. I have enclosed the address and directions. A friend of mine at Pharm-watch tells me that he has a contact and Deep Throat there named Colby Wood. He says you should call the enclosed number and ask if the man who answers has ever considered the importance of reserving a funeral plot. This sets up a prearranged meet for 8:00 P.M. at In and Out Burger. If you need anything I can be reached at 555-6440. It's a pay phone at the Syrian bakery downstairs. Just ask for Saddam. The Syrians love me.

Claudia is buried at noon in a hole dug primarily by a backhoe. The frozen ground is rough and slippery beneath their feet, the snow cleared in an uneven path from the parking lot to the grave. Linus walks with his shoulder under the pointed angle of his corner of the casket. Ford walks beside him, Claudia's uncle and cousin to the back. Linus has asked for a nonreligious ceremony but apparently this is out of the question. Claudia's mother looks pale and lost. A priest speaks of this life and the next. Madison clutches a rosary and a crucifix. Ruth looks stunned. Linus cannot figure out how he should feel. If Claudia had been having an affair, had been sneaking around behind his back for months, then what is he to grieve? The lie that was their marriage? Each act of sexual intercourse committed in grunting sweaty tandem on the beds and office furniture of a dozen nameless, faceless locales? Until last week he was a man in love with his wife, a man whose own children were imminent. Today he is a husk, a ragged question mark buffeted by frozen winds.

As the coffin is lowered and poor Claudia minus her two beautiful toes is laid in the ground, Linus strikes off on his own, steps from the shoveled path and wades out into the trees. He takes lunging steps through snow that climbs to his knees. The others watch in shock as he disappears behind a stand of oaks. He walks for three or four minutes, letting the funeral fade behind him. By a scarred sycamore he stops and looks out through the silhouettes of white and black, the skeletal tangle of branches and shrubs, at the houses of Arlington Heights. In the distance there is a 7-Eleven. People sit in their homes watching five hundred channels. They read the morning papers, turn on classical radio stations. Families shop for sporting goods. Teenagers carrying prophylactics and nitrous oxide board trains, climb into souped-up American cars for the ride to malls or into the streets of the city. Small children in strollers, dogs peeing on frozen lawns. The elderly in their nursing homes alone and together. A pride of lonely mothers huddle their baby carriages in the parking lots of supermarkets and speak of husbands who work weekends.

Linus sits down in the snow, feels it press up through the folds of his coat, fill the pockets of his pants. It is a cemetery after all. He has decided to simply die right here where he has collapsed. The world around him is silent, just the slow sound of snow compacting, the distant hiss of cars passing over roads slick with melting snow. He presses his face into the white, feels the cold bitter wet of it against his cheek, his eyes.

Agent Forbes approaches through a row of pine saplings. He is dressed in a long black overcoat. His face is flushed from the cold.

"Go away," says Linus. His head is turned to the side and he sees Forbes as a vertical line from the corner of his left eye.

"Get up, Owen. This is no time to quit."

"Consider the word *fuck* followed immediately by the pronoun *you*."

"I'm serious. Pull yourself together."

Linus sighs and sits up. He has snow in his hair. It runs down the collar of his shirt. He feels the cold moisture seep through to his underwear.

"My brother, Ford, used to get this gleam in his eye every time it snowed," he says. His nose begins to bleed, a small steady stream of red. "He would start to taunt me, to taunt Alice. His goal was to get us outside into the banks. He loved nothing more than picking us up and hurling us bodily into the snow. It held a special joy for him, this act of primitive power."

Forbes takes his hands from his coat pockets. He wears leather gloves, the kind hit men use when they slip weapons with silencers from hidden holsters. He wants to ask Linus where he went yesterday when he got on the A train and lost two of Forbes's agents in the crowds at Thirty-fourth Street, two agents now unpacking suitcases in the abandoned wasteland of the Yucatán. He leans against a crooked elm and watches Linus's nose bleed. It holds a certain fascination for him.

"My brother had a screw loose too," he says. "He liked to put bugs in empty paint cans and put the cans in this old paint-mixing machine my father kept in the garage. He liked the sound their exoskeletons made as they vaporized at one hundred jolts per second."

Linus licks his lips, tasting his own blood, but he does nothing to wipe it away or stop the flow. He sees it as a sign of extreme physical distress that his own blood would want to escape from his body.

"Ford started betting the stock market when he was eleven. He stole fifty dollars from my father and bought ten shares of IBM."

"My parents sent Glenn to the military after he stole a car and drove it drunk into a supermarket. My grandfather was a very influential man in our community in Pennsylvania. He had the charges dropped, but still, Glenn was clearly out of control."

Linus paws some of the snow from his hair, leans his back

against a tree. The air is so clean and cold and bright that he begins to feel dizzy. A clump of snow falls somewhere in the distance.

"My father used to go on strike. Sometimes we'd have nothing to eat for days except Saltines and rice. Ford would beat up kids at school for their lunch money. He ate candy bars and pretzels, drank orange soda and Yoo-Hoo. He felt no remorse in doing this."

"A bastard. He was training for life as a rich and powerful man."

"And Glenn?"

Forbes laughs.

"Glenn? Glenn's an alcoholic auto mechanic in Allentown. Last time I saw him at a family reunion I broke his fucking nose."

Linus is thoughtful at the suggestion of violence.

"I need to go to Ferndale, Washington," he says.

Forbes rocks on his heels.

"Ferndale, Washington."

"I have a lead on Danton."

"Tell me."

"If I tell you, then I won't be able to go. You will take my revenge away from me."

Forbes takes half a pill from his pocket and covertly places it on his tongue. The fear is getting worse.

"Where the fuck is Ferndale, Washington?"

"It sits just under the Canadian border. I hear they have some of the tallest trees in America."

"Is that where Danton is, in Ferndale, Washington?"

"I am following a lead. It takes me to Ferndale, Washington. I have no elevated hopes that this is where I'll find Danton, but it may provide more clues that *will* lead to them."

"So they exist? There is a Danton. How many members? Throw out some names."

"Jerry Bruckner, 555-6239."

Forbes takes out a pen and a sheet of paper. He scribbles the number down.

"What area code?"

"I don't know the area code. All I have are seven digits."

"Jerry Bruckner, you said."

"Also someone named Tony. I don't have a last name."

"Are these the guys you're going to see in Ferndale?"

"That information is given on a need-to-know basis. I'm not sure at this point you need to know."

"Ha ha ha. Very funny. Your nose is bleeding."

Linus nods, lets it go. Forbes stamps his feet to keep them from falling asleep. He has been a CIA agent for almost eleven years. When he was preparing to graduate from college his grandfather introduced him to some of his friends from the shop. Grandpa believed that Forbes's interest in politics and intelligence would take him far in the service of his country, and he recognized that a career in the Secret Service was a good step forward in any career in business or politics. Forbes, then known only as Richard Wermer, met with several recruiters and veterans. It was explained to him that his familial connections might afford him special privileges and placements. He spent a year in training before his first posting to Israel. He developed an interest in terrorism, joined a special task force, rose quickly through the ranks. By the early 1990s he had reached a position in which he was one of the few experts in the intelligence community with contacts in all of the government agencies, NSA, FEMA, NRO, FBI. Today he runs a task force with 107 special operatives under his command.

"I need a cigarette," he says. There is the fumble for the pack and lighter. He has learned to smoke with gloves on. It is one of the things they teach you at the agency. Linus puts up his hand and wipes the blood away from his lip. It has fallen in fat drops into the snow and seeps like murder toward the earth. Forbes coughs, puts the lighter in his pocket.

"I'll have a ticket delivered to your hotel room."

"Thanks, but I'll buy my own."

Forbes shrugs. He is excited by the idea of Ferndale, Washington, by the idea that his plan is working. The truth can never come out. This much is clear.

"I have been authorized to offer you a gun."

"Keep it."

"We're dealing with bomb builders. Bomb builders are classified in the armed-and-dangerous category. A gun is the first order of business."

"Jerry Bruckner," says Linus, "555-6239."

Forbes clamps his cigarette in his teeth.

"Still no area code?"

"You're with the fucking CIA. You can read mail padlocked inside a lead box. Don't tell me an area code is going to bring you to your knees."

"FBI. I'm with the FBI."

Linus climbs up out of the snow. His pants are drenched. He brushes halfheartedly at his legs. His fingers are red and refuse to bend, his face smeared with blood.

"Give me a break," he says.

Forbes drops the cigarette into the snow. He looks out toward the road, a black line in the distance.

"In Ferndale I'll be known as Bobby Collins," he says. "I'll wear a beard. When we meet I will tell you I am a trucker hauling pigs from Oregon. My opening line will be, 'Four hundred miles breathing pig shit.'"

"Get professional help."

"You'll say, 'Can you help me find the public library?'"

"A licensed psychiatrist with a permit to write oversize prescriptions."

"There'll be a ticket for Seattle waiting for you at your hotel. You'll have to rent a car. I have been authorized to tell you that all expenses are on the Bureau."

"You guys *are* the Keystone Kops." Linus is shivering. He is trying not to think of the men three hundred yards away throwing frozen earth on Claudia's coffin.

"Just stay away from me," he says. "Don't blow this by crowding me. These are sensitive people we're dealing with. If you get too close they'll know. Just let me work."

Forbes smiles, showing teeth.

"Linus Owen, you are a true professional. After careful consideration I have decided to continue feeling positively toward you."

"O joyous day."

"I have also been authorized to thank you for your extensive cooperation up to this point."

You are going on a wild-goose chase so big you can't even conceive, thinks Linus, rebuttoning his coat.

"I have your card," he says. "If I need you I'll call."

They both know that every move Linus makes will be tracked. Forbes offers his hand, but Linus shoves past him and stumbles back toward Claudia's grave.

There is a funeral reception at Astrid's house. People shuffle by to give their condolences. Ford and Madison shake hands and thank people for coming. Their clothes cost more than everyone else's combined. Linus hides out in the back bedroom that used to be Claudia's. He sits on a bed covered with coats and purses looking through her things, the high school yearbooks and faded photo albums. Alice comes in and closes the door. Her hair is tangled, her eyes red. She sits on the bed behind Linus and leans her head against his back. Linus refuses to cry.

"Brian wanted to come, but he couldn't get out of work."

"How are things? Are they still good?"

Alice shrugs. Her life seems so pathetic and small.

"He wants me to marry him. Our sponsors say to wait."

"He's a good guy."

"He's not smart like you or rich like Ford, but he's honest and he works hard. He's just weak. We're both weak. Together we're a little stronger."

"That's what together is for."

Alice puts her hand up and touches Linus's hair.

"Oh, Linus."

He grabs her hand and moves it away.

"Don't."

She sits up and stares at the clothes hanging in the closet. They are the outfits worn by high school girls in 1979, the bell-bottom pants and tube tops, the Olivia Newton-John half-jackets. Her own closet looked much the same. She stands and goes into the adjoining bathroom.

"You have to cry, Linus. You have to grieve." She comes out and plants herself in front of him. He stares into her belly button.

"I cried. I don't want to cry anymore."

Alice puts her hands on his head. They have gotten so old.

"It's something you live with, baby. Every day you wake up and there it is. For me it's drugs. You have to learn to turn it down.

Imagine it's a radio. Picture a volume knob, turn it down with your mind."

"She was leaving me. She was giving up."

"You don't know that. It's this really horrible rumor based on circumstantial evidence. It could have been a last-minute business trip." She stops. Neither one of them believes that.

They took her, thinks Linus. But who? Who took her and why?

Alice leaves the room. Linus goes through the pockets of jackets, purses. He takes credit cards from wallets, steals them from the friends of his in-laws, MasterCard, Visa, American Express. He takes a cellular phone from a small black leather purse. He starts to make a call, stops, looks out the window. Claudia's room faces the street. There could be microphones pointed at the house, helicopters overhead. He goes into the master bedroom, skirts the condolences of strangers, closes the door. Now he has placed the crowded voices of mourners between himself and the street. He locks the door, turns on the television, the radio. He takes the stack of credit cards from his pocket, calls the airlines. He books a flight for Salt Lake City, a flight to Washington, D.C., a flight to San Diego. He calls Southwest Airlines and books a flight to Tucson, to New Orleans, to Dallas. Each time he calls he uses a different name, a different card. He is counting on the fact that people don't notice a missing card for at least a week. He has taken cards only from people with three or more, trying to guess which card is the emergency reserve card, the unused. He goes back to Claudia's room, replaces the phone.

In the kitchen he throws his arms around Ford, buries his face in Ford's neck. Ford hugs him back, squeezes in the same cruel manner of his youth.

"It's okay, Linus. Your family loves you. Heaven has called her to it."

"How much money do you have on you?" Linus whispers. He puts all his strength into holding on to Ford, keeping him close.

"Excuse me?" Ford tries to move away. Linus squeezes with all his might.

"How much money?"

"Thirty-five hundred dollars."

"Cash?"

"Linus."

"Cash?"

"Cash."

"What about Madison? How much is she carrying?"

"Really, Linus, I don't see where this is going. If you need money."

"Ford," says Linus in a hiss, "I am going to ask you this one favor. I've never asked anything of you. You are a cruel, immoral man, but just this once I need you to do something and it is very important that you never talk about it, not with Madison, not with anybody. Too much is riding on this."

A woman in a black taffeta dress comes into the kitchen, stops, and exits when she sees the two men hugging.

"Fifteen hundred," says Ford. "She's got about fifteen hundred bucks."

"I need it. All of it."

"Are you in trouble, Linus? Is something going on here I should know about?"

"Don't, Ford. You and I aren't close enough. I don't trust you. I love you, but I don't trust you. Just give me the money. Don't tell Madison why you need it. Don't talk about it with anyone. Just bring it to me, put it in my pocket. Later we'll go back to the hotel. In the morning I'll be gone. You may never see me again. Are we straight?"

He lets go of Ford, steps back, looks him in the eye. For once, Ford feels ashamed. He has a sudden rush of emotion. The magnitude of his life comes upon him. His family is an accident of history, a random assortment of people brought together by birth and blood. He has always done everything to distance himself from them. The selfishness of this catches him in a sudden realization that it is now too late to take any of it back. He feels at this moment like an old, old man.

"I'm sorry, Linus," he says.

"It's okay, Ford. It's okay. Just do what I asked you."

Ford steps through the swinging door into the crowd. By tomorrow he will have spiraled back to his standard arrogant posture. Linus watches the door swing, aware of how alone he really is. He pours himself a glass of water and goes out into the living room to make his excuses.

At the hotel Linus finishes going through Claudia's things. He has brought them from New York, unable to search any bag for more than five or ten minutes at a time. Ford has gotten them rooms at the Ritz-Carlton. Linus's looks out over Lake Shore Drive. He stares out at the frozen expanse of Lake Michigan, the roiling fog whitening the horizon. He has pawed through the bottom of her bags, run his hands through the soft cotton spread of her underwear, the clumps of stockings. He has lingered over her T-shirts and bras. These clothes that still carry her smell, still carry a sense memory of her skin. Dresses and pants suits. He knows which socks were her favorite, which blouses. He recognizes the lipsticks. He feels his throat constrict at the sight of her toothbrush, its bristles flattened by cumulative contact with her teeth and gums. Aspirin, her brush and comb, a box of tampons. He knows where the scuff marks on her shoes came from, can identify each stain and wrinkle. Even her money seems familiar, the chaotic assortment of business cards and ATM receipts that jam her wallet.

In her carry-on bag he finds her date book. Inside are the numbers of their friends, the names of business contacts and service companies, the dry cleaner, the auto shop, the Ferry. She has written in her neat hand the numbers for his office on campus, the phone numbers and modem numbers at Edward's and Roy's. Linus picks up the phone, puts it down. He cannot call them. It is too dangerous and he hopes that if they are making progress they are aware of the risks and stakes involved. In order to find Preston he must go underground himself, disappear. Only an invisible man can find another invisible man. You must become what you are seeking. He relies on Preston to have the answers he is looking for. This is what happens to desperate men. They come to rely on hopes born from rumor.

Linus has no doubt that Forbes is lying to him. That he would believe this bombing was caused by the controversy over spy planes is as hard to swallow as if Forbes had told him the answer lay in UFOs. Somewhere in all this he believes he will find Hastings Pharmaceutical. He is aware that this may be a way of vilifying Jeffrey Holden, to remove him from the role of lover to that of villain, but he is positive that the root of this lies somewhere deeper than military hardware.

He goes through the calendar, circles entries that strike him as unusual or worth investigating. He goes through phone numbers, calling those with which he is unfamiliar. Most are offices, closed for the weekend, an answering machine, a recorded voice. He wakes three women from sleep, interrogates them as they struggle to regain consciousness. They are acquaintances of Claudia's, lunch dates, members of the Corporate Women's League. They can give him no clue, no indication as to why she's done what she's done.

He takes a pad from his own luggage. It is the one he stole from Holden's apartment. He looks at the clock. It is 4:31 A.M. In an hour he will be on his way to the airport, leaving Claudia's things spread across the bedcovers, scattered on the floor. They will be left behind with her body in the cold winter of Illinois.

There are two numbers on the pad. The first is a Chinese restaurant on West Seventy-first Street. Linus listens to a message in broken English that tells him what their regular business hours are. He hangs up the phone, crosses to the window, peers through the curtains down into the parking lot. The phone is surely bugged, the room as well. In the bathroom Linus has assembled the elements of his disguise, a blond wig, dark-rimmed glasses. From a costume store in Manhattan he has purchased a fake stomach, a foam pad with straps that will allow him to appear fifty pounds heavier than he is. He has collected oversize clothes, a ratty brown canvas jacket lined with fake sheepskin, hiking boots. He goes into the bathroom and washes his face. Once again he has gone without sleep for two days. He strips off his clothes, puts on a pair of jeans and a T-shirt. He slides the straps of the fake stomach over his shoulder, adjusts the waist belt. He puts on a button-down shirt. Over these he pulls on a second pair of pants, chooses to fasten them under the stomach, allowing it to hang ponderously over his belt. He applies some spirit gum to his bald spot and his hairline, places the wig on his head. He puts on the glasses, looks at himself in the full-length mirror. He stares at his image dispassionately, takes a plate of fake upper teeth from the bathroom counter, and puts them in his pocket.

He turns off the bathroom light, crosses over and sits on the bed, picks up the phone. He dials the second number on the pad. It rings.

"Hello?" It is not the voice of a man awakened from sleep. It is the voice of a man sitting by the phone waiting for someone to call.

"I'm calling about Holden," says Linus.

"Jesus Christ. It's about time."

Linus covers the mouth of the receiver with a handkerchief.

"I don't have long to talk. They're sure to be listening."

"You're going to get me killed. This whole thing has just gotten out of hand. I wish I'd never even discovered the damn thing."

"We don't have much time. We have to get our stories straight."

There is the sound of heavy breathing on the other line.

"Tell Forbes I'm not going to talk. Not in a million years. This whole thing never happened as far as I'm concerned."

Linus looks at the clock, tries to judge how long it would take for a man in good shape to travel from the parking lot to the fourteenth floor of the hotel. He figures he has another three or four minutes.

"Listen. I don't care about that. The one thing that's going to keep you alive is for you and me to understand each other as far as what happened is concerned. Tell me about the discovery. Leave nothing out. As far as you're concerned, I know nothing."

"You're talking hours. The whole thing. I mean it's too big."

"Think *Reader's Digest.* Condense. Compress. Ready, set, go."

"It's so hard to think. To get it straight. I discovered a synaptic inhibitor. Tests on rats were very promising, primates. It was a big discovery for me, just one research scientist invisible among the ranks of hundreds, of thousands. I knew Jeffrey from high school. We were friends. I kept him up to date. He said he had a friend at FEMA, an old college roommate. When the lab tests looked conclusive enough, he called this guy, Mills. The whole thing was set up from there."

Linus looks at the clock, curses. He puts the fake teeth in his mouth, slips on the jacket.

"What happened next? I need to know. The earlier stuff isn't important. The crucial bit is what happened after Forbes came in."

"We tested on inmates. Jesus Christ, can't we meet someplace? I need to relax. I haven't slept in four days."

"Tell me about the plan."

"Look, I don't know, okay? I just made the damn thing. They asked me questions about the effect on humans, proper doses, projected side effects. I had nothing to do with the rest of it. Nothing. This is bullshit, man. I'm going to be killed over nothing."

Linus stands, stretches the phone cord to the door. He imagines two men with side arms riding up silently in the elevator. Their weapons are equipped with silencers. He checks to make sure the wig is on firmly.

"What was the drug?" he says. "What did it do?"

"Who is this? What is going on here? Sam? Is this Sam?"

Linus drops the phone, slips out into the hallway. He heads

toward the stairwell, uses his elbow to break the glass of the fire alarm, pulls the lever. A great whooping noise fills the hall. The hall lights begin flashing on and off. As soon as the alarm goes off, the elevators stop between floors, then return to the lobby. Linus presses himself against the wall, waits for people to leave their rooms. The stairwell fills quickly with hotel guests in various forms of undress pushing in panicked fashion down to the lobby. Linus eggs them on.

"Is that smoke? Does anyone else smell smoke?"

He sticks close to Ford, hanging just behind his left shoulder. Ford does not recognize him. He is pushing determinedly through the sleep-stupid bodies, shielding Madison in one arm. At the third floor Linus drops back, pushes forward into the lobby surrounded by bodies. They mill in the parking lot, Linus placing himself near other men who have managed to struggle into coats and shoes before evacuating.

"I hear there are flames shooting into the hallways on fifteen," he says.

Fire trucks arrive. The firemen bring blankets for the underdressed. The guests are pushed back from the entrance of the hotel. They huddle out near the Dumpsters. As a third ladder truck pulls into the parking circle with its sirens blaring, Linus drops back into the shadows and walks off down East Pearson Street. On the corner of State Street and Chicago Avenue he hails a cab, takes it to the bus station, goes inside, buys a ticket to Milwaukee. He goes over to a vending machine, buys a pack of cigarettes, steps outside for a smoke, walks around the block, hails a second cab.

At the airport he checks in for flight 71 to Tucson, crosses to the United terminal, checks in for flight 95 to Washington, D.C. He goes to the duty-free shop, buys a bottle of scotch, a blue sweatshirt, and a Chicago Cubs baseball hat. At the American Airlines counter he gets his boarding pass for the 5:15 flight to Dallas. He goes into the men's room, walks to the last stall. He sits on the toilet, pulls his feet up onto the seat. He sits that way sweating under his fat-guy foam until 5:41, when, wearing the wig but without the fake stomach and oversize clothes, he walks in his sweatshirt and baseball cap to gate 61 and checks in for flight 105 to Los Angeles as the first call for general seating is being announced. He takes his boarding pass and mingles into the river of travelers making their way inside the plane.

He is carrying forty-nine hundred dollars in cash. He has no clothing other than what he wears. Rolled up in his back pocket are the articles written by Richard Preston. Next to him a woman with a hearing aid watches the flight attendants demonstrate the procedure for what to do in case of a water landing. Behind him a man with a cellular phone says, *By the year 2000, sixty percent of all solid waste will be made up of outdated technology.*

BOOK *two*

The Desert

We are put on this earth to launder money. This is Roy's philosophy. Humanity exists so that banks of varying sizes in multiple countries can transfer funds from account to account, bank to bank. Direct deposit, direct withdrawal, a steady flow of cash in and out of small theoretical waystations. There is the new millennium to consider. It is believed that 70 to 90 percent of all computers will crash in the year 2000. Up till now computers have been designed with room for only two digits to represent a year in any date field. It is the same with most software. On January 1, 2000, as far as all computers are concerned, the whole of humanity will have been transported back in time to the year 1900. Library books taken out on December 31 will not be due for another ninety-nine years, student loan payments will accrue negative interest, the principal shrinking with each succeeding month. We are staring at the collapse of the international monetary system.

Roy sits on the toilet thinking. Anxiety keeps his body still. His colon hoards the breakfasts, lunches, and dinners of seven days. Outside, the car is packed. This morning's visit from a team of pale men in dark suits has convinced them that they must seek a less public place in which to continue their investigation. There has been no word from Linus in three days. Roy has to assume that one way or another they will meet up at some point on the information trail. His toes are curled under the balls of his feet. He has taken off his pants and folded them neatly by the side of the toilet. The words *Kodak moment* enter his consciousness. He considers the pile of magazines in the basket by the tub, thinks about the growing industry of tabloid publishing, the proliferation of trade journals. A thousand magazines a month, a billion glossy photographs, a trillion descriptives, articles, captions. The personal ads of a million lonely men. How many words are written in how many tiny rooms by how many ambitious men and women? At any one time there must be seventy thousand essays, interviews, and opinion pieces sitting on shelves in newsstands and Barnes & Noble Superstores, surrounded by images of fashion models, products, slogans. What are we trying to communicate in such a desperate ejaculation of text and pictures?

There is a certain irony in Claudia's practice of advertising. For Roy, the glut of commerce, of saleable items and services, is a surrogate for human touch, the offering of feelings of safety and security. It is a placebo swallowed to stave off the fear of death, a kind of drug hawked by pushers, men with expensive suits and one milky eye, but like any drug, in the case of materialism the body builds a tolerance. This is why, as the millennium encroaches and anxiety percolates to higher levels, advertising has become so much more intrusive, infiltrating the very architecture of things. First just a placard on the side of a bus, then the entire bus itself. Billboards, blimps, the empty space on the back of a pack of matches. Soon Roy can envision whole buildings formulated to resemble cans of Coke, Pepsi, Sprite. Modern architecture itself will become the next wave of promotional material. Products will contain ads for other products, as the manufacturers and owners of varying product groups consolidate, as fewer and fewer corporations own more and more, as ordinary people own less and less.

Roy investigates a certain gurgling sensation in his gut, tries to decipher whether this is the sound of long-digested meals shifting. He readies himself in case of impending evacuation. Nothing comes. Outside, Edward finishes burning the paper evidence they have accumulated, barbecuing it on the grill. Roy leans over, picks up a book of crossword puzzles and anagrams. He stares at it blankly, then thoughtfully. He drops the book, picks up the passenger list with its highlighted names and creased, folded corners. He considers the idea that their mystery passenger may be more than just a name. Teddy Waren, middle initial O. Roy picks up a pen from the back pocket of his pants.

■

Edward sits in the kitchen thinking about Karen Silkwood. As soon as Roy is done in the bathroom they'll go. They have mapped out a convoluted escape route that involves changing cars, a long drive on a busy highway, a sudden turn onto an isolated off-ramp. They will meet Roy's cousin Henry, swap cars in a deserted underpass to avoid detection by helicopters or satellites. Edward swept their car for bugs the night before in the dark garage. He has collected two pin-size listening devices and a metal disk the size of a radio battery meant to track them wherever they go. These he has placed in the glove compartment. They will be discarded on the highway, thrown into the back of a pickup truck, and then a sudden deceleration, a right turn down a curving underpass. They have mapped it all out in a conversation scribbled on legal pads inside the bedroom closet. The pads have been burned. Excuses have been made to take the car out seven times in the last fourteen hours. Each trip to the car has brought with it a certain amount of equipment, hidden in garbage bags and old boxes meant to be discarded. At three o'clock Roy took three bags of laundry to the Laundromat. He carried two inside, with a third empty bag concealed in the first. At five-thirty he returned with two bags of clean laundry and one bag of someone else's clothes.

Roy comes out of the bathroom. He puts his fingers to his lips, shows Edward the passenger list. On the back side of the third page is written the name Teddy Waren. Beside it is the full Theodore O. Waren. The page is filled with a confusion of letters, deep black scribbles, and cross-outs. At the bottom of the page are three words circled in dark heavy lines: *Road to Nowhere.*

"What time are we meeting Christo?" asks Roy for the benefit of the listening devices.

"Nine o'clock. I told him to bring his essay on the real war on crime. I think we could use it in the next issue of *American Conspiracy.*"

On the pad he writes, *Nevada.* Edward nods. They both recognize the Road to Nowhere. It is a little highway in Nevada that runs from Naples to Clone. At least now they have a destination, as tenuous as it seems.

At the car they both take a deep breath, climb inside. Roy backs out of the driveway. He doesn't bother to look for a tail as he pulls out onto the street. He knows it's there. He thinks once again about the year 2000, the total reliance people have come to place on technology. The words *global village* suddenly seem prescient. Soon everyone will be plugged in, on line, connected to the great information mainframe of cyberspace consciousness.

"We are becoming the Borg," he says as beside him Edward paws through the pages of their road atlas planning a route to the Road to Nowhere.

■

They drive east to Nevada, traverse back roads and secondary highways, cutting a southern tear across the state. They scare themselves by flawlessly enacting their plan to deter pursuit, careening off the highway, switching cars. By late afternoon they reach Sacramento, by nightfall they skirt the southern Sierras. They drive through the sloping brown foothills, the highway cutting a slight black line into the rolling terrain. As the sun sets behind them they begin their ascent into the mountains.

"There were a few minutes back there, I don't have to tell you, I thought we might not make it," says Roy.

"An illegal right turn across three lanes of traffic. I felt like Bullitt."

"Downshift, brake. I repeat. There were some corners I didn't think it was possible to turn."

"I feel bad for your cousin Henry."

"I don't like my cousin Henry."

They wind their way up the peaks, reach the snow line. The air is sharp and cold. Edward closes his eyes and thinks of Claudia. As if reading his mind, Roy says,

"I never understood what he saw in her, really."

"In Claudia?"

"She was always so mean."

"I don't think she was mean. How was she mean? She just had her own way of doing things."

"She cut him down. Given the opportunity her comments to him were always skewed toward the negative."

"You have an example?"

"It's a Saturday afternoon. Linus has been to the grocery store. It turns out he has forgotten to buy paper towels. Linus, she says, why do you always do a half-assed job?"

"The paper-towel story again."

"She spoke in absolutes. Any minor mistake on his part was a colossal personality flaw."

"Her hours were long. She wore panty hose, sometimes around the clock. She operated under stringent deadlines. There was pressure. Sometimes she snapped."

"And the way she condescended about his job. It's not that I think she didn't love him—though the evidence at this point seems pretty conclusive—it's that she seemed physically incapable of accepting him the way he was."

"And yet they got married."

"Just because someone drives you crazy doesn't mean you don't marry them. My ex-wife was nuts. At the time, I found it endearing."

"I agree that she was hard on him sometimes, but there were other elements at play. I could see that they loved each other. It was obvious. Their personalities complemented each other. They were opposites. Isn't that always the case?"

"When was your last date, Ed? What do you know about 'always'?"

"Fuck you. In fact, fuck everybody that looks like you."

They wind their way down from the Sierras, past Lake Tahoe into Nevada. At Fernley they cut south heading for Coaldale. Even in darkness this stretch of road looks familiar to them. They have driven these highways a thousand times looking for answers in the great expectation of the western deserts. Outside there is just blackness smothering the windows of their car.

"Not that she wasn't beautiful," says Roy.

Edward stares at his reflection in the glass. Roy follows his headlights along the straight edge of the center line.

"Let's assume for now that she was sleeping with Holden."

Edward shrugs. It is not an assumption he enjoys making. Her infidelity with Holden makes his own secret wishes that much more illicit. It's a matter of proportion. To covet another man's wife when she is chaste is to entertain a harmless human fantasy. To long for a woman who cheats is to become a moral criminal. It is the element of possibility that changes the balance, the fact that Claudia was actually available for extracurricular romance.

"How long?"

Roy wipes his nose on the meat of his thumb.

"Let's say six months."

"She meets him in June."

"In New York."

"She's flown in for business."

"Maybe he comes to San Francisco."

"Is there any record of that?"

Roy shrugs.

"I haven't had a chance to look."

"My vote is for out of town. Distance is the main factor. The miles invite possibilities."

"They meet. At first it's just business. He's the head of marketing and product development."

"They work long hours preparing for the FDA hearings."

"What was the drug again?"

"Happidan. An antidepressant. Meant to compete with Prozac."

"This guy is married too, but it's rocky. The wife is a shrew."

"Not all wives are shrews."

"Fine, she was happy, but too needy, too easy. He wanted more mystery. He wanted a brunette with long legs."

"A California girl."

"Exactly."

"So he sees Claudia. He thinks, I'm interested."

"Maybe he's done this before. A womanizer."

"Too hard to check, given our current technology-free status."

"We're free-associating here. Let's say he's fooled around on his wife before. Mounts anything on legs."

Roy switches lanes to pass a silver tanker truck. Outside the temperature is twenty-one degrees.

"So she's in New York with Holden."

"There's a chemistry."

"Right. They go out. Both of them are starting to wonder if maybe this isn't dangerous."

"Except Holden, who we've decided is a womanizer."

"Right. Holden plans his move."

"A restaurant, two bottles of wine, an after-dinner cocktail."

"It's a classic story."

"Claudia begins to want something to happen."

"Things with Linus."

"Things with Linus are exasperating. He seems stuck in one place."

"Teaching voodoo to nerds for negligible money."

"She comes from heavy income, is used to a certain level of sophistication."

"Holden is as manipulative as a bee charmer."

"They end up in her hotel bar."

"Find a dark corner."

"Soon they are kissing in the elevator."

Edward swallows. He feels warm despite the winter air.

"It's been a long time since she felt that electricity rising from her toes, the spark of bodies coming together."

"She says, I can't do this. I can't."

"But she does."

They pass a sign that says COALDALE 51 MILES. They have entered the landscape of government secrecy.

"I just can't turn her into a monster," says Edward. His voice is quiet. "I see a lonely woman riding an elevator with the idea of filling a void."

"All obvious jokes will be bypassed."

"Put yourself in her shoes. She wants more than Linus will give her. She has ambition, and by saying this I don't want to stereotype her as a woman with ambition. I just see her as a person who harbors a deep dissatisfaction. Her life is not turning out how she wanted it. Linus's needs are simpler than hers. As far as he's concerned, they have everything they require."

"Except children."

"He said they both wanted children."

"I'm just saying."

"She asks him to find a better job, join a think tank, a political party. He's so smart."

"And yet he insists on a low-level teaching position."

"He is the star of the department. That's not nothing."

"Maybe she wasn't prepared for the level of paranoia she would find in a professor of conspiracy theories."

Edward pushes in the cigarette lighter, looking for something to do with his hands.

"Unlike you and me, I think Linus was relatively cautious," he says. "I wouldn't say paranoid."

"Even so, the dinners with kooks and radicals. She had a career to worry about. As she got older she became more mainstream."

"It happens to everyone. There's no crime."

"It didn't happen to Linus. There were government agents dropping by the house on a regular basis. *I'm sorry, ma'am, but have you seen this man?*"

"And she's just had him for dinner the week before."

Roy considers Linus his best friend next to Edward. To him Claudia is as evil as Klaus Barbie.

"Linus hated to go to her functions, the dress-up crowd, the conservatives."

"Even among advertisers, the liberals of the working world."

"So after five years she felt they were growing apart."

"Still, to have an affair. I have a problem."

"All I'm saying is let's not wrestle a scarlet letter from our position of moral superiority and sew it to her forehead," says Edward. "I'm saying, remember she was a person."

"A mean person."

"A mean person, but a person nonetheless. She had a right to happiness. Her actions in pursuing that happiness may be distasteful, but her right to be happy should not be questioned."

"Tell it to Linus."

Edward makes a halfhearted attempt to roll his window back up. He stops and instead rolls it back down, sticks his head out, where it is quickly frozen by rocketing winds.

"I'm sure he knows already," he says to the night. "Isn't that what love is all about?"

They drive for a while without speaking. Roy has begun to suspect that Edward has his own agenda in remembering Claudia. At ten o'clock they stop in Yerington for dinner. The restaurant is a rectangular truck stop populated by leather-faced men in dirty, defeated-looking baseball caps. At the table next to them an old woman sits across from her teenage grandson. Roy orders a hamburger and a Coke. Edward asks what kind of soups they have.

"Meatball."

"I'll have a salad and a glass of ice tea."

Next to them the boy begins to tell his grandmother about how he found Jesus.

"I've been saved for six years," he says. "Hallelujah."

"The Road to Nowhere," says Edward.

"Sooner or later," says Roy.

They drink. The water is cloudy and almost warm. The boy has speckly stubble centering primarily around his soft chin. He sits across from his grandmother with a comfort that betrays a like-mindedness beyond his years. Out the window Roy can see sand blow across the parking lot. Next door there is a gas station, empty but for the neon lights in the window and the stuttering fluorescents lighting the pumps. The night is clear, a blanket of infinite stars. Roy thinks about his divorce, the horrible fatalism of a love that has dried up.

"I say it's a drug," he says.

"This whole thing is about a drug?"

"That's what I'm saying. I'm basing this entirely on the words *pharmaceutical company* as they apply to this case."

"Even though we have defense contractors and CIA agents. You're going with Holden."

"I'm going with Holden."

"Despite the fact that the flight was to Brazil, a fact of which we have yet to determine the meaning."

"Say amen."

The boy and his grandmother look over from the next table and smile.

"Amen, brother." The boy drinks a vanilla milkshake from a dirty glass.

"My vote is for a covert operation," says Edward. "Advisers on their way to a South American country to train guerrilla warriors or state police."

"And the bombing was who?"

"Let's go with Danton. I'm willing to do that now."

"So what's in Clone? Other than tumbleweeds and heat."

"Danton headquarters, maybe? A cluster of mobile homes circled like wagons. Inside, the walls are filled with maps speckled with pins, technical schematics for seven large jet planes, the occasional pinup of a porn star or television actress. From there they run their secret campaign."

"My guess is we're on a wild-goose chase. I only hope Linus has better luck."

"Every time we come back to the desert I feel this wave of relief. A relatively bacteria-free environment, other than the small clusters of mouse droppings."

"Then again we could be buried in a dry hole by seven men with masks."

Edward begins wiping his silverware off with a paper napkin he pulls from a metal dispenser.

"I see your point."

The salad is an exercise in lettuce. Edward eats it, picking bits of dirt off his tongue with his fingers. Roy puts his right thumb and forefinger around his left wrist as if measuring. He stares at the counter, the 1940s-era cash register, the rotary phone nestled between a stack of receipts and a lopsided strawberry rhubarb pie.

"I feel so naked without the computers. Where do we get our information? How do we analyze data? I can't even start a fire with two sticks. I'm a man who's memorized so many seven-digit numbers he no longer remembers which way is clockwise. Is it to the left or the right? Being without electronics for more than a few hours is like being kidnapped by a cult deprogrammer in a cheap brown suit and taken to a fluorescent motel somewhere in New Jersey. What do we do now? Follow breadcrumbs, send smoke signals, listen to the ground for signs of approaching riders?"

"We ask people questions. We think about what they say." Edward leans over to the old lady and the boy at the next table.

"Evening."

The woman continues chewing, the boy looks over, smiles.

"Howdy." The old woman reaches up, removes a thumb-size piece of gristle from her mouth, and puts it on the side of her plate beside the others.

"My friend and I are on our way to Clone."

The boy raises his eyebrows.

"Don't blink pulling in or you'll miss it."

"They got a motel, someplace we could stay? One night, maybe two."

The boy looks at his grandmother. Her face resembles a scrotum as far as number of wrinkles goes.

"What would be the point?" she says.

Roy pokes at his food as if to ensure it's not just pretending to be dead.

"Nobody goes there, you're saying."

"Every two weeks a truck goes by full of water. I sit on my porch. Elvis the dog, he sits with me. Without the truck they'd all be dead in a matter of hours."

"Unless the Lord kept them alive," says the boy. "That is His prerogative."

"Dead as doornails in ten hours," says the old lady. "Maybe twelve. Lord or no Lord."

"So as far as lodging."

"Sleep in your car. That's my advice. You got windows?"

"In the car, yes."

"No windows you gonna freeze."

"Hear anything strange from Clone recently?"

The old lady looks at them, shrugs.

"Eat your fries, Jerome," she says.

"I heard the coroner from Carson City been down there almost every week." Jerome speaks with a mouth full of fried potato. "Billie Collins says."

"Billie Collins is dumber than a snake's ass." The old lady drinks what looks like scotch from a jelly-jar glass.

"That sure sounds peculiar," says Edward. "They must have a lot of people dying for the coroner to come out so much."

"Billie Collins says that folks is just wandering off into the desert."

"Then folks is dumber than Billie Collins," says the old lady. "Which personally I did not think was possible."

"How many folks they got down there?"

"Used to be about seventy-five. Now I think they down to forty-one. Billie Collins has a cousin down there. They speak sometimes on the CB." The old lady goes back to her chops, cutting a piece, lifting it to her mouth, chewing for forty or fifty seconds, spitting it back into her hand. She must survive on the juice alone, Edward decides.

Outside, a gleaming silver tanker truck pulls up to the gas pumps. A man in green coveralls jumps out, puts the hose into the gas tank, talks to the attendant, then walks over to the diner.

"There's the truck what brings water down to Colby and Naples and Clone. Like I said, every two weeks. Course, if they dumb enough to wander off into the desert I don't see why they gotta keep paying for water from Tahoe."

The driver comes in, sits at the counter, orders a burger and a glass of ice tea. Roy excuses himself, puts his napkin on the table, crosses over, and sits down next to him. The driver looks over and they nod to each other.

"Feel my arm," says the driver.

"Meaning?"

"Feel my arm. Tell me if I'm still humming from the road."

Roy puts his fingertips on the driver's forearm.

"Nope."

"What a ride, though. I love driving that big silver rig. I'm like a torpedo, a cruise missile streaking through the country. Driving at night too, that's the key. Most guys prefer day, but I'm a night man. There's something about two in the morning, you know? Something about the isolation. I tell 'em I only want the desert route, Nevada, Texas, New Mexico. I'm willing to go to Colorado, but only the south, same with California. I truck raisins, pigs, gasoline. I once drove a refrigerator truck full of lobsters from Los Angeles to Dallas. Think about it, lobsters in the desert. I truck office supplies to Phoenix, CD players to Reno. Every two weeks I pick up an eighteen-wheel bullet full of water, drive it across route 50, down route 376, stop in Colby, in Naples, in Clone. Sleepy towns. Towns with populations under a hundred, where people eat scrawny rabbits and low-flying buzzards, where they've got one store that sells ammunition and Pepsi. Sometimes I go days without saying more than three words to anybody. My record is fifty-seven. Back in 1973 I drove two tons of toasters from Montana to Florida, picked up a load of wicker baskets, drove them to Seattle, hooked up a trailer full of chickens, motored it to Wyoming, picked up a tanker full of gasoline, took it to Palm Springs. There's more, but just thinking about it I go into a trance. That whole time all I said was, Check the oil, at about day twenty-seven in Devil's Elbow, Idaho, and, I'm supposed to be driving peaches, day forty-six, eleven fifty-one A.M."

"Where do you get the water?"

"South Lake Tahoe Water and Light. I drive my rig up. They've got the tanker waiting. It's five blocks to the highway. I'm in Coaldale by ten forty-one, Clone by two-thirty in the morning."

"So Clone's the last stop?"

"Not for me. I mean, they've got their delivery, but I have to turn it around and gun it back. Most guys sleep at that hour, but I'm just getting started."

The driver takes his paper napkin, tucks it into the collar of his shirt.

"Ever see anything strange out there on the road in the middle of the night?"

The driver looks at Roy as if he's the grand-prize finalist in a low IQ contest. His face is a confusing mixture of chin and long gray eyebrows.

"Shit. Every driver's got stories. It's a question of experience. I been driving twenty-seven years. I've seen severed heads on signposts, burning crosses on the roofs of five-star hotels. I saw the Madonna once, seventeen feet tall and glowing white outside Durango. Let's not even get into spy planes and UFOs."

The burger comes. The driver finishes his second Pepsi, orders a third. Behind him Roy hears Edward say, Plastic surgery on a horse?

"How about in the last three months? Let's center on the southern Nevada region, maybe even these water runs of yours. Go back to November, December. You're driving down the highway. It's the middle of the night."

The driver removes the hamburger from the bun, takes a bite out of the onion, wipes his fingers on his napkin.

"December fourteenth. I'm ten miles out of Clone. I got two thousand gallons of purified water sloshing in the tanker. It's a clear night, the white sands are glowing against the darkness. All of a sudden my engine dies. I roll a hundred yards. I know what this is. This is magnetic pulse. This is space aliens or stealth technology. I get out of the cab, circle the rig. There's no wind, it's just silent. Cold. I take a piss by the side of the road. My piss steams on the frigid shoulder. I get back in the truck, check the clock. Somehow I'm missing an hour. It's three-seventeen. I get back out, circle the rig. Everything looks fine. What can I do? The truck starts right up. I'm in Clone by four. When you been driving as long as I have, you learn to live with those kind of phenomena."

"Anything weird since then? Tell me about the town itself."

"Henderson at the well talks about people walking off into the desert. He says seventeen people have cooked themselves since the army came. That's about one a week, sometimes two."

"Let's talk about the army."

Roy calls the waitress over, orders two beers. The driver sticks out his hand. It's got bits of tomato stuck to it. Roy shakes.

"Leonard Knuckles."

"Roy Biggs."

"You drive these roads as long as I have you get used to the convoys, the unmarked four-wheel-drive vehicles, the private-security goons. I show up in Clone on January third and Henderson starts in about how they was invaded the week previous. He's real matter-of-fact about it. I ask him what happened. He says they woke up one morning and found the town was full of soldiers. Says the soldiers broke into people's homes at gunpoint, took everyone to the dump. Says they took some people off to do some tests. I says, What kinds of tests, Hen? He says, They wanted to see if they could make us afraid. I says, That sounds pretty dumb to me. Soldiers break into my house, I'm already afraid. He says the whole thing was like a dream. That when the army showed up, everybody just went where they said, did what they told 'em. Hen said it didn't occur to nobody to get upset or angry or nothing. I said, You guys are just too laid back out here. He says after that people began having trouble getting out of bed. They get sick. He himself started wondering what the point of it all was. End of last month I went down there. I had to walk over to his house and get him to come open up the pump so I could off-load all the damn water."

"You think maybe the army gave them some kind of shot?"

"Beats the shit out of me. Henderson says his nephew, this guy Cliff Webb, came down the week previous with some other guys from this weird group, Anton or Branton or something. Says Webb told him it was a government test."

"Cliff Webb."

"Yup. All I know is, last time I went down there, Henderson tells me that people are packing up their cars in the middle of the night and taking off. He says everybody's spooked. I told him the dispatcher in Sacramento said he thought the army was bombarding them with electromagnetic waves, low-frequency signals. Henderson said people were getting out of bed and walking out of town, sometimes without shoes. He said some they'd find the bodies, but more often than not they just disappeared. I told him he should think about moving to a more populated area. He said maybe I was right."

Roy goes back to his table. Edward has pushed his salad up onto one side of his plate and is chewing ice cubes for their nutritional content. The old lady and the boy have finished their meals and the old lady is picking her teeth with the tines of her fork.

"Jesus has returned," says the boy. "Watch the skies. You'll see what I mean. In the Old Testament they had plagues. Plagues are a sign of God's wrath. We are approaching the time of judgment. If I were you, I'd think about repenting."

"We better get on the road," says Roy, to which Edward looks up with gratitude.

In the car Roy roots around under the seat looking for a forgotten candy bar, a half-empty bag of pretzels. He can't ever remember eating a meal in which he was hungrier after he ate than before. On the highway he drives about ten miles, then pulls over to the shoulder and turns off the lights.

"This is nice," says Edward.

"I'm waiting for the water truck."

"What do you make of this walking into the desert thing?"

"You haven't even heard the army invasion part."

Edward looks at his watch.

"We're in a lot of trouble, aren't we?"

After a half hour the long silver truck cuts through the darkness and passes them going 110 miles an hour.

"Hang on."

Edward finds a forgotten Fruit Roll-Up in the glove compartment and gives it to Roy. The desert races by.

"Plagues are a sign of God's wrath," says Edward.

"Fuck a duck."

At ten minutes to twelve they reach Colby, a town of 115. Roy watches the water truck pull into a small parking lot. The town is so small, it doesn't even have a traffic light. He drives about a hundred yards up the road and turns off his lights, coasts to the shoulder. The two of them get out, walk back along the side of the road. From a distance they watch Leonard Knuckles hook up the truck to a fat copper pipe. He lights a cigarette, stands by the front bumper of his truck smoking.

"Do you know how many mobsters are buried in shallow holes around the greater Las Vegas area?"

"We're a hundred miles from Las Vegas."

"The desert is where all the secrets are buried. That's all I'm saying."

They follow Leonard another forty minutes to Naples, exercise the same routine. At one-fifteen in the morning they pass a sign that says THE ROAD TO NOWHERE. Roy turns his lights off and pulls up close behind the tanker, trying to blend into the truck's shadow. Tailgating like that in the dark, they ride their anxiety for another fifty miles, silent, reflective. At two they pull into Clone, a crumbling spread of dilapidated wood cabins and mobile homes. One of the buildings has a sign hanging on it decreeing it the Nowhere Cafe. Not a single light shines. The water truck pulls onto a stretch of buckling asphalt. Roy parks the car behind the cafe. They roll up the windows, put the heat on. From the passenger side they can see Leonard Knuckles drop from the cab and stride over to the rear of his truck.

"They put something in the water," says Edward after a few moments.

"A drug."

"They stop Leonard between Naples and Clone. A foreign substance is introduced into the water supply."

"The point of which is what?"

"An experiment."

"The army invades a week later."

"A substance that has to build up in the body, reach a certain level."

"The invasion accomplishes what?"

"To test the effect of the drug."

"Whatever that may be."

"Whatever that may be."

Leonard unloads his water supply. Edward and Roy watch him climb back into his rig, start it up. They fall asleep with the heat blasting. Outside, nocturnal animals emerge from their burrows. The temperature collapses. Roy wakes up, turns off the engine, listens to the absolute silence, sits in the dark thinking about God. When he wakes up again it is six-fifteen and still dark. The tips of his fingers are blue.

"Holy shit," he says. "Ed, you gotta wake up."

The two stumble shivering and sleep-stupid from the car. They jump up and down, slapping their hands together. Lights are now on in the Nowhere Cafe. There is the sound of pots and pans. In the distance Edward can just make out the swell of desert ridges. The two of them stagger toward the cafe, open the door, step inside.

When Roy was twelve he watched a glass move across a table by itself in a motel room in Charleston, South Carolina. He was a boy in torn jeans with a blond crew cut, who had recently begun his growth toward adulthood with a sudden six-inch spurt. His knees were scabbed. He was sharing a room with his sister. His parents, Jim and Kathy, were next door at an Italian restaurant drinking jug wine. The motel was a dilapidated two-story Holiday Inn. The water in the pool was a disingenuous shade of green. They had come for a funeral, an uncle Roy had never met who had died in a nursing home next to a box factory on the dirty side of the river.

The glass in question had been used by Roy earlier that day for water from the bathroom tap. Now it was empty and dry, a squat, slightly spotty highball glass that had worn a little paper hat when Roy fetched it from the toilet tank. Leslie was on the floor, lying on her stomach kicking her heels. She was using a purple crayon to draw hair on a horse. She had made an olive sun and grass as blue as the ocean. When Leslie grew up she would harbor a secret longing for the comforting warmth of a woman's touch. She would drink vodka straight from the bottle one night at a frat party and end up naked and disoriented on a pool table. She would move to the countryside after graduation and study veterinary sciences. The local townspeople would know her as Dr. Biggs. Eventually she would marry Jeffrey Dobbs, who would later become a congressman. Lying on the floor of a motel room that smelled like feet, none of this was written, however. She was just a nine-year-old girl shellacking a coloring book with unpopular crayon colors, the awful greens and barbaric browns, the flesh-colored pinks and olive-tinted yellows.

Roy was sitting on one of the lax, concave beds. It was a humid summer day, a puzzled blue sky holding its breath, quietly longing for thunderstorms but finding only heat and light. The air conditioner in their room struggled and chugged. Roy put down his copy of *The Return of Tarzan*. He wore a T-shirt with a logo for the band AC/DC on it his father had bought him last spring. That summer he had started working on his cousin's fishing boat off Puget Sound. His mother said it was cute that he was developing little chest muscles and little arm muscles and little leg muscles. He was no longer just a little boy. He was now a little boy who ate like a horse. The funeral was tomorrow morning. All the relatives were flying in and checking into similar hotels and motels. The uncle had encountered the unfortunate circumstance of dying alone in a city none of his family regularly frequented. He'd lived his last few years afraid that his children would show up after his death and pry the gold from his teeth. To this end, at age eighty-one, he had had all his teeth capped at great expense and much to the puzzlement and delight of his dentist. Those teeth would be buried the next day with the rest of him, untouched. Perhaps this would be some comfort to him, if indeed there was an afterlife.

Roy stood up. A fly beat itself against a windowpane. The glass, which sat on a small round Formica table next to the television, began to slide slowly across the surface. Roy watched it with a growing sense of concern. It moved without hurry and with obvious deliberation toward the window. His sister began to draw orange ears on the head of a large dalmatian. The hair on Roy's arms stood up. He took a few tentative steps toward the table as the glass suddenly sped up, slid off into thin air, and bounced once on the carpet. Roy stopped. He felt electricity in the air. Over the tabletop the plastic chandelier started to sway. Leslie stood up from the floor and began to cry for no apparent reason. Roy picked up his book, grabbed his sister, and went out to the pool to cool off.

Later, on the ride to the airport, his parents told him to stop reading so many fantasy books. His father told him in great detail about static electricity. He said that lightning starts in the ground and jumps up into the sky. What Roy had witnessed, he explained, was an easily explainable occurrence, the manifestation of charged air particles. Roy, however, could only relate once more the feeling that had come over him watching the glass, the sudden sense of unreality, of some supernatural force. At the airport he said he thought the moving glass had been Uncle Charlie sending a message from beyond the grave. His mother took his Tarzan book and threw it in the trash.

Inside the Nowhere Cafe there is a bald man with a hairnet grilling potatoes on a long flat griddle. Only his torso is visible behind the long scarred-oak countertop. There are two customers hunched over the counter staring into their morning's first cup of coffee. A ceiling fan winds itself in sluggish circles, generating a negligible air current, offering the mostly visual relief of function. Over by the back door an old iron woodstove generates surprising heat. The man in the hairnet flips a pound of sliced potatoes with a spatula as the first rays of sunlight creep over the end of the counter and move quietly toward the two mute coffee drinkers. Roy takes in the scene and realizes that it is almost certainly a repeat of yesterday, of the morning before, of every morning. Towns like these are built on the routines of literal-minded people. Roy recognizes himself at the counter, a logger in flannel and steel-toed boots, younger, but still caught in that loop of 5:00 A.M. breakfasts at greasy spoons, the exhaustion of physical labor, the barrenness of a life spent living in a run-down trailer with dirty dishes in the sink and a television that can only perform two channels of static upon demand of the remote control. This was the refuge he took after Lorrie divorced him. He remembers how hard it was to leave the life of cutting trees, not because of any great love for it, but because of the fear that the return to society produced and because it was so difficult to conceive of change in a job that worked you from six in the morning until eight o'clock at night. Despite the drain, Roy spent his days breathing in the gas fumes of a roaring chain saw and considering more intellectual pursuits.

And then he saw the UFO.

Edward and Roy, frozen extremities in tow, hobble to the counter and sit on lopsided stools.

"Coffee," says Roy. "Preferably in a bowl."

"Tea," said Edward. His cheeks are red and the end of his nose is strangely white.

"Don't got tea," says the counterman. "Got coffee."

"Milk?"

"Sure. For your coffee."

"How about hot chocolate?"

The guy just raises an eyebrow. Edward nods.

"Coffee sounds great. I'll just have some coffee."

The two guys to Roy's right are squinty-eyed, leather-faced. One of them wears a collapsing baseball cap with the words CAT TRACTOR SUPPLY on it. The other has on a T-shirt that looks like it has participated in one too many meals. The counterman puts two chipped mugs on the counter, fills them from a blackened pot. Edward eyes his cup warily. Roy tries to tame the coffee with three teaspoons of sugar, tastes it, and adds a fourth. It's like drinking ink.

"You guys know where I could find Henderson?"

The two guys to his right exchange a look. The counterman drops seven link sausages onto the grill with a smoke-inducing hiss.

"Cemetery," he says. "You got to go see Bill Glover. He'll show you the grave."

Roy nods.

"That's a shame. Good old Henderson. He go recent?"

"Last Thursday."

"Heart, huh?"

The counterman looks at the two guys on stools. Nobody says anything.

"Last time I talked to him he was fine," says Roy. The locals continue to say nothing.

"My buddy Lenny Knuckles said he was thinking about moving to Reno."

The counterman, whose name is Walter Scruggs, begins cracking eggs onto the grill.

"Nobody here's got anything to say about that."

"I don't blame you. A man died. In fact, I bet the guys back in Washington are having a good laugh right now."

Walter takes a large metal spatula and holds it up in front of Roy's face.

"What the fuck is that supposed to mean?"

Roy picks up his coffee, takes a sip, grimaces.

"Man, this is the worst coffee I ever had."

Walter shrugs, goes back to flipping eggs.

"Money's tight. I gotta reuse the grounds."

Edward, who has just worked up the courage to put the coffee cup to his nose, sniffs at it once with suspicion, makes a face, puts it down, and asks for a glass of water, then thinks about what he's just done.

"You guys government?" asks Walter.

Roy snorts.

"Do we look like beady-eyed, pencil-pushing fat cats to you? That's some insult. Did I drive into town and shoot your wife? Am I hiding inside an armored vehicle teargassing your cows?"

"Shit."

"Me and Ed here are just a couple of guys who know what time it is. If I say more I'm saying too much."

Edward looks at the menu, decides he's in real trouble as far as food is concerned. It doesn't look like you can have breakfast in Clone without eating some kind of steak. Walter Scruggs shakes his head, scoops two mounds of eggs and three sausages onto two plates, and gives them to the two regulars sitting next to Roy.

"What do I care about time? As far I know it's the same hour for the last thirty-one years. Five A.M. and I'm cooking beef. All my hair fell out. I'm fat and my back hurts when I bend over."

"Nice, polite, friendly people. That's what Cliff Webb said we'd find out here in Clone. Salt of the earth, strong backboned, polite."

"Cliff told you that?"

"That's right. And we all know Cliff doesn't lie."

Walter focuses his eyes on the regulars. The sunlight has made its way down the counter and the three of them have taken on a glow that could almost be described as radioactive. Finally he wipes his hands on his apron and turns back to Edward and Roy.

"You guys eating breakfast or what?"

Edward and Roy exchange a look. Roy knows that there's very little here for Edward to eat. Edward feels a cold coming on. His palms are sweaty. His throat hurts.

"You got cereal?" asks Edward.

"I got eggs and sausage and potatoes and steak. If you cry like a girl I can make you some toast."

Edward mimics a smile.

"Get a lot of heart attacks around here?"

"I wouldn't know. Around here people don't live that long."

Roy muscles down some more coffee. It makes his heart race like Carl Lewis.

"Cliff says that's got a lot to do with the army."

"Cliff's got a big mouth."

"What he says."

"Well, I don't see Cliff around here. Do you see Cliff?"

"No," says Edward, who wouldn't recognize him if he were.

"Was Cliff here when the army came? Was he herded from his house at three o'clock in the morning? Was he taken to Henderson's barn and threatened with a rusty saw?"

"They threatened you with a rusty saw?"

"Was he here after the army left and his buddy Phil decides to take what we call around here the Clone walk? A little early-morning stroll out into the desert. Good old Phil, the first Clone Popsicle. I mean I feel bad for the guy, but that don't give him the right to go around shooting off his mouth."

"His buddy though. The guy's probably broken up. I'm sure he came right away when he heard the news."

"He came. He came with those other guys."

Aha, thinks Roy. He has a celebratory sip of coffee because there's nothing else around to have a celebratory sip of.

"Which guys?"

Walter makes a face. The population of his town has dropped to forty-one. This is his breakfast rush. In another week he won't even get enough customers to open. He's sick to death of the whole thing.

"I only got last names. Porter, McAndrew. There was another guy. A scrawny fuck like Mr.-got-any-tea over here."

Edward smiles and makes a big show of picking up his coffee cup and putting it to his lips.

"Cliff was pretty pissed," says Roy. "I'll tell you that. He said the army was putting some kind of drug in your water."

"Shit. I tell you this. Cliff was a fucking wacko when he lived here back in 'seventy-nine and he's still a fucking wacko. I'm not saying the army didn't pull some crazy shit on us. I mean, it could have been a drug. The way they clamped down on this town you'd think they had some crazy virus got loose like in that movie, or maybe this was just some drill. Who knows? The point is, people around here just stopped feeling right all of a sudden. Dolores over at number eleven went into some kind of trance for two days. Herb out at Red Rocks stood in the middle of the interstate and got himself run over by a semi. The army was really the least of our worries. I mean the army you can see, right? I'm talking about hardworking people who just stopped moving around like they used to. A whole town where people just get up in the morning and stare off into space."

"We're not talking a major coincidence though. I mean, the army just didn't drop in out of the sky for fun."

"Hey, I'm an American. I pay my taxes." Walter points to the regulars. "Red pays his taxes. Arnie pays his taxes. Arnie fought in Korea. Red used to be a fireman in Ely. I gave money in 'eighty-eight to the campaign to elect George Bush. You tell me why my government's got to invade my town and take me to the dump and hang me over the edge of a canyon by my ankles."

"Maybe they tasted your coffee," offers Roy.

The front door jingles. Agent Forbes comes in wearing jeans and flannels. He's got on a fake beard and a pair of boots in which the heel of the left is slightly higher than that of the right, an alteration that affords him a small limp. He hobbles up to the counter and sits down. Outside the cafe a small team of soldiers hides inside a covered truck that emits the prerecorded whines and grunts of two hundred hogs.

"Four hundred miles breathing pig shit," he says.

"Pardon?" says Edward, at whose left Forbes has chosen to sit.

"I said, I just drove four hundred miles breathing pig shit."

Edward thinks about this for a minute, chews his lip.

"I don't know what to say to that. That's a greeting I have never thought to prepare an answer for."

Forbes orders coffee, lights a cigarette.

"I'm just getting the hang of hellos myself. You'd think they'd come pretty natural after forty-one years, but I always get tripped up with nice-to-meet-you and the handshake thing."

"So instead you say four hundred miles breathing pig shit."

"Bobby Collins," says Agent Forbes, born Richard Wermer, holding out his hand.

"Telly Savalas. You know, like the actor."

And Forbes, who knows exactly who he's talking to, says:

"Hey, there's an unusual name."

"It's Greek."

"You from around here?"

"No. I live down in Phoenix. Me and my buddy run a model-train store."

"Model trains, huh?"

"That's right. We specialize in pre–Civil War cabooses."

"I once rode a real train from Oregon to Ohio."

"Is that right?"

"Took three days."

Edward looks over at Roy, who has just ordered two fried eggs and four strips of bacon. Forbes's entrance has pretty much stopped all conversation inside the Nowhere Cafe. Beside him the two regulars finish up their food, push aside their plates. Walter Scruggs buses them, takes some singles off the counter, hands back some change. Roy decides that after breakfast they will drive over to the cemetery and see if they can talk to Bill Glover.

"I hear some crazy shit's been going on around here lately," says Forbes. Edward finally decides he will skip breakfast after Walter pulls a big block of bacon out of the refrigerator and dumps it on the counter.

"What kind of crazy shit?"

"UFOs, I hear. Alien invasion. I got my camcorder ready. I figure I could make a million dollars selling footage of that shit to CNN."

Roy looks over.

"Where do you hear this?"

"On the CB," says Forbes, who loves to use the expression *CB*. His right leg is moving up and down at a steady pace. He popped a couple of pills before he came in, but they don't really seem to be working as well as they used to. The bottle's getting low, and he feels he's going to have to up the dosage to three. Right now the cafe feels a little small for him. Too many walls and not enough windows.

"Well," says Roy. "We're only a stone's throw from Nellis. You got a pretty good chance of seeing some saucers, though it may be our boys who're flying them."

"Christ. You think so?" Out in the truck the soldiers are waiting for Forbes to come out. The oldest is twenty-four. In ten years he will become a consultant to arms manufacturers and defense contractors. He will become an influential platform author for the Republican party. The other soldiers have futures too, except for Douglas Crow, who will be killed in a helicopter crash just two weeks from today. They have orders to take Edward and Roy into custody. The army has been watching Clone since two weeks after the invasion, when the mortality rate shot up through the roof.

"Well, saucer sightings out here in Nevada are pretty routine."

"Hey, listen," says Forbes, "I found something weird a few miles up the road. You know, I pull over to take a piss and I'm letting go into the brush and this thing catches my eye. It looked like a briefcase. I didn't want to touch that shit since I watch a lot of episodes of *Tales from the Crypt* and whenever guys find shit and take it, something bad always happens to them, but I really feel curious, you know."

Edward looks over at Roy.

"A briefcase?"

"Looked like it." Forbes takes out a cigarette and puts it in his mouth. If he can't get Edward and Roy out of here of their own free will, the soldiers are going to have to pistol-whip them in the parking lot.

Roy's breakfast comes. He starts in on it with the luxury that comes from a steel stomach. Edward considers letting out a sob so he can get that toast. Walter Scruggs is washing dishes. The two regulars get up and leave, letting in a breeze of cool air.

"I was up in Ferndale, Washington, last week," says Forbes. "It's near the Canadian border."

Edward nods. He's thinking about the briefcase.

"How far up the road you see this briefcase?"

Forbes shrugs. His left hand is in his pants pocket, fondling the bottle of pills.

"Six miles maybe."

"I think I'd be interested in taking a look at it."

"Hey, sure. Let me just take a piss." He stands and limps into the restroom.

"What do you think?"

Roy shrugs, spoons his last corner of egg into his mouth.

"It's worth a shot."

After a moment Forbes comes limping out of the restroom.

"All set."

Roy throws five dollars on the bar, motions for Edward to go ahead of him.

"Thanks for the breakfast."

In the parking lot Roy offers to drive them, but Forbes says he's got to take the truck.

"Company rule. I can't be more than a hundred feet from my pigs at any time."

The pig truck is a long semi full of computer equipment and gleaming stainless-steel walls. It is temperature-regulated to a cool 55 degrees at all times. It sits on the cracked macadam emitting pig noises from two speakers hidden under the chassis. There is also a small canister on the underside of the truck that emits a pungent mist of pheromones at five-minute intervals.

"How can you drive with that smell?"

Forbes grins, climbs up into the cab.

"I can't smell a thing. It's a medical condition. No sense of smell. No taste either. Food is just like cardboard to me. What are you gonna do?"

On the road heading back out of town Edward and Roy speculate on the contents of the briefcase.

"I say it's full of pornographic playing cards."

Roy shakes his head, keeps the gas down to keep up with Forbes's truck, which is cruising at seventy-five miles an hour.

"Don't they usually transport pigs in open trucks?" asks Edward. Roy shrugs. The reflection of the sun off a distant airplane catches his eye. We are not alone, he thinks. He has read every book and article there is on extraterrestrial life, recognizes the different types of aliens, the grays, the Vikings, the Men in Black. His own experience with a hovering saucer started him on the road that has led him here, to an empty desert road chasing a conspiracy of drug manufacturers and government officials.

If you were to ask him about that night, about the sudden silence in the woods, the flashing lights, he would try to reconstruct it for you from the fragmentary memories he has. There is a substantial period of missing time. He is convinced there was an abduction, has flashbacks of uncomfortable medical procedures. The color blue stands out in his mind. He could not tell you why.

There is something about the helplessness of knowing that there are far greater powers in the universe than he that has made Roy a suspicious person. Those who have been taken come to understand the essential lie of modern life. It is as if a man in a small town sees a large pink elephant on a traffic island while driving to work one day. He says, Hey, did you see that elephant on Elm Street this morning? His friends clear their throats, wait for the punch line. The man drives to the police station and asks the same thing of the police, who greet him as if he is a lunatic. Something is going on. A two-ton pink elephant doesn't just sit on a traffic island at rush hour and go completely unnoticed by a town full of people. The man begins to believe that everyone has seen the elephant but is conspiring to keep it secret. Why would the elephant come to just him? Is it a sign from God? Is some higher power at work?

The next day on his way to work the man sees the elephant again. He pulls over to the side of the road, gets out of his car. The elephant sits on a park bench reading a newspaper. The man goes to find a cop. When he returns, the elephant is gone. Now what is going on here? Maybe the man is crazy. Maybe the elephant is simply a chemical code in his head that produces the pink pachyderm at a certain time each morning. But let's say that other people begin seeing the elephant. Mrs. Jones at 311 Cleveland Avenue sees the elephant on her swing set after dinner one night. She calls to her husband, but when he comes up from the basement the elephant is gone. Bill Ford sees the elephant on a highway overpass after a high school basketball game. The police deny the existence of the elephant. The mayor issues a statement that the sightings of the elephant can be explained by the existence of a pink moving truck with the words PINK ELEPHANT MOVING COMPANY on it. It's just the power of suggestion. But the elephant sightings continue. Now the elephant sighters go underground. A pink elephant newsletter is put out every month by the original man using a home PC and the local Kinko's.

People in other towns come forward to say they too have seen the elephant. How can the elephant exist and go unnoticed by the authorities? Years pass. The number of sightings grows. A poll is taken in which a majority of the country's population believes in the existence of the elephants. And yet the government continues to deny it. How are we to trust a government that denies the existence of things we have seen with our own eyes? This would be a grand leap of faith. And so we begin to suspect that there are other agendas at work.

For Roy that period of missing time began a transformation, much the way victims of violent crimes undergo transformation from being regular people with regular lives to becoming people obsessed with the threat of dark streets and unlocked doors. It is a rape of safety. We begin to watch the skies.

"Where the hell are we going?" Edward says a moment before the truck begins signaling, slowing down, pulling over onto the shoulder. The two of them climb out, walk around the front of the car. The sun has crested distant mountains and shines a cold detached light down on barren scrub land. Forbes drops from the cabin and limps around to the back of the truck.

"You know what I like about the desert?" he says. "There are no walls. It's just open space. There are no buildings with little rooms, no elevators, no constricted stairwells." He shudders. He has popped another three pills while driving here. He knocks on the back of the truck three times and Edward and Roy find themselves facing the barrels of five guns. Edward puts his hands up without having to be asked. Roy shakes his head, spits into the dirt.

"Typical," he says.

Inside the truck are two metal chairs with wrist and ankle restraints. The walls are a shiny nickel-plated alloy. Forbes, with his beard and artificial limp, walks to the front end of the rig and knocks on a metal door. Two men with masks come out. Edward and Roy, strapped into the chairs, experience a certain sinking sensation in their stomachs.

"We need to know where your friend Linus is," says Mr. Yee. "We don't have much time."

"I really couldn't tell you," says Roy as sincerely as he can.

Forbes watches the soldiers close the big metal doors of the rig, digs his fingernails into his palms, forces a smile.

"I've decided to take a real liking to you boys," he says, coming forward and putting his hands on their shoulders.

"Please don't," says Edward.

"So I'm going to level with you. Your buddy Linus, who I also like a great deal, has disappeared on us."

For once Edward and Roy are silent. Forbes wipes his forehead on his sleeve.

"Now we need to get some information, *need* being the key word to pay attention to here. You guys have been snooping around here all morning. You probably realize that some strange things have been going on around here recently and you've probably jumped to all sorts of very exciting and mysterious conclusions, as I would expect you always do."

"What exactly have you been poisoning these people with?" asks Roy.

"You see. This is just what I'm talking about. You know how hard it is these days to recruit good people into government service. There's just so much bad PR floating around out there."

"And why send in the army? How did you expect to keep that a secret?"

"As far as I'm concerned we're just a couple of guys sitting around in the back of a really big truck. Washington, D.C., is an extraordinary number of miles away. By wagon train it would take whole seasons to get there."

"We don't know where Linus is. Nobody's talked to him in two weeks."

"Ferndale, Washington, he said. Jerry Bruckner, he said. He gave us a phone number. That Linus is a very gutsy guy. When this is all over I'd really like for the four of us to go out, get a few piña coladas. I see you all as guys I could really have a good time with."

"Are you insane?"

"The thing is, we got this letter. We're no longer talking about a simple airplane bombing. We have a much bigger situation on our hands now. You guys have been driving around the country looking for this group Danton. Personally, I approve. The more people we got out there looking, the better. I mean, you guys are probably going to end up in a cardboard box the size of a toaster oven, but you may help the rest of us out in the long run."

"Just tell us what we can do, sir. Roy and I want to help."

"I knew I could count on you two. You're patriotic guys. I can tell that just by reading those interesting little newsletters you put out. But let me cut to the chase before I let Mr. Yee and Mr. Clean have a go at you. We know now that Danton is most likely located in the four-corners area. We figure there may be ten to twenty guys. Some kind of militia. Militias are big now. People tend to get carried away. It happens. We know that. We can sympathize. Where was I?"

"A letter."

"Right. So a letter comes yesterday. It's addressed to me personally by my given name, which is strange since the only people who know my given name are my mother, who's as loopy as a color Xerox, and my grandfather, who's as dead as Francisco Franco. So already I'm impressed. The letter pins down the bombing. We got the bombing now. It's definitely these guys, and it seems pretty clear that it's some kind of revenge thing for our little adventure here in Nowhereland."

"What kind of adventures are we talking about?" asks Edward. "Two words. Sounds like."

"The business of government is to protect the nation. The details of one particular operation are irrelevant."

"Can I get that embroidered on a pillow?"

If Roy could free his arms he would clamp his hand over Edward's mouth to keep him from talking. Forbes sighs and looks over at Mr. Yee and Mr. Clean, who today wear the masks of ex-Soviet premiers Khrushchev and Stalin. Edward begins to think he can't feel his toes. He tries to move them inside his shoes. He's afraid of gangrene. His chest is crisscrossed with scars from the operation, doctors' probes and instruments, the reinflation of his lungs. The scars have receded to a pale pink, a vaguely sluglike set of burrows, but looking at them there is the suggestion of the grim inner workings of the human body, the blood and tissue, the sloppy wrestle of heartbeats and pulse, the stringy muscle and mottled fat. Once you've had another human being tear open your body, master your organs, your bones, your blood, you are never again under the mistaken impression that the human body is a machine made up of cool gears, of wires and brightly flashing lights. Once your body has been invaded by infection, has drowned itself in fluid and fever, once you've felt the chest-cracking pain of the jaws of life, you never again look at yourself as anything more than a frail and temporary organism. Edward walks around every day aware of his liver processing toxins, aware of his heart beating, the breath entering his lungs, leaving. He pays attention to the movements of his fingers, the workings of his joints, the movements of his eyes. He considers the synapses necessary to raise his arms, the flow of blood up his neck to his brain. He worries about his sinuses, the health of his colon, his prostate. He examines his testicles for lumps. He avoids high-tension power lines, uses only nontoxic cleaning products. And now he is going to be tortured in a soundproofed truck by men in rubber masks.

"So you get a letter," he says.

Forbes nods.

"From Danton. It's clearly them."

"What were the names you used—Jerry Bruckner? Is this his letter?"

"We're starting to think Jerry Bruckner might have been a ruse. We think that Linus may have gotten a little creative on us in the information department, but we're confident that the two of you have accumulated one or two more credible names by this point, and Mr. Yee and Mr. Clean will be along shortly to extract those from you."

Edward doesn't want to think about what that means.

"Before I read you the letter I want to show you something."

Forbes goes over to a metal tabletop that hangs on one of the metallic truck walls. He opens a briefcase, removes a folder.

"This is a matter of national security, so I don't think I have to remind you that what you hear in this room cannot be repeated outside." Forbes puts on his grimmest face. He has no intention of letting Edward and Roy return to their car. As if sensing this, Roy's mouth is already dry and he has to swallow once or twice before he can manage to say:

"Naturally."

Forbes crosses his arms and examines them both, first Roy, then Edward. They look pale and tense. It's the truck. The idea that the government has a moving vehicle masked by technology that roams the country, a rolling interrogation station. It makes those who are taken feel helpless. He smiles.

"Good. Well, then, I'll begin. The truth of what's been going on around here is the following. In December of this year we got word of a planned terrorist attack, a biological agent to be introduced into the water supply of three major cities, Washington, D.C., New York, and Chicago. The drug was to be a chemical compound, in many ways like sarin nerve gas. We believed the attack could come at any time. Security was beefed up at all local water-processing plants. The reservoirs were monitored. Then came an anonymous phone call. The compound was being tested in a small town in Nevada to check for chemical effectiveness, solution dilution, solvent-ratio issues. We mobilized a strike team. The local population was rounded up and tested. Time was of the essence. The water source must be traced back, the contamination point identified. We found a chemical agent in the water, though not a nerve gas. The new substance had to be tested. We were not authorized to inform the local population of the reasons for our interest. It was decided that the risk of widespread panic was too great. The threat to the nation's water supply must remain a secret until we can be sure we have identified the agent and either eliminated the threat or devised an antidote that can be introduced preventively into the water."

Forbes holds up a notarized form that neither Edward nor Roy can read. He puts it back in the folder.

"Your government conspiracy, therefore, gentlemen, is actually an attempt by the government to save the American public from a terrorist threat."

"So what is this chemical?" asks Roy.

"It's still unknown. We believe that in sufficient quantity it can be lethal, but it is obvious that here in Nevada the proportion was small enough that it induced instead some debilitative, but in and of themselves nonlethal, effects."

"Dementia," says Mr. Yee.

"Loss of fear response," says Mr. Clean.

"Sluggishness, extreme suggestibility, paralysis of the aggressive centers of the brain." Forbes closes the file, returns it to his briefcase.

"And you think Danton is responsible for this?" Edward entertains a brief hope that he is engaged in a reasonable situation with reasonable men that can be resolved by a simple exchange of ideas.

"We believe that Danton is planning to use this compound on over three million people sometime in the next month. We are in a race against time. You friend Linus has shown the misguided inventiveness which may actually find Danton, but which will surely get him killed. You see, gentlemen, we are dealing with a very dangerous element here. This is one of the instances in American history where I would think that even severe skeptics of the government such as yourselves would agree that a strong and swift government response is in the best interest of all people interested in living to a ripe old age."

"What's the connection to Hastings Pharmaceutical?" asks Edward, who has been called a dangerous element himself for more than five years.

"Hastings Pharmaceutical has been helping us identify the substance. Some of their scientists were killed on flight 613, along with members of our task force on their way to a chemistry and biological sciences conference in Brazil. It is clear that Danton is trying to impede our efforts to identify and neutralize the compound."

"Read us the letter," says Roy. He remains unconvinced that Danton is responsible for what has been happening here.

Forbes shrugs. He looks down at the unfolded letter. He is sweating under his arms in such great quantity that were he to lift his arms his shirt would be wet from armpits to waist.

"The letter is unimportant. We need to know the names of Danton's members and their location. I don't have any more time to chat. I think I've been very cooperative in giving you an idea of why we need to know. I think it's clear that millions may die if you insist on keeping quiet. Now that you understand the importance, I'm sure you both want to be as helpful as possible."

"Can I see the file?" Roy moves his head toward Forbes's right hand, because his arms are secured to the chair.

"No, you may not."

"It just seems like this is a very credible story in which all blame is placed conveniently on faceless terrorists."

Forbes licks his lips. He looks first at Mr. Yee, masked today as Khrushchev, then at his Russian counterpart, Mr. Clean.

"Gentlemen," he says. "It seems that our subversive friends here are opting not to help the American people in their time of need."

"Look, Mr. . . ." says Edward.

"Agent Forbes."

"Look, Agent Forbes. Try to understand our position."

"I don't have to understand your position. People are already dead here and you guys are too cynical to do the right thing. I would have expected more from men of your caliber. If Linus were here and he understood the lives at stake I don't think he would hesitate, do you?"

Edward takes a deep and shaky breath. He is afraid of dying. He is afraid of being tortured in a sterile refrigerator truck in the middle of a desert. He glances at the bank of computer consoles linked to the far end of the trailer. For once the absence of dust, of the smallest evidence of natural elements, makes him distinctly uncomfortable. There are men with masks opening small metal cases full of gleaming instruments. He wonders what life must have been like in the era of dungeons and religious inquisitions, the analogue age of the heretic and the purifying flame. Progress in all things, he thinks.

"Who is Teddy Waren?" he asks.

Forbes laughs.

"The mysterious passenger 101." He nods to the soldiers at the truck doors, who throw back the bolt and swing open the big bay doors, letting in a sudden sense of place, an outdoors that Edward and Roy, their backs to it, aspire toward with great desperate hope. Forbes closes his briefcase, loosens his collar. Now that he can see the outdoors he relaxes, his mood turns weightless.

"Someone had to carry that bomb on the plane," he says. He pats them on the shoulders and walks toward the exit. "We are in a new age of martyrs, gentlemen. Do me a favor, will you, and don't become two of them." He walks to the back of the truck and jumps down into the dirt. The sun is a round orange fireball scowling at the earth. Behind him the soldiers close the doors with a hard crash of metal. Forbes climbs into Roy's cousin's car, starts the engine, and pulls out onto the highway. The truck pulls out behind him with a great shuddering of gears. On the radio a man says, *Only in redemption can there be forgiveness.*

Los Angeles is a city that appears to have been built to satisfy somebody's desire for a cigarette. It hangs with a particular mixture of poverty and glamour on the cusp of the Pacific Ocean, just one pretentious cafe and trendy restaurant after another, separated by asphalt and the gurgling fumes of Jaguars and dilapidated Oldsmobiles. As with any major city, the airport is the first thing most visitors see, stumbling off of intercontinental flights, oxygen-deprived and surly from their predigested meals. Like other airports, the Los Angeles airport sits on the highway, an electronic animal poised in the underbrush of some urban savanna, lurking mechanically, feeding off the spastic regurgitations of airplanes. It is an airport like all others, an automated conspiracy of moving floors and revolving luggage, where desperate clots of bodies in wrinkled clothes struggle to break out, fighting their way through crowds of suitcase-laden optimists grappling to break in.

The airport is proof of humanity's surrender to machines. It is a place where bodies go to pee in bathrooms with two hundred stalls, to drink corrosive coffee served from unnatural kiosks built of plastic and adhesive foam. It is a country with a population of zero but an immigration problem of obscene proportions, its borders overrun at all hours by persecuted people seeking temporary asylum from the violence of flight. People sleep in uncomfortable chairs, haunted by unnatural neon daylight, kept awake by the monotony of artificial voices and the static electricity that jerks from the flame-retardant carpets. The airport is a clock, a calculator, a lever used to lift the wingless from the earth and fling them at the receding horizon. It has no soul, nor does it have heart, just an ever-changing portrait of faces and a collection of traveling art exhibits that appear interesting on first examination and then prove to be the aesthetic equivalent of an in-flight magazine.

Linus's airplane descends to feed from the mechanical mother at eleven o'clock. He is squeezed from the narrow opening at the front like a small turd and flushed through stadium-size corridors and down escalators whose jagged metal teeth appear to have been designed solely to aid in some sinister digestive process. He emerges onto the street squinting into the morning sunlight. It is hot, crowded. He is disoriented by the urgency of moving bodies and raised voices. Linus throws his sweatshirt into a trash can. He has never been to Los Angeles before now, knows it by reputation only. He has always thought of it as a beach town with beaches you can't swim at, full of gourmet restaurants you can't get into, a mystical movie-star tax bracket built from conceptual currency and celluloid credit cards, where beautiful blond starlets longing for infamy are made to feel ugly, and lopsided-faced action Neanderthals are bribed to act beautiful.

From a disorganized line of multinational taxidrivers, Linus hails a yellow cab. He tells the driver he is interested in buying a used car. The driver, whose name sounds like two different kinds of South American fruit, explains that, by luck, he happens to have a cousin who is selling a Buick Skylark from 1981. Would Linus perhaps like to see it? The cousin lives not far from the airport. Through a stream of semiparked vehicles they careen out toward the highway. Linus stares at the palm trees, closes his eyes. This may as well be Florida. The car he's in may as well be on its way to a makeshift morgue crowding a lonely junior high school. There is no backward, he tells his brain. Only forward. Behind us is simply a thin gray fog, but Linus can still make out certain faces in the haze. They take a highway off-ramp, wind through questionably middle-income houses. With a sudden deceleration and a squeal of brakes they arrive at the house of the cousin. In this way Linus comes, within his first hour in L.A., to own a monkey-shit-brown two-door with double-size tires and ragged fabric seats.

He buys a map of L.A. and an orange soda. He plots a course heading east, threads his way onto the highway toward San Bernardino. He feels he has a lot to learn about Hastings Pharmaceutical. Information about their products and their practices, their lobbyists and political action committees. Information that may lend some insight as to why he is a widower.

From a pay phone at a Shell station he calls the number Cody left for him. He asks if the man who answers has ever considered making arrangements for his own burial plot. He is told, without minced words, to fuck off. He is in San Bernardino by two o'clock. There are six hours until he is to meet Colby Wood, a man with a name that sounds like the film capital of Connecticut. He stops at a shopping mall and buys a sandwich and a root beer. He examines the address Cody has given him for Hastings Pharmaceutical, examines his map. He is a tourist with strange priorities, who looks not for directions to Disneyland or Universal Studios but to a small office building buried among a series of shopping malls.

Half an hour later he is sitting in his car in a parking lot across the street from the Hastings Pharmaceutical building. It is a squat cube of glass that resembles in many authoritarian ways the mirrored sunglasses of the Highway Patrol. The building itself has no plaque or sign identifying it as Hastings. It displays no visible owner. Yet the parking lot is accessed by a key card and sits full of blue and gray automobiles. This does not strike Linus as unusual in any way. He is familiar with the anonymous office buildings of government contractors like Wechtel, which provides security for most major secret government bases. These are structures filled with flat-featured men with top-level security clearances. They are dummy corporations, hiding the agendas of industry and government. Their employees will not tell you whom they work for or what is inside. Linus often imagines that when children disappear, this is where they end up: in innocuous-looking office towers in suburbia, where men in gray suits and sunglasses use the children's untapped psychic powers to predict the rise and fall of the stock market.

He parks his car in the shade of a eucalyptus tree, where the shadow will obscure his figure to anyone looking through the windshield. He rolls down his windows, succumbs to the elevated temperature that makes the newly poured black asphalt shimmy with the illusion of heat. At noon he watches clusters of secretaries emerge from the revolving doors. A catering truck arrives. The sun paints a reflection of the surrounding hills in the facade of the building. For Linus, a native of Brooklyn, the sparseness of the Southern California landscape, with its freeways and shopping malls, swimming pools and prerecorded coyote cries, has always seemed a visual precursor to bland citizenry.

He sits the rest of the afternoon sweating in his still-unfamiliar vehicle. He explores the glove compartment, feels around under the seat. He finds a discarded pack of Marlboros and a torn pair of women's underwear. He watches for anything suspicious, tries to ascertain a pattern or routine to the comings and goings. Every half hour a security car glides down the street, pulls into the Hastings parking lot. A uniformed security guard climbs out and confers with the guards at the front desk. Linus envisions the air conditioning that must cool them inside, the constant arctic winds. His own shirt is soaked through. Soon he will have to drive back up the road to Macy's and buy some new clothes, for he can't spend the next few days dressed in one pair of jeans and a sweat-stained shirt. He still has thirty-eight hundred dollars, most of it tucked into his right shoe. It is damp and smells of feet, but Linus prefers this to the cold, crisp half truths of newly printed money spat from an ATM.

Colby Wood turns out to be a woman. The two meet at a picnic bench bolted to the parking lot of In and Out Burger. Linus sips his soda under the irradiated glow of streetlights.

"I don't like doing this," she says to him before he can manage a hello.

"I wouldn't ask you to if it weren't important."

"I don't know you. I don't even know your name. All I know is I get a message on my answering machine that tells me you're going to call. You could be FDA. You could be internal security."

"I'm a very sad man whose wife was blown up on an airplane. It makes me distracted and irritable, but not a cop."

Colby eyes him warily. She seems reluctant to sit down, as if doing so is an admission of compliance. She turns her head quickly from side to side. She is looking for a setup.

"I can tell you right away that though Hastings does a lot of ethically questionable things, I don't believe they blow up planes. I think I would have to draw the line at that, blowing up planes."

She is a forty-year-old woman with short curly hair and thick ankles who has resigned herself to the fact that she will probably never get married or have children. Instead she has appliances. She has a ten-slice toaster, an espresso machine, a bread-baking machine, three Cuisinarts of different sizes, a four-hundred-dollar juicer, an electric cheese grater. She orders devices hewn from plastic and steel from catalogs. Her pants are pressed by a machine that looks like a coffin she keeps in her garage. She is only happy when something in her house is whirring or spinning or toasting or liquefying. She sees this as a metaphor for the womb. Her house is a body and the sounds and motions are those of the blood pumping through veins, of a giant heart beating. Her coworkers call her a gadget freak, but she has resolved to replace the comfort of human contact with the reliable performance of machines.

"I don't work directly for Hastings," she says. "I mean I do and I don't."

"I have no information one way or the other. I cold-called. It was suggested you could help me find out things about Hastings Pharmaceutical. No other data was given."

"I work for an independent body that coordinates the efforts of several major pharmaceutical conglomerates to address the needs of the market and create opportunities for growth and increased market share."

"Make more money, in other words. Plus the whole world-domination itinerary."

"In a nutshell."

"You have a lot of competition, in case you haven't read the paper recently."

"Drug 'em," she says, and gives a slightly bitter laugh. "That's our motto back at headquarters."

"Which is where?"

"I can't tell you that. I can't even tell you the name of the organization. I'm not sure it has a name, to be frank."

"But you're here. You obviously have something to say."

Colby takes out a pack of breath mints. She puts one in her mouth. Next to appliances, her greatest concern is fresh breath. She goes through four packs of mints a day. They are her placebo in a world of multimillion-dollar decisions.

"I'm here because I have certain ethical concerns about the work I do."

"This is true about most people anymore, I would think," he says. "It has a lot to do with the centralization of wealth. After everything that's happened we're back to Karl Marx."

"The business of healing people who eventually die anyway is a losing proposition unless you also invest in the technology required to treat them. Sometimes I think we forget that these drugs are supposed to treat specific sicknesses and we end up with pharmaceuticals themselves as a metaphor for health."

Linus watches the cars go by on the road, a constant whir of gliding light. Colby chews her mint. Tiny sparks are created in her mouth. This gives her the illusion of supernatural power. Linus goes to the take-out window to order some food.

"Jeffrey Holden," he says when he returns.

"A creep. Try me again."

"Jerry Loyal."

"An egotist and a putz."

"What about a synaptic inhibitor secretly tested on inmates?"

"Which one?"

Linus nods and considers his burger. Colby drinks a sip of 7-Up.

"Look," she says, "let me just give you a kind of overview of where the pharmaceutical industry stands at this point in time. To be blunt, pharmaceutical companies are engaged in a campaign to purchase HMOs. Right now between us we control about six thousand doctors and over six hundred thousand patients. The rationale is that with the doctors working for us, we can increase the amount of prescriptions. We can increase the likelihood of drug therapies recommended over other methods of treatment. This makes good business sense. Drug companies now pay doctors for prescribing drugs in trial phases. They're paid per prescription. Every year we develop hundreds of new drugs. Only a handful are approved by the FDA. It's an enormously expensive proposition, which is why we were all relieved when we successfully lobbied to reduce the FDA waiting period for new drug approvals down from thirty-three weeks to nineteen."

Linus remembers that he still has reservations at a bed-and-breakfast in Marin to celebrate his anniversary. He hates himself suddenly for living. Across the table, Colby Wood frowns.

"Last year Eli Lilly held a National Depression Awareness Day at a suburban Maryland high school. The day was billed as an educational forum, but actually turned into a Prozac referral seminar. I think it's safe to say that the pharmaceutical industry believes that the lives of every man and woman in the world could be bettered by the use of prescription and over-the-counter drugs for everything from Alzheimer's disease to feelings of general dismay."

Colby swallows her breath mint, unwraps another.

"The big market right now is in mood modifiers, antidepressants. People have anxiety. They feel depressed. You could say it's part of being alive in the modern world, but to the drug manufacturers it is an alarming sign of the increase of chemically treatable mental illness. We're trying to take the stigma out of depression and to let people know that these drugs aren't only for psychotics. They can become a staple part of the American diet. No complicated side effects. No painful withdrawal symptoms. Just feel better about yourself. That's all we want. For people to feel better about themselves. The competition is stiff, though. There are hundreds of new antidepressants under FDA testing right now."

"What kind of testing?"

"Oh, you know, tame stuff. Control groups, volunteers. We've tested this stuff on monkeys and convicts. In fact, mental hospitals in third-world countries provide a fertile testing ground for a lot of this stuff, but that's just between you and me."

"What about work with the government?"

"A few companies do it. Hastings is the biggest. They've been working with the CIA since Vietnam and the LSD tests."

"Mind control?"

Colby shrugs. She picks a french fry off her plate and examines it like it's a cigarette butt.

"So you're a nut. Is that what this is all about? Did you drag me all the way out here to talk about microwave technology and how drug companies are planting suggestions in your mind to kill sitcom actresses?"

"You don't think a pharmaceutical industry with an agenda to physically medicate millions of people a year constitutes some kind of mind control?"

"That's not mind control. That's drug therapy. Treatment. You have an industry responding to a sickness. We want to make people well again. This is the published agenda."

"I can't believe you drove all the way out here just to recite the published agenda. You could have mailed me a brochure."

"Hey, I don't know you from Leslie Stahl. You could be wearing a wire. You could be print media. There could be a hidden camera in your hat."

"I'm not wearing a hat."

"All I know is I get a couple of phone calls. It could be anybody. I wasn't even going to come."

"But you did."

Colby unwraps another mint. The moon suggests itself in a cascade of glowing clouds.

"That's true," she says reluctantly.

"And I can't believe it was for the food."

A small smile like a reluctant admission of pain.

"We're talking about an industry that brings in over seven hundred billion dollars a year, six billion in antidepressants alone."

Linus closes his eyes, opens them again. He's still the same man in the same place. Behind them a man on a cellular phone says, *It's just a small part, but I get my own hairdresser.* Linus tries a bite of something in a bun.

"And you work for it," he says.

"I'm well paid. I feel my opinion carries weight. I'd like to think I'm helping steer us away from policies based on greed."

Linus rubs his eyes with the palms of his hands.

"I'm going to tell you a story," he says with spots flashing in his eyes. "It's a short one. There are a lot of details missing. Consider it a work in progress. I'll take any editorial suggestions you care to make."

Colby takes another pack of Life Savers from her purse. She peels off two and places them on her tongue. Later, driving home, she will notice a car with tinted windows pulling into her driveway behind her. A man will get out and stuff her into a large canvas sack. After three days her coworkers will report her missing. The police will come up with no leads. She will reappear a week later, resign her position, and move to a small one-bedroom house on Maui.

"Go ahead."

"A man works for a pharmaceutical company. He's a research scientist. His job is to develop new drugs. Let's call him Dave. Dave knows that his company, let's call the company Hastings, has hundreds of research drones just like him working in labs all over the country. They're recruited right out of graduate school, fresh and eager and lured by the promise of big money. Dave works hard. He wants to make a name for himself. He wants a career full of discovery and promotion. Now, he happens to have a friend named Jeffrey Holden, who works in the corporate offices. They're not great friends, but they know each other, maybe have some friends in common. So Dave works hard in his little lab and he discovers something. He gets very excited about it. He stumbles on a synaptic inhibitor, something which to a layman like me sounds routine, a thing scientists with multiple degrees discover in their sleep, but for

Dave it is a great discovery. Sensing his approaching fortune and promotion, he goes straight to the top. He doesn't want some research pit boss taking credit for his discovery. He calls his buddy Holden. He tells him, Hey, I've got something here. Something unique. Holden listens, jots down a few notes, and, always looking for an angle, says, Let's have dinner.

"They meet at a restaurant, have a couple of drinks. Dave lays out his findings. He draws pictures on napkins in ballpoint pen. Holden asks him a few questions. He wants to know what the potential applications are for this drug. Dave is prepared. He can name ten. By the end of the meal Holden feels he may just have something. In fact, this sounds like the perfect thing for a little relationship he has going with the government. So Holden calls up a guy he knows at FEMA, named Mills. He tells him he has something he thinks Mills might be interested in. A presentation is set up, a meeting held. Without much fanfare Dave is given the floor. He's brought charts and models. He is as excited as a kid in the Hershey factory. He talks about chemical properties, about the effect of his new drug on the brain of a rhesus monkey. He shows slides. There are other men there besides Holden and Mills. Men whose faces I can't see, whose names I don't know.

"Dave fields questions. He has no idea what he's doing talking to guys from an unnamed federal agency, but he's young and energetic and he's got car payments to make. The meeting ends. Mills and Holden retire to Holden's office, perhaps to discuss a finder's fee. I assume there are other high-ups from Hastings there, vice presidents, board members. 'Looks good,' says Mills. 'Let's start some tests and see how she performs.' Cut to a maximum-security prison in some rural state. A new doctor has been hired to care for the inmates. He begins to administer the drug to a control group of prisoners. He sees them every week, gives them a shot or a pill in a cup. He takes notes, blood samples. He talks to them about how they're feeling. He tells them there's a hundred bucks a month in it for them if they're willing to jerk off into a cup. Whatever. The point is, he does a field study and presents his findings back to the development team.

"Mills at FEMA feels good about how things are going. He sees it as time to make a phone call of his own. He goes back to his office, picks up the phone. He calls up another guy at a different goverment agency who goes by the name of Forbes, who is reachable at a phone number with no corresponding address. Forbes sits down with him and they go over the hard data. They both agree that this thing could be very useful to the government. The story gets fuzzy from here. The details thin. All I know is the ending. In the end my wife gets on a plane in New York and ends up scattered across the Florida Everglades."

Linus chews the ice in his cup. It tastes vaguely of wax. He stares at a stand of trees just behind Colby's right shoulder.

"Anyway," he says, "you can see I need some help finishing it. The story is only halfway done and I'm experiencing writer's block that's starting to make me nuts."

Colby chews at her lips, methodically working from the left lower across and up to the right upper.

"This is not a story you want to hear. This is a story that will give you nightmares."

"I don't sleep."

"Daymares."

Linus drops his burger in the trash, wipes his hands on his jeans.

"As far as you're concerned I was born to hear this story. This story is my birthright."

More lip chewing.

"This isn't what I do. I sit down with someone from Pharmwatch every few weeks. We talk about trends in the industry. I don't divulge information about secret projects."

"The line is pretty thin. I'm just asking you to take a baby step forward and back."

"There's the issue of professional ethics. I have an allegiance to the industry."

"People have died. There are FDA protocols set up for the testing of these drugs. We're talking about bypassing them entirely, about exposing human guinea pigs to chemical compounds that nobody knows the long-term effects of. Is that what you stand for?"

"This isn't my area."

"But you know things."

"I work for a consulting group with no name. Of course I know things. It's speaking about them with strangers that makes me nervous."

"I'm running out of clues. Soon I'll just be a man with a dead wife and no good reason why. These things go cold. Evidence is buried. I don't want to topple an industry. I just want to know."

Colby opens and closes the clasp on her purse. She looks over at her car, a green Volvo. It too is filled with appliances, audio technology and temperature-regulation systems. She likes to sit inside and listen to the engine hum. The white noise makes her calm.

"A synaptic inhibitor, the one in question specifically, is used to prevent people from having certain neural activity. It is a behavior and emotion blocker, in layman's terms. You isolate a part of the brain that controls a particular function. You then tell that part not to communicate with any other part. You isolate it. In this way, theoretically, you can keep people from feeling sad or stealing groceries from the Kwiki Mart. It is generally a very imprecise science, because there is still so much about the human brain we don't understand."

"And this particular inhibitor?"

"Is a pacifier. It's meant to control two things, fear and aggression."

"And."

"And it was tested unsuccessfully and has been shelved."

"Shelved."

"There were fatalities."

Yes, thinks Linus, there certainly were.

"And why blow up an airplane?"

"About that I have no information. I do know that other than Holden at least two other Hastings employees associated with this project were on the plane. Other than that..."

"Do you know anything about a group called Danton?"

Colby picks up a packet of ketchup, squeezes the contents first to one side and then the other, a methodical pressing of fingers. It feels vaguely medicinal, like the manhandling of a boil or a burn. She has a degree in biochemistry but prefers policy to lab work. She lives in a house that is modern and sparse. She is afraid even to have a pet, for fear that she might not love it enough and that it might become haughty and aloof and leave her alone with her appliances. Sometimes people go too long without acting and find themselves stuck in a routine or mindframe they can no longer break free from. For Colby Wood there are her catalogs and her TV.

"I have heard rumors that they're a group devoted to the ending of all human-related testing, including drug and chemical. These groups are often monitored by the industry and their government affiliates. It has been suggested that the bombing of your airplane was done by them as retribution for the Nevada test."

Linus leans across the table and covers her hand.

"What is the Nevada test?"

Colby pulls her hand away, rubs it on her pants. She looks again at her car, as if for reassurance. She does not encourage the touch of others and feels vaguely threatened by it when it happens. She stands up, brushes her jacket flat.

"That's all I'm going to say. Your next step is probably to find Danton and ask them. I highly doubt anyone at Hastings is directly responsible for the death of your wife."

"It's all connected."

"Yeah, but that philosophy doesn't get you anywhere. What I'm saying is, your real culprits are either the wackos or the government."

"Isn't that always the case?"

Linus watches her start her car. She flicks on the lights and for a moment he is blinded by their searing glare, but instead of covering his eyes he leaves them open, looking for some kind of inspiration. Neither of them realize that for the next twelve days she will join the ranks of the disappeared, though if you were to tell Linus right now in the parking lot, watching her taillights recede, he might say that he wasn't surprised. There is, after all, just a thin piece of paper between all of us and the questionable power of the state. After she's gone he stands up slowly and makes his way back to his car. He is a man alone in a fast-food restaurant parking lot in Los Angeles, hundreds of miles from home. As he climbs into his car he decides that this is probably a metaphor for the mechanical isolation of his time.

He drives east into the desert, spilling coffee onto the thinning seats of his new car. For a long time there is just the road and his perception of civilization. White lines cutting through him, yellow lines perforating his sense of time. He begins to lose his identity. The most indifferent side effect of solitude is that it can either inspire memory or encourage forgetfulness. To drive, one man alone, across desert highways, to roll up and down windows, fumble with a broken radio, to troll a two-lane blacktop void of all vehicles except your own. In the backseat are wrappers from food you should never have eaten, the half-empty bags of chips, the discarded boxes of doughnuts. It is a landscape in which the only meal you will remember well into old age is the single piece of fresh fruit devoured under a blazing sun on a flat jut of red rock. The way the juice runs over your fingers and falls onto the bone-dry dust. It is the sticky hands you lick clean, the sweet taste an anomaly in a tableau void of all blossoming, flowering, visible life.

The highways are straight and flat, cresting distant jagged hills. Snow dusts the higher elevations. Dusty roads and troubled, glowering skies. This is the great western desert, hoarding acres, Nevada, Utah, Arizona, the home of jerky black-and-white movies from the past, the rushing walls of destruction brought on by nuclear testing, the pigs in cages, the houses vaporizing, scattering under the force of unthinkable blasts. It is the birthplace of radioactive winds, where downwinders in Utah and New Mexico woke on 1950s' mornings or looked up on lazy weekday afternoons to a bright flash in the distance, a faraway rumble, a hot, sudden wind. It is where the prediction of wind patterns and dispersal schematics failed and a new kind of science was born.

At a gas station outside Fort Defiance, Arizona, Linus stands on a cracked asphalt island putting gas into the dusty Buick Skylark he purchased from Hidalgo Kokonot for $329. It is March 1, but what does that mean? Linus's hair is matted down by wind and dust, eyebrows confused and disoriented, his left arm sunburned from elbow to wrist. He has been driving for two days, winding his way southeast along two-lane highways, across reservations, over pitted gravel roads and dirt shoulders, stopping before midnight each night, sleeping in his car or inside invisible motels lost on back roads, run by toothless men part Navaho, part Scandinavian, part Peter Lorre.

His pilgrimage is to Victory, New Mexico, just outside the White Sands missile range, home of the first atomic explosion, open to tourists twice a year. A fenced-in expanse of lifeless dirt, where the radioactive topsoil has been plowed under, but odd-shaped stones composed of the first man-made element, trinitite, can be found scattered across the brutalized terrain.

Linus leans his hip against the trunk of his rusting two-door vehicle. He shakes the last greasy drops of gas from the hose and places it back on the pump. Other than the gas station there is only a dilapidated trailer crippled in the sagebrush a hundred yards back from the road. Dusk is gathering, a hot flush rising to the sky, highlighting the lengthening shadows, the temperature dropping steadily like a plane reaching for the hard comfort of earth. The red clay turns, like a man in rising anger, a blinding cadmium. One or two confused white clouds race across the upper atmosphere, like young animals who've wandered too far from the herd and are pursued by cackling jackals. Inside the gas station a small dark man in dirt-encrusted overalls squints toward the horizon, a tiny black-and-white television glowing beside him, antenna wired with tinfoil, as baseball teams in a distant world filled with lush green grass and pretty girls play a silent game to the soda machine.

Linus is surprised, in retrospect, to find out how important to him the institution of marriage really was. As a boy he had considered the long parade of women from real life to television with a certain greed. He dreamed big, from Sally Motion in ninth grade to Charlie's Angels busting crime syndicates with feathered hair and hip-hugging polyester pants. His girlfriends before Claudia were scrawny adolescents with questionable skin. They were angry graduate students with hacked hair and a tendency to make sudden dangerous gripping motions in the vicinity of his genitals. He had loved them all in one way or another. Lois with her impossible clumsiness. Dianne with the Coke-bottle glasses and one long, lonely nose hair. He'd dated five girls before he met Claudia, slept with three. They were a parade of women hiding dark emotional secrets, given to sudden outbursts and furious blushes.

In Claudia there was the sense of impossible luck, that someone so desirable could ever consider a man of his small stature attractive, even intellectually, much less marriageable. But Linus had made up for looks and charm with passion and humor and the disarming insight that he actually listened when people talked to him. He was the New York boy and she the midwestern girl. She was gestapo about cleanliness, had only socks that matched, carefully wrote the amount and date of each check into her checkbook as she wrote each check.

"I can't stand forgetting things," she said. "It drives me nuts. Car keys, people's names, paychecks. I've forgotten the combinations to every combination lock I ever bought, even though I carefully write down the number on a piece of paper, which I store in a very sensible place that I later totally fail to remember. One time when I was in college I lost a plate of spaghetti. I cooked it in the kitchen, put it on a plate. I went to get a glass of water. When I came out of the kitchen it was gone. I found it two hours later on top of the toilet seat being eaten by the cat. Once I've misplaced something you might as well write me off for the rest of the day. I'm too distracted."

"Try losing your hair," Linus would say. "Once you misplace that you never get it back."

During their courtship, before they moved into a two-bedroom apartment in the Sunset district of San Francisco, they would meet spontaneously, suddenly spying each other across streets or in crowded bars. It was as if they'd been drawn to each other magnetically. Linus would go to a movie at the Castro, would ride the bus home and see Claudia on a street corner with her friends. She'd leave work, drive to the supermarket, and see him in the parking lot shoveling grocery bags into the trunk of his friend Iggy's car.

"Stop stalking me," he'd tell her, and she would just laugh.

"I'm carving soap puppets with your name on them. Tonight I begin inserting pins. If you feel a sharp pain in your ass, that'll be me starting my campaign of voodoo and supernatural harassment."

They would go on dates and stop under flickering streetlamps to kiss. He would hold her face near his and breath in her unlikeliness, the surprise of her. He was urbane and she was disarmingly honest and together for some reason they made one sane, happy person and so they got married at a vineyard in Napa, surrounded by an odd collection of Chicago WASPs and Brooklyn unionites, who stood blinking at the rolling green foothills and sprawling California vineyards as if trying to remember if grass was the thing you walked on when concrete wasn't around or something you stayed off of because it was dangerous, though whether to the grass or the pedestrian they couldn't decide.

There had been a gurgling fountain and a band made up of some of Linus's friends from college, and Claudia in her long white wedding dress had been a pillar of pure light, with perfect hair and perfect lipstick and her face had been so smooth and happy and brilliant that Linus suddenly realized what it is that makes two people cling to each other for the balance of their lives, that makes them choose to endure the bulk of their time together, even if only to sit side by side on a couch and stare at the wall, and who, when apart, can do little more than wait from one phone call to the next.

The road descends in a gradual curve. A rusty pickup truck full of Indians passes him with one dull headlight pointed off at a crooked angle. Linus turns on the radio and tries to dial in KBYE in Truth or Consequences, New Mexico. The static pattern of shifting stations reminds Linus of cellular phones and computer modems, fax machines and walkie-talkies. It is the mechanical noise of technology, the language of robots and androids. Linus always resisted the growing importance of plug-in items in his life and work. Though he and Claudia have the money, he has never upgraded his PC past the lethargic 386 that squats sluggishly on his desk. He is not connected to the Internet, does not own a fax machine, a beeper, or a cell phone. When using an overhead projector in class he still fumbles around for the On switch. His VCR flashes zeros at him insistently.

On the other hand, Claudia has a beeper and a phone in her purse. *Had* a beeper and a phone, Linus must remind himself. Now there is just the purse and the beeper and the phone with no one to use them. She was a woman with tools, who brought to their marriage a mysterious knowledge of electric drills and levels. She understood the basic elements of construction, knew why wall studs were always placed sixteen inches apart. She knew what a monkey wrench was and how it differed from an Allen wrench. This knowledge in and of itself was compelling to Linus, who realized that people who understood how to use tools were somehow more adaptable, more likely to survive in the eventuality of a national emergency or nuclear war. He understood that the knowledge of tools was the difference between those people who saw life as a series of surmountable challenges and those who felt that control of their lives was always just beyond their reach. The understanding of hammers and screwdrivers. The familiarity of rulers and staple guns. The importance of power sanders and tabletop saws.

For Claudia technology was just another tool, like her glue guns and tire chains. A computer was a word processor, a data-storage device, a design aid. A phone was a communications device. None of these objects had any intrinsic value other than their usefulness. They held no mystery, no life of their own.

At night in the desert there is only the diffused glare of his headlights, the occasional road sign, the gleaming eyes of animals scattered across the swelling flats. Linus drives with the windows up, hypnotized by the muffled roar the Skylark makes as he eggs it up past sixty, the droning hum of the balding tires on pavement. Back in Tiburon he owns a 1983 Duster. It is his credibility car, the car of the left-wing college professor. Claudia drives a Saab, a trade-in from her last Saab, only seven months old. He considers it now in his mind, gleaming black, soft top, leather interior. It is a car he always felt like a fake riding in, let alone driving. He realizes that just as he needed his appearances of poverty and rusting integrity, she needed her sense of creative energy breeding wealth, intellectual confidence breeding class and style. It is the car they would take to dinners and parties with her friends from work, her business functions, his lopsided Plymouth hidden in the garage. For Linus it was this difference in class that was most dangerous between them, the unspoken struggle of all Americans. For him, integrity was in some way tied intrinsically to poverty. For her, achievement deserved reward, and she was proud of the fact that her family was reasonably wealthy, proud that she had managed in her education and career to maintain her life in the manner to which she had become accustomed.

Linus, on the other hand, became awkward around issues like savings accounts and mortgages. His parents had never owned a home. His father had never taken a vacation. They had never gone to Europe or even left the tristate area. Linus and Ford were the first of the Owen family to go to college. For Linus, money was something you kept in the bottom of a drawer, the underside of a mattress. Before Claudia he lived in student housing, a series of small, cluttered studio apartments with industrial carpeting and water stains on the ceilings. He ate food from cans, spent whatever money he had on books. He was aware of every penny his father never had, aware of how his parents would seem to his classmates, like uneducated dockworkers from Brooklyn. Linus struggled throughout high school and college to lose his Brooklyn mouth. There is still a New York flavor to his words, a Brooklyn inflection, unlike Ford, who seems now as if he had been born in a Connecticut villa and raised by English lords in Cambridge.

When Claudia and Linus were married he was dismayed to find that their combined salaries brought them in at just over ninety thousand dollars a year. Gifts arrived throughout their engagement, expensive cookware, glasses, china. They found a large two-bedroom apartment in the inner Sunset with a backyard and fireplace. Linus began to feel out of place. He had accustomed himself to wiping off dirty spoons and eating hummus from cans. Now he had silver and china and cobalt-blue water glasses. They had framed art and throw rugs. They would drive to the supermarket on the weekends in Claudia's Saab and buy over a hundred dollars' worth of groceries, whereas before, Linus could never remember spending more than thirteen. They ate out in nice restaurants. Claudia would bring him presents, jackets and slacks, a pair of oxblood wingtips. He understood that she was trying to mold him, to make him more presentable, but he didn't mind. For Linus, the clothes were not the point. He would wear slacks and jackets if it made her happy, as long as she understood who he was and where he came from.

"You know, I bet Ford wears socks like these," he might say as he was coaxed into throwing away his torn white sweat socks and wearing dress socks with shoes.

"They're socks. Are you telling me a pair of socks is going to turn you into an inside trader?"

But Linus never felt comfortable in gabardine. Dress socks reminded him of old men close to retirement who've had all the hair on their calves eroded away by years of shiny black stockings, pulled up and sagging, pulled up and sagging. He fought with Claudia to keep the T-shirts with moth holes, but over the years they ended up as rags used to stain tables and change tires. He turned thirty and found on his own that he no longer felt comfortable walking around in sneakers. One day he opened his closet and found that the uniform of his youth was missing and for a moment he felt, not like a sell-out, but like an old man who has grown out of his youth without realizing.

At eleven-thirty in the morning Linus pulls into a dirty driveway in Victory, New Mexico, just outside of Radium Springs. His mouth tastes of dirt and debris; his forehead is sunburned from the glare of the windshield. His plan is to speak to Cody's friend Luther, then drive north to Truth or Consequences, where he will begin to track Preston from his last known location. The house is a double-wide trailer with a tarp porch. There's a big propane tank hooked up to the side of the trailer and a collection of animal skulls of various sizes sitting on a blanket. A hand-drawn cardboard sign says ALL SKULLS $5.00. A small crooked dog lies in the shade on its stomach panting. There is a water dish a few inches from its head. The screen door of the trailer is open. Linus checks the address Cody gave him, looks at the mailbox. A man in shorts and sandals comes out of the trailer. He's in his forties, a few days unshaven.

"The snake skulls are two dollars. They're real rattlers, though this one's a garden snake, I think." He nudges one of the skulls with his toe.

"I'm looking for Luther K."

"FBI?"

"FFC. Friend of Fisher Cody."

The man nods.

"You Linus."

"That's right."

"Me and Fisher got a system. He wants to get in touch with me he sends a letter to Freddie Baker over at the gas station. Nobody reads Freddie's mail. He's a sex junkie. Yesterday he comes over with a copy of *Backdoor Beauties* and a letter from F.C. saying you was coming. Says you want to know about Preston."

"That's right."

Luther nods, looks at his watch.

"Let me put the skulls inside and then we can go over to Harvey's and get some lunch."

They drive a half mile into town with the skinny dog standing in the bed of Luther's pickup. Harvey's is a dark narrow bar with mostly meat on the menu. Linus has a beer and a burger. Luther orders ribs. The waitress is a tired blonde with crow's feet and a ratty apron. Inside is a scattered collection of old men and young who Linus, in his romanticizing of the West, assumes are ranch hands, but are mostly truckers.

"I moved here in 'seventy-one," Luther says. The dog sits on the floor under his feet and pants. It has seven toes on its front right paw. "I had a degree in physics from MIT. I went to work at Los Alamos, building better bombs, et cetera, et cetera, et cetera. It was fine. A little awe-inspiring. I was pretty cocky, you know. Top of my class. Sometimes when you're that smart you think you understand God. Everybody else seems so slow. It was hard for me to even talk to anyone not in my field. I had a tendency to yell *Eureka* in crowded theaters. In nine months I had designed a detonator delivery system that was years ahead of what we'd been using. I began experimenting with various types of cold fusion. I had a vision of creating black-hole bombs. I was intrigued by the question of antimatter. Six months later I went native, moved into a trailer. I felt my first priority was to get a dog."

The food arrives. Linus begins on his beer.

"Did Cody tell you why I'm looking for Preston?"

"Nope."

Linus talks into his beer.

"He killed my wife, but I don't really want to go into it."

Luther shrugs, pours ketchup on his plate.

"Have you ever seen an atomic accelerator, a cyclotron?"

Linus shakes his head.

"Scientists have no business uncovering the secrets of the atom. This much is clear to me now. We're like children playing with matches. Sure we can do it. Sure we can design a device that can force isotopes of uranium into each other with enough force to blow up twenty-one miles of city streets, but why would we want to? It's just arrogance."

"My main concern right now is what's wrong with Preston and where do I find him. Other people will have to wait."

"He's nuts is what's wrong with him. Everybody on this planet is nuts, though. Fluorocarbons destroying the ozone and people are still flaring Aqua Net at their heads."

"I drove four hundred miles in three and a half days. I need something more specific than fluorocarbons and Aqua Net."

"He's bald. He's a bald man. Is that specific enough? Maybe five-eleven, blue eyes. He wears a lot of hats, because he doesn't like being bald. And he's fucking nuts."

"I'm with you. You've hooked me with your clever opener. Don't let me up for air. Press on."

"I haven't made love to a woman in six years."

Linus shakes his head, picks up his burger.

"You need to work on your continuity."

"I made a lot of sacrifices when I left Los Alamos. There were choices. Hard choices that had to be made. I was disillusioned by science. I considered pursuing religion. I thought about going back to New Hampshire and starting a landscaping business. I needed time to listen to the wind, think things through."

"Who wouldn't."

Luther picks up a rib, gnaws the meat off the bone. He has stubble maybe a week old.

"I was humbled. I saw myself in relation to the amazing powers of the universe. A fly, a speck."

"And therefore unlayable, is that what you're telling me?"

"Last time I saw Preston was three months ago. He was with a guy he called Porter. Told me Porter was ex-CIA, a former employee of the Area 51 military complex. I told him I'd be more impressed if he laughed milk out of his nose."

"Good. Keep talking. I'll get us more beer."

"Porter was short, stocky. One eye was a little higher than the other. He kept a knife in his boot. I'm used to men with knives in their boots. Out here in the great Wild West, who doesn't have a knife in their boot?"

"Focus."

"Preston and I met in 'eighty-five. I went on his show a few times to talk about nuclear practices at Los Alamos. He was interested in history, in details. He wanted to hear about accidents during the Manhattan Project. He wanted to talk about the nuclear mystique of the desert. We took phone calls from housewives in Nebraska whose sons lived in missile silos eleven months out of the year. He was up in Truth or Consequences and I'd drive up sometimes and we'd have dinner. If he had some especially famous kook in town to do the show he'd throw a big party, have some Mexican girls cater. They'd spend the night talking about alien technology and Jewish bankers. I told them the problem was more basic. It was the presumption of science. I told them that the biggest problem was curiosity. We should all be satisfied to know our immediate world, I said. Learn the names of the trees on your block, understand the annual rainfall. What is the population of your town? Why does a car run? Who invented the chemical fireplace log? I am an enemy of a universal theory of everything. I hunger now for uncertainty. Otherwise we are looking at the death of imagination."

"But we'll have the fanciest CD players you ever saw."

Luther wipes barbecue sauce on his leg and the dog climbs to its feet and begins to lick it off.

"For the most part no one wanted to talk about science. For them, mystery itself was the enemy. What they wanted were facts, hard knowledge. I argued that the complete absence of facts was a far more preferable way of life."

"And then he disappeared."

"Yes."

"Tax problems, extramarital activity? He was a well-recognized personality, had a profitable mail-order company for Question Authority merchandise. Why walk away?"

"He started taking longer trips into the desert. He was arrested once or twice for trespassing on government property. He wanted to get inside government bases. I think the secrecy was eating at him. He wanted to know, once and for all."

"Does he belong to a group called Danton?"

Luther shrugs, drinks his beer.

"People obsessed by secrecy often start secret groups of their own."

"Where is he?"

"He moves around."

"He was here three months ago. Did he go north or south when he left, east or west?"

"If I had to guess I'd say Utah or Nevada."

"That narrows it down."

"Try Canyonlands. Try the small towns near Nellis. He'll hide near a base. He's a fan of irony."

"What is the obsession, the motivation? I need to understand."

"He is both fascinated and terrified by the devices we've created to engineer our own destruction. It's just the wait is driving him nuts."

"He's not alone?"

"Other than Porter I hear he's got maybe one or two more guys. He likes to keep a low profile. He's done the public doom-crying. A smaller group frees him to act. He told me that originally they had considered calling their group the Guinea Pig Militia. The point is a revolution of patients against the arrogance and clinical detachment of doctors. He is moved by a fear of secret government testing, nuclear, chemical, viral."

"Why blow up a plane flying from New York to Brazil?"

"If he did it, then there must have been a reason. I wouldn't stray too far from theories that surround the issue of covert experimentation."

"A new drug. This is the rumor."

"Think of him as an animal backed into a corner. His rationale would be one of self-defense. When I knew him during the radio show he walked around with .357 magnum strapped to his hip. He slept in a locked room with no windows."

"What's in it for this Porter guy?"

"Question not the motives of the seriously disturbed. Other than the knife in the boot, this guy had a collection of semiautomatic weapons in the trunk of his car. I wouldn't doubt he knows all the terrible karate chops made famous by Mr. Spock on *Star Trek*."

"What about the others?"

"He talks sometimes when he stops by. I sell him a couple of skulls. For me there's a lot of loneliness. I tend to get drunk and throw myself emotionally at women. I have an embarrassing tendency to cry. Darla here in the apron. I can't tell you how many times I've propositioned her through a blubbering veil of tears."

"A man alone never betrays himself."

"Isn't that one of those lines from *Kung Fu*? Listen carefully, Grasshopper, a man alone never betrays himself."

"My point is, if you stay out of love then you avoid a world of pain."

"The thing I love about Darla is her feet. You can't tell now in those shoes, but all her toes are exactly the same length, from the big toe to the pinkie toe. It's the symmetry I love. She is a woman with absolutely even feet."

"And the others, besides Porter?"

"Sometimes he talks about computers. He talks about fighting viruses with viruses. I would guess he has some kind of computer pro and maybe a local to sneak him around."

"A local of where? Here?"

Luther shrugs. He feeds pork to his dog.

"Try St. George, where the downwinders live. Try Los Alamos. Look for a bald man in a funny hat walking around with a psychotic WASP."

"Is there any reason for me to go to Truth or Consequences?"

"Cold trail. Forget the radio program. The radio program is ancient history. Think about irony. Preston is a man for whom the ultimate revenge is the most ironic. The bomb, if it was him, was heavy-handed. Maybe he was short on time, or maybe he didn't do it at all. He's more the type to buy a test tube full of anthrax from a disgruntled scientist and put it in the refrigerator of the president of the Centers for Disease Control."

Linus stares at his half-eaten burger. He has lost five pounds in the last week.

"This is like a needle in a haystack."

"If a man really wants to disappear, then the desert is the place to do it. My impression, though, is that Preston has an agenda. He hides, but he resurfaces. I wouldn't be surprised if there wasn't a manifesto somewhere."

"Will he come back here?"

"Last time I saw him was three months ago. Before that, six months. There's no guarantee."

Linus wonders what he's doing sitting in a diner in the middle of New Mexico talking to a former nuclear physicist who now sells animal skulls out of a trailer. He takes a deep breath, lets it out, and realizes that these kinds of meetings are as routine to his life as shaving. He understands suddenly that without the outcasts and disgruntled paranoiacs he would have no friends, no work, no grounding. No wonder Claudia was leaving me, he thinks. I am a small man who exists on the fear of other people.

"Do you know where I could get a gun?"

"Rifle or pistol?"

"What's the difference?"

"Rifle's easier. Pistol has a waiting period."

Linus finishes his beer, looks down at the cuffs of his jeans.

"Do you think that every American life eventually comes down to a question of bullets?"

"It's the capacity for destruction. I think when you finally meet Preston you're going to have a lot to talk about. Imagine me, a skinny kid from New Hampshire designing detonators for hydrogen bombs. It all comes back to Oppenheimer's 'Now I am become death, destroyer of worlds.' I see it as the frustration of mortality, the fear of death manifesting in a fundamental need to control life. Why do people become doctors, policemen, soldiers? It all has to do with the saving and ending of life. Who am I to build a better bomb? Don't I know better? Didn't my mother teach me anything? In my case the answer is yes, but it took time to sink in.

"For Preston I think the vision of death has made him worship death. Just as he couldn't stand the mystery of not knowing the secrets of the government, so is he fundamentally unable to live with the ultimate mysteries of life. He needs facts. I think Preston has worked to strip the extraneous from his life, but he can't forget it's out there. It gnaws at him. He becomes suspicious of it. Modern life has an agenda to absorb him, to control and manipulate him. He imagines executives from Nike conspiring with SWAT teams to parachute into his stronghold and force him to wear fluorescent high-tops, death squads from Fortune 500 companies. I must strike first, he thinks. Only then will I be safe."

Linus pays the check and he and Luther and the dog drive back along pitted roads to Luther's trailer. Linus stands on Luther's fried-dead lawn, throws a ball for the dog. Luther goes into his house, comes out with a shovel. He circles to the back of the trailer, digs a hole. In a few minutes he comes back with a dirty clump of what looks like clothes. He hands it to Linus, who stares at it suspiciously. On closer examination what Luther is proffering is an old dirt-encrusted T-shirt wrapped with string. Luther cuts the string with a knife he pulls out of his boot. Inside the crusty T-shirt is a gun.

"So you don't end up disappearing into the desert," says Luther. Linus takes the gun and puts it in his jacket pocket. It's a revolver that looks like it may be from the 1940s.

"Does it work?"

"That's the funny thing about guns. With the proper maintenance they last forever."

"Yes, but this one has been buried in a shirt under your house since maybe 1981."

Luther crumples up the T-shirt and drops it on the ground. He wipes his hands on his pants legs.

"It works."

Linus sighs, stares at his battered old car, the rust spots like lesions in the sun. He has chased a rubber ball to the edge of a cliff. He considers opening his own scavenged-skull shop in the trailer next door. I will change my name to Barney, he thinks. When people ask me about my past I will say simply that I served my adult career in the food service industry. The purpose of my life is to forget more than I have ever had to remember.

"Any last thoughts on where I might look next?" he says.

Luther scratches at his beard. His skin is brown and dry. He is a man who has turned his back on math to embrace chaos.

"Preston is a great believer in the apocalypse and a big fan of irony. That's the most I can say."

So Linus gets back in his car, makes a wide U-turn, and drives toward Doom Town.

As he drives, sweating, half blinded by sunlight, Linus considers what he has learned about Preston. Scraps of innuendo, the character assassinations of kooks. Near an indolent mugging of cattle he pulls onto the shoulder of a two-lane road, reviews Fisher Cody's letter. It has a different resonance now that he is sitting in a red clay valley surrounded by silence and stone. He rolls down his window, feels the dry wind on his face. The radio emits only static. From Cody's jagged handwriting no real clues arise. He has nothing in the way of facts, in the way of leads. If Luther K. says Preston is a fan of irony, then Linus's hunch is to drive to Nevada, to the Nellis Air Force Base, where in the early fifties a town was built for the sole purpose of explosion. Rows of houses, stores, schools, churches inhabited by mannequins, filled on the morning of each atomic test with food flown in from San Francisco, Texas, New Mexico. Here the army blew away suburban American communities on sweltering days in June, little Billy on his bicycle, Dad with his hose watering the lawn, Mom in her modern kitchen glazing a swollen ham. It was necessary to understand the potential for damage, for death and the destruction of property. It was important to test the exposure to radiation, the punishing wind and brutalizing glare. This was Doom Town, now just a cluster of architecturally unsound buildings, sunburned, seldom visited, long forgotten. This is where Linus envisions the enemies of government testing might be hiding.

In Ash Fork, Arizona, he succumbs to a sudden stabbing pain in the gut. At a roadside Chevron station Linus sits on a filthy toilet, clutching the edge of the sink for support. The scene is a painting from the modern Bible, *Job with Ragged Mop;* a forsaken man, gray, shadowy, matched wanly against a gray backdrop. The single bulb swings slowly from the ceiling, encrusted by dirt, throwing a cloudy light. The corners of the room are dark. Water dripping from sweating ceiling pipes. The smell of ammonia and anonymous human waste. A rusty bucket cups a moldy mop in a filthy corner. Outside, the sun slips magnificently into the horizon, an aging diva putting on a stunning performance to an empty house. Linus has reached the void here in Arizona, home of John Glenn, senator, astronaut, and also of the biggest hole known to man. What fullness remains to him must be expelled now, purged finally in this filthy rest stop. He holds his nose, chokes. His own smell nauseates him. He wonders if there are any answers left that can make suffering these indignities worthwhile.

He stumbles out of the restroom feeling weak. A second car sits at the pumps, a blue Volvo. Next to it is a man in a black windbreaker and gray Perry Ellis pants. He has an expensive Nikon leveled at the collapsing gas station. Linus wanders over to the withered attendant, who sits on a stool in a dark booth watching an old color television with a dent in the top. Linus asks him if he should pump the gas himself. Do I have to pay first? The man looks up. One of his eyes is milky. He shuffles out to Linus's junker, screws off the gas cap. Linus hovers around him, trying to decide whether to help or duck back into the corroded restroom.

"Ever been to the Grand Canyon?" says the man in the windbreaker. He has taken the camera from around his neck and rested it on the roof of his car.

"Pardon?"

"The Grand Canyon. It's a big hole in the ground."

"Yes. I know what the Grand Canyon is."

"Ever been there?"

"No."

The man in the windbreaker picks his teeth with the nail of his right pinkie.

"Me either."

Linus opens the passenger door of his car, takes out a plastic water bottle. He considers drinking, feels his stomach gurgle, puts it back on the seat. As he waits, dusk settles, creating an ambiguous glow. Depth perception fades and becomes finally impossible, except perhaps for looking inward. The man in the windbreaker picks up his camera, takes Linus's picture, the flash shattering the growing sense of visual calm. Linus jumps.

"Jesus Christ."

"Sorry. I just bought the thing. I haven't got the hang of it yet. Sometimes it just goes off."

The old man slides the hose from Linus's car, puts it back on the pump. He moves around with audible effort, his breath coming in little huffs and grunts. He asks Linus for seven dollars and eighty cents. Linus gives him a ten and he shuffles back to the booth for change. A dark dust stirs up, blows across the cars. Over the roof of the gas station the moon begins to rise, full and orange. It is swollen, a luminescent orb larger than Linus has ever seen. He leans against the hood of his car and stares at it. For a brief moment he feels awe, a sense of beauty that pushes through his hardened skin, blows into his lungs like a sudden wind.

"Look at that," he says. "Would you look at that."

The man in the windbreaker's answer is to stick Linus with a hypodermic needle.

He wakes up in the passenger seat of the Volvo. The car is streaking across a dark highway. Linus grabs the door handle, claws at the lock, manages to pry it open against the resistance of automotive velocity. Cold wind batters him, a roaring noise. He is prepared to jump out onto the road, whatever the speed. The man in the windbreaker reaches over and clubs him on the back of the head.

The next time he wakes up, his hands are tied behind his back with plastic bag-tie handcuffs. His head is throbbing, feels cracked. His fingers are numb. He thinks about the gun sitting under the passenger seat of his car back at the gas station. Next time he should keep it on him, though given his current predicament next time may be a different life.

"What time is it?"

The man in the windbreaker looks at his watch.

"Eleven."

Linus nods. His mouth tastes sour. He catches his own eye in the reflection of the windshield, turns his head, ashamed.

"Is this for something I did, or just a random kidnapping?"

The man in the windbreaker takes out a cigarette, lights it.

"Something you did."

Linus nods again.

"I guess you're supposed to tell me to stop nosing around things that don't concern me. You're supposed to say, 'You know what happens to nosy parkers, Mr. Gittes?' "

The man in the windbreaker smiles. It's so rare to get a subject with the thoughtfulness to joke.

"They get their noses cut," he says.

"They get their noses cut. That's right."

The man in the windbreaker rolls down his window and blows smoke into the night. The jacket makes a crinkling noise whenever he moves.

"The rental car company doesn't like people to smoke in the cars," he explains.

"Oh," says Linus.

"I should quit anyway."

"Hey, don't let the politically correct masses get to you," says Linus. "What about your personal freedoms? Smoke on, I say. It may be the last politically rebellious act we have."

The man in the windbreaker shrugs.

"I could lose my deposit."

Linus moves his fingers to see if he can feel them. He tries to sum up his life in a few simple sentences. Here lies Linus Owen, always chasing shadows.

"You know what I want to know? Why are people so preoccupied by conspiracies? Here I am running around in the middle of the desert chasing smoke."

The man in the windbreaker grunts. His name is Wiley Lutts. In high school he was voted most likely to disappear without a trace.

"You're the professor."

Linus shrugs.

"Sure, and if I'm so smart, how come I'm sitting in this car trussed up like a rodeo bull?"

The man in the windbreaker reaches into the glove compartment and takes out a dark red McIntosh apple, wipes it on his sleeve, takes a bite out of it.

"Good point."

They drive for a while, a lone flare sputtering through the night.

"I guess it's got something to do with superstition," Wiley says, after a pause so long that Linus has assumed the conversation is over.

"How so?"

"Well, you know, believing in conspiracies is like the last piece we got left of believing in ghosts or vampires or shit like Frankenstein."

Linus tries to rub an itch on his face with the shoulder of his shirt, turning his head into it, once, twice, three times.

"And politics? Talk to me about politics. And how about money while you're at it."

The man in the windbreaker shrugs.

"I don't follow politics, but I pay attention to people. In my job you got to pay attention to people."

"Your job being?"

"I take people for long drives, ask them questions. Mostly they don't come back."

Linus watches the darkness float by.

"You must dig a lot of holes."

Wiley scratches his head, windbreaker crinkling. The sound is beginning to wear on Linus, its artificial qualities, synthetic on synthetic.

"It's the filling them in that's bad. After you've dug them and done what you have to do to put the person in there. Usually you're tired. I try to bring a meat sandwich with me to keep my strength up."

Linus considers this last sentence and tries to decide if it is a thing a rational person might say.

"So you put a bullet in a guy and then sit on the hood of your car and eat a sandwich?"

"I tried protein shakes and them—what do you call 'em—power bars, but it's like eating dirt."

Wiley shudders. Having spent seven years burying bodies, there's nothing more unsettling than the thought of eating dirt. Another silent minute passes. Linus tries to remember what life was like when he was a child, the things he thought about, the way the world looked. There is a sense of overwhelming relief in some part of him that he will soon cease asking questions altogether, that he can finally follow Claudia and not have to face an endless life alone.

"There's God, right," says Wiley. "And some people believe in Him, but they mostly believe these days in science. And it's the science part that keeps them from accepting that mysteries don't always have an explanation. So bad things happen and they got to find a reason. Somebody's got to be responsible."

"Even when they've got somebody to blame, though, people still look for them. They turn over every rock. Look at me. Look at my life. At least try to tell me, before you put me in a hole, why it is I spent my whole life trying to prove that for every evil there is some nefarious, elite group secretly plotting."

Wiley picks a piece of apple peel from between his molars.

"All right, buddy. You're getting a little blubbery now. They just pay me to ask questions, not to philosophize."

"Who pays you?"

"Rowdy Roddy Piper. Now will you shut up."

Linus looks at his own reflection in the windshield of the car. He moves his head gingerly, feels something slosh, thinks, Maybe I have a concussion.

"I bet you get a lot of last requests," he says.

"You wouldn't believe."

Linus closes his eyes. Wiley steers the car with his right knee, adjusts his mirrors. Linus leans back, tries to arrange himself so he can be comfortable sitting on his numb hands. He rests his head against the seat and for a minute is surprised to find that he could almost fall asleep. He watches the white lines shooting under the car, listens to the hum of the wheels turning against pavement. He thinks about Claudia, her long delicate hands. It is the sense of finality that relaxes him, the knowledge that everything is drawing to a conclusion.

"I guess you have some questions for me," he says.

Wiley takes another bite of the apple. He chews.

"You gonna answer them?"

"Sure, why not. That's what I do. I learn things and then I teach them to other people. It always seemed like a sort of noble thing to do."

"My sister's a teacher. Fifth grade back in Queens. Kids today. Shit."

"I was going to have kids myself someday. I kind of looked forward to teaching them. I thought I might be good at that, you know?"

"I got a boy and a girl. The boy's eight years old. He's got some kind of gift for chess. He beats guys five times his age. Some kind of kid."

Linus pulls his knees up, puts his feet on the edge of the seat. His arms feel like they might twist out of the sockets. He wonders if anybody will miss him after he's gone the way he misses her.

"We were going to have kids soon. I can almost close my eyes and turn back the clock and see her, you know."

"Your wife?"

Linus nods.

"She was in the wrong place at the wrong time," says Wiley.

There is a certain unarguable quality to this kind of statement. Linus sighs.

"She was always scared of planes."

"I take buses. Trains too. I had to fly out here. Drank six beers before I got on the plane."

"But they called you, so you came."

"The phone rings. You pick it up and you've already made a deal. The next step is small by comparison."

"You work for Forbes."

Wiley snorts. It's his way of laughing.

"Forbes," he says derisively.

"Hastings?"

Wiley bites, chews again. He checks his rearview mirror, then his sides.

"They want me to ask you some questions. Then I'm supposed to introduce you to the ground."

Linus turns his head to look into the backseat. He can't see the shovel. Wiley pulls out a cigarette, pushes in the lighter.

"It's in the trunk."

Linus wipes his face on the shoulder of his shirt again, hunching his shoulder, turning his head.

"Forbes'll be pissed," he says. "I'm working for him, you know."

Wiley shakes his head.

"First of all, I doubt very much you're working for Forbes, and second, even if you are, big deal. Forbes is not a player in this scenario."

Linus gives his own tiny snort, thinks, Isn't it always the case. He feels pulled in every direction.

"We could call him, maybe. See what he has to say."

Wiley makes a face, disgust and impatience.

"Give me a break, will ya? I thought you were gonna be, what, classy maybe. The begging wears on a guy's nerves after a while."

Linus sits forward, leans his forehead on the dashboard.

"This is really uncomfortable," he says.

"I could pull over right here, put you out of your misery."

Linus thinks about it.

"Did you kill my wife?" he says.

"No. Bombs ain't my business."

"But somebody from Hastings?"

Wiley rolls down his window, flicks his cigarette butt into the night. It flies back, bounces along the road, a tiny cinder quickly fading from sight.

"I don't want to have to put you in the trunk."

Linus sits back slowly. His forehead is red where he placed weight on it. He sighs.

"You want to know what I know?" he says. "I know Hastings made a drug. I know they sold it to the government. I know the government tested it on people, whom it killed. I know that a group named Danton is somehow involved in all this. That's what I know."

"Who'd you tell?"

"Nobody."

"You told Colby Wood."

"That was just fast food. There was no information exchanged. She's an old friend of my wife's."

"Don't lie."

"A college girlfriend."

"I said, don't lie."

"I hate to break it to you, son, but there is no Colby Wood. She's just a figment of your imagination."

Wiley smiles.

"She I had to put in the trunk."

Linus chews his lip. His nose starts to bleed, the blood running over his lip and down his chin. He's actually kind of happy that it does so, as if the nosebleed is an old friend who has surprised him in an airport or bowling alley.

"That's too bad."

"She was distraught."

"Who wouldn't be. A sudden kidnapping. A strange, violent man. A long drive."

Wiley considers the apple, chooses to smoke instead.

"When it's a rental car you worry about damage. If there's damage you don't get your deposit back."

Linus considers breaking something like a window or a dial, then decides that might go badly for him. He figures he will just bleed quietly onto the floor in the dark, passive-aggressive to the end.

"I guess I should say I wrote this all down and mailed it to different people."

"Most people say shit like that. They offer me money. That's number one. Number two is they tell me that if they don't make a call by a certain time, an unnamed party is going to release information. It's like a threat, except a threat you have to believe for it to work and I don't."

"So they just go in the ground."

Wiley shrugs. His face is free of ethnic identifiers. He has a high hairline, keeps his hair short. His teeth are straight and white. At home he drives a Porsche. His wife thinks he's a traveling salesman who works for a large cable-television distributor. He could tell you the names of the players on every New York Yankees team since 1941.

"I don't take people for a ride unless I'm sure they aren't going to come back from the grave and kick me in the butt. I'm hired to provide a service. That service is to bury the issue along with the guy. I don't do that, some other guy comes looking for *me*."

Linus looks at the dashboard, watches the apple turn brown where it has been bitten.

"You know every place I've been, don't you?"

"Since you left Loyal's office over a week ago."

Linus licks his lips, tastes the familiar flavor. Blood. The carpet under his feet is starting to stain, small drops spreading into bigger clusters.

"Does Forbes know?"

Another look of disgust.

"I would hope a major corporation could afford better help than the fucking government."

"Civil servants, you're implying."

Wiley picks up the apple, takes another bite, chews quietly, then nods. Linus swallows blood.

"So Forbes doesn't know where I am?"

"Forbes wouldn't know his own ass if he sat on it."

Linus shrugs. Everything seems to have jumped out of his league. Wiley clears his throat, hawks something up, spits it out the window.

"He's distracted lately, you mean?"

"It's those pills. Never sample the merchandise. They teach you that day one. Never sample the fucking merchandise." Wiley once spent two summers living in California. He broke into people's houses and stole things while they slept. Usually he just did it to prove it could be done.

Linus tries to focus on what Wiley is saying.

"Drugs, is it?"

"Guy's got a fucking crate of untested medicine in his house. He pops those fucking pills like they were going out of style."

"The ones from the Nevada test?"

"That shit killed people. You wouldn't catch me doing drugs I know kill people. What am I, a dumb ass?"

Linus shakes his head.

"Definitely not a dumb ass."

Wiley nods, face serious.

"Damn right."

Linus thinks about Forbes taking pills meant to paralyze the fear and aggression centers of the brain.

"Aren't you ever afraid?" he asks.

Wiley checks his mirrors. They haven't seen another car for ten minutes.

"Two times I been afraid. Once when I'm five years old my brother's fucking tarantula gets out of the tank, ends up in my bed. The second time I'm fourteen. I'm about to lose my virginity with a thirty-two-year-old lady whose pool I just cleaned."

"I'm afraid all the time."

Wiley rolls up his window, fixes his hair, which has become windblown.

"Takes all kinds."

They pass a sign for a historical monument. Wiley starts to slow the car. Linus feels a sudden panic in his chest, is surprised to find that when it comes right down to it he wants to live. The car pulls off the road onto a dirt trail. The ride is bumpy, Linus's teeth chattering against his tongue.

"Fucking hundred-thousand-dollar hit and I'm driving a goddamned Volvo," says Wiley, watching the road for sudden dips and craters.

"A blue Volvo."

Wiley makes a gesture, as if to say, *Thank you,* or maybe, *Exactly. I'm glad at least you can understand the indignity.*

Linus pulls his wrists at the restraints. They cut into his skin but won't snap. He considers ways he might escape. Most of them involve having free hands and the gun that's sitting under the seat of his monkey-shit-brown car. Through the darkness he can make out the stunted forms of Joshua trees and bounding brush. The car makes a sudden quick left turn and comes to a stop, the headlights illuminating a long hole in the ground. Wiley puts the car in park, turns off the engine, leaving the lights on. He turns to glance at Linus. His eyes don't seem to look in the same direction.

"You told nobody, right?" he says.

"Actually, wait. It's coming back to me."

Wiley opens his door, spits into the dirt.

"Yeah, yeah."

The open door lets in the scent of the cold, dry desert wind. Linus thinks about Edward and Roy. He wouldn't be surprised to see two holes next to his own. He has never hit a man in the face, an oversight in his life that will probably get him killed if the opportunity to fight arises, which he can't foresee its doing. Wiley circles around the front of the car, cutting through the two long beams of light. He opens Linus's door.

"Let's go," he says.

"Hold on, let me fix my makeup."

"Out."

Linus climbs out painfully. He is glad that his knees don't buckle under him. This would be a sign that the fear had won out, and if he is to be Job he at least wants to be Job with dignity. Wiley closes the door behind him, goes to the trunk and gets his shovel. He rests it against the passenger-side door. He has yet to notice Linus's bloody nose.

"I've got a last request," says Linus.

"Save it."

Wiley walks over to the hole, inspects it. He called ahead to Phoenix, left a message on an answering machine. A man named Lamar drove out here this morning and dug it. Wiley eyes the hole, looks at Linus.

"It's a little short."

"I've been growing recently."

"No shit?"

"Two inches since October."

Wiley unsnaps his shoulder holster, thinks about whether he wants Linus to stand in front of the hole or in it.

"See, I bet you want to blame that on some fucking conspiracy too."

Linus smiles, is grateful for the opportunity to do so one last time.

"The thought had occurred to me."

"Look, Professor. I like you. I don't want to put you in the ground feeling bad."

"So I can go?"

"Hey, right. I don't like you that much. No, I'm gonna tell you something my dad told me when I was ten. Something that makes a lot of sense to me and might help you feel better about why things happen."

Linus takes a deep, shaky breath. He is afraid, in the end, to die. What if Claudia's not waiting for him on the other side? What if she's standing on a Charmin cloud with Holden? The risks seem too great.

"I'd appreciate that," he says.

Wiley takes a pistol out of his jacket, slips out the clip, checks to make sure it's fully loaded.

"I was ten, right, like I said, and my dad comes in to me and my brother's room. He's got to tell us our grandma's dead. It's his own mother, so he's been crying. Me and my brother, we've never seen our dad crying, so right away we know some heavy shit is up. He sits us down on the bed, takes our hands. He tells us that Bubby—that's what we called my grandma—he says, Hey, kids, Bubby's passed on, you know. And my brother, he's twelve, he says, Like died? Like she died? And my dad says, Yeah, but he says, I don't want you kids to be sad. You should know that your Bubby had a real long life and she did lots of stuff she really liked and she had five great kids and twenty grandkids and so she died happy. But he could see that me and Robby were really upset and he felt bad and so he hugged us and sat down on the bed and he said, I want to tell you something about life that my dad told me when I was a kid. So we wiped our eyes and shut up, and he looked us right in the eye and said..."

A gray-haired man in a black sweatshirt pops up from the far side of the car and puts two bullets into Wiley, knocking him back two steps, the sound of the gun astonishingly loud. For a minute

Wiley looks intensely shocked, almost comically startled. He holds up his own gun, but only so he can put his hand to his chest to feel the bullet holes. His feet do a weird sort of shuffle dance in the dirt, his heels going over the lip of the grave. He opens his mouth, and his eyes lock on Linus's. For a second they are thinking the same thought: What's happening to me? Am I dying? And then he loses his footing and falls back into the hole. Linus's heart is racing, the blood roaring in his ears. He realizes that he has gone involuntarily into a sort of half crouch. He looks up at the man with gray hair, who's come out around the front of the car and is staring into the hole. He turns back toward Linus, puts his gun away.

"Fucking hell," says Linus.

"I think he's dead."

"Fucking hell."

"You said that."

"Shit. How about that? How about shit?"

The man shrugs, goes around behind Linus, cuts his cuffs off with a knife he takes out of his boot.

"You're Linus Owen."

Linus rubs his wrists. He does it to give his mind time to get working again. The man puts his knife back into the top of his boot.

"And you have to be Porter."

Porter raises an eyebrow, an affect lost to Linus, who stands panting in the dark. Exhaling cold air, Porter rubs his hand against the stubble on his cheek.

"Luther K. called me. He wanted us to know someone was snooping around."

"That was me. The snoop."

"Yeah, great."

Porter rubs his hands together, looks over at the hole. He claps his hands together and turns back to Linus.

"Okay, now that we've gotten the introductions out of the way, I'm going to have to ask you to take off your clothes and climb into the trunk of my car."

Linus considers this for a moment. There is a man lying dead in a lopsided hole fifteen feet away.

"What kind of car?"

"Huh?"

"What kind of car is it? It's a question of trunk space."

"Acura Legend."

"I'm definitely not getting into the trunk of an Acura."

Porter shrugs, begins to walk away from the Volvo back toward the road.

"Fine," he says, "but you're going to have to climb into the hole to get the keys to this yuppie's blue Volvo."

Linus thinks about that. Porter stops just outside the range of the headlights.

"And you'll never get to see Preston."

Linus feels a growing sense of anger. One that's been building since this whole thing began. He walks to the back of the Volvo and squints into the darkness.

"Why do I have to take my clothes off?"

"I have to check you for devices."

"And the trunk?"

"Nobody can know where we hide."

Linus takes a step away from the light. His eyes try to adjust to the dark.

"And I'll get to see Preston," says Linus, then realizes he doesn't have his gun. He will have to find some other way to kill him. This thought from a man who has never once struck a living thing in anger.

"Preston is writing the manifesto, but he'll take a break to speak to you."

Ah, the manifesto, thinks Linus. End of the twentieth century and every well-armed constitutionalist thinks he's Martin Luther.

"How do I know you're not just going to kill me?"

Porter points to the hole. Linus sighs.

"Couldn't you have waited until he was done with his story? It might have meant a great deal."

Porter is getting impatient. If it had been up to him Linus would be the one lying in that hole and Porter himself would be back at the compound pushing Preston to go public already, for God's sake. Preston, however, lives for an audience, a trait that Porter figures will get them all killed. He taps his foot gently on the ground, looks at his watch.

"He wasn't going to tell you anything you didn't know already. The guy's a hit man, for Christ's sake. What kind of advice is a hit man going to give you that doesn't sound like a comic book or a Hallmark card?"

Linus sighs again, shrugs.

"I gotta see Preston," he says.

Porter picks a sesame seed from between his teeth with his car key.

"Then let's go."

The trunk of the car is like a coffin. Porter drives northwest, changing from paved to dirt roads, sometimes traversing open fields to avoid detection. The car jerks and bucks, bruising Linus's back and legs and his already sensitive head, sending him ricocheting around the black interior. He becomes disoriented quickly, the cold constricting his extremities in toward center. The first hour passes. On the straightaways he feels around at the unfamiliar objects sharing the cramped boot with him. He can make out a set of road flares, which feel waxy and phallic and could be dynamite, a thought that comes to him as he carefully touches the capped tops and bottoms. There is also something that feels like a pie tin and a small length of rope. In the front, Porter listens to country music. Linus can make out the strains of Patsy Cline, of George Strait. The road makes a rubber hiss under the tires, a sound that merges with a feel, velocity and vibration. Occasionally there is a flood of red light when Porter brakes or a flashing yellow glow when he signals a right or left turn. In these uncomfortable illuminations Linus studies the inhuman qualities of his skin, glowing as if from radiation exposure or neon light. He puts his hands up before his face, places them against the tail end of the trunk, watches the red glow illuminate the webbing between his fingers, the gold wedding band. He remembers the circus flashlights from when he was a kid and his parents would take them to Ringling Brothers up at Madison Square Garden. Palm-size red plastic rectangles snaked with a thin red cord, devices he and Ford and Alice would swing over their heads along with a hundred thousand other children as elephants and strong men lumbered in the three rings below, the crowd above making the world's first electronic wave.

In the front, Porter drums his fingers on the steering wheel. He has never been a great believer in words. He was a stammerer until fifth grade, a condition that robbed him of any real appreciation of language. Words for him became a source of embarrassment. I think in pictures, he tells people today. I dream in voices. Words are a form of deception. I think one thing. I say another. I do a third. What's the truth? It is this status as a cynic of language that makes him the most uncomfortable with Preston's decision to write a manifesto rather than act. There is only so much time, Porter told him last week as they crouched in the storm cellar waiting for the sounds of black helicopters. Preston remained unswayed. A thing not done well, he said, may as well not be done at all. Porter covered his ears with his hands like a four-year-old and made a series of dronelike noises with his mouth.

He crosses the border into Nevada, heads north to Las Vegas. He drives at speeds in excess of one hundred miles an hour, crosses the nuclear landscape, the desert miles. In a Kmart in St. George two weeks ago he saw two pale girls with bandannas on their heads, staring out of drawn faces. Welcome to the land of leukemia, he thought through pictures in his mind, images such as this, of tiny bald children in shopping carts and ice cream parlors wearing faded colored kerchiefs.

He stops in Las Vegas to buy supplies for the compound, drives the neon strip in the electronic alarm of night, the black pyramid, the casinos and theme parks, a million flashing lights. It is a gold sequin dress of a town, as tacky as 1975. Pure oxygen and risk. A million volts of air conditioning, a thousand electric-blue swimming pools, a hundred crazy blondes with cocaine addictions and no identifiable scruples. He sees bearded men in hair shirts carrying signs announcing the apocalypse, obese pedestrians in overburdened electric wheelchairs struggling up the inclines of handicap on-ramps, hookers with unrestrained bosoms hurling their final seconds of beauty at the passing cars of alcoholics and soldiers on paid leave. He burns oil. A fly inside the car rebounds from window to window, looking for salvation or a way out. He stops at a red light. Cars behind him honk. What the fuck? he shouts. The light is red, but he has been fooled by the clever ploy of one casino, which has set up a supplemental traffic light of its own to try to lure business. A large black man in a raincoat throws half a cheeseburger at his car. Porter can appreciate the story of Gomorrah. A man (or woman) in a food-encrusted chicken suit staggers out of a bus stop and for a moment appears to take flight, though this is just an illusion created by a large stuffed animal falling off the curb.

The group's needs are simple, camping supplies, an adequate

source of groceries, and paper for Preston's typewriter. Webb needs his comic books and titty magazines, Dent needs a portable generator for his laptop. Porter likes to listen to the hits of the sixties, seventies, and eighties. McAndrew doesn't like a damn thing except shooting cans with a .45 and intimidating Webb and Dent. The five of them are growing impatient. One can only hide from a manhunt for so long. Statistically this has been proven. Lately Porter has been reconsidering his allegiance to Danton. He had assumed he would have more control than he does. It is Preston's power over the others. Porter has a bad feeling about where all this is going, but what are his options? Copies of the documents have been made. He has told Preston that if they have not acted by April 1, he will go forward on his own. An April Fool, is what Preston called him. I should have shot him right there, thinks Porter. He wonders if there's still time to jump back to the other side.

In a landscape of parking lots Porter chooses one and brings his car to a halt. He leaves it unlocked, walks across heated asphalt. Linus lies confused in the trunk, anticipating. He waits for the sound of the key, the narrow window of light. It does not come. Porter enters Outdoor World. It is the land of the gun and the fiberglass beer cooler. He buys ammunition and two semiautomatic assault rifles. He stocks up on water and dehydrated-food packets. Outside once more, he ducks into the Super Food Co. Market, trolls the aisles with a cart, his eye out for canned goods and boxes of cereal. He stops for one last cup of coffee at a kiosk shaped like an Indian-head nickel. It is sour and black. He stares out the window into the parking lot at his car. This is not the ocean, he thinks. Behind him a man on a cellular phone says, *Money is the sound of one hand clapping.*

In the trunk, cramped, teeth chattering, Linus reflects on his last conversation with Claudia. Something he has, until now, been unable to do. This is either a sign of progress or evidence of a deep-seated masochism, and given his captured predicament he leans toward masochism, but the rift with Claudia has become a regret he worries like a bone, struggling to figure out what strange accident of speech and silence has led him so far from understanding. She called from Chicago. Their hellos were brief. I miss you, he said pretty much right away. He was sitting on the kitchen counter absorbing radiation from the microwave, which spun and heated something store-bought. I miss you too, she said. True? False? He opened the cabinets behind his head, pulled out a box of Wheat Thins, searching the contents by feel, food made in factories by underpaid workers who themselves ate greasy meats and rice or nothing at all. Let's go away this weekend, he said. I've made reservations in Calistoga, a spa. This is meant to be a concession on his part, for anarchists are not known to frequent spas, not often seen soothed by mud and hibiscus tea leaves lying among the bourgeoisie, drinking sweet liquors from tall scalloped glasses.

Oh, Linus, she said. You hate Calistoga.

And you hate dinners with Reverend Alexander of the United Church of Alien Promise, but you still cook.

How are the boys? she said, changing the subject. "The boys" is what she calls Edward and Roy.

Oh, fine. Edward says he is exhibiting all the symptoms for pre-Renaissance consumption. Roy drove all the way to San Francisco with his groceries sitting on top of his car.

Well, I'll be back in the next couple of days. Mom wants to take me to the antique show. I'm considering feigning death myself.

What about Calistoga?

Linus.

We could drive up on Friday. I can have Farley cover my classes.

Linus.

I just think we need to spend some time together.

Don't sound so desperate, Linus. It's...

It's what?

Unattractive.

The microwave emitted a ding as loud as the horn of a crosstown bus. Startled, Linus banged his head on the cabinet behind him. He saw stars.

Jesus fucking Christ.

Look, Linus. I don't want to fight with you. I just need a couple more days off.

What? No. I hit my head.

What?

I hit my head. The microwave. Never mind. Just come home sometime. We're supposed to be in love. People who are in love like to see each other every once in a while.

Don't lecture me about love, Linus. I'm not the one who hides his emotions until they're like trip wires.

Linus takes the food from the microwave. A home-cooked meal constructed by ex-cons in a flame-retardant factory in Trenton. He throws it in the trash and opens a bottle of wine.

I had Jerry Young in English lit recommend some good Napa cabernets for us, he says. There's a short silence. Linus pours a quarter of the bottle into a large water glass. The only light in the kitchen comes from the porch outside, a vaguely yellow glow that makes the wine look black. Linus is not a drinker, but when he hangs up with Claudia he will drink with a deliberate fervor that borders on violence.

Don't try so hard, Linus. Just be yourself. It's okay.

But Linus feels a sudden self-loathing, wonders briefly how he has descended from the cocky young academic to this person he does not recognize, who will compromise his own dignity for the smallest attention.

What do you want from me, Claudia?

Progress. I want a collective sense of advancement. I want you to grow like I'm growing, to experience new things. I want more than just routine.

I like routine. Routine is restful. It is the natural state of couplehood, the state toward which all marriages gravitate. When you get married it's with the understanding that you will watch more television with this person than you will ever again watch alone or in the company of others. It's with the knowledge that you will develop rituals that surround Sunday breakfasts and Friday nights. You will grow to anticipate each other's wants. You are volunteering to abandon mystery and slip into a comfortable understanding. That's marriage. I'm sorry if I'm just Linus who teaches college students the same basic principles year in and year out. This is my field. I write. I publish. I like it. Between you and me now on the phone, after you've made me feel about as low as I can ever remember feeling, I hope to stay doing what I'm doing until I am a crazy old man with seven feet of white hair growing out of my ears wandering around bus stations muttering about the ghost of William Casey. Now get your bony ass home and stop being such a child.

It seemed the appropriate thing to do at that point was to hang up the phone with a conclusive crash, which he did. His heart was beating rapidly and he had the cold metallic taste of anger right on the front of his tongue. He stood holding the glass of wine, staring at it, a black beverage on a dark night. He lifted it to his face and forced it down, all of it in one gulp. He had no idea if he would ever see Claudia again at that moment. He had lost the understanding of what marriage was supposed to be like. All that was left, it seemed, was the silence of different lives.

Porter returns to the car. He has bought a blanket at the army/navy store, which he tosses quickly into the trunk before Linus has time to comprehend that the trunk has opened and then closed. Suddenly he is struggling with a smothering weight. He lets out a yell, wrestles the blanket for a full minute before realizing what it is. He lies there, letting his breathing return to normal, and covers himself, shivering from cold and an emotion he recognizes easily as fear.

Edward wakes up nauseated. He is in a narrow room with high ceilings, big enough for a single metal-framed bed (this one bolted to the floor) and for a person to walk five paces from a heavy metal door (with a small wire-mesh peephole) to a concrete wall that holds a sweating metal toilet. The room has been painted an industrial green, which under the fluorescent lights makes it resemble the inside of a germ cell. His head feels cloudy, as if while he's been sleeping someone has filled it with syrup. He lies on his back sweating. Using hands that don't seem to belong to him, he touches his body to make sure it's still there. His mouth is dry, tongue feels swollen. The clothes he's wearing are flat green hospital scrubs. The thin gray blanket he has been given has been kicked down to the bottom of the narrow, concave bed, metal springs stabbing up around him. He tries to focus his eyes on a spot on the ceiling.

Using disembodied fingertips, he touches his face, traces the length of his nose, his dry, chapped lips. He considers sitting up, ends up repeating the words until the act itself becomes meaningless. The thought occurs to him that he has been drugged. On his body there are small black-and-blue marks that discolor the bottoms of his feet, the insides of his thighs. When he coughs, which he does as soon as he tries to sit up, his body makes a wet sound that produces liquid. His sinuses hurt him, eyes feel hot. He lifts his legs off the bed and places his feet on the floor, which is ice cold and shocks him slightly from his daze. Edward sits there staring at the wall eighteen inches from his face. Outside the door he hears sounds of speech and movement, electronic noises, the closing of doors. He coughs again into his hands, studies the wetness, clear and without real viscosity. He moves slowly. He would like to jump to conclusions but finds himself unable to get his mind off the ground.

"Ah," he says, studies the sound in the room. "Oh."

He is disoriented and slow-witted. Without the drugs he would certainly be extremely anxious, but instead he feels detached, adrift. He stares at the wall. He begins to think he has transformed into a machine, an android, an electronic life form incapable of feeling, of fearing, of loving. The room has no windows. Other than the bed and toilet there is no furniture, no decoration, just the specter of the door, its single metal eye. When he tries to stand, Edward becomes aware of a certain sensation in his feet. A sharp, insistent jangling. He stops, rests his weight on the bed, and thinks it through. He decides that what he is feeling is pain, the bright, stabbing sensations of damaged nerves. He considers this. Maybe if he figures out what the pain is from. Once he recognizes the feeling, however, it is as if all the other aches and bruises step forward clamoring to be recognized. Before he realizes it, he is lying down once more, looking up at the long fluorescent bulb. His teeth hurt, back, arms, neck. He decides he will encourage the pain, see if it can distill the syrup coating his brain. He thinks about where the pain came from, swims back through gray matter. Thinking is a matter of chemical exchanges, he tells himself. He blinks his eyes. The synapses fire clumsy messages. His foot twitches. He bends one leg until it makes a right angle. There is a memory of a face. He licks his lips slowly, moves his fingers. He understands suddenly where these ambiguous signals of pain originated. It is a question of electricity and sharp, jarring blows. Mr. Yee and Mr. Clean.

He sits up again. The floor remains cold.

"Roy," he says, clears his throat, tries it again. He is alone.

He lifts his right hand, touches his hair, his forehead. I have been tortured, he thinks. There is no feeling accompanying the words. They just hang in the air in front of him, dissolve into the ambiguous green wall. In a moment he has forgotten them. He tries to remember what he has said and to whom. He coughs again. His lungs are full of water inhaled in the course of drowning as two men held his head down in a metal bucket until he bucked himself into unconsciousness. He remembers with considerably less detachment now the desperate struggle for oxygen. Through the haze, a certain sense of anxiety begins to penetrate. He shakes his head, slaps his own face. He reaches out, touches the wall. He thinks he will soon try to stand up. For now, though, he lies back, closes his eyes. His breathing is rushed, heart rate high. He needs a drink of water.

When he wakes up again, it is with the understanding that there has been a noise. He turns his head, watches a big man in white scrubs come in through the door. The man checks a clipboard.

"Six-one-three. Dinnertime."

Edward struggles up onto his elbows, still foggy and weak.

"Edward," he says. The orderly grabs him by the armpits, helps him to a sitting position.

"You must learn to respond to six-one-three. This is how you will be addressed. Six-one-three. It's here on your uniform." He taps Edward on the chest above his heart, where his number has been sewn onto his shirt, then navigates him from his room into a wide, brightly lit corridor. Other figures are emerging from similar holes. They all share a look of stunned submission, hobbled by a chemical club.

"This is a prison?" asks Edward.

"Hospital."

Hospital, thinks Edward.

"Was I in an accident?"

"No, unless thinking so helps you to adjust to your new surroundings. If that is the case, then yes, you have accidentally lost touch with reality."

Edward tries to figure out what this might mean.

"If this is a hospital, then I'd like to see a doctor. I mean, I demand to see one. I'm not supposed to be here. In this hospital. People...people die in hospitals."

The orderly pulls Edward into line behind another man. A third falls into place behind him.

"Tomorrow the doctor will come. He will show you pictures and ask you questions. He will request that you describe the room you inhabited as a child down to the smallest detail. You will talk about your mother and how she held you back or loved you too fiercely. He will want to know things about your mind, the inhibitions you have, your ability or inability to love. He will want to hear about any pets you may have had, any feelings of guilt or remorse you have experienced, feelings of sexual inadequacy, or homosexual impulses you may have suppressed. You must help him understand the inner you. This inner you will make you well again. But that's tomorrow. Tonight we will feed your body."

Edward shakes his head, shakes it again. He feels a reluctant adrenaline, like anger struggling against his chemically induced calm.

"It's so hard to think with these drugs."

The orderly shrugs.

"The drugs keep you calm. They are meant to place you in a meditative state. You must think about getting better. Let us take care of your body so you can focus on your mind. We feed the machine so the mind gets stronger."

A group of thirty or forty patients has formed a sloppy line in the middle of the hallway. They are led by a small number of orderlies past open doorways beyond which are nothing more than narrow beds and dirty toilets.

"I need to find Roy," says Edward.

The orderly has struck up a conversation with another orderly revolving around basketball statistics. The veneer of hospital rhetoric is forgotten. Edward tugs on his sleeve. The orderly gives him a menacing look.

"Six-one-three, do not force me to strike you."

"I need to find Roy," repeats Edward. His feet have managed to affect a shuffling motion and he moves along in the line. The hallway reaches a T. The line turns right, moves past a common area with faded couches and TVs. The orderly goes back to talking basketball.

In the dining area, industrial metal benches, a row of aromatic steam tables, trays filled with plastic spoons, Edward is deposited in line by the orderly, who then moves away to rest against the wall with the other orderlies. The room seats about two hundred but is only half full. On the far side of the hall Edward notices a small group of women, separated from the men, lined up with plastic trays and muddy expressions at the steam tables. Grim-faced locals in hairnets shovel ambiguously colored items onto plastic plates, hand them off without comment. At the head of the line Edward spots Roy. He starts to call out, then reconsiders. He looks at the orderlies lined against the far wall, burly men with crew cuts and tattoos circumnavigating their biceps. Edward picks up a tray from the pile, gets on the back of the line. His wrists ache, feet. The backs of his legs are undergoing a peculiar burning sensation. He makes a vow never to talk to Linus again should the opportunity to speak to him ever arrive, which it seems unlikely to do. He is served in turn, an anonymous collection of parts and pieces drawn together by a menacing brown liquid. The smell does nothing for his nausea, and he gags, but manages to curb his desire to throw up out of a desperate need to remain anonymous, to avoid drawing attention to himself.

In front of him a man demonstrates the steady patience required to drool in thick ropes. Edward is almost positive that he told Mr. Clean about Cliff Webb, about the water truck and Leonard T. Knuckles. He's almost positive he held nothing back. In the end the information didn't seem to make a difference.

"The electricity has already been budgeted," said Mr. Yee. "We may as well proceed."

Edward takes his tray of food and shuffles his way over to a table near the women. Two men with plastic goggles sit down across from him. One is skinny, Caucasian. The other is wide-bodied, looks like an Indian.

"They don't let us have regular eyeglasses," says the Caucasian.

"The glass," adds the Indian, making a cutting motion across his wrists. He notices Edward looking at him quizzically. "People always ask," he says.

Edward watches Roy sit down at a table on the other side of the room. He picks up his fork, pokes at the unidentifiable objects on his plate.

"What kind of hospital is this?"

"We're not allowed to talk about it," says the short, flat-featured Indian. The right side of his head has been shaved recently. There are track marks between his toes. The other man has a narrow face with an impossibly long neck. He makes a clockwise motion with his index finger around the circumference of his temple. Edward feels an irrational wave of relief. A mental hospital. In a regular hospital there are diseases, open bodies, the opportunity for infection. This relief is followed closely, however, by a certain understanding that at least in a medical hospital there are doctors who are trained to treat the subversions of the body. Here there will only be shrinks. Through drooping eyelids he examines the dirt under his fingers.

"I'm Foop," says the narrow man. He inclines his head at his partner. "This is Navaho Ned." Foop leans forward, holds his face inches above his plate. He whispers to Edward, "They put transponders in his head."

Navaho Ned looks at Edward and puts his finger to his lips. His goggles have started to fog up, making his eyes look shiny and distant. Edward nods, looks across the room at Roy, who is eating alone at a table in the corner.

"I have to talk to my friend."

Foop and Navaho Ned exchange a look. Foop scratches the outside of his nose, working his finger covertly inside. He roots around for a minute, examines the results.

"There are no friends here, though we have been asked to participate in the buddy system. For example, Navaho Ned is my buddy. I am Navaho Ned's buddy, but we are not friends. That would be against the rules. They have told us that we are not supposed to think about what this means for too long."

Edward looks over at the orderlies. Most of the patients have finished eating, pushed their plates away.

"I need to get my friend a note," he says.

"No paper," says Foop.

"No pens," says Navaho Ned.

"No crayons or pencils or felt-tipped markers. No chalk, no yellow or pink highlighters."

"I get the picture," says Edward.

Foop shrugs. Navaho Ned shrugs. Edward looks at the wall behind the steam tables, where wire-mesh-covered windows reflect a certain blue sky, unplaceable by state or country. He watches a heavy cloud squeeze its way across the bars. He thinks about the drugs he must be on, finds himself hoping for anything already FDA approved. He doesn't want to be here, a man disappeared to a mental hospital undergoing clandestine experimental drug treatments, whatever the rationalized benefit to humankind.

"Do we ever get to go outside?"

Foop smirks. Navaho Ned has become distracted by something he has found between his teeth.

"TV," replies Foop, nodding, indicating that here there will only be traveling of the virtual variety.

One of the orderlies blows a whistle and the patients stand up and begin to carry their trays over to a large metal dolly by the steam tables, stacking them at impossible angles, gluing them together by force and gravy. Edward holds back, tries to wait for Roy to approach the dolly. One of the patients at the front of the line is caught in the press of bodies, begins to shove people around him. The robots revolt. A melee breaks out, a combination slapfest and food fight, which brings the orderlies charging over and finds Edward sitting on his ass with a surprised look on his face and his tongue bleeding where he has bitten it. He feels hands on him from behind, turns, and sees Roy crouching behind a folding table.

"TV from six to nine," says Roy.

"I'll look for you."

Roy turns to crawl away. Edward hears the sound of scuffling feet. Something drips off the table onto his hand. Roy moves away, stops, turns back to Edward, who stares in horror at the brown gravy on his skin. The rough hands of an orderly haul Edward to his feet, reactivating the pain of a hundred bruises. The room is covered in food and the collapsing resistance of the drug-stupored. Edward is pulled through the obstacle course of tables toward the dining-area door. He reaches up and rubs the remaining brown liquid on the back of the orderly's uniform. This garners him a smack, the reflexive backhand of a far bigger man. A certain sense of clarity returns to Edward with the connection. His drug-laden brain pops into focus, encouraged by the sharp sensation of violence, which is why Edward will later tell Roy he's positive he saw Claudia being led from the dining area with the other female inmates just before he was dragged once more into the hallway.

Edward dreams about machines. He dreams he's in the dayroom watching television. On screen is a documentary on the history of the world, millions of quick-cut images demonstrating every inch of earth from pole to pole, from the craggy recesses of Inner Mongolia to the metropolitan hubs of Paris and Rome. It is a statement of size and complexity. In the dream he is sitting beside Navaho Ned and Navaho Ned is talking, but in the voice of Richard Burton. He says,

"Now that we have set up the postindustrial age, we realize that it could continue to operate without us indefinitely. The world has become a self-perpetuating machine."

On screen are the images of women squatting by muddy riverbanks, men riding glass elevators into the depths of atrium lobbies. In the dayroom metal plants begin to grow.

"The free market economy," says Navaho Ned, "the advance of molecular technology and genetics, the development of sophisticated weapons systems, the interactions of governments, government contractors, lobbyists, politicians. These are all examples of modern machines, machines built from technology and human labor, a new biotechnology."

In the dream, Claudia sits naked on a surgeon's table. Doctors have just finished implanting a television in her head.

"In the machine," says Navaho Ned, "our individual identities are irrelevant. It is this feeling of removal, of expendability, that breeds fear, for once you realize that the world itself is now a type of technology, then you realize that if you can't claim to be part of the machine you are redundant."

On screen, Hutu and Tutsi tribesmen promenade on the deck of the *Love Boat,* the words I LIVE TO SHOP, a dramatic re-creation of the Last Supper with George C. Scott as Jesus and Linus as Peter the apostle. Above Edward's head there is a giant red arrow with the words YOU ARE HERE. Edward in the dream. Edward on the television. Edward in the machine.

He opens his eyes. What day is it? What time? He has fallen asleep in the TV room, smothered by the cushions of a well-stained sofa chair. He blinks away the dream, stares at the sky, visible through the gated windows. There are fourteen inmates sitting around the television. He wonders if he and Roy have been abandoned here or if this is just another stage of their interrogation. He will never forget the fact that underneath his mask Mr. Yee resembled in some terrifying way the grinning Christian specter of John Denver.

An orderly leads Roy into the room, positions him in a chair at the back. Edward notices but remains where he is, disabled by muscle relaxants. He stares at the television set, which emits a certain off-key song and displays the frantic affability of children's programming. A big purple dinosaur named Barney expresses his love for everyone in this room, in all rooms, preschools and mental hospitals across the world. What a benevolent creature, to be so free in its distribution of good feeling. Appreciative, some of the inmates voice their reciprocal love in scattered shouts and murmurs, a nonunanimous cacophony of misplaced affection.

In front of him, Foop slumps on the couch beside Navaho Ned. Both are staring at the ceiling-mounted television set through scratch-resistant plastic goggles. At the same time Foop is scratching his right palm with his left index finger. He has been doing so for thirty minutes. The palm is raw and will soon begin to bleed. Navaho Ned is drooling slightly onto the collar of his scrubs. His responses are sometimes grunts, but most often silence. Roy sits in an old green easy chair with pee stains on the cushions. He has managed to palm his after-lunch pill, disposing of it between the cushions of the chair. His mind has almost returned to full clarity and with it has come an overwhelming sense of claustrophobia and abandon.

"Magilla Gorilla was a gorilla," says Foop. Navaho Ned grunts.

"Snagglepuss was a mountain lion."

Another grunt.

"Or was he a cougar?"

Edward stares at the back of Roy's head. He has been unable to avoid the afternoon drugging. He has trouble concentrating and his short-term memory seems to have been disabled. The whole world seems comprised of slow-moving images. His teeth feel fuzzy.

Roy gets up and comes to sit down next to him.

"Are you drugged?"

Edward nods. He is staring at Navaho Ned's thick head.

"I saw Claudia."

"You are drugged."

Edward turns his head and looks at Roy, fixes him with the darkest stare he can muster.

"I saw her."

Roy looks out the window. He's afraid he will cry. He holds his hands up in front of Edward's face.

"Edward, listen. I can still feel the electricity in my fingertips. They won't stop tingling."

Edward nods.

"I saw her. She's not dead."

"Maybe she's undead. Maybe this is the afterlife."

"I saw her."

"Ed, there's no way. Now stop it, you're scaring me."

Edward raises an eyebrow. Roy exhales, closes his eyes.

"Okay, you saw her. I believe you. What the hell do I know? Nothing in this fucking thing has been what you thought it was going to be."

In front of them, Foop, speaking into his hand as if it is a phone, says, *Unless he was a lemur.*

Edward tries to clear his head. He stammers, "Any idea where we are?"

Roy shakes his head.

"They told me New Jersey."

Edward smiles with alarming slowness. *Barney* ends and for a moment there is the promise of a different show. Foop says something that sounds like *aw-ya.* Navaho Ned sneezes. Another episode of *Barney* begins. Edward looks away, rubs his nose, then his eyes.

"I have to talk to her."

"They keep the women separate."

"Well, we'll just have to find a way."

Roy leans back in his chair, rests his head against the wall. He closes his eyes and pretends to be asleep. He wonders if he will like Claudia any better this time around.

"There are some people here from Clone."

"How do you know?"

Roy keeps his eyes closed, lets his jaw go slack.

"I spoke to them. They were kidnapped and brought here. They didn't just wander off."

Edward watches the moon appear in the chicken wire of the window. He feels like a liquid.

"I saw her. I saw Claudia" is all he can manage to say, repeating the words, the image of Claudia's face coming back to him over and over.

Roy pretends to snore, making a rumbling noise in his throat. Edward continues to stare at the back of Navaho Ned's head. Something about the wideness of it, the jet-black hair, is hypnotizing.

"What are they going to do with us?"

Roy's answer is to pretend to wake up and go back to his chair by the window.

■

That night Roy lies under sheets that stink of bleach. He holds his hands up in front of his eyes but can see nothing. He has no doubt that if they desire to, these people can make him crazy. It is just a question of dosage and the proper environment. The next morning he will be taken to room 400, where he'll encounter the victimization of psychotherapy, anonymous, industrial, where through focused discussion of his childhood and his parents' divorce, Roy's suspicions and political actions will be reduced to symptoms of mental unbalance expressed through talk-show buzzwords and Freudian catchphrases. A short man like a glazed ham will interrogate him about his repressed sexuality: "When we rebel against the state, we are really rebelling against our parents, Mr. Biggs. Tell me about your mother," he'll say, "your father. You were an only child, a loner, an orphan. How did losing your virginity make you feel, scared, alone? Tell us about the UFOs, the secret government plots. Does chewing aluminum foil help to block the radio waves peppering your head?" "I am a political prisoner," Roy will insist. The ham will shake its head. "How can we help you if you won't help yourself?"

A second day passes, a series of lonely moments of startled waking for both Edward and Roy, separated by narrow corridors and steel doors. They are unaware of the rising and setting of the sun. Their bodies strain to follow some internal clock, drugged into a motionless sleep. Edward establishes a routine of pacing, of staring through the peephole at the tiny patch of outdoors, of feeling dizzy and lying down. Lunch is a sinister sloppy joe and a can of grape soda. As he walks the corridors looking for Roy, Edward's heart strains. He searches the halls and dining area for another sighting of Claudia. He has almost convinced himself that she was a vision, a drug-induced hallucination. At lunch he sits at an industrial dining table, beside Foop and Navaho Ned, who have somehow recognized him as a man of like-minded antipathy and stick close when they are able. They talk in couched terms about the tests they have been subjected to. The whole thing seems insane. They sound like crazy men. At times Edward himself feels unbalanced, mentally agitated, paranoid. He hears voices, detaches from social situations. He forgets his name, the names of his family and friends. He looks for Roy, though he has forgotten what he looks like, but Roy does not appear.

At dinnertime he manages to hide in a narrow closet meant to hold janitorial equipment. The canvas shoes he has been given soak through with potentially toxic liquid that makes his feet itch. Edward refuses to think about it. If he is meant to die in this place of infection or disease, he thinks, then that is what he will do. For the first time since 1991 he feels a reckless disregard for the power of germs. He is at the tail end of his afternoon dose, as rational and clearheaded as he will ever be during a day inside. He stares out through a narrow crack between the door and the jamb. Minutes pass. Orderlies file by with the male inmates. The women approach next, defeated blondes, jittery black women, and sluggish Mexicans. He sees her, the woman who could be Claudia. For the ten or fifteen seconds she is visible he studies her, the angle of her jaw, the slope of her nose, the color of her eyes. She stares ahead with her mouth drawn, eyes flat and unfocused. Edward feels an elation that is like freedom. It is she. Unarguably, absolutely she. Claudia.

After the women have passed he makes his way to the dining hall, sneaking in at the end of a line of disparate septuagenarians. He approaches the steam table, darts his eyes to the orderlies, back to the tables where the women have assembled in loose-knit clusters. He accepts his industrial meal, approaches his usual table. Foop and Navaho Ned are already there, chewing celery stalks.

"Columbus Day," says Foop.

"October twelfth."

"How about Martin Luther King."

"January twenty-first."

"Uncanny."

It is possible that both Foop and Navaho Ned are really secret agents. It is possible that they work for unnamed government agencies. It is possible that everyone in this hospital is an actor, that the whole situation is a reenactment, that none of it is real, that they are not even here. It is possible that the whole thing is a dream, a continuation of Edward's midnight hallucinations. It is also possible that everything is what it seems, that the world is a truculent, evil place, that men in suits are really out to get them, that they have only moments to live. If you think about it too long, anything is possible, and that fact alone could drive a man insane.

Edward sits down, keeping his eyes on Claudia. He does not want to draw attention to himself, but he must let her know he is there.

"Are the women always kept separate?"

Foop smirks, punches Navaho Ned in the shoulder, once, twice, three times.

"He wants to know if the women are always kept separate."

Navaho Ned scoops a clump of rice onto his celery stalk, takes a bite. Foop looks first left, then right, leans forward.

"Something could be worked out maybe. For a price."

Edward rubs his eye. His tongue feels thick and ungainly.

"What kind of price?"

Foop takes a big bite of loaf. He chews for a while, starts to talk.

"There is a guard. I can't say more. He came in maybe six months ago. That's all I can comfortably disclose. He likes the ladies. To reveal more is to say too much. If you really want something over there, you let him know and he can sneak you out in the night to a room behind the kitchen."

Foop clamps his right hand over his own mouth.

Edward nods, keeping his eyes on Claudia. She has grown pale and thin in the past two weeks. Her hair has been hacked off at uneven angles. It seems incredible to Edward that less than a month ago he was sitting in Linus's living room drinking ice tea while Claudia worked at her desk in the living room and Edward stole glances at her over Roy's shoulder.

"What makes it worth his while?" he wants to know.

Foop grimaces, uncovers his face, reaches into his mouth, pulls out a gray clump of something half chewed. He puts it under his plate, coughs into his napkin. Navaho Ned lifts up the side of Foop's plate, examines the lump.

"Could be cat," he says.

"Hello," says Edward.

Foop grimaces again, wipes his forehead.

"We can't say. I mean, I can't say." He smacks Navaho Ned's hand, which is poking at the clump visible under the edge of the raised plate. Navaho Ned goes back to his meal. Foop rubs his jaw.

"Between you and me, he likes to listen."

"To what?"

Foop puts both hands over his mouth this time. He begins to turn bright red. He stares Edward in the eye, drops his hands into his lap.

"What do you mean what? He likes to listen to you doing your business. He likes how it sounds. In out, in out. Now don't make me say another word. They can hear our thoughts. Just to think about it gives you away."

Edward rubs the back of his head. His bruises have started to heal, but the memory of the electricity still wakes him from daydreams.

"How soon?"

Foop slumps forward, puts his head in his hands, rests his elbows on the table. He sighs, exasperated.

"Tomorrow night. Tell me which one you want. Don't say it out loud. Just think it and my transponder will pick it up."

The whistle blows. Edward picks up his plate, steps over the back of the bench. From here it's a short walk to the pharmacy, where he has to go to pick up his afternoon dose.

"The young one with the lopsided hair. I don't know her number."

Foop pushes pieces of food from between his teeth with the tip of his tongue. He nods to Navaho Ned, who is busy cleaning his plate with a piece of bread.

"Yes, I understand. The princess. It all makes sense. I'll give you a choice, though. Would you trade her in for what's behind door number three? Don't speak. Just nod once for yes, twice for no." He makes a sucking sound, trying to force more reluctant morsels from his molars by the creation of a vacuum.

Edward shakes his head.

"No. Her. She's the one," he says, dumping his tray and stepping back toward the hallway. He turns to look, but Claudia is gone.

▪

The next day there is a fight in the common area between Navaho Ned and a man with seven teeth. Navaho Ned is taken to solitary confinement, doped up on Thorazine. For the third straight day, Roy is kept in his room without food, unsure of time's passing, assaulted by colored lights. Edward looks for him, begins to fear the worst. Foop stops by the lunch table to tell him that the encounter with Claudia is set for that night. Edward returns to his room, nervous. He can't think of what he should say. He can offer her no hope of rescue, no attempts at escape. He loves her but can think only of the joy Linus will feel when he learns she is alive. Where is my beautiful wife? he wonders. Where is my intimate, my confidante, or will I live out the rest of my days locked into a chaste but questionably homoerotic relationship with Roy? The drugs send him into an agitated slumber. He wakes up to the sound of a key in the door. The orderly who comes in is a giant.

"Six-one-three, let's go. Be quiet about it."

He leads Edward down the long hall, around the corner, past the mess hall, encourages him with grunted profane whispers. Edward stays quiet. He walks with shuffling steps. He feels anxious, off balance. The drugs make him jittery. When they reach the room, the orderly, Klaus, stops him by putting a hand the size of a ham on his chest.

"She bites. She claws. She screams. She kicks. This is fine with me. I appreciate that in a woman from an acoustical standpoint, but you're the one inside. If you want to come out in relatively the same shape you went in, I suggest you pay attention to her moods."

Edward nods. He stares at the door, at what it hides, a cramped, moldy closet harboring a pee-stained cot smelling of ammonia. The orderly puts his hand on the doorknob.

"You've got half an hour." He turns the knob.

Inside, the room is dimly lit, a dirty twenty-watt bulb hanging from a string. Claudia crouches on the warped cot with her back to the corner, knees drawn up against her chest.

"Don't you fucking touch me," she says. She looks like an animal.

"Claudia, it's Edward."

She kicks out at him. He flinches, puts his hands up, shows her the palms.

"It's Edward, remember? Linus's friend."

At the sound of Linus's name she stiffens. She licks her lips, squints through the haze.

"Edward?"

He sits on the edge of the bed. His heart breaks to see her here like this.

"That's right."

She feels the cool cement of the wall against her back, touches it with her palms. She thinks, They'll never stop punishing me. She relaxes her body, opens her arms. There is a part of her that believes she deserves this room, deserves the things they try to do to her here.

"Well, here's your chance, Edward. Did you bring the mistletoe with you this time?"

"What? No. Claudia, you have to listen to me."

She thinks, What else is there but grief? After enough of it the body goes numb. The doctors tell her one day she will understand that she deserves more, but right now the only thing she deserves is punishment.

"Come on, Ed. They only give you so much time. That fucker outside has rules."

She undoes the buttons on her blouse. Edward stares at her.

"Claudia. What the hell happened to you?"

She drops her hands, her blouse fastened by one last button.

"What happened? Edward, what do you think happened? Linus died and I went crazy. I went crazy and they locked me up, and now I spend most of my time biting the ears off of men who want to have sex with me."

Edward stares at her. The scrubs they've given her are frayed. He can see the naked skin of her clavicle, the inner curves of her breasts. He turns his head, can't begin to imagine what he should say.

"Linus didn't die, Claudia."

Claudia nods.

"In a car crash. He was crushed. His head. His chest. His legs. The men who came to the airport showed me pictures." She chews her cuticles. "Poor Linus. I told him that Duster would kill him."

Edward sits on the edge of the bed.

"No, Claudia. You don't understand. Linus isn't dead. We thought *you* were dead. We thought you'd been killed in a plane crash. Linus and Roy and I have been looking for you."

"That's nice of you to say, Edward, really, but it's okay. I've accepted it. He's dead. I had an affair and he died. I fucked another man in a hotel room in New York and Linus flipped his automobile seven times across an empty highway. Cause and effect, effect and cause. The doctors say it's not my fault, but I know."

Edward grabs her hands, holds them still.

"Stop it. He's not dead. We don't have much time. I need you to listen to me."

She pulls her hands away, moves back against the wall.

"You want to know the funny thing, Ed, if you really are Ed? If this isn't just my insanity bleeding onto the floor. The funny thing is, I only did it once and it wasn't even that good. Jeffrey, Jeffrey, Jeffrey. He had a short, fat penis he couldn't even use, all talk, all lead-in, and when it was over I felt hollow as if he'd just cleaned me out, as if I'd hired some kind of professional cleaning service to come in and sterilize my insides, empty my rooms of furniture, of decorations, of memories. So I went back to Linus, stumbled back, wandered back in a daze like a zombie, what a mess, what a fucking mess, and every time I opened my mouth I wanted to tell him, I mean, how big a deal is it if I still loved him, if we could work it out, if I was there now, but I never did. I never told him and so he died."

"Claudia, you have to listen to me."

There is the sound of the doorknob turning. Edward's head comes around. He thinks, Oh, shit, not yet, and then Klaus's face appears through a crack in the doorway. He has the look of murder in his eye, but when he sees the two of them his face lightens and he withdraws and shuts the door. Edward, confused, turns back to Claudia and finds she has finished undoing her top, has lowered it across her arms. Her breasts are pale and flat under the flickering lights. He turns his face away, ashamed by his arousal.

"Claudia, Linus isn't dead. You've been tricked. Listen to me. I wouldn't lie to you. You were kidnapped and brought here under the pretense of mental health, but what is really going on is much worse. Will you listen to me? Put your shirt on and listen."

She closes her eyes, concentrates on the rhythm of her breathing. When she was flying to New York she was a nervous wreck, sitting in an aisle seat, making anxious trips to the bathroom. The sky was a clear, bright blue. The plane had a single aisle, flew booked to capacity. She sat packed in among the bodies of businessmen and harried flight attendants, breathed in the stale air of the modern commuter. Beside her a woman on a cellular phone described the intensity of an orgasm as better than clitoral but not quite vaginal. Claudia tried to figure out if she was leaving Linus, if the affair had been a sign of leaving or a way of waking herself up. Why can't I tell the difference? she wondered. If I don't know what I'm thinking, what I'm feeling, then who else can tell me?

What would she say to Holden? The thought of him repulsed her now, his jovial eyes, the racquetball muscles. How shallow can a person be, she wondered, and how shallow she by association. Somehow she had to keep him from destroying her life. In the bathroom she splashed chemically treated water on her face, watched the blue liquids in the toilet escaping the bowl. Stuck inside the tight coffin of the lavatory, she stared at her face in the warped metal mirror. Who is this person? she wondered. She looks so familiar and yet why don't I know her? She would have to ask Tony to drop her from the Hastings account. She would have to try to tunnel her way back inside her own marriage.

At the airport Jeffrey was all smiles. He hugged her, though she resisted, grabbed her hand, swung it as if they were high school sweethearts.

"I don't love you, Jeffrey," she'd said, before he could speak. "I'm going back to my husband."

Holden stuck out his lower lip, made a sad face, then laughed. He didn't love her either. She was just a plaything. What she didn't know was that the only reason she was there was that Forbes had called Holden the day before and told him to get her to New York. We know about your little fling with the professor's wife, he'd said. Call her. There's something I need her to do for me.

"I bought two tickets for us," he'd said. "I think we need a romantic week in Rio to reignite that spark."

She'd pushed him, thrust a finger in his face.

"Are you crazy? The only reason I came was to tell you that if you think you're going to call my husband and tell him about your forty-five seconds of bliss, then you should know that I'm going to hire a man named Bruno to shoot you at your country club."

Holden had made a face of mock alarm, then checked his watch, shrugged.

"I think you've misjudged which one of us has friends in dangerous places," he'd said. Over the PA came the boarding announcement for flight 613. Holden had picked up his bag, slung it over his shoulder.

"Last chance," he'd said.

Claudia's response was to walk away, shaking. She made it as far as the bathroom before breaking down. She'd sat shivering in the far stall until she'd gotten hold of herself, then walked out to the row of sinks to wash her face. She would have to tell Linus, that much was clear. Then she would say that she wanted to take a leave of absence from her job. She thought maybe they could take a trip for the summer. Take three months and go to Greece or Italy. She wanted to find her way back to being the Claudia she was when she had married, confident, happy, with a great life ahead of her. She no longer wanted to be a woman who broke down in airport restrooms after confronting her infidelities in public places.

She'd pulled a wad of paper towels from the dispenser, held them to her face. When she looked up, there was a woman behind her spraying perfume. The smell was like rosemary. Outside the bathroom she'd come face-to-face with Forbes.

"Claudia Owen?" he'd asked her, and when she'd nodded said, "I'm sorry to have to tell you this, Mrs. Owen, but there's been an accident at home," and Claudia had allowed herself to be led to a waiting car.

Edward tries to reach out to her across the dirty cot.

"I know you never really believed in this stuff, Claudia, in conspiracies, in secret government plots, but I think now you're going to have to start. Your life has been ruined because of one. Your marriage has been broken. You have been taken against your will, lied to, and abandoned here in a run-down mental hospital. This isn't the drugs. I'm not a hallucination. You are not mentally ill. Are you with me so far?"

"Edward."

"Listen. A bomb was planted on a plane from New York to Brazil. A plane the airlines said you were on. It was flight 613 to Rio. You were sitting next to Jeffrey Holden. There's surveillance camera footage of a woman who looked like you boarding the plane with a man who looked like Holden. The plane blew up over Florida.

Agents of the FBI told Linus that a secret left-wing group planted the bomb. This is absolutely true. These people were in hiding. The FBI wanted Linus to find the group for them. You'd been killed. We all believed this, and so Linus is looking, we're looking, because we thought this group had killed you. I don't have all the details of why they took you, why you're here. You're going to have to trust me."

"Linus?"

"Linus is alive. You're alive. Nobody here is crazy. This whole thing is about a drug invented by Hastings, by your client at the agency. They were using your death to get Linus to help them find this group."

"They? Who's they? Now you sound like Linus. Always with some unnamed they. God, that drove me crazy."

She sits up, challenges him with her posture, her expression, and Edward begins to feel he may be getting through.

"They the government. They Hastings Pharmaceutical. They Jeffrey Holden. They Mr. Yee and Mr. Clean. They Agent Forbes."

Claudia touches Edward's arm.

"Forbes? Did you say Forbes? Edward, Forbes is the one who met me at the airport, who told me about Linus's accident. He showed me pictures."

"Believe me, I'm not trying to be cliché when I say that pictures can be faked."

Claudia chews at her cuticles, which are bloody and raw. Her hair is dirty and has been cut by the imprecise hands of an impatient orderly. With no context in which to understand this new version of events, she has trouble concentrating. If she is no longer a woman suffering a nervous breakdown, then does this mean she is sane, healthy? She feels neither. One thing she knows is that she will not cry.

"I'm not dead," she says quietly.

"I know."

"I'm just a little lost."

"Well, we found you, Claudia. It's okay."

Claudia wavers, struggles, tries to remain detached, then gives in to hope. She comes out of her corner, pushes up against Edward, allows him to engulf her in his narrow arms. He feels her warmth, smells the industrial odors of her hair and skin. This could very well be a dream for him as well.

"Is Linus here?" she asks, scared at once that he is and is not.

Edward shakes his head.

"I came in with Roy, but he's disappeared."

"But he's alive? Linus? He's alive?"

"He's alive."

Claudia shuts her eyes and tries to picture her husband's face, allows herself to remember his voice, the feel of his skin. Maybe there's still a future she can look forward to.

"What are we going to do? How are we going to get out of here?"

Edward shakes his head. He reclines slowly until his back is to the wall, kisses the top of Claudia's head. He can't begin to imagine how they can escape, can physically surmount the walls and fences, can tunnel through earth or rappel from windows, so he too closes his eyes. He feels the heat of Claudia's form, breathes her in, and for a few minutes, trapped there in that angry, forgotten room, he escapes in his mind.

In a small ghost town just outside of Ely, Nevada, a black sedan pulls into a ramshackle barn. A man with gray hair climbs out and closes the lopsided barn doors behind him. He steps into the dusty morning light, places both hands on his hips, stretches his back. A smaller man comes out of an old wooden house, approaches him squinting.

"Did you get him?"

Porter nods. He's been driving for eight hours straight. Cliff Webb stands barefoot in the dirt, takes a wristwatch out of his pocket, checks the time.

"How's Preston doing?" asks Porter. Webb shrugs.

"He's in that room now twenty hours a day. Last couple of days he's been yelling out how he's almost out of paper. Good, I say. That means you're almost done." He shrugs again. "But he just keeps writing."

Porter spits. He is thinking about a *National Geographic* special he once watched on the islands of Palau, a series of small soup-bowl-like rock formations in the South Seas filled by natural lakes. He shakes his head, rubs his eyes.

"Well, if the professor here could find us, I doubt the gestapo is far behind."

Webb nods. He looks at the barn, worries about the likelihood of capture. This must be an omen. They have to figure out how to turn it to their advantage. The variable in the trunk of Porter's car makes them all nervous. Except Preston, who sees this all as some kind of game.

"Well, we'd better haul him out of there, see if he's still breathing."

Porter nods, spits into the dirt.

Linus comes out of the trunk without much of a fight. He is naked, shivering, half awake. His stomach has let go again sometime in the night and the smell of his intestines greets the two men as they open the trunk.

"Jesus," says Webb. "What did you do to the guy?"

Porter scowls, hauls Linus out onto the dirt. He closes the trunk with a crash. The two men hustle Linus inside before they can be caught by satellite photography. Inside, they rub him down with burlap, making his skin red and raw. Porter gives him a pair of jeans and an old T-shirt, which Linus dons quietly. They sit him down in the makeshift kitchen area on an old metal diner stool.

"I'll get Preston," says Porter, and walks out of the room.

Webb goes into the cupboard, comes out with a bottle of Pepto-Bismol. He hands it to Linus.

"Drink this."

Linus takes two or three swallows, wipes his mouth with the back of his hand. The taste is chalky and too sweet. He is dying for a real drink.

"Could I get some water?"

Webb shrugs. No one has told him how they're supposed to treat the variable, this scrawny anarchist from San Francisco. He goes back into the cupboard, comes out with a liter of water.

"Drink it slowly," he says. Linus takes a big gulp, then another. In the distance he can hear the clacking of a typewriter.

Dent comes into the kitchen, sees Linus, stops. He is a tall, nervous-looking teenager with thick plastic glasses. He looks at Webb.

"This him?"

Webb nods. Dent walks up to Linus, looks him over.

"How much time do we have?" he asks.

Linus shakes his head.

"I don't know. It could be a year or they could be right behind me."

Dent nods, scratches his head.

"What do you think?"

Linus shrugs, scratches at some of the dried blood on his chin.

"I don't think we were followed."

Dent decides this will have to be good enough. He goes over and leans against the counter.

"I read that article you wrote on corporate welfare," he says to Linus.

Linus considers the irony of this comment spoken by this kid in this context. He supposes it's a sign of desperation that a man in a life-or-death situation such as this would want to try to instigate an intellectual conversation.

"So what did you think?"

Dent shrugs. He is here developing computer viruses that Preston envisions will be used to cripple the entire federal government. His primary political concern is for the environment. The others are focused mainly on medical testing. It amounts to the same thing, he tells them. Don't think all those pesticides are doing you any more good than they're doing the bugs.

"Sounds like you're on our side."

Linus gives him a tired smile, not entirely believable in its good-humoredness. Right now he doesn't know if there are any sides he would be willing to join. He coughs into his hand, rubs his mouth, takes some water and wipes away the rest of the dried blood that has crusted on his upper lip. In the back of his mind he listens for Preston's approach. It's hard to believe that these men are responsible for the death of his wife. They seem so ordinary and ineffectual, so much like him really, and yet he steels himself to the thought that he may have to try to kill them too, which shows how far from reality he has come, a man alone, burlap-burned and weaponless, leaning against a splintering wall in the middle of a ghost town.

Webb looks over at Dent. Neither man has shaved for three days. The apprehension is like caffeine driving them all. They've got the evidence, the means of distribution. They have the plan. All they need is Preston and he stays locked in that room watched over by the giant McAndrew.

Porter comes back into the kitchen, takes a granola bar out of the cupboard. Though he hasn't slept in twenty-four hours he looks alert.

"He'll be right out."

Linus looks at the three of them evenly spaced across the dirty kitchen. He feels a certain detachment that could be the result of the head injury, but is more likely a kind of shock at having ended up where he needs to be. He wonders which one of them built the bomb, taping clock parts to C-4. He thinks about Porter driving to New York with the bomb in the trunk of his car, the rope, the pie tins.

"Who's Teddy Waren?" he asks.

At this moment Preston walks into the kitchen preceded by a behemoth.

"Professor Owen?" Preston is bald, as Luther K. described him, and Linus's height, with heavy black eyebrows that make him look in many ways like a cartoon villain. He sticks out his hand to shake. Linus ignores it. Faced with his quarry he becomes strangely silent, as if sensing that anything that happens from now on will be a disappointment. Preston narrows his eyes.

"It's been a while," he says. "You may not remember, but you were supposed to appear on my show."

"Oh, I remember."

Preston smiles.

"Good, good."

There is an awkward silence. The big man behind Preston takes the opportunity to crack his knuckles one at a time. Everybody calls him Clive. He stares at Linus with studied detachment.

Preston looks at his watch.

"Well, Professor Owen, what can I do for you? I'm a busy man."

"Of course. The manifesto."

Preston clears his throat.

"That's right."

"Well, I won't take up too much of your time. I just want to know why you killed my wife."

Preston looks at Webb, then Dent, then Porter. He shrugs.

"I'm sorry."

"Sorry doesn't do it."

"No, I mean I don't understand."

"You planted a bomb on a plane. My wife was on the plane."

Preston nods, looks at the floor.

"Professor Owen, I can assure you that neither I nor my associates were responsible in any way for the death of your wife. None of us has left the compound for more than a day since January."

Linus tries to decide if he expected Preston to deny it all along. He would have thought that a megalomaniac like him would be the kind to boast.

"Who is Teddy Waren?" he says.

Preston looks up, surprised, meets Linus's eyes.

"Teddy Waren is an anagram devised by me. It decodes as the Road to Nowhere."

An anagram, thinks Linus. He considers the implications.

"But clearly there was a passenger by that name. Even an anagram has to be somebody."

"His name was Roger Leeds. He was a member of our group."

Linus shivers. He is barefoot and the T-shirt is thin.

"And he took the bomb on board."

Preston shakes his head.

"No."

Linus sees red.

"Look, I rode half the night naked in the trunk of a fucking car. My wife has been killed and I've been dragged into the middle of a power struggle between a government dope fiend and a bunch of desert revolutionaries. Now I think you owe me an explanation for why you blew up that plane. Is this about the Nevada test?"

Preston nods.

"Yes. In part."

"All right. Well, why don't you start by telling me, what the hell was the Nevada test?"

Preston goes over to Linus and tries to put his hand on Linus's shoulder. Linus shrugs him off, gives Preston a shove. McAndrew steps forward and pins Linus to the wall with one hand. He pushes on Linus's chest until Linus feels he might die. Preston recovers his balance and taps McAndrew on the arm, signaling that he can let Linus go.

"Professor Owen, are you willing to be calm about this?"

Linus seethes. He rages with a desire to kill and die, to recover in some way his own quiet dignity and finally sleep.

"Yes," he says.

Preston nods.

"Well, let's go into the living room and I'll explain it all over a drink."

■

"Part of the reason I agreed to see you," says Preston, "is that given your background I thought you would understand what we are trying to accomplish here."

They sit on an array of worn and broken chairs that have been patched with splints or brackets. The windows are covered with dusty white sheets, letting in translucent light from the morning sun.

Porter and Dent sit by the window. Webb has gone to stand watch on the back porch, where he stays with an automatic weapon under the shade of the splintered porch roof. The monster McAndrew sits at Preston's side. Linus has yet to hear him utter a single syllable.

"Don't be so sure," says Linus. "I can be very dim-witted when I want to be."

Preston shrugs.

"You're an intelligent man. When faced with the evidence I'm sure you'll see that there's only one way to interpret it."

Linus looks them over one by one, wonders what their bedrooms look like, whether they sleep in pairs, in shifts. He thinks about how they must have lived here the past few weeks, what they must have eaten. There is the overwhelming sense of fear in the scenario he creates: a small clot of men desperately trying to conceive of ways in which they can keep their identities alive after the government storms their compound and they're never heard from again. His headache has returned with a steady throb that crouches behind his eyes.

Preston leans forward, clasps his hands together. "First of all, I want to reiterate that we did not kill your wife or anybody else for that matter. Roger was on that plane as part of a reconnaissance mission, which I will explain shortly. Your wife's death is just another in a long line of senseless killings carried out by our government and their corporate puppet masters."

Linus looks at Porter, then at Dent. He tries to figure out why these men, who seem at least partially rational, would follow a man like Preston. Preston sips water from a chipped coffee mug, licks his lips. He rubs his bald head with his right hand.

"Let me go back a few years though. When I was doing my radio show in New Mexico I spent a lot of time traveling, talking to the people who lived in the four-corners area. I took trips up into the Nevada desert to the towns surrounding Nellis Air Force Base. These people have the highest cancer rates in the world, and it's because they've all been subjected to incredible amounts of radioactive fallout from the over nine hundred nuclear weapons tested at White Sands and the Nevada test site."

"Downwinders."

"Exactly. Downwinders. I also spoke to hundreds of former test site employees, all sick and dying, and hundreds of ex-GIs forced to crouch in dirty pits near ground zero and watch those terrifying blasts. After a while I reached what I considered to be a rather sane conclusion based on the overwhelming evidence: that our government engaged in a carefully planned campaign of lethal nuclear testing on the people of this region, and, truth be told, on the country itself, because there's not a county in America that hasn't seen a fallout cloud carried overhead by jet stream or wind pattern."

"You blew up my wife's plane because of nuclear testing in 1950?"

Preston scowls.

"We didn't blow up the damn plane," says Porter. "If you don't stop saying that I'm going to drive you back to Arizona and put you in the hole."

Linus shuts up, but he can't help but think that the most effective way to convince a man you're not a killer is not to threaten to kill him. Preston has another sip of water, pats McAndrew on the leg, gives him a small, brave smile.

"No, Mr. Owen, though we are here no doubt because of the thousands of people dead and dying from needless radiation exposure, that, in and of itself, is not what prompted us to do what we are about to do."

"Which is?"

"Be patient. I'll get there."

Preston has a sip of water, rubs his head.

"I don't think I have to tell you that this country has for the last fifty years conducted secret medical experiments on the American people. The syphilis injections in 1932, the spraying of bacteria from navy ships off San Francisco and the dispersal of biological agents in the New York subways in 1950 and 1966. For over fifty years they have worked to develop the ultimate biological weapon. Why would a government do this? You of all people should know that the United States of America is not a democracy. It is a corporation that exists for one purpose and that is to further the profits and power base of all major corporations."

Linus rests his head on his left hand, rubs his eyes.

"Are you going to start talking about the New World Order? The U.N. shock troops poised on the Canadian border, the concentration camps on former military bases, the salt mines beneath

Detroit prepared to hold thousands of Soviet troops. Because if you are, I'm not sure I can handle that."

"It's not a joke, Professor Owen. It is definitely real. We have assembled the proof."

"What proof? That the world is run by major corporations? That's no secret. That corporations have no sense of social responsibility? I'm shocked."

Clive McAndrew leans forward, places his hand on Linus's leg.

"Shut up."

Linus considers this briefly, then complies.

Preston rubs his head, picks up the chipped mug.

"What do you know about Gulf War syndrome?"

Linus looks at McAndrew, as if to say, May I? McAndrew nods.

"It's an immune deficiency brought on by a combination of chemical and biological agents used in the Gulf War."

Preston shakes his head.

"Gulf War syndrome is a man-made disease, a tool introduced to cut the world population and allow the United States Corporation to set up a medical emergency dictatorship."

Linus looks at Porter, who nods, moves his eyes back to Preston. He uses his incisors to chew the skin of his cheek.

"Get to my wife on the plane."

"Slowly but surely, Professor. Slowly but surely." Preston clears his throat, rubs his head again, a gesture that seems to Linus a nervous habit or for luck.

"For a number of years Mr. Porter here worked for the CIA. One of his responsibilities was to oversee the security of quasi-corporate, quasi-military buildings and bases. Working with consultants, he designed and installed a number of very advanced security systems. One of those systems was built and installed at the Hastings Pharmaceutical research facility in southern New Jersey. Another was installed at a small compound of anonymous buildings out in Nevada utilized as a project headquarters for a number of secret military projects."

Linus stares at Preston's throat, the almost invisible blue vein throbbing on the left side of his neck. He thinks about the spa he should be at with Claudia, basking in hot mineral water.

"My wife had an aisle seat. When I identified her body it was missing several toes."

Preston nods.

"In 1989 a company in Boca Raton, Florida, called PIT, began developing a particular strain of hydrogen cyanide called Prussian Blue, which they sold directly to the Iraqi government. We have acquired documents that show that they tested Prussian Blue two years prior to the Gulf War on gas-mask filters to judge its effectiveness in filter penetration."

"A series of unconnected facts. Conspiracy theory as Faulknerian stream of consciousness."

Preston sips his water.

"I think we both have learned that nothing our government is involved in is unconnected."

Linus sighs.

"What does this have to do with the Nevada test, which, I might add, remains a mystery?"

"It's all in the manifesto," says Preston.

Porter gets up from his chair and crosses over to Linus.

"The bottom line is this: population control."

Preston clears his throat.

"We've been expecting the New World Order for years, but until recently have not known the guise under which it would come, how the Constitution would be suspended and a dictatorship put in place. In the past year Porter has accumulated documentary and conversational evidence that the plan all along has been to introduce a deadly virus into both the American and world communities and then, under the guise of a medical emergency, impose a totalitarian order, utilizing medical ID chips to track all citizens. They tried with AIDS, but AIDS is too slow."

Linus has heard some of this before in different conferences and correspondence. It seems so far removed from one man and his grief, but he sits still and lets them talk. His desire for information has been reduced to the physical details of one bomb and the man who planted it.

"The Gulf War," says Preston, "was arranged by the United States Corporation with the aid of the Iraqis. Under the guise of chemical attack they introduced a biological agent into a large population of American soldiers."

"Not just American," interjects Porter.

Preston nods.

"Among all the chemical and biological cocktails detonated by missile or spread by the detonation of captured warheads, what has emerged is evidence of a single biological agent that breeds in the human body for two years before exhibiting symptoms. It is an agent that can live in clothes and equipment for up to seven years. It passes from soldiers to their family members, from old army surplus to the teenagers who buy fatigues at the army/navy store, from the jeeps and trucks, blankets, and gas masks of Gulf War soldiers to soldiers at Fort Bragg, Camp Pendleton, from Bosnia to Somalia."

"Forty-nine thousand U.S. troops who served in the Gulf War have been discharged," says Porter. "That's over seventy percent. They have gone back to the general population, infected their wives and children. They are encouraged by the Pentagon to give blood. We are seeing increasing numbers of people unconnected with the war coming down with chronic fatigue syndrome and other symptoms of GWS."

Preston leans back, puts his hand on McAndrew's arm.

"Clive here is my sister's son. He grew up in Montana, joined the army. He served in the Gulf, active duty on the front. He was given the experimental vaccinations to anthrax and other viruses, took the bromide pills made from experimental nerve agents lethal enough in their own right. He had no choice, and this is a drug, I might add, that the government pushed past the regular FDA approval process. It could have been cyanide for all the FDA cared. Like the other soldiers, Clive was exposed to sarin nerve gas and toxins from the oil-well fires. He came home sick, headaches, blurred vision, muscle spasms. He lost control of his bladder, experienced memory losses. He went to live with his mother, my sister. Somehow he infected her. How was this possible? Soon afterwards she began having symptoms, chronic fatigue, bloody diarrhea, severe cramps, a telltale rash. She died over a year ago for reasons no one has been able to identify. Despite his illness Clive got married to his high school sweetheart. A year later she gave birth to a baby with no arms or legs." Preston leans forward. "Sixty-seven percent of all babies born to Gulf War veterans have birth defects. Sixty-seven percent. When Porter and I decided to act, I called Clive and despite his illness he joined us. He knows that this is a battle for our lives."

Porter crouches down beside Linus. The three of them have him surrounded, have closed in on him. Linus looks over their heads at

Dent, who still stands staring out the window. Preston rubs his head violently.

"Think of all the emerging diseases that have appeared since 1991—the flesh-eating bacteria, the hemorrhagic fevers, the hantavirus and filoviruses. Don't think these things are unconnected. We are dealing with a world plague."

"And so the Nevada test," says Linus, barefoot and slightly claustrophobic. He leans back in his chair to get away from them.

Preston leans back. Porter stands up. McAndrew sits giant and mute.

"Well, here's where it gets interesting," says Preston. "Porter and I have known each other since 1986. As I've told you, Porter used to do security work for the government. Well, last year he calls me and tells me that he's discovered some very interesting information about a certain drug being developed at Hastings Pharmaceutical. He says it ties in directly to the coming of the New World Order. I am living at the time in a grain silo in Indiana. We meet in a bowling alley in Cleveland."

Linus squints as the light coming in from the windows gets brighter. He wants to ask for some aspirin. He wants to ask for his life back. He covers his eyes for a moment with his hand. Preston finishes his water, puts the mug on the floor.

"It appears that Hastings is developing a drug that disables the anxiety and aggression centers of the brain, while leaving the rest of the brain functions unaffected. As the man who designed their security system, Porter has kept an ear to the operations of all his former clients. He knows how to set up wiretaps, how to access their mainframes. He has learned that a special branch of the CIA headed by Chris Forbes is working with Hastings to perfect a drug that can be prescribed along with symptom-treating medication, or disseminated through a water supply, to neutralize the threat of widespread revolt and panic. You see, the new plague that will trigger the national emergency that brings with it martial law involves certain risks. Just as you have proven yourself to be an unpredictable variable, so there is a big risk that a panicked population of millions may overwhelm or overthrow the shock troops of the New World Order. This drug will be used to sedate a nation."

"So the Nevada test."

"Was a trial run, where the drug was introduced into a small town of seventy-five through the water supply, and then the town was invaded by special forces and certain residents were taken away for testing."

Porter goes to the window and parts the curtain over Dent's head, making Dent look up. Porter turns around.

"We found out about the test from Cliff Webb, who had an uncle who lived down there. We went down, snooped around. It's clear that this thing is escalating quickly. We have the documentation. We need to release it soon. Now would be best."

Preston shakes his head.

"The documents alone can be covered up, downplayed as fakes. We need to provide the American people with context. They need to understand the full implications. A manifesto must be written explaining the facts and calling for worldwide revolt."

Dent comes away from the window. He looks at Linus. Nobody has yet addressed the issue of Linus's wife's death, he thinks. They're all too caught up in the fate of humanity to worry about what happened to one woman.

"Roger Leeds joined us in November. He was a journalist, sometimes wrote articles for *Covert Action Quarterly.* When we learned that the folks at Hastings were going down to Brazil for a conference on biological and chemical agents, Preston sent Roger to tag along. He was supposed to pose as a chemist from Texas A&M. We gave him an assumed name. Porter and I forged his papers."

Linus feels as if he is at the end of a long tunnel looking into a faraway room.

"What about the bomb?" he hears himself say.

Dent shakes his head.

"We're on your side, Linus. We're just like you. People like us don't plant bombs. I think you know that."

Linus stares at Preston's mug on the floor, studies the pattern of the chip, the rough ceramic surface.

"Who?"

Porter moves to stand behind Dent.

"We think it was Forbes."

Linus nods.

"Why?"

Preston stands up, indicates to McAndrew to do the same. The four of them circle around Linus again, making him feel as if he is a small child at the bottom of a deep well.

"The most obvious answer is that he wanted to use you to get to us."

"By blowing up a plane?"

"He knew your wife would be on board, maybe even arranged for her to be. He knew he was running out of time to find us before we distributed our evidence, evidence that would expose him and the government. He needed an insider, one of our own kind, to find us. He killed your wife to motivate you."

Linus assembles these details as if they are building blocks too large and heavy to be moved by one man. He takes a deep breath, thinks it through. Outside, the sun angles for its transition into afternoon.

"Then why did you bring me here?" he asks finally. "He could be right behind me."

Preston rubs his head furiously, claps McAndrew on the shoulder. He is excited. They are all excited by any change, by the prospect of acting after so many months of preparation.

"Because we want to turn the messenger against his sender."

"Meaning?"

"We have a plan."

Linus stretches his legs, stands up from his chair. He thinks of poor Edward, deathly afraid of even the common cold, of Claudia resting under six inches of virgin snow. He nods at Preston. He no longer knows what to believe.

"Let me see what you've got."

It takes Linus twelve hours to reach San Francisco. He rides Interstate 80, lumbering through Sacramento in a '78 Honda without working taillights. The car is a junker rescued by Porter and Dent from a scrap pile outside Las Vegas. It hemorrhages oil onto the highway. Linus leaves at night after reviewing Danton's documents, after reading Preston's manifesto. He is deposited, blindfolded, on the shoulder of the interstate, given the keys to the Honda, which Dent has driven out behind Porter's car. Despite his plans, Linus has killed no one, shot or stabbed, strangled or bludgeoned. He has not struggled with makeshift weapons, mastered the fear and adrenaline of a fight, crossed the line between innocence and the crimes of Cain. The burden of murder has been lifted and with it a great sense of relief has come.

He is not surprised to learn that he has been manipulated. It was to be expected, all things considered, but in a way this whole ordeal has been an exercise in fate. Still it is with a keen sense of revenge that he grips the steering wheel and masters the many miles, crossing the border between states, leaving behind the great western desert, emerging once more into the land of foothills and the routine of concrete shopping malls, fast-food houses, and secure suburban neighborhoods. He rides with the windows down, worshiping at the temple of sleep.

As he reaches the alarming maze of intersecting freeways that make up the East Bay, Linus begins to whistle nervously. He checks his mirrors. The freeway overheads glow their jittery fluorescents, washing the road clean of mystery and detail. He rockets through the towns of Vallejo and Albany with their seven-dollar barbers and disgruntled antique shops, loops his way down past the Shell refinery, skirting the inlets of the Bay, the mothballed fleet. He is going home and the thought makes him both nervous and calm.

At a gas station in Piedmont he calls the number on the card Forbes gave him. He reflects on the things he knows about drug addicts, the half truths of television documentaries, Alice's downfall, and a long-ago reading of Jim Carroll's *The Basketball Diaries*. The phone rings. Linus stands shivering on the abandoned asphalt of deepest night. The phone is picked up by a machine, no message, just a beep. Linus leaves a brief message.

"I have met Danton. The documents are secure. Meet me on the ferry from Tiburon to San Francisco at seven A.M."

It is 3:08 on Friday morning.

■

The message reaches Forbes in five minutes. He is sitting in the living room of a nondescript brownstone in Tribeca, amid open-mouthed cardboard boxes filled with Styrofoam peanuts. The lights in the room are on, a lemon-yellow glow against hardwood floors. Outside he can see the scaffolded bulk of City Hall, lit from the front. Nomadic taxis, dispatched, unloved, prowl the empty streets. The morning rush is poised and ready to begin. Forbes too has gone without sleep for three days. It is a side effect of the drug. Untested medicine breeding unforeseen reactions. The windows are open, though the March wind that rushes in is solid cold and Forbes is barefoot and wears only a thin T-shirt. He is thinking about a girl he knew in college, her wide mouth and lonely blue eyes.

It has become harder to conceal his drug habit of late, though he has been fooling himself if he thinks it has gone unnoticed up until this point. The drug has produced an array of disturbingly random responses from his body, including the aforementioned sleeplessness and an increase in saliva production, which prompts him to spit quite frequently. He is also plagued by headaches and a constant ringing in his ears. The fear is almost overwhelming now. Despite his best efforts to conserve, he is running out of pills. The small window of euphoria grows shorter with each dose. He has chewed his fingernails down to the cuticle. Like other drug addicts, he has convinced himself that he can clean up anytime he wants. He just isn't ready yet. Sometimes he sits at his desk unable to move, unable to decide what to do. Despite this floating paralysis Forbes has developed an unrealistic sense of how much control he retains over the Danton situation. He is unaware that Mr. Yee and Mr. Clean have been retained to shadow him and, if necessary, to kill him. He is similarly unaware that Hastings Pharmaceutical has hired hit men of their own, that his bosses are already planning to use his addiction to this experimental drug as a way to further study its effects. In the next room his wife sleeps, arms and legs akimbo.

On the coffee table in front of him Forbes has opened an old, fading photo album. There is a handful of pills scattered on the table and as he looks at the pictures he pops them like candy, chewing one at a time, their bitter taste making his eyes water. The pictures are of his parents when they met, their wedding. His father is the tall Burt Lancaster in the navy uniform, just eighteen, the son of a captain of industry about to marry the daughter of an automobile emperor. Forbes turns the pages, listens to the crinkle of plastic. Some of the photos have slipped from their mountings, clustering in the album's binding. His father served the duration of World War II on the U.S.S. *Indianapolis*. He was a lieutenant at the time and used to tell Forbes stories about watching the device be loaded, an atomic bomb headed for a small island in the Pacific. He called it Fat Man, recounted its innocuous shape and size, the sense of unease it raised in his crew. They were glad to get it off the ship, glad to set sail back out to sea. He never spoke of what happened afterward. It wasn't until high school that Forbes learned the details, the sinking by a Japanese submarine, seventy-two hours clinging to life preservers, being picked off in clusters by hundreds of hungry sharks. The thought gave Forbes nightmares. It also explained why his father refused to swim in lakes or pools, why he would never take his family to the beach. This fear of water was passed on to Forbes, either through genetics or conditioning. Ever since the tenth grade the thought of the ocean has sparked his imagination to the grotesque.

Forbes's cellular phone hiccups under his jacket. He pops a pill, answers it.

"The professor has resurfaced. He suggests a meeting in San Francisco."

Forbes nods, uses the palm of his hand to sweep the remaining pills into his jacket pocket. He puts on his shoes, stands up, leaves the apartment without kissing his wife.

■

In Tiburon the sun has come up, muscled its way through a low bank of fog. Linus stands on the wooden dock of the marina watching the boxy white ferry mount the small swells of the Bay toward him. He is surrounded by men and women in business suits. He stares at the distant geometry of San Francisco, seen as if through a tearful mist. He has come to offer a diversion, but is struck suddenly by the notion that while they are on the ferry he should push Forbes into the Bay. Another uncharacteristic impulse toward murder. The freezing waters and swift current. Let him know how it is to feel threatened. Overhead a swatch of seagulls circles and dives.

On the boat Linus chooses a spot on the top level looking out from the stern. He stands at the railing, rubs his hands together. He has given Forbes four hours to reach him. He wonders what he has interrupted him from, a light interrogation, a damage-control meeting, or maybe a slow shudder in the stuttering light of a bathroom stall, fumbling on his hands and knees for dropped drugs. Linus wonders suddenly what has become of Edward and Roy, then puts those thoughts from his head. He feels responsible for whatever has occurred.

Understanding that Forbes is not in control of himself has reduced the amount of anticipation Linus feels as he waits for their meeting. He has experience with the frazzled sensibilities of drug addicts, has watched his sister, Alice, dance through her desperate need. Forbes will not be the challenge, he thinks. The challenge will be in getting past Forbes to the men upstairs. The challenge will be in convincing those he has not yet met. He turns up his collar as the ferry begins to escape the moorings of Tiburon. Behind him a woman on a cellular phone says, *Test the formula on your arm before you give it to him.* A man with a tiny mustache throws bread crumbs to the seagulls. Once they are moving, Linus scans the boat, making random assumptions about which passengers are government agents or corporate hit men. Behind him a gull lands on the rail, gives Linus the attention of one pink eye.

Forbes sits on a bench ten feet from Linus drinking coffee from a paper cup. He wears a wig of curly red hair, sports an auburn Fu Manchu. He has been flown in the back of a fighter plane at speeds in excess of Mach 4 to reach the meeting, forced inside the tight cavity of the F-15 screaming inside to get out. He is shivering still, but at the same time sweating. The ferry plods on into deeper water. He thinks of his father safe aboard his ten-ton steel battleship until a Japanese submarine sank it to the bottom of the Pacific with one well-placed torpedo. The pills do nothing. His hands won't stop shaking, tremors that by now he has almost ceased to notice.

When Linus's back is to him he takes off the wig and mustache, leaves them on the bench. He stands up, smooths his hair, places the coffee on the rail. There are exactly seventeen Secret Service men on board, including Mr. Yee and Mr. Clean, who call themselves Agents Bones and Hooper and have pigmented their skin to look Puerto Rican, ensuring that Forbes, preoccupied with his own fear, will not notice them.

"Do you realize it used to take Puritans in horse-drawn buggies a whole year to make the journey from coast to coast," he says, his voice as warbly as that of a man freezing.

Linus turns around, looks Forbes in the eye.

"People used to know the names of their neighbors."

Forbes puts his back to the rail so he won't have to stare into the impenetrable green water.

"A town had a mayor, a sheriff. There was a telegraph clerk everybody called Lefty."

"In Salem they burned witches. The Donner party ate each other in the blizzard-covered mountains of California."

Forbes shrugs.

"So maybe I'm romanticizing a little."

Linus puts his hands in his pockets. He studies the height of the railing, wonders how much force it would take to launch Forbes into the cold dark water. The wind blows their hair like trash around an empty parking lot.

"I've decided to take a very intense disliking to you," says Linus.

Forbes smiles.

"You don't have the bargaining power to dislike me."

Linus raises an eyebrow, says nothing for a moment. Then,

"I have Danton. I have the documents."

Forbes pulls his coat around him, fighting off the wind.

"Paranoia. These are enemies of the people we're talking about."

"Let's not start in with speculation as to who's an enemy to the people."

"All right, Linus. I don't have time for your shit today anyway."

"You seem tense. Why don't you take a pill and relax."

Forbes studies Linus's face. He looks around the upper deck of the ferry.

"Excuse me?"

"I'm just saying, maybe a small blue pill to take the edge off."

Forbes grabs Linus by the collar, brings their faces together.

"Who's been telling you lies about me? Is it Porter? That little shit. He couldn't pull his weight before and now he's making all these crazy accusations."

Linus sniffs, decides Forbes's breath is mainly coffee and stomach acid.

"There was a hit man from the drug company. He said you had a whole case of untested medication in your apartment."

Forbes lets go of Linus's collar, tries to regain his footing. Maybe he's not as in control of the Danton situation as he thought. The fear makes him weak. A sudden, intense feeling of claustrophobia overtakes him. He sweats in earnest, decides he may be able to put the drug issue aside, but there's still the matter of this hit man that just came out of nowhere. Linus leans in to him. He can smell Forbes's perspiration, bitter on his neck.

"What are you so afraid of, Richard?" he says.

Forbes feels his heart start to race. He looks around the deck again. For a minute he's certain that one of the passengers is Mr. Yee. He loosens his tie, unbuttons his collar. He's almost certain he died in the screaming confines of the F-15, the unconscionable weight of G force pinning him to his seat. That this is all some sort of punishing limbo, the sick dream of a vengeful God.

"Tell me where Danton is," he says. He repeats it: "Tell me where Danton is." But his voice is thin and shrill.

"You killed my wife."

Forbes brushes his hair back with his hand. He rolls his head on his neck, takes a deep breath. From his breast pocket he takes a Polaroid, hands it to Linus. Linus stares at it.

"What is this?"

"This is a picture of your wife taken this morning."

Linus stares at it, a picture of Claudia, hair cropped, looking gaunt and savaged. She is holding up a copy of the *Washington Post* with today's date. It is the cheap work of a kidnapper. Linus looks up at Forbes. He is temporarily speechless.

"Claudia's dead," he says.

Forbes rebuttons his collar, pulls up his tie. Back in control, he thinks. He feels his composure returning. With his right hand he smooths his hair again.

"I don't think so, Linus. You see, Claudia is there to keep you from getting any ideas. Now tell me where Danton is."

Linus licks his lips, swallows.

"I'm sorry, who?"

Forbes takes out another Polaroid.

"We have your friends as well. Tweedle Dumb and Tweedle Dumber."

Linus nods. He should never have assumed he might get the upper hand.

"The manifesto is complete," he says. "The mailings have begun."

Forbes wipes his nose, which has begun to run.

"If that's true," he says, "then everybody dies, including you."

Linus nods. He stares at the tic that has begun fluttering on Forbes's temple. He would have to hit him high and with all his weight to get him over the rail.

"It's possible an exchange can be worked out," he says.

Forbes grunts.

"I thought so."

Linus watches the gulls circling the back of the ferry. Behind them the foothills of Marin recede, the statuesque span of the Golden Gate Bridge.

"Tell me about Richard Wermer," he says.

Forbes wipes his nose again. He decides that if he can remain focused on the approaching dock he may be able to fight off another panic attack.

"Don't know him," he mumbles.

"Come on, Richard. You are him."

Forbes shakes his head.

"In the New World Order, all our pasts will be forgiven." Forgotten. That's what he meant to say.

"You know what the guy from Hastings said before I put him in the ground?" Linus says.

Forbes thinks about the likelihood of Linus killing anyone. He smiles.

Linus scratches at his three-day shadow.

"He said, 'I don't think Forbes is as important as you think he is.'"

Forbes clears his throat, spits over the side of the boat.

"Is this the same one who said I was a drug addict?"

Linus leans over the rail to his right, sees the city fast approaching. He turns back and looks at Forbes with disdain.

"Aren't you?"

Forbes's right leg is shaking. He takes his hands out of his pockets, blows on them. This is the signal that says Linus is to be taken as he leaves the boat. Agents take up positions downstairs at the ferry exit. Forbes, mouth dry, begins to pray that if God will take him off this boat, he will stop taking the pills. He will love his wife and rededicate himself to his job. I just need to get off this fucking boat. When he looks down into the water all he can see are the fins of monstrous sharks.

At the same time Linus too is undergoing an emotional overload. There is a wild sense of elation at the notion that Claudia is still alive, coupled with the certainty that he just won't be good enough to save her. It is clear that this attempt at double-cross has been for nothing, stupid to think it could have worked. Somehow he will have to find a way.

"Tell me about the Gulf War, Richard," he says. "Tell me about the Nevada test. I want to hear about this New World Order of yours."

Forbes zips and unzips his coat. The pier is in sight.

"We'll have plenty of time to talk about that later."

Linus watches the dock. There are men in suits waiting on the pier to meet them.

"There is no later, Richard. Later is just an excuse for not answering the question."

"Stop calling me Richard."

"I want my wife back, if she really is alive."

"I want my documents."

Linus feels the boat slow down, start to turn. He breathes in the exhaust voided by the ferry as it applies reverse engines. The passengers in their designer suits stand, fold their newspapers. A man on a cellular phone says, *Hey, we don't dictate terms to the new technology. The new technology dictates terms to us*. Linus takes a deep breath.

"Well, then, you better stay near the phone." He begins to move.

Forbes turns to grab him, but Linus has already vaulted up over the railing and, as Forbes watches, he drops smoothly into the roiling water.

■

Two hours later Linus meets Porter in a nude bar on Ellis and Hyde. He has changed clothes at the bus station south of Market, shivering and soaked. They sit in a sticky booth in the back. Porter has a beer. Linus orders a bloody Mary.

"We have to figure that the police have your picture," says Porter.

Linus takes out the Polaroid of Claudia, damp and folded in at the corners. He studies it in the low lights.

"It won't work. We need a new plan."

"Stopping is not an option. Everyone is in position."

"What does that mean? Why does everybody talk like they're tough guys in some cold-war film?"

Porter drinks his beer. He still has the knife in his boot.

Linus holds up the picture as if its existence is proof of some higher consciousness.

"We have to find her."

"What we have to do is get these documents out."

"I don't care about the documents. I want my wife and my friends back."

Porter drinks his beer.

"Stupid," he says. "Selfish."

Linus looks at him for a long time. The sense of recklessness he felt before today has been replaced by an overwhelming need to be careful.

"They'll die," he says.

Porter is unperturbed.

"We've come too far. The truth will get out. In fact, the whole issue of finishing is nonnegotiable."

Linus meets Porter's eyes. He sees something in them he's never found in his own eyes even at his most radical moments, even during his most extreme days: Porter has broken free from the world of people and entered the world of ideas. Linus may as well be on television as sitting right here across from him, a real person, flesh and blood, whose life has meaning, whose existence should be protected if only because of the unmistakable implications death has on the living.

"What's the value of truth if you've given up your humanity?" he asks quietly.

Porter finishes his beer, wipes his mouth on his napkin.

"This is how it always is," he says. "This is why we always lose. The weakness. We start along a course we know will end in tragedy, but we do it because the outcome could have real meaning, and then we start to think about humanity. We start to question our morality. This is what they count on. I know. I've been on the other side. When standoffs like these get close to their finale, the CIA starts to relax. They have another cappuccino and look at their watches and say, Well, those kooks should be infighting about their humanity about now."

He stands up and leans his knuckles on the table.

"We don't have time for this. If you're not willing to go forward, then I walk out of here and you're on your own. We can't afford your weakness. We can't afford your wife or your friends. You have to get past your own selfishness. There's a greater good we're striving for here. I think you know that. I think that has meaning for you."

These are more words than Porter has used together since he was sixteen years old. Linus looks up at him, fascinated by the way Porter's mouth doesn't move when he speaks. What am I doing? he wonders. He's surrounded by fanatics, and yet how can Linus just let Forbes get away with this? Claudia's freedom is paramount. That is what's truly nonnegotiable, but there has to be some way they can all win. Linus squeezes his hands into fists, closes his eyes, but he just can't see it. He watches a cockroach ascending the back of a wooden chair. There seems to be only one option. Porter has turned his attention to the strippers on the bar, has deposited a soggy twenty on the tabletop. Linus reaches over and touches his arm.

"How long until our next move?"

Porter checks his watch again.

"Six hours."

Linus nods.

"I'll meet you back at the hotel."

Porter cocks his head.

"Why?"

"There's something I have to do."

"What?"

"It's nothing, but it's private."

"Are you fucking me?"

Linus stands up.

"Look, Porter. We both know that this distribution is something I've been working toward all my life, to finally challenge a government, to clue people in to the deceptions. I'm ready to do this, but if I'm going to do it at the sacrifice of my wife and my friends, I need a few minutes to work it through." He touches his head and his heart. "In here and in here."

Porter, who's never been incredibly preoccupied with remorse, shrugs. He tries to bore into Linus's head with his eyes, to soothsay whether or not Linus can really be trusted here at the most dangerous part of the game. The music from the bar is the return of the seventies. Linus meets his eyes, keeps his face expressionless. In the end, for Porter, it's a question of flipping a mental coin.

"If you're not back in an hour, I'm doing it without you."

Linus nods. And if your ass wore a skirt you'd fuck yourself all night long. He smiles.

"I'll be there."

■

After Porter leaves, Linus sits for a moment staring idly at the smoke from the afternoon drinkers curling in waves toward the ceiling. He remembers the taste of his father's muttered exhalations, the blankets of secondhand smoke that warmed their house. He thinks about his mother. Onstage the popularity of nipple tassels begins to make a comeback. He orders another beer, sits for a minute chewing his lip. When the waitress comes back Linus gives her ten dollars, asks her if there's a pay phone he could use.

"Near the john," she says.

He wipes his mouth, stands. Back past the narrow pool tables is a hallway. He makes his way there, removing a card from his wallet as he goes. He picks up the phone, stares at the receiver, hangs up. He paces in the tight hallway. What am I doing? What the hell am I doing? he wants to know. The card is Forbes's, just a name and telephone number with no area code. Linus picks up the phone again, cradles it to his ear, places his back to the wall, stares out along the empty corridor of the bar. His eyes move to the card. The betrayal is like striking matches on his tongue. Every once in a while he can make out a tassel swinging in a quick circle just at the end of his peripheral vision. The dial tone is a warm voice humming in his ear. He wipes the mouthpiece on his sleeve, puts the phone back up to his ear, and dials six digits of the number written in pencil on the face of the card, then hangs up again. He just can't bring himself to do it, to turn them in. This is what hell must be, he thinks. The torture of impotency. He kicks the wall, once, twice, three times, and hard, the shock traveling up his leg into his torso. He tears the card into little pieces, drops the pieces on the floor. An incredible wave of isolation descends on him, remorse. How can I save you? he thinks. How?

He is about to make his way back to the bar when he has a thought, an insidious and dangerous thought. He stares at the pay phone, its hand-worn numbers. The risks are just as grave, but there is a chance he can do it. He picks up the receiver again and this time dials a number from memory.

The man who answers the other end is terse.

"Yes."

"Is this line secure?" asks Linus in a voice deepened to attempt anonymity.

"It depends on what this is about."

"It's about Linus."

"Then no. Call back at the following number."

Linus hangs up, redials. This time the voice is more aggressive.

"Who is this?"

"I'm a friend of Linus's."

"How can I be sure?"

Linus flinches at the familiar voice, the tone, but keeps his own voice icy.

"You can't be, but I have to be brief, so here are the details. The wife is alive. She's being kept somewhere along with two guys called Edward and Roy. They'll be killed unless you do something. So will Linus." This much he knows is true.

"What makes you think I can do anything?"

"You're a man with powerful friends."

"In my business there's no such thing as a friend."

Linus squints toward the front door, checks out the two men who've just come in.

"Get them out. He needs your help. He won't admit it, because he's too proud and too stubborn, but he does. He has no other way out. Tell his wife and friends to go to the Space Needle in Seattle. They'll be contacted there."

The man at the other end pauses. There is a possibility that Linus's voice has been recognized. He holds his breath. Finally there is a response.

"You're pretty sure I'll help."

"Brother, I'm just throwing rocks at trains."

At one o'clock in the morning Porter and Linus pay a visit to the Fairmont Hotel. They enter through the side, ride a service elevator to the tenth floor. Pushing a metal and canvas laundry cart, they pad the halls looking for room 1051. Linus is wearing a new pair of Nike high-tops to give him the advantage of stealth. When they reach the room Porter takes a copper passkey from his pocket. He has been collecting keys for the past ten years, keys of all shapes and sizes, keys to storage lockers and music boxes, keys to people's homes, keys to cars, and, most important, keys to special government bases. The thought of doors he cannot open makes him extremely claustrophobic.

Inside room 1051, Agent Forbes is watching television. A documentary on the industrial revolution. He sits in a cheap hotel desk chair at the foot of his bed, wearing only a pair of Jockeys and his skinny black knee socks. He took his last pill an hour ago, savored its bitter flavor. From now on he has resigned himself to fear. Even now the chemicals in his brain are lurking, looming. He can see them if he closes his eyes, a dirty red tide, splotchy, floating. If he can just make it one more day, he thinks, he can have this whole thing wrapped up. Mr. Yee and Mr. Clean have made it clear that the fiasco on the ferry will ruin him in Washington. Forbes's status as a golden child could soon disappear completely. While they were lecturing him in a ratty office near the airport, Forbes excused himself to go to the bathroom to throw up. He can no longer remember what it was like before the fear, can no longer picture in his mind what triggered it.

At the sound of the key in the door he looks up, reaches back toward the bedside table for his gun. The door opens. He stretches back, tips the chair, grabbing for it, realizes too late that it is lying on the table by the other side of the bed. He shifts his weight, turns toward the door, but because of his backward lean the chair tips over, spilling him gracelessly to the floor. He scrambles to his hands and knees. Porter crosses behind the bed, saps him with a roll of quarters wrapped in a sock. His last vision is of a watercolor lobster trap floating in a blue-green cove. Together they lift him into the laundry cart, push it into the hall. Porter closes the door behind them. Linus wheels Forbes back down the hall to the service elevator. They ride down in silence. At the loading dock Linus looks both ways, checks the stairs. Forbes is lifted gracelessly from the cart and dumped into the trunk of Porter's car. In with the road flares, the pie tins, the rope. Linus considers the irony.

They are on the highway by one-thirty, Porter checking his mirrors every few moments in search of police, Linus working to contain the hope that has blossomed in him since he hung up the phone six hours ago. He has rolled the dice and must proceed as if he's already a winner, though he is relying on someone who has never come through for him in the past. All he can think is that if Claudia is not dead, then maybe she never had an affair, that the whole thing has been a ruse since the beginning. It is a chance to have his life back, miraculously unbroken.

In the trunk, Agent Forbes comes to with the feeling that he is being pummeled by icy mallets. He puts up his hands to ward off the blows, presses them against the roof of the trunk. His next thought is that he has been buried alive. He lets out a panicked yell. The loose rope in Porter's trunk manages to work its way over his shoulder and onto his neck. He struggles with it as if it is a snake. It has been three hours since his last pill. Forbes's mind is alive with the delusions of nightmare. He pisses himself, lets out another yell. In the front seat, Linus and Porter exchange a look. Porter changes lanes. Linus reaches down and turns on the radio. They drive for an hour in silence, just the sound of one song giving way to another, the occasional rush of air from an open window, the rumble of trucks roaring past. In the trunk, Forbes continues to demonstrate his inability to relax in enclosed spaces. Finally, Linus, no longer able to endure the sounds of Forbes's distress, says:

"What do you really expect to get out of him anyway?"

"Confirmation."

"You have the documents."

"We want a statement from the horse's mouth."

"Whose idea?"

"Webb's."

Linus shakes his head.

"They'll come after you now for sure."

Porter shrugs.

"They were after us anyway."

"Now it's a federal crime, kidnapping across state lines."

Porter yawns, covers his mouth with one hand.

"They were never going to let us live. What have we got to lose?"

In the trunk, Forbes beats a desperate rhythm. Linus turns up the radio. They drive north.

"What did you think of Preston's manifesto?"

Porter shrugs.

"Haven't read it."

Linus coughs into his hand.

"You're risking your life for a moral philosophy you haven't read?"

"I'm not a manifesto person."

As Porter speaks, the car crosses some invisible line and the radio station changes from all country music to Spanish religious programming.

Linus slips off his new sneakers, rubs his feet.

"The idea of disheveled men in small rooms eating trail mix and making humorless demands?"

"Too many words. Not enough doing."

"It's sort of fascinating though. The idea that in this day and age we still have these solitary souls living in isolation working by candlelight to pound out the path to human equality. The idea that even today there are people who believe in the inherent value of political acts."

"And in their spare time they're building bombs out of manure and three-inch nails."

"Well, yes, but not all of them. Look at you."

Porter rolls down his window, spits into the wind.

"Preston says there's nothing valuable in murder."

"And what do you say?"

Porter checks his rearview mirror.

"I sleep better the nights I don't kill someone."

Linus listens to the sound of the wind pushing through his cracked window. On the radio a woman says, *Act now and receive one hundred dollars cash back.*

"I don't see what the big deal is," says Porter. "They tell me you write books."

Linus yawns, hangs his arm out his open window.

"I have academic credentials. My audience can afford to buy books. The manifesto writer is more of a literary terrorist. He's saying, Make room for me, the disenfranchised, the outcast. Make room for my people."

Porter's reply is to pass a lumbering tanker truck.

They reach the Portland safe house in seven hours, pull into a gravel driveway. The sky is an angry gray, looming cumulus clouds threatening rain. As the car slows, Forbes renews his frantic beating on the trunk. Porter thumbs the button of a garage-door opener and pulls the car into a beige and black garage. He rented this house three months ago under the name of Boone. Here they will meet Preston, put the finishing touches on their package. The others are waiting in cities across the country. They have synchronized their watches. The distribution is now a deadline to be contemplated in terms of hours. Linus climbs stiffly out of the car, bends at the knees. He catches Porter's eye, nods toward the back of the car. Porter takes a snub-nosed pistol out of his jacket, opens the trunk. Forbes stares up at them, blinking against the light. His arms and legs are stuck in a defensive posture, much like a roach flipped onto its diaphanous shell.

They haul him to his feet, this ridiculous man in socks and underwear, move him quickly up the three short steps and through a flimsy wooden door into a rustic kitchen. He trembles in random waves. Linus finds himself moving furtively, as if he's being recorded on grainy black-and-white film. This is his first federal crime and rather than feeling liberated, he feels dirty. That Forbes has become such a pathetic creature, hunched over in sagging, damp drawers, only makes him feel crueler, as if the revenge he thought so sweet is really a sour persimmon on his tongue.

They dump Forbes onto a flimsy kitchen chair, his back to a curtained window. Porter hands Linus the gun.

"I'll get Preston," he says.

Linus nods. He holds the pistol awkwardly, pointed in the general direction of Forbes's torso. The kitchen smells of mildew and unsafe dairy. The linoleum floor is green, speckled with gold flecks. There is a kitchen table, topped with the same linoleum, standing on dull aluminum legs. The room is lit by a diamond-shaped ceiling fixture, unwashed for many years. The refrigerator is an old, rounded Westinghouse, and though Linus can't see inside it he knows that if he could the shelves would be aging metal, the freezer contained in the main box, covered with a block of ominous ice, the white crisper drawer faded yellow. Forbes, in his tighty whities and black socks, seems an incongruous apparition against the sense of home the kitchen implies. He is like the aging, defeated traveling salesman crying to an empty house on the morning of his suicide.

"Don't fall apart on me now, Richard," says Linus, and he wonders if all their conversations are destined to be played back in reverse order.

Forbes stares at the floor. His nose is running.

"It's cold."

"Yes, it is. It is cold. And you're a son of a bitch."

Forbes nods. He is retreating in on himself. The fear is like a hammer pounding him small.

"You have to do the right thing now, Richard. This is a fact. You have to do the right thing."

Forbes wipes his nose, looks up.

"I am the great and mighty Oz," he says, and he emits a short laugh, a thin, desperate expulsion of breath.

Porter comes back into the room followed by Preston. The two are grim-faced. Preston carries a small video camera on a tripod. He gives Forbes a brief look, then moves past him to set up the camera over by the sink. Linus forgets himself for a moment, ends up pointing the gun at Porter, who takes it away from him with a curse. Preston stoops behind the camera, puts his eye to the viewfinder. He adjusts the focus. With the entrance of Preston, Forbes seems to perk up. He straightens slightly and watches as the bald man clicks off the lens cap, taps the external microphone.

"Pete, Linus, I need you to move out of range of the camera. Come stand back here by me."

Forbes watches them like a monkey in a zoo staring through bars. He tries to pull himself together, to keep his cool. Never mind the underwear. Never mind the fear. He could wrap this thing up here. He could take control of the situation, get back his prestige. He stares into the camera with a look of anxious boredom.

"It's freezing in here," he says, with more authority this time.

Linus shouts, "Where's Claudia?"

Forbes looks at him, shrugs. Porter spins the wheelhouse on his pistol. Preston straightens from the eyepiece, looks at Porter and Linus, nods. He finally turns his attention to Forbes directly.

"Please state your name."

Forbes shakes his head.

"You sit here accused of crimes against humanity. How do you plead?"

There is no response from Forbes, who has fixed his eyes on the cabinets above Preston's head.

Preston nods. He reaches over and pauses the camera. Porter turns around, opens a kitchen cabinet, pulls out a jar, moving too quickly for Linus to judge the contents. Porter steps into range of the now silent camera, holds up the jar so that Forbes can see what's in it. Forbes makes a small noise in response. The jar is full of bugs. Porter puts his hand on the lid.

"These are African army ants. They can strip the flesh off a pig in just under thirty minutes."

Forbes's heart begins to race. He feels a sudden desperate need to crawl out of his skin. The truth is, the jar is filled with regular garden ants Preston has collected from a hill out back. What they are counting on is Forbes's inability to control the fear. The power of suggestion. Forbes shrinks back in his chair, his eyes begin to move rapidly around the room. To him the ants look huge. The implication is of death, of being eaten alive. He tries to scramble up onto the table but Porter lifts the gun, menaces him back into the chair.

"Hey, hey, hey," says Forbes. "Woah, wait a minute. This is bullshit. Don't put those things on me."

Porter looks at Preston, who motions him back. The camera is turned on again.

"Please state your name."

But Forbes is staring at the ants. He shakes his head, forces his eyes down, scrutinizes the dirt on the floor. Once he gets an idea in his head it's hard to drive it out. Preston prompts him again. Forbes looks up, checks the walls.

"It's Forbes, Chris Forbes."

"You work for what agency?"

"FBI."

"Are you positive that it's the FBI?"

Porter mimics tossing the jar to Forbes, who jerks, brings up his hands. He is breathing rapidly.

"CIA, okay. I work for the CIA. Just keep those bugs off me."

"Tell me about the Nevada test."

Forbes licks his lips. The camera records him staring at something just above and to the right of the lens. He starts absently scratching his arms, turns, smiles at the camera. In the kitchen light he looks slightly green.

"I don't want to."

Preston bends, looks through the eyepiece.

"Let's try this again. In the fall of last year you were contacted by scientists at Hastings Pharmaceutical."

"Not true. Not true. I was called by Mills from FEMA. See, you don't know anything."

"Well, Agent Forbes, we're here so you can tell us." Preston pauses the camera. He steps out into the center of the room. "I have pills for you, Richard." He pulls a small pill case from his pocket, pours five blue pills into his palm.

Forbes stares at the hand as if terrified that it may disappear suddenly in a puff of smoke.

"Give," he says.

Preston shakes his head.

"You have to tell us what we need to know. If you do, you can have the pills. If not..." He turns his back on Forbes and goes back to the camera.

Linus has begun to sweat, leaning up against the ironing board. Preston switches on the camera. It captures Forbes looking left, then right. There is hair growing from his clavicle. He swallows visibly, exhales. His eyes blink seven times in rapid succession.

"We ran some tests."

"What kind of tests?"

"Tests, you know, on inmates."

"It's illegal to test drugs on inmates. Do you know that?"

"Hmm."

"Do you know that it's illegal to test drugs on inmates, Agent Forbes?"

"Yes, sure I know that. But they're fucking convicts, for Christ's sake."

"As long as you know."

The camera records Forbes wiping his nose, then rubbing at it with the palm of his hand.

"The tests looked good. It's mostly dosage. There were some side effects, swelling of the hands and, uh, feet, some apathy. We thought these effects stayed within acceptable, you know, parameters."

"And what are acceptable parameters?"

"Well, that's not my area."

"What is your area?"

"I am responsible for defensive-scenario planning."

The camera records a moment of silence.

"Which means?"

"Crowd control."

"Martial law, in other words."

"Yeah, right. Martial law."

"Describe how this drug could be useful to you in this area."

The camera records Forbes rocking back, wiping his face again.

"I really need a pill," he says. "I think I'm dying."

There is another moment of silence.

"Describe how this drug could be useful to you in this area."

The camera records Forbes staring at the jar of ants, scratching at his torso.

Preston clears his throat.

"Let's skip to the Nevada test. Now you decided to test this substance on the town of Clone."

"I need a pill."

"Your hair's on fire," says Porter.

The camera records Forbes pawing at his scalp.

"Agent Forbes, you need to stay focused."

"I can answer your questions a lot better if I could just have a pill."

"In December of last year you tainted the water supply of Clone, Nevada, isn't that right?"

"Yes. They have their water delivered. We stopped the truck."

"The town was exposed."

"The dosage was too high. After a few days people started having, uh, seizures."

"You could get in a lot of trouble."

"Only two people died."

"Only two."

Forbes's left leg now begins to twitch. He has drawn blood from his abdomen with his fingernails.

"It came to my attention that there were some potential whistle-blowers on the Hastings staff."

"Whistle-blowers."

"Yes, and then I found out that somehow some of the documents had been leaked."

"What did you do? Agent Forbes, wake up. What did you do?"

"I needed to trace the documents, to shut down the whistle-blowers."

"So what did you do?"

"There was a conference in Brazil. A drug thing."

"Yes."

"Men from Hastings were going to attend."

"You blew up the plane."

"I needed to find the documents. And, uh, and it came to me that Holden was sleeping with this radical professor's wife."

"Liar."

A smile flickers across Forbes's face. He wipes his nose, hacks at it with his hand.

"I called him up and told him to take the wife to Brazil."

"Did you think she would go?"

"It didn't matter. If she didn't we could make it look like she did."

"So you told Holden to board a plane you intended to blow up."

"These are matters of national security."

"You told Holden to board a plane you intended to blow up."

Forbes nods.

"You picked the wife up at the airport."

"The husband. We said there'd been an accident."

"What do you know about Gulf War syndrome?"

Forbes shakes his head. The camera records him smiling.

"You're stumbling around in the dark."

Preston straightens, turns off the camera.

"Lock him in the basement with the jar. We'll give him some time to think this over."

Linus turns around and looks at the wall. He can hear Forbes yelling as Porter muscles him down the hall and downstairs into the basement.

"Do we have what we need?" Linus asks as Preston goes into the living room and parts the curtains. He stares out into the street. A few parked cars, the sounds of children with Hot Wheels. A slow rain has begun to fall.

"We have enough. Remember our purpose here."

Linus nods. He wonders when this will finally be over. Somewhere his wife may be waiting. May be. May be. The not knowing could kill an elephant, thinks Linus.

Preston checks his watch.

"It's begun," he says.

Then it is Forbes's nineteenth hour without a pill. He sits on a dirty basement floor in his underwear, losing his mind. Next to him is a jar brimming with ants. An oval fluorescent light stutters against the ceiling, making the objects in the room appear to move, the shadows come and go. He is too afraid to move the jar, and yet its nearness is terrifying to him, the bugs crawling on one another, moving in mounds. They appear to eye him through the glass, to organize in teams, some trying to topple the jar, others to tunnel their way from the bottom. If he kicks the jar away it will break, but the only alternative is to pick it up gently and move it to the other side of the room, and he feels sure the jar would slip, or the ants would crawl out through some invisible hole onto his hand, his arm, up onto his face.

The basement itself has been shrinking steadily for the last hour, closing in on him, the smell of dirt and kerosene, the bitter taste of his own sweat. He has lost almost everything that made him a man. Under the weight of so much fear, Forbes has reverted to something less than human. The fear ceases to be of specific items, becomes instead an overwhelming terror, almost as if the thought of existence itself were a monster. Finally the ants disappear. He enters a catatonic state. It is in this state that Linus finds him as he descends the stairs.

"I want to know who she was," he says.

He stands at the foot of the stairs staring at Forbes, half collapsed, wide-eyed, drooling in a dirty corner. Forbes continues to stare at the jar, though he has ceased seeing it. He has chewed his fingers until they bled. Linus regards him with disgust, but perhaps also pity.

"Who was the woman on the plane next to Holden? If it wasn't Claudia, who was she? Somebody else's wife? Is another man sitting in an empty house because of you?"

Forbes's only reply is silence.

Linus stares at him for another minute, then turns and climbs back up the narrow wooden stairs and closes the door behind him.

Preston is in the kitchen with Porter.

"The package is away," says Preston.

Linus nods. Any relief he expected to feel is late in coming. Manifestos have been nailed to church doors before. Today we don't even remember their authors.

"How?" he asks.

Preston grins.

"Spit into the great maw of cyberspace is what they tell me. I insisted on physical mailings as well. I don't trust the new technologies. People use words like Internet or E-mail. I don't know what it means. So when young Dent tells me he has established several international web sites, I say good, though I have no idea what he's talking about. When he says he has done a mass electronic mailing, has scanned images of the documents into something called jaypegs, I shake my head. They assure me this is the best way to reach the people directly, which I'm all for. They say this manifesto will be read by everyone from the president of Egypt to grade-schoolers in Kansas. If this is so, then I say hurray for the new technology. Take the power of information back from the state and put it in the hands of the people."

"Will you all meet up again later?"

Preston pulls back the curtains, checks the street. Porter stands silently against the refrigerator thinking about the smell of oil.

"It was necessary to split up for the delivery. We need to make ourselves a smaller target. There is a place to meet, but you'll forgive me if I keep it secret."

"And this video?"

"The video will follow the manifesto. We will wait three days, then follow the manifesto with footage from the tape. An anonymous foundation has been set up overseas. The web sites will channel people's responses directly to the media and the federal government. If we are not all killed, we will come forward publicly. There is a small chance that this information will provoke a serious political response from a country crippled by apathy. I can't say I'm hopeful, but I'll try to remain optimistic. The manifesto is out. That alone is a great weight off me."

Linus checks his watch again. Soon they will climb into separate cars, he in one, Preston and Porter in another. Where will they go? Linus isn't sure. If nothing changes he will open his car door nervously, possibly dropping the keys, will fumble with the ignition, check the mirrors once or twice. He will hold his breath when he starts the car, perhaps close his eyes in case Porter or unidentified secret policemen have placed a bomb under the hood. He will point his rusty vehicle toward the highway, toward Interstate 5 heading north. Linus will drive with his heart in his throat to Seattle, where Claudia, Edward, and Roy should be waiting—please let them be waiting—shell-shocked, underweight, wondering what will happen to them next. He is an atheist relying on a miracle. A fool for hoping. He clenches his jaw, prepares himself for disappointment, but it's all he can do not to leave immediately.

"Dent said something about viruses, computer viruses, I mean."

Preston drops the curtain, smiles.

"It was Dent who suggested we respond to a virus with a virus. He's such a clever boy. He's devised all sorts of really ingenious bugs that we hope will aid in the downfall of the United States Corporation. I can't explain them. All I know is, one is supposed to turn off their phones and another is meant to reset their clocks. I asked him how this would topple a government and he said, 'It's the little things they take for granted that are our best weapon.' So we shall see. In about an hour I believe the phone company will lose all records of any phones registered to a national security agency. Porter has provided us with the cover names these agencies do business under, so this will help make the attack more successful. That's about all I can say without sounding like a boob."

Linus crosses to the kitchen door, looks out onto the back walk.

Preston stands up, rubs his head.

"Porter and I are going down to see Forbes and then we should go."

"Don't bother. I was just down there. He's gone. I don't know what those pills were, but they don't appear to have been very good for his brain."

"Still," says Preston. "It's how they find him that matters, and Porter, I think, has a personal matter he'd like to resolve."

Linus looks back at them over his shoulder.

"You are not going to kill him?"

Porter shrugs. Linus turns, opens his mouth to speak. Preston puts up his hand.

"Nobody's going to kill anyone. We just want to leave him with a copy of the manifesto in case he wants to do some reading while he waits to be rescued."

Linus looks them both in the face, turns back to the screen door.

"Well, I said my good-byes," says Linus. "I'll wait here."

He listens to the sound of their feet receding down the hall. He stands at the kitchen door staring out at the back walk, shaded by trees. More than anything he just wants to be home again. He wonders if he'll ever even see the building. Where can they go from here? He has become a fugitive, married to a small group of paranoid men. As he stands there staring into the road he sees an apparition. A ghost from his past, floating out of the trees. He blinks at it, but it remains, Ford turning into the walkway from the street, walking toward the house. Linus's heart starts beating fast. His first thought is, It worked. His second thought is, How did he find me? Linus's eyes move past Ford, searching for Claudia, for Edward and Roy. He allows himself to hope for a moment that love has triumphed unimaginably over greed and hatred as Ford makes his way up the walk and stops just below the porch steps. With one hand he motions for Linus to come outside. Linus turns to look behind him into the kitchen. It is a moment with strangely fantastic qualities. He feels detached from any sense of reality. He has lost all sense of grounding. He pushes open the screen door, steps outside, stops at the top of the short steps staring down at his brother.

"Ford, is that really you?"

Ford places his finger to his lips, indicates with his head that Linus should follow him back to the street. Linus shakes his head, makes a head indication of his own that he has to wait for Preston and Porter before he can go. Ford frowns. He reaches up and grabs Linus's arm, pulls. Linus pulls back, shrugs him off. Whatever the spell was, it is broken by this contact, and Linus, with a sudden burst of sinking fear, turns back toward the house. Ford grabs his belt loop, tries to pull him off the porch. At that moment Linus hears the first gunshot. He struggles free, throws open the screen door, rushes back into the house. Ford yells after him. Linus runs, hearing his own breath loud in his ears, his heartbeat. He moves in what seems like half time, pushing against the molasses of his own anxiety. In the front hall he stops dead. A soldier in black fatigues and a gas mask is pointing a rifle at him. Behind him are two men in rubber Halloween masks.

Ford bursts into the hall behind Linus.

"No," he shouts. "He's with me."

Linus pushes past the soldier, forces his way to the top of the basement stairs. Other soldiers, breathing loudly through respirators, are securing the house. They sprint silently up the stairs to the second floor. Linus steps down onto the top basement step. Everything is coming in frames. The basement smells musty. He looks down. At the bottom of the stairs Porter lies prostrate, blown backward with one leg up, resting on the banister. He is bleeding from the head and chest. Preston and Forbes have collapsed together, caught in an embrace like lovers. Forbes's naked legs stick out from under Preston's slumped body. His head rests on Preston's narrow shoulder. The jar has been smashed and the ants are now free to make their way over Forbes's legs, scaling up the two bodies, navigating their way around the spreading pool of blood. There is the haunting smell of gunpowder. Linus turns back to the hallway. The men in the Halloween masks are stripping off rubber gloves.

"You have him?" asks the one who looks like Nixon.

Ford nods.

"I'll take care of it."

Again Linus pushes past the soldiers, still camouflaged by flak jackets and head cover, stalks back to the kitchen. Ford catches up behind him, walking purposefully. Linus's only thought now is to escape, to get to Claudia. On the back porch Ford grabs his arm.

"Linus."

Linus shrugs him off, descends the stairs.

Ford catches him again at the front walk. There is a black BMW parked at the curb.

"Get in the car, Linus."

Linus turns right, walks away from the automobile.

Ford stops at the passenger door.

"If you don't get in the car, Linus, they're going to shoot you. That's the arrangement."

Linus stops but doesn't turn around.

"You have no idea what you just did," he says.

Ford snorts.

"Get in the car, Linus. You're the one who's in over his head."

Linus stands under a Japanese maple tree. He is buffeted by the sound of its leaves rustling in the wind. The sun has moved to the other side of the hill, casting the street in shadow. Though there have been gunshots no one has come into the street to investigate. Ford pushes a button on his key ring and the BMW emits a throaty clunk, door locks sliding open.

"I'll take you to Claudia."

Linus stiffens.

"It's the only way, Linus. It's the deal I made to get you out of this."

Linus turns around, looks at Ford standing next to the car. Even now Ford is dressed in gabardine pants. He wears a white shirt with a Nehru collar. His shoes are polished to a shine.

"That's the deal?" says Linus. "That? Three men are dead. You're telling me that was the deal."

Ford makes a face of disgust.

"Get in the car, Linus. If you don't, you and your friends are going to end up permanently missing. 'The end zone of a major football stadium' is how they put it. I have no control over that after you walk away. I get back in my car and you're dead. I'm telling you right now, this is your one chance."

Linus stares at the ground. An old yellow school bus rolls by, the children leaning out the windows, their voices raised, their small shiny faces. Though it's March the air smells like fall. Linus walks to the BMW. Ford opens the door for him, closes it once he's inside, then looks around for a moment, the quiet residential street, the slow turn of clouds. He decides that when he gets back to New York he will spend some time at their house in Connecticut. Jingling his keys, he makes his way around the back, climbs into the driver's seat. He starts the engine, adjusts the internal temperature control to seventy degrees. The car rolls slowly away from the front walkway. Linus watches the house recede in the side-view mirror.

"What kind of person are you?" he says quietly.

Ford pinches his nose, makes a left turn onto a major avenue.

"What are you asking, Linus? If I'm a crook? I wasn't the one hiding out with two dangerous fugitives and a kidnapped FBI agent."

"He was a CIA agent."

"I suppose he told you that."

"As a matter of fact, he did."

Ford shakes his head.

"You just can't see the mess you're in."

"Ford, do you have any idea what this is all about?"

"I'm sure whatever ideas I have are nothing like the ones you've cooked up."

"We're talking about a deliberate campaign to create and transmit a plague. We're talking about using disease as a weapon to control the population, using drugs to pacify people into not minding."

Ford opens the top button of his collar, lowers the temperature a single degree.

"Another unbelievable plot, Linus. Another paranoid delusion."

"There are documents this time, Ford. We have documents."

"It's not *we* anymore, Linus. It's just you."

"Forbes."

"I think it's safe to say that Agent Forbes was a very disturbed man who took it upon himself to mastermind some unsavory projects."

"Oh, no. This isn't the kind of thing you can write off like that. We're talking about an organized campaign going back fifty years, medical testing performed before Forbes was even born."

Ford stops at a red light, checks the gas gauge. He turns on some light classical music. Linus turns it off. Ford grunts.

"Oh, yes, the webs of intrigue, the government within governments."

"I think the fact that I'm sitting in your car right now is evidence of that."

Ford grimaces.

"Linus, *you're* the one who called me, okay, and don't pretend you don't know what I'm talking about. Did you think I'd fall for funny voices? Do you really think I'm that thick? My God. You called me and that's the only reason I'm here. Just try to think clearly for a minute. I put my ass in some very hot water because of you. You think I wanted to approach these people? You think I want to owe them a favor? Those guys in the masks? You know, I met Agent Forbes once, a few years ago. He was a very scary man, but in my business you sometimes have to deal with men like that. I don't *like* doing it. They're dangerous and it's not smart to get involved with them too deeply. I don't wake up every morning and say, Gee, I hope I can ask some trained killers for a favor today, but you called me. You said you needed my help, and you've never needed my help before, so I did what I could, but don't turn around and attack me just because it didn't turn out how you wanted. I got you out. I got your wife and your friends out. Why can't you just say thank you?"

Linus is still vibrating from the sound of shots. He feels an immense hatred for every living thing, himself included.

"Have you seen them? Have you seen Claudia, Edward, Roy? I mean alive and well, healthy and whole?"

"No, but I have assurances."

"Assurances? Jesus Christ, Ford. You can't trust these people."

Ford feels an overwhelming fury at the ingratitude.

"Linus, I'm a businessman and this is a business deal. I won't bore you with what my side of the deal was or how much it cost me. I'm sure you wouldn't care, but if they tell me Claudia's out, then she's out. If you can't trust them, you'll have to trust me."

Linus can't stop his leg from bouncing. He is a rocket breaking up on reentry.

"People are dead, Ford. They're dead. We just killed them with one telephone call. I can't let that roll off me. This whole thing has driven me irreversibly insane. I'm sure of it now. A lunatic. For three weeks I thought my own wife was dead. You let me think that. What can I think except that you set me up. Not Forbes. You."

"I didn't know. Believe me. I am not the mastermind of one of your stupid conspiracies. I don't stand for that kind of thing. I came because *you* called. I had no idea about any of this until *you* called and asked me to help you get Claudia out. How many times do I need to repeat that? It was Forbes."

Linus shakes his head.

"I don't think I'll ever believe that this whole debacle was masterminded by that floundering drug addict."

"You didn't know him in his prime. He was a dynamo."

"Please."

"He was. A twisted Machiavelli they tell me."

"Ford, it doesn't matter. There's no way the buck stopped with mixed-up Richard Wermer. He was a dolt who thought he was a genius."

"Linus, I've spoken with these people. After you called I made some phone calls. I had a few meetings. Things were explained to me, and as always you have no idea what this is all about. There are interests here that must be protected."

"The rich, the elite, whose interests? Not mine. Not Claudia's. Not Preston's or Porter's. Who protects our interests?"

"It's not like that. You're always making me out to be some kind of monster. You have no idea how the world works."

"How does it work? Tell me so that once and for all I know."

Ford signals, changes lanes. He follows signs for the highway.

"It's a question of order," he says.

Linus holds his breath, turns to look at Ford.

"Order?"

"And stability. Order and stability. It's a matter of protecting people."

"By shooting them."

"Will you try for one minute not to be a complete moron, Linus? You don't understand the responsibilities of the free market. This world isn't about individuals. It's about societies. It's about people working together."

"People working together? Ford, you sound like Karl Marx."

Ford scowls. He flushes.

"We have created this wondrous civilization, this incredibly interconnected chain of people and government and business, and you know what keeps it together? You know what keeps us from sliding back into barbarism? Money. That is the one constant. The world can come apart at the seams, morals eroding, homosexuals in the streets, but the value of money will always remain. Even in depression-era Germany it was not a question of how little the money was worth, but a question of how one could assemble enough of it to rise above the chaff. Wealth is a relationship, Linus. It's not something to be taken lightly. Do you know how many people there are in this country without even a hundred dollars to their name? Tens of thousands, maybe hundreds of thousands. How can we let those people decide what happens to the rest of us? If it were up to them, Barney the fucking dinosaur would be president. I mean, look at them. They're uneducated, they're dirty, they're violent. Democracy is about a strong economy. People can't be free unless they earn. A thriving business creates jobs. People don't understand these simple rules. That's the level of stupidity we're dealing with. That people wouldn't understand that money will make money for everyone if you nurture it, if you feed it and take care of it. How can we expect people who've never had the responsibility of money to understand the complex decisions of the world?"

"Ford, you are an imbecile."

"Oh, I am, am I? What about, Thank you for saving my ridiculous life? What about, Ford, I hope going out on a limb for me didn't jeopardize your position or your own damn family?"

"I'm sorry, but you talk about the responsibilities of money in the same sentence as protecting your country. Money doesn't have borders. It doesn't understand the struggle of people for freedom, for equality, for food. Your money will never care what happens to you, no matter how much you care what happens to your money."

Ford grins, accelerates the BMW onto the highway. Inside the car he can't even hear the road. This whole incident has reaffirmed his own power in his mind. He thanks the money. It has made him powerful enough to interrupt the workings of government.

"Look, Linus, we can no longer fool ourselves that any one country matters. We have to accept that. Business is done on an international level. As we speak, corporations are losing their ability to distinguish between what is America and what is any other nation. This is the future. You can't fight it."

"People, Ford. I could have been killed. Your own wife and children could be run down tomorrow. What is the value of wealth without humanity?"

Ford adjusts the temperature in the car to sixty-eight degrees. Linus feels that his whole life has come down to this one exchange. Ford shrugs.

"Linus, *you* called me. I know you hate it when I remind you, but I did help. I negotiated a deal in which you get Claudia back and your friends. I think that's pretty fucking impressive given the circumstances. Doesn't that make me more human?"

Linus opens his window. The car's temperature gauge struggles to adjust. He exhales.

"Yes, it's worth something. I appreciate it. I mean, I'm not crazy, but other people are dead. I feel responsible."

"You're not. This was their deal and they knew the risks."

"But I'm the one who called. I'm the one who set them up."

Ford shakes his head.

"Don't be stupid, Linus. The FBI knew where you were all along, since the minute you kidnapped Forbes. They were coming in with or without your call. What you did was save yourself. You feel guilty because you survived, but don't forget, you were dragged into this against your will. I understand that, at least. You just saw an opportunity to turn the situation to your advantage. I can respect that. I'm glad I could help. So now you get your life back. Can you handle that? Can you handle winning for once?"

Linus watches the trees rocketing past, the chassis of other cars. There is the sound of the road. His voice, when it comes, is quiet.

"I need to know things, Ford. The world doesn't make sense. I need to know why I'm growing. I need to know why my nose bleeds so much. I need to know, Who was that woman on the plane?"

Ford brakes, accelerates, switches lanes.

"The woman was a federal agent. Just like Forbes. That's what I'm told."

"Did she know? Did she know she was getting on a plane that was going to explode?"

"It was a terrorist bombing, Linus. Do you think they would have sent her if they knew?"

Linus shakes his head, looks out the window.

"Things are happening to me, Ford. Things that don't make sense."

"Some mysteries can only be solved by God, Linus. If you're really getting taller, if you're having nosebleeds, my first advice would be to see a doctor."

"The doctors know nothing. They talk about my pituitary gland. They confer in cluttered rooms and then diagnose me as a man with skinny capillaries."

"Well, maybe they know what they're talking about, Linus. Maybe it's not a government plot to control your body."

"I just don't trust them, Ford."

"Then all that's left is the Lord."

Ford pushes a button on his own door and Linus's window rolls up with only a slight murmur of a whir. Linus watches the white lines. Each one that floats under the car feels like it's cutting him in half.

"The manifesto went out, you know." He sounds like a small child sulking.

"Who's going to believe it?"

"People will listen. The evidence is right there. Does the government really think I won't say anything, that Edward and Roy will keep quiet?"

"That's part of the deal too. You all need to think about alternative careers now."

Linus shakes his head.

"I can't stop being who I am, Ford. I can't stop believing what I believe."

"Well, then, I should have just left you back there, because you clearly have no interest in living."

"The proof is out there now. The knowledge is power. We could make things happen."

"They have all the power, Linus. All of it. Knowledge is nothing."

Sitting there, strapped in with his seat belt, protected by hidden air bags, by metal and glass and whispering automotive technology, Linus feels trapped, tortured.

"So we're just supposed to forget, to pretend."

"It's called survival."

"Ford."

"Linus, you have no choice. What else can you do? Your friends are free now, but for how long if you start shooting your mouth off again?"

Linus tries to think of a way out but can't. He has the irresistible urge to weep. Maybe just living is enough. Maybe dogs can write software.

Ford reaches out and squeezes his shoulder.

"I want to give you some money to help you get settled. It's the least I can do."

"I don't want your money."

"Linus, be smart. There's no other way to go. Let me help you."

Staring at the highway, Linus is certain he can see his own future, a future with a man and wife in a two-bedroom house with a faded Welcome mat petting a golden retriever maybe, a subscription to *Time* or *Newsweek* on a maple coffee table, watching sitcoms when darkness comes, identifying with the voices on the laugh track, the man and the woman making their own mouths grimace into smiles, their own vocal cords barking out the chuckles and guffaws. Pretending. Pretending they have no past. Pretending they aren't afraid all the time. Pretending money can make them invulnerable, that conformity can make them immortal. Linus sees the future and it's a cartoon. His face will crack under the force of his own artificial smile. In the car, as they draft the breezeless corridor behind an eighteen-wheeler, hug the guardrail through turns and narrow straightaways, Linus realizes that though he's escaped he's still a pawn, a tool like a bevel or saw, who will be stored in an empty shed with the other outdated tools, Edward and Roy, Claudia, and who knows how many others. Their silence will become their function. They will evolve into instruments whose meek retreat gives them their greatest value and their complicity in this fashion will make them responsible for all the unforgivable acts they once sought to unveil. At that moment Linus decides he would rather not live at all if the only option is to surrender. He sits up suddenly, as if realizing he is late for an appointment he'd completely forgotten.

"Stop the car, Ford."

"Linus."

"Stop the damn car."

Ford opens his mouth to scold, but Linus lunges over, grabs the wheel. They wrestle for control, Linus struggling to get his foot across the divide, to push down on the brake. The car swerves, dovetails across two lanes.

"Jesus Christ!"

Ford struggles to keep the car out of a spin. He touches the brake. The car jerks over onto the shoulder. As soon as it's stopped, Linus opens the door and jumps out. Ford leans over, tries to coax him back inside. The car has come to a stop on a low overpass overlooking a river. Linus stands at the railing looking down at the slow, dark water. Ford steps out onto the macadam. He yells something at Linus about ingratitude. He orders Linus to get back in the car. Linus doesn't look up. He stands staring down the incline at the way the water bends around a curving jut of rock. Ford comes up behind him, grabs his arm. Linus sets his weight, grabs Ford's wrist, and pivots. Off balance, Ford stumbles. Linus keeps turning, sends Ford tumbling down the hill. He stalks down after him. Ford rolls, ends up sitting at the bottom trying to get his bearings back. He gets to his feet slowly, looks up. Linus comes barreling down the hill, slams into him. They fall back into the riverbed. For Linus it has come down to this. He has been used, manipulated, tossed aside. His marriage is in shambles. His friends are in danger. All for the placation of money. He takes it all out now on Ford, the bully of his youth, Ford, who struggles under him, uses his weight to try to roll Linus off him. Linus hangs on, throws his first punch, catching Ford on the temple. He throws another, a third. Ford's white shirt is muddy and wet. The two roll over rocks and broken branches. Ford manages to get an elbow into Linus's stomach. He rolls on top of him. Linus brings his knee up, catches Ford unprotected, brings it up again. Ford falls into the dirt, retching. Linus grabs his hair, sinks his fingers into Ford's scalp, and pulls his head up. Ford makes a sound of animal protest. He tries to bring his hands up, but before he can pull them from under his body the hair comes away in Linus's hand, peels back like the top of a sardine can, and Ford's face falls back into the dirt.

Linus squats for a minute looking at the hair, a long strip sticky on the underside with glue. He looks down at Ford's angry red scalp. The sound of the river moving past. Linus stands up, drops the toupee onto Ford's back.

"Where's my wife?"

"You'll never make it."

"Where is she?"

Ford rolls onto his side, keeps his eyes away from Linus's face.

"There's a bus stop north of Seattle, in Innis Arden. I had them take her there."

"And Edward and Roy?"

Ford nods.

"Them too."

Linus looks up at the sky, puts his hands on his hips. The sun is sending colored light to the clouds, alerting them to the approach of sunset. He looks down again. Ford hasn't moved. Linus holds out his hand.

"Give me your hand."

Ford shakes his head, turns over on his other side, touches the corner of his mouth, where the lip has swollen.

"Be smart, Linus. Please, for me, for your family."

"I can't do it, Ford. I can't. I appreciate everything you've done for me, really. I never would have thought, I mean, you really tried, but it's the seduction of Faust to surrender now, to trade in my identity just for the chance of survival. I don't mean to disappoint you, but that isn't who I am. Please. This is my soul you're selling. Claudia may have a different opinion, and Edward and Roy, who knows, but right now I have to make the choice and I choose to take my chances. We might make it. I wouldn't bet on it, but we might."

Ford licks his lips. His face is smeared with dirt. What happened to that sense of victory? he thinks.

"Linus," he says.

Linus shakes his head.

"They didn't stop us, you know. The documents went out. The manifesto will be read. I have to let that fact push me on. There's a real chance now, but it has to be followed up, otherwise the truth will just disappear."

Ford moves to sit up, touches his pink scalp tentatively, as if noticing it for the first time.

"Linus, for the love of God, nobody believes in all that conspiracy garbage. Please. You're killing yourself for nothing."

Linus wipes his mouth. His nose begins to bleed.

"You'd be surprised," he says. "In fact, I'm sure you will be."

He turns around then, the smell of trumpet lilies like sirens luring him toward the promise of great beauty, makes his way back up the hill with the river roaring under the overpass beside him. He doesn't look back when Ford sits up and calls his name. He climbs. Nor does he look back when he reaches the top and Ford has climbed shakily to his feet. He just walks to the driver's door of the BMW, which is still open, making its plaintive electronic pleas for closure, and climbs inside. He turns off the automatic temperature controls, rolls down the window. Humming a tuneless tune, he begins to drive.

For more information on Noah Hawley and A Conspiracy of Tall Men, *visit the author's web site at: www.26Keys.com*